DARKNESS
DIVIDED

DARKNESS DIVIDED

JOHN SHIRLEY

STEALTH PRESS

PUBLISHER'S NOTE
This is a work of fiction. Names, characters, places and incidents either are a product of the author's imagination or are used fictitiously, and any resemblance to actual persons, living or dead, events, or locales is entirely coincidental.

ISBN 1-58881-016-X

FIRST STEALTH EDITION MARCH 2001

Stealth Press books are published by Stealth Media Corporation. Its trademark, consisting of the words "Stealth Press" and/or bomber logo is registered in the U.S. Patent & Trademark Office and in other countries. Marca Registrata.

FOR TIM POWERS and SERENA "SIX GUN" POWERS

CONTENTS

indicates previously unpublished story

INTRODUCTION

With few exceptions, every writer in every field would like to be considered *sui generis*, unclassifiable, reinventing his own eponymous genre every time he puts pen to paper or fingers to keyboard. Very few are actually capable of this. John Shirley seems to achieve it with every story he writes.

When you think of John Shirley, you may think gonzo, cyberpunk, Subgenius. Probably you don't think first of his vivid, expertly drawn characters, and that's a shame. Sometimes a writer's flashy or controversial reputation can obscure his truer skills. Philip K. Dick is one example that comes readily to mind. John Shirley is another. Both these writers' work is populated by unforgettable characters trapped (often trapping themselves) in inescapable circumstances, which is pretty much the essence of a great story. From the young predator-in-training (and his equally well-delineated victim) of "My Victim" to the broken children of "Tricentennial," all of these characters have not just obvious back stories but entire *lives*, of which these tales are clean-cut but still bleeding slices.

Shirley's work asks brutal questions about things like addiction and responsibility. Once a thing has its hooks in us, are we ever able to get free of those hooks entirely? How much flesh do we leave on them? And didn't we willingly swallow the shiny, baited hooks in the first place?

There are two collaborations here. In my opinion, collaboration is one true test of a writer's stylistic strength. Does his voice come through clearly, without seams but also without drowning out that of his collaborator? In both cases, Shirley's voice does—and these collaborations are with William Gibson and Bruce Sterling, either of whom might easily overshadow a lesser writer.

I first encountered John Shirley's work in one of the *Hot Blood* erotic horror anthologies. I always felt that these anthologies were wildly uneven, but that there was invariably at least one story that was worth the whole price of admission. In this case it was Shirley's "Pearldoll." There were other good stories in the volume, but "Pearldoll" was the one that made me say, "OK, I'm glad I spent the money on this book." You now hold in your hands an entire collection of Shirley's stories, any one of which is well worth the whole price of admission. I hope you enjoy them as much as I have.

Poppy Z. Brite
New Orleans, November 2000

PART ONE

'Til Now

My Victim

I'm watching my victim set up a shot, in the crooked, crosshatch shadow of the Santa Monica beach boardwalk. My victim is Corey Hart, early thirties, lean, with nervous movements that suddenly vanish when he says "Action!". Then, during the shooting he becomes still as a lizard relying on its camouflage; he wears a white short-sleeved shirt, khaki pants, Converse high tops that don't quite go with the pants, glasses that would be horn-rim but for transparent frames; there's a clipboard under his arm as he talks to the cameraman.

On this waning September day there are only four people in his crew, a chubby, earnest black cameraman in an alligator shirt; two acned, long-necked college interns, boy and girl, as production assistants, and a bored-looking middle-aged white guy carrying the sound-recording gear, microphone boom in his hand.

A group of, sickly teenagers, the runaways this documentary is about, stand in the shadows of the pylons under the boardwalk, waiting to be called for camera interviews. The word is, this guy will pay them $20 each to talk for a few minutes. Other kids are sitting with their back to us on the yellow sand, looking out to sea as they pass a joint, the wavelets sticking dirty foam to their feet.

I'm sitting with my arms around my knees, about twenty yards behind my victim; I'm basking in the late afternoon sun, watching him openly sometimes, other times appearing to let my attention wander; my mouth slack, eyes unfocused, so that I'm just another gawker with nothing else to do. I'm sitting on a faded Universal Studios towel, barefoot, wearing grimy, shapeless clothes I'd never ordinarily wear; got a jug of the cheapest Gallo, half empty. Like I'd ever drink Gallo: I poured half of it out before I came. Normally I'm tailored; normally I drink mostly imported cabernets. Even as an undergrad, last year in the frat, I drank only the best. The frat brothers gave me a lot of crap about it.

My brother Jeremy's first victim is not really as interesting as mine. I'm in the studying phase, following my victim, never letting him know I'm watching him, and it's like studying a Frank Lloyd Wright building, with all its levels and spaces—whereas Jeremy's victim, hell, it's equivalent to studying a mid-western high school gym. I mean, Jeremy's victim has one big ambition: to be the owner of a video arcade. *My* victim? Mine is a guy who makes documentary movies about street poets and all kinds of other stuff. He even won an award for one of his films. Now, *there's* someone worth killing.

The film maker and his crew never even glanced at me, when I first came over and sat down with my towel and jug. It occurs to me now that the disguise might yet be a problem—I might seem colorful enough for them to want to film me, for a quick background shot of other people on the beach: part of the seamy atmosphere these beach-bum kids live in, or something. If they take any notice of me, like they might want to film me, I'll walk away.

It's one of the *Principles of Safe Victimization*. A PSV, my father calls it. He made us memorize the Principles—they aren't written down, that'd be bad security. The operating PSV in this case is pretty obvious: don't be seen stalking the victim. If you're going to be visible, blend into the background. Be anonymous, but make that anonymity different every time.

You don't want a detective locating you through what Dad calls "the incremental use of collateral factors," for example non-connected witnesses, like somebody watching from the boardwalk, the detective nudging them into remembering "a kind of ordinary looking guy, except he was sort of grimy, with a bottle of wine, watching the documentary people the whole time..." And maybe th

ticing a guy about the same height and weight and rac

in the vicinity of the victim some other time. From ther

starts to put together a picture of a possible stalker: me

Being truly, really anonymous, Dad says, is a great art.

Dad taught me to take mental notes, never to write anything down, or record anything. Never to use videotape. All that stuff can be used as evidence against you. It happened to Granddad: he kept a written journal, and they found it. It was cryptic, but still, it connected him with the victim. His big money connections got him off, but it was a near thing.

So I'm noting everything mentally; taking mental snapshots. Click: My victim has assistants, but no bodyguards. No one is expecting trouble—My Victim was chosen, partly, for having no enemies.

"There's a trade-off," Dad told me. "If he had no enemies, then his being killed stands out, and that's bad, it makes them look for someone anomalous, like you. If he had enemies then there's a good chance those enemies would be blamed instead of you, should you fall under suspicion. That'd be good. But... the Principle that applies here is of never letting yourself be *known* to be in the victim's life—so you can't possibly fall under suspicion no matter what. As far as anyone knows, in the context of your victim, you don't exist. They can't suspect someone who doesn't exist. And a guy who has no enemies is not looking around, he has no bodyguards looking around, no paranoid hirelings. And that's worth more than having somebody who can be blamed. It's worth way more, son."

Another mental snapshot. Click: my victim has an easy, comfortable way with strangers. He's now interviewing one of the teenagers, a slack-faced kid whose eyes keep wandering to anything but Corey.

Corey being comfortable with strangers means—if that comfort extends to all strangers and not just interviewees—that I might be able to talk my way into his house, say, on one pretext or another, if I'm sure he's alone. To murder him, of course. To murder him in his home, which is out in the country, in privacy.

Click: he's drinking a can of *Coors Lite* as he talks to the guy. Drinks *mildly* on the job, three cans a day: obvious poisoning applications. Drinking on the job and from a beer he's packed in a cooler, at home, too, gives me another arena for a possible poisoning.

Dad recommends poisoning. You don't get blood on you; you don't have to be there when your victim dies, which of course means less opportunity for some haphazard, unexpected witness (Fifth *Principle of Safe Victimization*: always expect an unexpected witness) to tie you into the Execution Zone.

Poison sounds good to me too. Jeremy, now, wants to kill his victim with a gun. Dad will allow it, but doesn't advise it. In fact I can see he finds it distasteful. I tried to tell this to Jeremy when we went horseback riding along the beach north of Malibu, the day after his birthday.

"Dude," I said to my brother, "it's not just that he doesn't like the mess and it doesn't matter how careful you are not to get blood on you or to use an untraceable gun or to take care with the fingerprints or whatever. The whole point is not identifying with the killing. If you want to use a gun, it means you might like killing just for killing. And that's bullshit. It's not about liking or not liking."

"Oh come on," Jeremy said. He's a short, chunky, blue-eyed guy with Mom's curly shiny black hair. He carries himself like a pimp entering a pool-hall, Dad told me once, when he was pissed at Jeremy: High-stepping arrogance. But that's how Jeremy moves through the world. Thinks he's way adult by now but he isn't. "We get all this training so we can destroy people, so we can kill—you're supposed to like what you're good at. Dad even said so. 'Love this art' he said."

"The art is the preparation, the not-getting-caught, the chess game of it—like you're playing chess with all the cops in the world at once. It's not the moment, the actual act of making the victim dead. That's why he doesn't let us kill girls, man. You might..."

I broke off. I could tell he didn't like the way this was coming out. "I might what?"

"Not you. I mean anyone. Anyone might get off on that—Dad says there's some kind of sexual thing when you kill any kind of female. It's all subconscious."

"Hey bro, Freud was discredited."

He's proud of getting a 3.8 majoring in psyche his sophomore year: Psychology as a preparation for going into marketing later. Behaviorism. We're both heading for the best MBAs we can get, of course. Dad and the family made that part of the Sworn Tradition, in the '80s. Given my choice I'd have been an American Lit major, but Sworn is Sworn.

"It's not Freud, its more like sociobiology or something. Or—I don't know, I just know there's automatically a sexual . . . a sexual part to it."

I'd started to say "sexual component" but said "sexual part" instead because, with Jeremy, if you use a phrase like "sexual component" he'll scowl and come back at you with something like "the elasticity of post-structuralism", some string of ten dollar words that won't mean a whole lot. He's competitive like that. Especially in the context of talking about Dad. He's always worried more about impressing Dad.

"I don't give a goddamn about that," he said. "I kill who I'm assigned to kill. If it's going to be male, fine, whatever. But don't say I'm a fag if I happen to . . . to love the art of it."

"What? No, I wasn't going that way at all—I'm talking about identification with the killing. It's as important to not like the killing *particularly* as it is not to care about the victim."

"Oh come on. Nothing's more important than not identifying with the victim. That's primo, that's tops. Otherwise you blow everything. That's the whole point of doing it in the first place."

I decided to let it drop. He was stating the obvious; he wasn't getting the subtle, and the art of victimization is subtle. "Subtle understanding of setting and situation is what keeps a man from being caught," Dad had told me.

Dad killed three Random Personal Victims, chosen at twenty year intervals. Sometimes, see, you need more than one. He says you'll know if you need another one; if you need to re-commit. It may be a man only needs one Random Personal Victim. I never asked Dad why he needed three, but I have my suspicions. I figure I'll only need the one—

because I'll know I'm killing various other people, routinely, as part of the business, anyway. It's all about not hiding from that knowledge. Having the courage to do *anything* necessary. People use the phrase "moral courage"; there's also such a thing as amoral courage.

But that day, all I said to Jeremy was, "Race you back to the limo, bigshot."

And we did, raced the horses back to the beach parking lot where the limo was waiting. I let him win. The groom put the horses in the trailer behind the truck, and we got in the limo, and played Nintendo 64 in the back, all the way home to the winter house.

Now, in Santa Monica. The edges of shapes around us grow dull; colors become less colorful: dusk is coming. The shadows are reaching out from the pylons. Another young boy is talking to Corey's camera about how he likes living on the sand under the boardwalk, it's usually warm enough, it's never *too* warm, "and it don't smell too bad, and there's always some shit happening, somebody's got something, or they can figure out where to get something", and he doesn't mind "renting" himself to some of the guys on the Venice muscle beach strip, some-times, "because, I mean, people ask me, and I go: Who cares? I mean, shit, whatever."

I wonder how many thousands of years prostitutes have been saying that, in a thousand different languages. I had a good history prof, Mr. Delany, he really gives you a perspective. He doesn't know about the Sworn Tradition, though. No outsider does. But he knows about P-2, and the Cosa Nostra—.

But no—Cosa Nostra—that's so very, very different. We don't in-volve ourselves in crime, as people understand the word, apart from the Victims. We shear the sheep legally. And, too, the Sworn Tradition is all in one extensive family, or intertwined families, which is never something that can be entered by anyone outside the family, not even by marriage; you have to be a descendent of the original bloodlines, which was Northern Italian and Austrian. And still is. *Only* Northern Italian, and Austrian. *Only*. It goes back to just before the Renaissance; to the great Italian conspirators, some of whose names became household words. "Machiavelli was a simpering weakling," my father once said, chuckling.

Anyway, our family doesn't interfere in the broader outline of history, unless it serves us financially. It's all about accruing wealth, of course. "What for others is crass materialism is for us a sacred trust," Uncle Tino once said, after his third Remy. "If we worshipped a god, it would be toothy old Mammon." But of course we worship nothing but "pleasure in survival, survival in pleasure".

I am careful to appear to go to sleep on the sand, with my back to my Victim; to be sure he's gone before I leave. Sixth sub-PSV: *Movement calls attention.*

Dad began eradicating my "non-familial empathy" early, very early. Three years old.

"I wish to God my Father had started me early," he said, when I asked him about it five, six years later. I was around nine. Asked him, with a sudden and uncharacteristic boldness, why he'd made me kill my Lhasa puppy with the piano wire when I was three. On one level I knew why—he'd explained it to me, he'd been training me all along—but then again I didn't know; in some other way, some deeper way, I didn't understand, not then.

I had expected the question to make him angry. But instead he began, "I wish my Father . . ." He broke off and shook his head. He got that odd sort of ghostly look in his eyes, at such moments. I'm only beginning to understand that look.

We were on the back lawn, between the topiaries and the main house of our summer place in Eddington, England; we were watching the trainer work with the hunting dog, in the early morning. The sun was pulling the dew into gossamer streamers. Father was standing there with his hands in his pockets. I had heard one of his hired wives screaming with almost convincing joy from the guest house the night before and thought I'd see him pleased this morning, but he looked almost in grief.

"You see, my father didn't start me until I was twelve, son, and by then a man has too many opportunities to create the capacity for non-familial bonding. And it was hard when he made me kill my little brother."

I looked at him in real shock: Silent and resonant, I can still feel it, more than a decade later.

He smiled wearily. "Yes. He was only four. Well, you understand: He had spina bifida. He could not have been allowed to reproduce. He ... was a symbol of family decay—so long as he lived. But once dead, he was, you might say, transformed into a symbol of vitality: to cut away the sickly limb is to renew vitality. However ..." I remember his hand raised to express something inexpressable; a cryptic gesture, like signing for the deaf, but signing a non-word, something not found in any lexicon. "Somehow I had become identified with him, son ... though I had been warned that his sickliness made him—we never told him this, of course—it made him non-family. And even within the family we permit only the Higher Bonding. The Higher Bonding is undertaken with a clear vision, and so it is provisional ..."

So in making me kill the puppy, my father was saving me from what he'd suffered when he'd had to kill his brother by smothering him with a pillow, his father supervising. He was snuffing the candle of empathy for anything outside the Sworn, because that candle grew, over the years, unless you snuffed it early, snuffed it small. The pain was less, after that, and the forgetting, the annihilation of caring came easier.

Dad and I, that day, watched the trainer yank the dog up short on a choke chain. A sense of masculine communion with the trainer, with Dad.

That conversation on the lawn, more than a decade ago, is on my mind as I get out of a bus a few blocks west of downtown L.A. I can't drive myself here, or take a limo, of course, since I'm here to watch Corey. A cab driver would remember me.

Corey will be on the far side of the old, ragged park, near the reeking duck pond, interviewing runaways. Today I won't be close enough to be noticed. I'll watch through binoculars—

"Son?"

Dad is rolling down the window of his Porsche, at the curb just behind me. I'm surprised to see him so near a stalk-zone. He tilts his head, summoning me into the car. He's wearing a linen Armani sports jacket, collarless offwhite shirt, sunglasses. A classical music station plays on the car radio. He closes the windows of the car, as I sit beside him, turns on the air conditioning. "You're going to let him see you again, son?" he asks, looking across the park. Three cholo kids throw broken glass at plastic pop bottles bobbing in the pond.

"He won't see me. I'll use binoculars. Won't get within two hundred yards."

"You might be noticed by someone in the park: a white guy, here, watching another white guy with binoculars."

"Well, I have a way to do it, that . . ."

"Whatever you've got in mind won't work. Strikes me you're taking a long time at this stage. Makes me wonder how serious you are."

My mouth goes dry. "Um . . ."

"We'll talk about it another time. You know, your brother date-raped a girl, last night, at school. He might face charges."

I look at him in real amazement. Why would Jeremy do that? He can have some of the finest women available. He gets laid all the time. And it's so fundamental, not drawing attention to the family by breaking society's laws.

He chuckles dourly. "I was just as surprised. Well, almost. He's growing . . . undisciplined. It happens sometimes. It's usually a genetic defect. We do have to struggle with inbreeding. When it happens, the unruliness has to be weeded out."

I look at him. I made myself ask without a quaver, "Are you sure?"

"No, no I'm not. It could be an aberration. We can arrange for this thing to be smoothed over. A million, two million dollars spread out here and there. And if he reins himself in . . . It might not be necessary for you to prove yourself well and truly Sworn."

I have felt it coming. I try to pretend that I was prepared. I want badly to swallow but I wouldn't let myself. "But—it might be?"

Dad nods, looking at me. "You might have to kill your brother. Say it."

I wet my lips so I could say it. "I might have to kill my brother."

"Good. Sub Rosa, all this, of course. You don't even know about the date-rape accusation."

"Yes. Of course."

"And son? I think, today, you will not follow your victim. It may be that your victim will not be this man Corey. It may be your brother instead. If it's Corey—you won't have to kill your brother. But for today—let the stalk-and-study go. Today doesn't feel right for this . . ."

He taps the binocular case on its strap over my shoulder. I nod.

"I'll give you a ride home."

The crisis passes. My brother was truly penitent; but in a controlled way. Dad tells me I can go back to choosing The Moment with Corey. Picking the Execution Zone. Today, I'm watching my victim at the mall. And of course I'm looking very different from the way I looked on the beach. I come off young for my age: clean shaven and grunged out, I pass for a teenager who's in the mall because there isn't any other place to go.

My victim is in the sporting goods store, picking up a fresh supply of target arrows. Corey is one of these the Zen and the Art of Archery guys. I've been watching him for about two months—the limit of observation time, if you do it right—and I've seen him here twice before. After he buys the arrows he goes to the tobacconist and gets some Balkan Sobranies; an expensive cigarette he only allows himself when he hits the target near enough the center. Never smokes except during archery. He's a good archer, and I'm glad the *Principles* are totally opposed to giving the victim a square chance. He'd kill me sure.

At the range I have to be in complete concealment; there aren't enough people here for comfortable camouflage; he might well notice me. But concealment isn't hard, with lots of trees and brush around the range. The oak tree I'm squatting under still has most of its leaves, but the ones that have fallen crackle when I shift my weight from one hunkered leg to the other. Spiders squat in web tunnels, hundreds of webs like little fishing nets in the tangle of junipers that hides me. A bluejay screams like a British soccer fan overhead. It's getting on my nerves and I'd like to chuck a rock at it but I know better.

Soon I'm engrossed in watching Corey.

We're required to think of our victims by their first names. It's a deliberate invitation to empathy; a sort of test. *The victims are not to be thought of as 'it': think of them as three-dimensional, living breathing human beings, with parents and children and feelings. As former children. If this brings up a pang in you, then you're at the secondary stage in your Life-training.* And it's all the more reason you must kill the man.

I watch him choose an arrow from the quiver on the rack beside him; I watch him nock it, with the second-nature deftness of long practice; I watch him draw the bow and fire, and somehow it's all one movement even though there are two or three seconds between drawing and firing. The arrow flies to just outside the bullseye. He takes another arrow, nocks it, draws, seems to become very still, as still as the target, and lets fly. To either side of him other archers are cursing, chattering, laughing, muttering, squinting, tensing; in comparison Corey is a study in relaxed self-containment. This time his arrow strikes the bullseye, and he allows himself to light a cigarette, to inhale once, deeply, before nocking, in a way, the cigarette, too, in the ashtray he's brought along.

After four more arrows, three striking the bullseye, the lady next to him—a big-assed, sourfaced woman with short clipped hair and a workshirt—asks him not to smoke anymore. His nod is almost a bow, and doesn't smoke any more. It doesn't interfere with his shooting, this abstention; it doesn't seem to make him tense, there's not even quiet irritation in his body language.

I let out a long, deep breath and shake my head in admiration. The guy really has something. Talent, skill, grace and imperturbability. Dignity.

I know, of course, that all the Victims have noticeable good qualities, or good people dependent on them. Sweet-looking children waiting at home, say. What's the point of trying to burn out empathy where none is likely to be generated? If you aren't instinctively reluctant to kill the victim, then he's probably not challenging enough. Of course, if you've got to the Fixity Point, the aim of our Lifetraining, where you can kill and *genuinely* feel nothing—feel nothing *and without repression*—then your killing is only a necessary ritual, an affirmation of the Sworn Tradition. And something more: it's the Tradition's hold over you, of course. Even if you become infected, diseased by "conscience", you can't report the Tradition without reporting yourself. Not that you'd live long if you tried.

So I let myself feel the admiration for my victim. Repression makes a man "guilty", and that makes him sick. He must kill randomly and consciously and this frees him from repercussions. So it is in theory. But sometimes I see that ghostliness around my father's eyes and wonder.

I think again that a guy like Corey, he's seriously worth killing: it completes him, in a way. This guy, he really is like architecture: you can see the philosophy of the builder in the building's design. This guy blueprints his whole life according to some kind of philosophy. Zen, I think, or something like it. His documentaries are all about raising consciousness of the underprivileged and the lost. I tell myself that uncreation is an art form too.

I saw him with his girlfriend only once—a pretty Asian-American. She's studying film at NYU, back east, and they are being patient and faithful while they wait for her to get through it. They see each other when they can.

She's a feminist but somehow Corey is almost chivalrous around her without seeming to put her down with it. I still haven't figured out how he does it.

I remember feeling a real ache when they kissed. Because you could see him communicating something to her in the kiss. It's something I can't do. I'm allowed to have sex with the best call-girls in the world; at those prices, they'll kiss you, and with passion. You can like them— the expensive ones are educated and pretty and charming—and they can like you. But I'm not allowed to feel *close,* of course. It's against the Sworn Tradition. And when, from the select families, a wife is chosen for me, I am free to feel a passion for her; but to actually fall in love would be foolish. Her life with us is provisional, in so many ways.

I break off surveillance, and trudge through the woods, climb over a barbed wire fence to cross a field where cattle graze. My limbs feel heavy, somehow, and I don't understand why. An old man in a plaid shirt and work-boots, a cranky old rancher, pulls up in his truck and shouts at me to approach with my hands up, he's sick of people wandering over his land, he's going to press charges. I approach him and give him seven one hundred dollar bills, without a word. His mouth hanging open with surprise, he lets me go, just as wordless.

I walk down the gravel road to where the limo is waiting. The driver, of course, is an Initiated Servant. They're all Sworn, on their own level; picked very carefully. They are paid well for their loyalty, and usually retire with at least a million dollars after taxes.

Dad gets out of the limo. He must have come in his own white stretch, and switched over, waited here for me.

We walk down the road together, talking, hands in pockets. The driver is an old man from Corsica; he waits. He'd wait for days if he had to, and not make a sound.

Dad deepens the chill already gathering in my belly when he asks, "Son, why follow him to archery, again, after two months? Are you thinking of arranging an accident there? That'd be tricky. You'd have to be in complicity with someone . . ."

Having anyone help you with the kill is, of course, forbidden; a grievous violation of both the *Principles of Safe Victimization* and the *Basic Articles of Understanding*.

"No, it's just general surveillance."

He looks at me. It's never any use lying to him.

"Well," I add, with an apologetic smile, "I guess I'm feeling pangs, feeling empathy, and I figure I have to *really* feel it before I can 'let the rose wither' . . . I mean, you said don't suppress . . ."

"Yes. But—not at two months. At one month, yes. But son—how long have you been feeling this thing?"

Another lie springs to mind. I dismiss it. "You're right. At least a month."

"So it's gone beyond 'letting the rose wither'. It's stalling, son. You don't want to kill him . . . because *you really like him.*"

I feel the tears coming. My father doesn't chasten me for the tears. He knows they're tears of shame.

Corey is drinking *Coors Lite* as he sits on his redwood deck, out behind his two bedroom place at the end of a long, lonely road East of Thousand Oaks. He's sitting in a wooden deck chair, writing a letter to his girlfriend. He always writes to her in his own handwriting, on stationery: Long letters in flowing freehand. He hasn't looked closely at the can; hasn't seen the needlehole in it, and after he takes another sip of the beer, he begins to choke. He lurches to his feet and flails toward the back door, trying to get to the bathroom, or the phone, I'll never know which, and then he staggers once more, and he falls.

He is convulsing face-down, the pen gripped in his fist stabbing the redwood planks, his legs jerking, as I climb over the wooden railing and come to stand over him. I flip him over with my foot, so I can look into his face as he dies, as my father has ordered me to do.

There's yellow foam around his lips. His mouth opens and closes soundlessly but it is his eyes that ask the question.

"You'd never understand why I killed you. But I will say I'm not the stranger you think I am."

His head shakes, or maybe it's convulsion, and the ancient, untraceable, traditional poison, which in our family we call only Number 317, moves inexorably into its final stage, and he shivers once, decisively, and stops breathing.

After a moment, tentatively feeling my inner self, I realize the "rose" is withering. I am becoming Fixed. It is a profound relief.

Father comes out of his place of concealment, on the far side of the rocks. Smiling. "Congratulations, son. Now, and only now, are you fit to run the world's biggest multinational." He embraces me. I feel nothing as he embraces me, except pride of accomplishment. The rose is withered.

Nineteen Seconds

Someone nudged Alan from behind. In his turn, he nudged his little brother, ahead of him. "Move up." Two more steps because another kid had gone down the Drain.

"I timed the slide," Donny said, moving the two steps. "It takes about nineteen seconds to go down the Drain if you're laying down when you do the slide. Sitting up after the tunnel, it's about twenty-one or twenty-two seconds . . ."

How many seconds in a year, Alan wondered. *How many seconds have I been alive?* Alan was fifteen today. His Dad had arranged the birthday party. Alan hadn't wanted a birthday party at the waterslides, that was something you did for a ten-year-old, or twelve oldest. It was just one stroke up from jumping into a bin of plastic balls at the Kiddie Zone.

Donny, his brown hair thatchy from repeated wettings, was staring deeply into his watch, his lips moving, practicing the stopwatch mode.

Trying not to think about the spider, or his asthma, Alan wondered why kids around ten and eleven got into timing things. How fast to run ten yards, how fast to go down a slide. They loved watches with built-in stopwatches.

Donny was nut-brown—he had his Dad's skin, seemed to tan easily. And he had Dad's easy carriage, his coordination. More than once Alan had caught the look of relief and hope in his father's eyes when he watched Donny play softball: This one wouldn't be a disappointment.

The line of chattering, squinting kids in bathing suits was moving slowly up the wet, winding fiberplastic stairs; step, step, stop—wait— step, step, stop—wait. Alan and Donny were two-thirds the way up the stairs edging the Drain, the fastest twistiest waterslide in the Wet City waterpark. Alan felt the Central California sun pushing on him; its heat seeming to ricochet directly at him from the flat, dusty fields around the waterpark. He savored the occasional gusts of chlorinated mist from the little waterfalls feeding the blue and green fiberglass tubes of the waterslides. The dust, the heat, the unseen clouds of pollen threatened to close off his chest again, and he was afraid of having an asthma attack in front of the others. He'd left his inhaler down at the picnic table—he'd look like an even more pathetic geek, carrying it around in his swimming trunks. The rest of the birthday party were local kids his father invited, high school freshmen like him; they'd said yes just for a free trip to the waterslides—last chance to get wet in the heat before school started. He didn't want to crumble in front of them: Yancy Stephens and his girlfriend Lani and that Danya with the twisty little smiles when she looked at you, like she was trying not to laugh. If he crumbled in front of them with an asthma attack, or lost it to his fear of spiders and toy animals, they'd all try not to laugh. Like they had when they'd seen him come out of the changing rooms, long and skinny and pallid and reeking of the strongest possible sunscreen. And they were good at things that people cared about, they were not defective, it was as if all their parts worked so smoothly together, inside them. They were smoothly functioning machines, there was nothing wrong with them. They were even good enough to try not to laugh.

"I'm gonna push, see if I can get it down to eighteen or seventeen seconds," Donny said.

"Could depend on when you manage to look at your watch, after you crash into the pool at the bottom," Alan said.

Donny made a disgusted face; Alan was raining on his parade.

"You could keep your finger on the clicker thing on your watch and hit it just when you hit the water," Alan suggested.

Donny brightened.

They were nearly at the top level now, a few minutes from making their plunge. You could see the whole park from here twenty-five acres of what used to be a wheat field, now it was nine waterslide structures and the Wild Sprinkler area for the little kids to play in. The waterslides were eccentric, complex structures, looping blue Dr. Seuss edifices, an apparent whimsicality underpinned with engineering rigor; flashing streams and waterfalls, laughing voices merging with rushing water. Sometimes vagrant breezes invaded the chlorine and sunscreen smell, betrayed the rot and blood of the slaughterhouse, down the highway a few miles.

Alan was increasingly aware that the asthma threat—the tightening in his chest, the shallowing of his breath—was entwined with naked fear. This particular slide, the Drain, scared him as no other did and for no good reason at all. He liked roller coasters, he liked the Top Gun at Great America, which could prise tooth fillings loose with its sudden G-forces. He liked the other water slides. But the Drain seemed to be designed by whoever had designed the night terrors he'd had when he was ten and eleven. It had an innovation: those animal faces that popped out at you, and three short waterfall drops. Then there was nature's own innovation: the black widow he'd seen just after the Tunnel of Darkness, as his brother called it. The spider that no one else had seen.

"When I go through the Tunnel of Darkness, this time," Donny said, his voice given a kazoo quality by the finger in his nose, "I'm gonna make myself really straight like those luge guys so I just shoot through like a bullet through a barrel . . ."

"What kind of tunnel, anyway, *isn't* a tunnel of darkness," Alan said, eyeing the entrance to the slide as a blonde girl in a bikini, her breasts just big enough to justify the top, hesitated in its entrance until her friend gave her a shove and she went squealing down . . . maybe to run into the black widow. "I mean, it's redundant. All tunnels are dark, pretty much."

"Redund what?"

"Never mind." He turned away from Danny to look out over the fields around the park.

"You're getting a burned spot in the middle of your back, dude."

"Great. Just great. That's the spot I couldn't reach . . ." Usually Dad or Mom would've put the sunscreen on his back but there wasn't a chance to do it without the party guest kids seeing and he'd look even geekier getting gunk smeared on his back like a baby getting baby oil.

They were only five kids away from the top of the slide. A bored college jock in shorts and shirt, whistle on a string around his neck, was supervising the kids going down. The college kid's nose was peeling from sunburn and he kept gazing longingly over the alfalfa fields around the waterpark, toward Sacramento.

The little farming community of Central Corners, where Alan went to high school, was about thirty miles from the outskirts of Sacramento, the nearest big town. Everybody knew everybody, and everybody knew that the teenagers all wanted to get out of town.

Two kids now. "You didn't even see a shadow hanging in that bush over the slide that could be a spider?" Alan said suddenly, looking at the dim mouth of the tunnel opening of the slide.

"Get over that spider thing," Donny said, too loudly. The two middle school girls in front of them looked at them, then grinned at each other.

"Shut up, fag-ass," Alan said, his face reddening.

"You shut up, Shovel Boy," Donny retorted.

"Shut up about that," Alan muttered.

"Then you don't call me names neither."

Shovel Boy. He'd spent half the summer shoveling manure for the Corral of the Doomed, as the local kids called it: the pen where they kept cattle, waiting to go into their own chutes, their wooden slides into the slaughterhouse. The cattle lifting their heads, smelling blood in the air, lowing, their eyes rolling. Knowing.

The idea had been to earn enough money for a car, but they paid you by the loadful, and it was a lot harder than he'd thought. He'd quit after three weeks with only seven-hundred-forty bucks. And what could you buy with that?

Now it was Donny's turn to go down. "Okay, checking watch," he said, climbing up onto the little launching seat at the tunnel mouth. "Okay, checking watch, checking watch, five four three—"

"You're holding up the line," the jock said.

"—two one!" And then he was gone, Alan's little brother sucked laughing down a drain into the darkness. Maybe the spider would get on Donny.

The jock glanced at Alan, made a keep-it-moving motion with his hand. Alan bit his lower lip, and told himself, in his mind, *Get over it, dude, for real.* He climbed up onto the seat. . . .

Shit, you know that the fiberglass bears and cougar are the park's lame attempts to copy something the owner saw at Disneyland and they don't even scare three year olds . . . And the spider isn't—

"You going, dude, or what?" the jock asked.

Alan held his breath, which was his first mistake, and leaned back, pushed off with his hands, onto the stream of water and down the blue fiberglass slide, into the tunnel.

Big fucking deal, in nineteen seconds . . .

Down into darkness of the slide, slipping through his mother's fingers, like in the night terrors—later he'd worked out that each incident in the hollow crackling pith of the night, each night terror lasted maybe two minutes and seemed like hours . . . and hours.

Alan eleven years old, waking for the fourth time that year with what one doctor had said, later, was "classic night terrors" and what one had said was "sleep apnea complicated with a mild seizure of some kind." For him it was being awake in a body that was going on a shambling ride without him, feeling like his blood had been replaced with hot wax that was cooling, thickening; and he had sat up in bed, watching the pee welling out the side of his underpants, seeing it as if it were something completely different, just a phenomenon of color and liquidity, an expression of his insides, coming in pulses that seemed completely disconnected, though he could feel each pulse of release; and taking so long, an hour, it seemed to him. Then he found himself walking down the carpeted hallway, trudging away from the taste in his mouth, but you couldn't get away from a taste, it was like metallic shit with burning electricity in it, that taste, and it was spreading through his jaw, making his jaw soft as it spread so that when he tried to shout for someone to help him, the bones of his jaw flopped around, only gargling noises coming out, and the trudging went on for hours, till he felt that coldness dripping from his scalp and he started to touch the back of his head but stopped when he realized the back of his skull was gone, and his brain was exposed, wet, don't touch it, you'll break something and make it even worse, just get down the hall to the light, but now something was oozing from the dark borders into the trapezoid of yellow light, like a stain of motor oil (he could taste the motor oil) spreading into urine; now the spreading stain was taking shape, was a silhouette of a bear, a man in a bear suit, or just the bear suit alive, yes just an empty bear suit, empty but alive, turned half away from him; it was the mascot of that team that his Dad and his brother watched on TV, its head revolving slowly on its shoulders toward him, its face trying to find an expression, contorting as it tried to make a beckoning grin, but its horrible, diseased nature forcing the expression into a murderous leer, one glassy bear-mascot eye drifting way higher than the other. And Alan rooted himself in place, in the hallway, so he wouldn't get any closer to the bear, but the floor was moving like one of those slow moving rubber sidewalks in the airport drawing him toward the bear which was splitting open down its fat middle to rattlingly spew the white granite gravel that Grandma Ellsby had fallen on when she had that stroke that killed her, Grandma's hand clutching the gravel. Her yellow hand opening and closing. His mother was yelling at him with a megaphone voice, distant and fuzzy like the voice of the vice principal at school coming through the intercom, when you could only make out every third word the vice principal said except you could always hear him say, at the end, *You are expected to remember this.*

"AlAn, dAmMit, lOOk AT mE, WhAt aRe yOU DOinG!"

His mom's teeth seemed yellow, mossy, in her mouth, extending to become an endless wall of mossy teeth stretching away into the yellow trapezoid distance, the teeth curving around to wrap her head, thousands of crooked, green-yellow teeth in a rippling, dancing ribbon, and the smell of burning iron; then the smell of that "just a little off" hot dog he hadn't wanted to eat that his Dad had made him eat because he thought he was just being "a prima donna about his food again" that had given him food poisoning, the teeth dancing, his mother shouting—

He was slipping to his wobbly knees as Mom shook him, in that hallway; he was sliding through Mom's fingers, and he heard himself saying, "I had a service station man putting teeth, putting teeth, if that bear comes, the smell of Mr. Green Things for a thousand points..." He was trying to say something else, not sure what, but that's what came out, and then sinking to the floor and jerking upright as Dad poured ice water on him to shock him out of it... The sudden blaze of the hall light as Dad hit the switch—

—Blaze of sunlight as he came out of the first set of waterslide corkscrews and rushed feet-first toward the end of Donny's Tunnel of Darkness, the urine-yellow light up ahead—something sliding into it from the side, running along a web, taking on shape as it lowered itself, dangling, quivering down: the black widow, seeking, perhaps, to extend her web, her bulbous abdomen no bigger than a cherry-pit but it seemed to swell in his sight like a black balloon instantly expanded on a balloon-filling machine, as she dropped lower and he kicked at her, missed, and then she dropped on an unseen thread at his crotch—some part of his mind noticing that all this was taking too long, though it must have been under a second from seeing the spider and seeing her drop, it seemed to take five minutes of rushing toward the spider, his limbs leaden-heavy as he tried to move to avoid her, the weight of slowed perceptions fighting high speed—then she'd dropped—

She must've missed him, must've gone under him, when she—

Dropped, down the first waterfall, the slide angling enough so it wasn't a complete drop but a sudden plunge into steepness, the sunlight exulting in a blast of rainbows, cloud of mist, and his heart gave a leap, the protraction of time now a kind of grace as it opened up his plunge into this pool of shine and cerulean water, the thought that he was getting past his fears, he was halfway through the slide, he could hear music echoing from somewhere, celebrating him, singing *You got past the spider*—!

Then he was plunged again, was twisted to the left, slamming his shoulder on the smooth, gripless surface, jerked right with the switchback to slam his right shoulder and cheek achingly on the wall, yelling at the unexpected pain. A mouthful of water, tasting chlorine, swallowing it, coughing—what if the black widow were in the water and he swallowed her alive—

Another plunge, a spin past the herky-jerky movement of the leaping plastic cougar, which looked to him not threatening but scared itself, as if the cougar were running from the next thing to come, warning him of the next plunge, even as it came, thump and choke, and there! the rearing animatronic bear, too much like the mascot bear, muzzle wrinkled in fury as it jerked toward him on its turntable; he saw Grandma's hand reaching from a split at the lifesize plastic bear's middle, plaintively reaching out, the hand no more yellowed or clawlike than it had been in that final year of her life, skin the color of tobacco stain, trembling out for him: if he could grab her hand he could pull her out, he clutched but missed and he heard her reproachful cry as he passed, and then the bear's icy shadow fell over him, from the trapezoid of yellow, its face meshing with his father's face, shouting at him, *Cut this bullshit out Alan* and then the sinking into the rug, with the sinking a great weight on his chest, closing around his bronchial tubes, the wheezing begun, and as he opened wide on the final spurt of the drainslide he saw a long black spider's leg extruding from the edge of his bathing suit she had—

She had got on him—

She was on him—

And the knowledge was stronger than the time he'd thought his hair was on fire, had awakened slapping at his hair, convinced, sure with a noontime certainty, that his hair was aflame and he was going to burn to death starting from the top—

More certainly than that: Knowing that the spider was on him as he spun through the blue half-tube, shouting, clawing at himself, someone laughing on the stairs beside the slide, Alan trying to shout *Get it off, get it off*, his jaws too heavy; if only the bear would call its spider back, the spider was one of the bear's eyes but with teeth to bite . . . Each breath so far from the last one, farther yet from the next, as he clawed his trunks off him and ripped at his crotch with his fingernails, maybe the black widow has got under his foreskin, she was going to get up his—*Get it off*—

A sweeping, slushy swish, a single bass-note, and then he was in the pool at the bottom of the slide, turning over in water only three feet deep, thrashing, seeing his feet above, they were framing the sun and a black crinkled spot on the sun—a spider sunspot—

The spider—!

The bear gripped his upper arm, yanking him upright.

No. It was a tall girl in shorts and 49ers T-shirt and short red hair and quizzical look and a whistle around her neck, "Whoa there guy," she was saying, leaning back so she could lift him to his feet...

Yancy, Lani and Danya were standing in a group beside a mortified Donny, near the edge of the landing pool at the bottom of the Drainslide; Donny's mouth open, he was staring as if he'd forgotten how to blink, Yancy and Lani and Danya were trying not to laugh, Yancy not quite succeeding, shaking his head silent with laughter—

Alan knowing he'd clawed off his swimming trunks, was standing there naked and bleeding, looking down to see his foreskin torn, clawmarks on his stomach.

He tried to say, *There was a black widow, look, there it is, floating in the water! I had to get it off—*

But he was wheezing with the asthma attack, crumbling in front of them, unable to speak and the turbulence in the pool had swept the spider into a little black dot that was sucked, as he watched, into the filtering trough, along with his swimming trunks.

He looked at Yancy and Lani, and Danya and knew that his insides had become transparent to them, they were looking into him, seeing the disconnected parts inside him, and knowing, the three of them, forever knowing with a concrete certainty that he was fundamentally defective, he was defective, he was just defective.

Jody and Annie on TV

First time he has the feeling, he's doing 75 on the 134. Sun glaring the color off the cars, smog filming the North Hollywood hills. Just past the place where the 134 snakes into the Ventura freeway, he's driving Annie's dad's fucked-up '78 Buick Skylark convertible, one hand on the wheel the other on the radio dial, trying to find a tune, and nothing sounds good. But *nothing*. Everything sounds stupid, even metal. You think it's the music but it's not, you know? It's you.

Usually, it's just a weird mood. But this time it shifts a gear. He looks up from the radio and realizes: You're not driving this car. It's automatic in traffic like this: only moderately heavy traffic, moving fluidly, sweeping around the curves like they're all part of one long thing. Most of your mind is thinking about what's on TV tonight and if you could stand working at that telephone sales place again . . .

It hits him that he is two people, the programmed-Jody who drives and fiddles with the radio and the real Jody who thinks about getting work . . . Makes him feel funny, detached.

The feeling closes in on him like a jar coming down over a wasp. Glassy like that. He's pressed between the back window and the wind-shield, the two sheets of glass coming together, compressing him like something under one of those biology-class microscope slides. Everything goes two-dimensional. The cars like the ones in that Roadmaster video game, animated cars made out of pixels.

A buzz of panic, a roaring, and then someone laughs as he jams the Buick's steering wheel over hard to the right, jumps into the VW Bug's lane, forcing it out; the Bug reacts, jerks away from him, sudden and scared, like it's going, "Shit!" Cutting off a Toyota four-by-four with tractor-sized tires, lot of good those big fucking tires do the Toyota, because it spins out and smacks sideways into the grill of a rusty old semitruck pulling an open trailer full of palm trees . . .

They get all tangled up back there. He glances back and thinks, *I did that*. He's grinning and shaking his head and laughing. He's not sorry and he likes the fact that he's not sorry. *I did that*. It's so amazing, so totally rad.

Jody has to pull off at the next exit. His heart is banging like a fire alarm as he pulls into a Texaco. Goes to get a Coke.

It comes to him on the way to the Coke machine that he's stoked. He feels connected and in control and pumped up. The gas fumes smell good; the asphalt under the thin rubber of his sneakers feels good. *Huh.* The Coke tastes good. He thinks he can taste the cola berries. He should call Annie. She should be in the car, next to him.

He goes back to the car, heads down the boulevard a mile past the accident, swings onto the freeway, gets up to speed—which is only about thirty miles an hour because the accident's crammed everyone into the left three lanes. Sipping Coca-Cola, he looks the accident over. Highway cops aren't there yet, just the Toyota four-by-four, the rusty semi with its hood wired down, and a Yugo. The VW got away, but the little caramel-colored Yugo is like an accordion against the back of the truck. The Toyota is bent into a short boomerang shape around the snout of the semi, which is jackknifed onto the road shoulder. The Mexican driver is nowhere around. Probably didn't have a green card, ducked out before the cops show up. The palm trees kinked up in the back of the semi are whole, grown-up palm trees, with the roots and some soil tied up in big plastic bags, going to some rebuilt place in Bel Air. One of the palm trees droops almost completely off the back of the trailer.

Jody checks out the dude sitting on the Toyota's hood. The guy's sitting there, rocking with pain, waiting. A kind of ski mask of blood on his face.

I did that, three of 'em, bingo, just like that. Maybe it'll get on TV news.

Jody cruised on by and went to find Annie.

It's on TV because of the palm trees. Jody and Annie, at home, drink Coronas, watch the crane lifting the palm trees off the freeway. The TV anchordude is saying someone is in stable condition, nobody killed; so that's why, Jody figures, it is, like, okay for the newsmen to joke about the palm trees on the freeway. Annie has the little Toshiba portable with the 12" screen, on three long extension cords, up in the kitchen window so they can see it on the back porch, because it is too hot to watch it in the living room. If Jody leans forward a little he can see the sun between the houses off to the west. In the smog the sun is a smooth red ball just easing to the horizon; you can look right at it.

Jody glances at Annie, wondering if he made a mistake, telling her what he did.

He can feel her watching him as he opens the third Corona. Pretty soon she'll say, "You going to drink more than three you better pay for the next round." Something she'd never say if he had a job, even if she'd paid for it then too. It's a way to get at the job thing.

She's looking at him, but she doesn't say anything. Maybe it's the wreck on TV. "Guy's not dead," he says, "too fucking bad." Making a macho thing about it.

"You're an asshole." But the tone of her voice says something else. What, exactly? Not admiration. Enjoyment, maybe.

Annie has her hair teased out; the red parts of her hair look redder in this light; the blond parts look almost real. Her eyes are the glassy green-blue the waves get to be in the afternoon up at Point Mugu, with the light coming through the water. Deep tan, white lipstick. He'd never liked that white lipstick look, white eyeliner and the pale-pink fingernail polish that went with it, but he never told her. "Girls who wear that shit are usually airheads," he'd have to say. And she wouldn't believe him when he told her he didn't mean her. She's sitting on the edge of her rickety kitchen chair in that old white shirt of his she wears for a shorty dress, leaning forward so he can see her cleavage, the arcs of her tan lines, her small feet flat on the stucco backporch, her feet planted wide apart but with her knees together, like the feet are saying one thing and the knees another.

His segment is gone from TV but he gets that *right there* feeling again as he takes her by the wrist and she says, "*Guy*, Jody, what do you think I *am*?" But joking.

He leads her to the bedroom and, standing beside the bed, puts his hand between her legs and he can feel he doesn't have to get her readier, he can get right to the good part. Everything just sort of slips right into place. She locks her legs around his back and they're still standing up, but it's like she hardly weighs anything at all. She tilts her head back, opens her mouth; he can see her broken front tooth, a guillotine shape.

They're doing 45 on the 101. It's a hot, windy night. They're listening to *Motley Crue* on the Sony ghetto blaster that stands on end between Annie's feet. The music makes him feel good but it hurts too because now he's thinking about *Iron Dream*. The band kicking him out because he couldn't get the solo parts to go fast enough. And because he missed some rehearsals. They should have let him play rhythm and sing backup, but the fuckers kicked him out. That's something he and Annie have. Both feeling like they were shoved out of line somewhere. Annie wants to be an actress, but she can't get a part, except once she was an extra for a TV show with a bogus rock club scene. Didn't even get her Guild card from that.

Annie is going on about something, always talking, it's like she can't stand the air to be empty. He doesn't really mind it. She's saying, "So I go, 'I'm *sure* I'm gonna fill in for that bitch when she accuses me of stealing her tips.' And he goes, 'Oh you know how Felicia is, she doesn't mean anything.' I mean—*guy*—he's always saying poor Felicia, you know how Felicia is, cutting her slack, but he, like, never cuts me any slack, and I've got two more tables to wait, so I'm all, 'Oh right poor Felicia—' and he goes—" Jody nods every so often, and even listens closely for a minute when she talks about the customers who treat her like a waitress. "I mean, what do they think, I'll always be a waitress? I'm *sure* I'm, like, totally a Felicia who's always, you know, going to be a *wait*ress—" He knows what she means. You're pumping gas and people treat you like you're a born pump jockey and you'll never do anything else. He feels like he's really *with* her, then. It's things like that, and things they don't say; it's like they're looking out the same window together all the time. She sees things the way he does: how people don't understand. Maybe he'll write a song about it. Record it, hit big, *Iron Dream*'ll shit their pants. Wouldn't they, though?

"My Dad wants this car back, for his girlfriend," Annie says.

"Oh fuck her," Jody says. "She's too fucking drunk to drive, *any*time."

Almost eleven thirty but she isn't saying anything about having to work tomorrow, she's jacked up same as he is. They haven't taken anything, but they both feel like they have. Maybe it's the Santa Anas blowing weird shit into the valley.

"This car's a piece of junk anyway," Annie says. "It knocks, radiator boils over. Linkage is going out."

"It's better than no car."

"You had it together, you wouldn't have to settle for this car."

She means getting a job, but he still feels like she's saying, "If you were a better guitar player . . ." Someone's taking a turn on a big fucking screw that goes through his chest. That's the second time the feeling comes. Everything going all flat again, and he can't tell his hands from the steering wheel.

There is a rush of panic, almost like when Annie's dad took him up in the Piper to go skydiving; like the moment when he pulled the cord and nothing happened. He had to pull it twice. Before the parachute opened he was spinning around like a dust mote. What difference would it make if he *did* hit the ground?

It's like that now, he's just hurtling along, sitting back and watching himself, that weird detachment thing . . . Not sure he is in control of the car. What difference would it make if he *wasn't* in control?

And then he pulls off the freeway, and picks up a wrench from the backseat.

*   *   *

"You're really good at getting it on TV," she says. "It's a talent, like being a director." They are indoors this time, sitting up in bed, watching it in the bedroom, with the fan on. It was too risky talking out on the back porch.

"Maybe I should be a director. Make *Nightmare On Elm Street* better than that last one. That last one sucked."

They are watching the news coverage for the third time on the VCR. You could get these hot VCRs for like sixty bucks from a guy on Hollywood Boulevard, if you saw him walking around at the right time. They'd gotten a couple of discount tapes at Federated and they'd recorded the newscast.

". . . we're not sure it's a gang-related incident," the detective on TV was saying. "The use of a wrench—throwing a wrench from the car at someone—uh, that's not the usual gang methodology."

"Methodology," Jody says. "Christ."

There's a clumsy camera zoom on a puddle of blood on the ground. Not very good color on this TV, Jody thinks; the blood is more purple than red.

The camera lingers on the blood as the cop says, "They usually use guns. Uzis, weapons along those lines. Of course, the victim was killed just the same. At those speeds a wrench thrown from a car is a deadly weapon. We have no definite leads . . ."

" 'They usually use guns,' " Jody says. "I'll use a gun on your balls, shit-head."

Annie snorts happily, and playfully kicks him in the side with her bare foot. "You're such an asshole. You're gonna get in trouble. Shouldn't be using my dad's car, for one thing." But saying it teasingly, chewing her lip to keep from smiling too much.

"You fucking love it," he says, rolling onto her.

"Wait." She wriggles free, rewinds the tape, starts it over. It plays in the background. "Come here, asshole."

Jody's brother Cal says, "What's going on with you, huh? How come everything I say pisses you off? It's like, *any*thing. I mean, you're only two years younger than me but you act like you're fourteen sometimes."

"Oh hey Cal," Jody says, snorting, "you're, like, Mr. Mature."

They're in the parking lot of the mall, way off in the corner. Cal in his Pasadena School of Art & Design T-shirt, his yuppie haircut, yellow-tinted John Lennon sunglasses. They're standing by Cal's '81 Subaru, that Mom bought him "because he went to school." They're blinking in the metallic sunlight, at the corner of the parking lot by the boulevard. The only place there's any parking. A couple of acres of cars between them and the main structure of the mall. They're supposed to have lunch with Mom, who keeps busy with her gift shop in the mall, with coffee grinders and dried eucalyptus and silk flowers. But Jody's decided he doesn't want to go.

"I just don't want you to say anymore of this shit to me, Cal," Jody says. "Telling me about *being* somebody." Jody's slouching against the car, his hands slashing the air like a karate move as he talks. He keeps his face down, half hidden by his long, purple streaked hair, because he's too mad at Cal to look right at him: Cal hassled and wheedled him into coming here. Jody is kicking Cal's tires with the back of a lizardskin boot and every so often he kicks the hubcap, trying to dent it. "I don't need the same from you I get from Mom."

"Just because she's a bitch doesn't mean she's wrong all the time," Cal says. "Anyway what's the big deal? You used to go along peacefully and listen to Mom's one-way heart-to-hearts and say what she expects and—" He shrugs.

Jody knows what he means: The forty bucks or so she'd hand him afterward "to get him started."

"It's not worth it anymore," Jody says.

"You don't have any other source of money but Annie and she won't put up with it much longer. It's time to get real, Jody, to get a job and—"

"Don't tell me I need a job to get real." Jody slashes the air with the edge of his hand. "Real is where your ass is when you shit," he adds savagely. "Now fucking shut up about it."

Jody looks at the mall, trying to picture meeting Mom in there. It makes him feel heavy and tired. Except for the fiberglass letters—*Northridge Galleria*—styled to imitate handwriting across its off-white, pebbly surface, the outside of the mall could be a military building, an enormous bunker. Just a great windowless . . . *block*. "I hate that place,

Cal. That mall and that busywork shop. Dad gave her the shop to keep her off the valium. Fuck. Like fingerpainting for retards."

He stares at the mall, thinking: That cutesy sign, I hate that. Cutesy handwriting but the sign is big enough to crush you dead if it fell on you. *Northridge Galleria*. You could almost hear a radio ad voice saying it over and over again, "Northridge Galleria! . . . Northridge Galleria! . . . Northridge Galleria! . . ."

To their right is a Jack-in-the-Box order-taking intercom. Jody smells the hot plastic of the sun-baked clown-face and the dogfoody hamburger smell of the drive-through mixed in. To their left is a Pioneer Chicken with its cartoon covered-wagon sign.

Cal sees him looking at it. Maybe trying to pry Jody loose from obsessing about Mom, Cal says, "You know how many Pioneer Chicken places there are in L.A.? You think you're driving in circles because every few blocks one comes up . . . It's like the ugliest fucking wallpaper pattern in the world."

"Shut up about that shit too."

"What put you in this mood? You break up with Annie?"

"No. We're fine. I just don't want to have lunch with Mom."

"Well goddamn Jody, you shouldn't have said you would, then."

Jody shrugs. He's trapped in the reflective oven of the parking lot, sun blazing from countless windshields and shiny metalflake hoods and from the plastic clownface. Eyes burning from the lancing reflections. Never forget your sunglasses. But no way is he going in.

Cal says, "Look, Jody, I'm dehydrating out here. I mean, fuck this parking lot. There's a couple of palm trees around the edges but look at this place—it's the surface of the moon."

"Stop being so fucking arty," Jody says. "You're going to art and design school, oh wow awesome I'm impressed."

"I'm just—" Cal shakes his head. "How come you're mad at Mom?"

"She wants me to come over, it's just so she can tell me her latest scam for getting me to do some shit, go to community college, study haircutting or something. Like she's really on top of my life. Fuck, I was a teenager I told her I was going to hitchhike to New York she didn't even look up from her card game."

"What'd you expect her to do?"

"I don't know."

"Hey that was when she was on her Self-Dependence kick. She was into Lifespring and Est and Amway and all that. They keep telling her she's not responsible for other people, not responsible, not responsible—"

"She went for it like a fucking fish to water, man." He gives Cal a look that means, *no bullshit.* "What is it she wants *now?*"

"Um—I think she wants you to go to some vocational school."

Jody makes a snorting sound up in his sinuses. "Fuck that. Open up your car, Cal, I ain't going."

"Look, she's just trying to help. What the hell's wrong with having a skill? It doesn't mean you can't do something else too—"

"Cal. She gave you the Subaru, it ain't mine. But you're gonna open the fucking thing up." He hopes Cal knows how serious he is. Because that two-dimensional feeling might come on him, if he doesn't get out of here. Words just spill out of him. "Cal, look at this fucking place. Look at this place and tell me about vocational skills. It's shit, Cal. There's two things in the world, dude. There's making it like *Eminem*, like Jim Carrey—that's one thing. You're on a screen, you're on videos and CDs. Or there's shit. That's the other thing. There's no *fucking thing in between.* There's being *Huge*—and there's being nothing." His voice breaking. "We're shit, Cal. Open up the fucking car or I'll kick your headlights in."

Cal stares at him. Then he unlocks the car, his movements short and angry. Jody gets in, looking at a sign on the other side of the parking lot, one of those electronic signs with the lights spelling things out with moving words. The sign says, *You want it, we got it . . . you want it, we got it . . . you want it, we got it . . .*

He wanted a Luger. They look rad in war movies. Jody said it was James Coburn, Annie said it was Lee Marvin, but whoever it was, he was using a Luger in that Peckinpah movie *Iron Cross.*

But what Jody ends up with is a Smith-Wesson .32, the magazine carrying eight rounds. It's smaller than he'd thought it would be, a scratched grey-metal weight in his palm. They buy four boxes of bullets, drive out to the country, out past Topanga Canyon. They find a fire road of rutted salmon-colored dirt, lined with pine trees on one side; the other side has a margin of grass that looks like soggy Shredded Wheat, and a barbed wire fence edging an empty horse pasture.

They take turns with the gun, Annie and Jody, shooting Bud-Light bottles from a splintery gray fence post. A lot of the time they miss the bottles. Jody said, "This piece's pulling to the left." He isn't sure if it really is, but Annie seems to like when he talks as if he knows about it.

It's nice out there, he likes the scent of gunsmoke mixed with the pine tree smell. Birds were singing for awhile, too, but they stopped after the shooting, scared off. His hand hurts from the gun's recoil, but he doesn't say anything about that to Annie.

"What we got to do," she says, taking a pot-shot at a squirrel, "is try shooting from the car."

He shakes his head. "You think you'll aim better from in a car?"

"I mean from a moving car, stupid." She gives him a look of exasperation. "To get used to it."

"Hey yeah."

They get the old Buick bouncing down the rutted fire road, about thirty feet from the fence post when they pass it, and Annie fires twice, and misses. "The stupid car bounces too much on this road," she says.

"Let me try it."

"No wait—make it more like a city street, drive in the grass off the road. No ruts."

"Uh . . . Okay." So he backs up, they try it again from the grass verge. She misses again, but they keep on because she insists, and about the fourth time she starts hitting the post, and the sixth time she hits the bottle.

"Well why *not*?" She asks again.

Jody doesn't like backing off from this in front of Annie, but it feels like it is too soon or something. "Because now we're just gone and nobody knows who it is. If we hold up a store it'll take time, they might have silent alarms, we might get caught." They are driving with the top up, to give them some cover in case they decide to try the gun here, but the windows are rolled down because the old Buick's air conditioning is busted.

"Oh right I'm sure some *7-11* store is going to have a silent alarm."

"Just wait, that's all. Let's do this first. We got to get more used to the gun."

"And get another one. So we can both have one."

For some reason that scares him. But he says: "Yeah. Okay."

It is late afternoon. They are doing 60 on the 405. Jody not wanting to get stopped by the CHP when he has a gun in his car. Besides, they are a little drunk because shooting out at Topanga Canyon in the sun made them thirsty, and this hippie on this gnarly old *tractor* had come along, some pot farmer maybe, telling them to get off his land, and that pissed them off. So they drank too much beer.

They get off the 405 at Burbank Boulevard, looking at the other cars, the people on the sidewalk, trying to pick someone out. Some asshole.

But no one looks right. Or maybe it doesn't feel right. He doesn't have that feeling on him.

"Let's wait," he suggests.

"Why?"

"Because it just seems like we oughta, that's why."

She makes a clucking sound but doesn't say anything else for awhile. They drive past a patch of adult bookstores and a video arcade and a liquor store. They come to a park. The trash cans in the park have overflowed; wasps are haunting some melon rinds on the ground. In the basketball court four Chicanos are playing two-on-two, wearing those shiny, pointy black shoes they wear. "You ever notice how Mexican guys, they play basketball and football in dress shoes?" Jody asks. "It's like they never heard of sneakers—"

He hears a *crack* and a thudding echo and a greasy chill goes through him as he realizes that she's fired the gun. He glimpses a Chicano falling, shouting in pain, the others flattening on the tennis court, looking around for the shooter as he stomps the accelerator, lays rubber, squealing through a red light, cars bitching their horns at him, his heart going in time with the pistons, fear vising his stomach. He's weaving through the cars, looking for the freeway entrance. Listening for sirens.

They are on the freeway, before he can talk. The rush hour traffic only doing about 45, but he feels better here. Hidden.

"What the *fuck* you doing?!" he yells at her.

She gives him a look accusing him of something. He isn't sure what. Betrayal maybe. Betraying the thing they had made between them.

"Look—" he says, softer, "it was a *red light*. People almost hit me coming down the cross street. You know? You got to think a little first. And don't do it when I don't *know*."

She looks at him like she is going to spit. Then she laughs, and he has to laugh too. She says, "Did you see those dweebs *dive?*"

Mouths dry, palms damp, they watch the five o'clock news and the six o'clock news. Nothing. Not a word about it. They sit up in the bed, drinking Coronas. Not believing it. "I mean, what kind of fucking society *is* this?" Jody says. Like something Cal would say. "When you shoot somebody and they don't even say a damn word about it on TV?"

"It's sick," Annie says.

They try to make love but it just isn't there. It's like trying to start a gas stove when the pilot light is out.

So they watch *Hunter* on TV. Hunter is after a psychokiller. The psycho guy is a real creep. Set a house on fire with some kids in it, they almost got burnt up, except Hunter gets there in time. Finally Hunter corners the psycho-killer and shoots him. Annie says, "I like TV better than movies because you know how it's gonna turn out. But in movies it might have a happy ending or it might not."

"It usually does," Jody points out.

"Oh yeah? Did you see *Terms of Endearment*? And they got *Bambi* out again now. When I was a kid I cried for two days when his Mom got shot. They should always have happy endings in a little kid movie."

"That part, that wasn't the end of that movie. It was happy in the end."

"It was still a sad movie."

Finally at eleven o'clock they're on. About thirty seconds worth. A man "shot in the leg on Burbank Boulevard today in a drive-by shooting believed to be gang related." On to the next story. No pictures, nothing. That was it.

What a rip off. "It's racist, is what it is," he says. "Just because they were Mexicans no one gives a shit."

"You know what it is, it's because of all the gang stuff. Gang drive-bys happen every day, everybody's used to it."

He nods. She's right. She has a real feel for these things. He puts his arm around her; she nestles against him. "Okay. We're gonna do it right, so they really pay attention."

"What if we get caught?"

Something in him freezes when she says that. She isn't supposed to talk like that. Because of the *thing* they have together. It isn't something they ever talk about, but they know its rules.

When he withdraws a little, she says, "But we'll never get caught because we just *do it* and cruise before anyone gets together."

He relaxes, and pulls her closer. It feels good just to lay there and hug her.

The next day he's in line for his unemployment insurance check. Him and Annie. They have stopped his checks, temporarily, and he'd had to hassle them. They said he could pick this one up. He had maybe two more coming.

Thinking about that, he feels a bad mood coming on him. There's no air conditioning in this place and the fat guy in front of him smells like he's fermenting and the room's so hot and close Jody can hardly breathe.

He looks around and can almost *see* the feeling—like an effect of a camera lens, a zoom or maybe a fish eye lens: Things going two dimensional, flattening out. Annie says something and he just shrugs. She doesn't say anything else till after he's got his check and he's practically running for the door.

"Where you going?"

He shakes his head, standing outside, looking around. It's not much better outside. It's overcast but still hot. "Sucks in there."

"Yeah," she says. "For sure. Oh shit."

"What?"

She points at the car. Someone has slashed the canvas top of the Buick. "My dad is going to kill us."

He looks at the canvas and can't believe it. "Mu-ther-*fuck!*-er!"

"Fucking assholes," she says, nodding gravely. "I mean, you know how much that costs to fix? You wouldn't believe it."

"Maybe we can find him."

"How?"

"I don't know."

He still feels bad but there's a hum of anticipation too. They get in the car, he tears out of the parking lot, making gravel spray, whips onto the street.

They drive around the block, just checking people out, the feeling in him spiraling up and up. Then he sees a guy in front of a Carl's Jr., the guy grinning at him, nudging his friend. Couple of jock college students, looks like, in tank tops. Maybe the guy who did the roof of the car, maybe not.

They pull around the corner, coming back around for another look. Jody can feel the good part of the feeling coming on now but there's something bothering him too: the jocks in tank tops looked right at him.

"You see those two guys?" he hears himself ask, as he pulls around the corner, cruises up next to the Carl's Jr. "The ones—"

"Those jock guys, I know, I picked them out too."

He glances at her, feeling close to her then. They are one person in two parts. The right and the left hand. It feels like music.

He makes sure there's a green light ahead of him, then he says, "Get 'em both," he hears himself say. "Don't miss or—"

By then she's aiming the .32, both hands wrapped around it. The jock guys, one of them with a huge coke and the other with a milkshake, are standing by the driveway to the restaurant's parking lot, talking, one of them playing with his car keys. Laughing. The bigger one with the dark hair looks up and sees Annie and the laughing fades from his face. Seeing that, Jody feels better than he ever felt before. *Crack, crack.* She fires twice, the guys go down. *Crack, crack, crack.* Three times more, making sure it gets on the news: shooting into the windows of the Carl's Jr., webs instantly snapping into the window glass, some fat lady goes spinning, her tray of burgers tilting, flying.

Jody's already laying rubber, fish-tailing around the corner, heading for the freeway.

They don't make it home, they're so excited. She tells him to stop at a gas station on the other side of the hills, in Hollywood. The Men's is unlocked, he feels really right *there* as she looks around then leads him into the bathroom, locks the door from the inside. Bathroom's an almost clean one, he notices, as she hikes up her skirt and he undoes his pants, both of them with shaking fingers, in a real hurry, and she pulls him into her with no preliminaries, right there with her sitting on the edge of the sink. There's no mirror but he sees a cloudy reflection in the shiny chrome side of the towel dispenser; the two of them blurred into one thing sort of pulsing ...

He looks straight at her, then; she's staring past him, not at anything in particular, just at the sensation, the good sensation they are grinding out between them, like it's something she can see on the dust-streaked wall. He can almost see it in her eyes. And in the way she traps the end of her tongue between her front teeth. Now he can see it himself, in his mind's eye, the sensation flashing like sun in a mirror; ringing like a power chord through a fuzz box ...

When he comes he doesn't hold anything back, he can't, and it escapes from him with a sob. She holds him tight and he says, "Wow you are just so awesome you make me feel so *good* ..."

He's never said anything like that to her before, and they know they've arrived somewhere special. "I love you, Jody," she says.

"I love you."

"It's just us, Jody. Just us. Just us."

He knows what she means. And they feel like little kids cuddling together, even though they're fucking standing up in a *Union 76* Men's restroom, in the smell of pee and disinfectant.

Afterwards they're really hungry so they go to a Jack-in-the-Box, get drive-through food, ordering a whole big shitload. They eat it on the way home, Jody trying not to speed, trying to be careful again about being stopped, but hurrying in case they have a special news flash on TV about the Carl's Jr. Not wanting to miss it.

The Fajita Pita from Jack-in-the-Box tastes really great.

While he's eating, Jody scribbles some song lyrics into his song notebook with one hand. "The Ballad of Jody and Annie."

They came smokin' down the road
like a bat out of hell
they hardly even slowed
or they'd choke from the smell

Chorus:
Holdin' hands in the Valley of Death
(repeat 3X)

Jody and Annie bustin' out of bullshit
Bustin' onto TV
better hope you aren't the one hit
killed disonnerably

Nobody understands em
nobody ever will
but Jody knows she loves 'im
They never get their fill

They will love forever
in history
and they'll live together
in femmy

Holdin' hands in the Valley of Death

He runs out of inspiration there. He hints heavily to Annie about the lyrics and pretends he doesn't want her to read them, makes her ask three times. With tears in her eyes, she asks, as she reads the lyrics, "What's a femmy?"

"You know, like 'Living In femmy.'"

"Oh, infamy. It's so beautiful . . . You got guacamole on it, you asshole." She's crying with happiness and using a napkin to reverently wipe the guacamole from the notebook paper.

There's no special news flash but since three people died and two are in intensive care, they are the top story on the five o'clock news. And at seven o'clock they get mentioned on CNN, which is *national*. Another one, and they'll be on the *NBC Nightly News*, Jody says.

"I'd rather be on *World News Tonight*," Annie says. "I like that Peter Jennings dude. He's cute."

About ten, they watch the videotapes of the news stories again. Jody guesses he should be bothered that the cops have descriptions of them but somehow it just makes him feel more psyched, and he gets down with Annie again. They almost never do it twice in one day, but this makes three times. "I'm getting sore," she says, when he enters her. But she gets off.

They're just finishing, he's coming, vaguely aware he sees lights flashing at the windows, when he hears Cal's voice coming out of the walls. He thinks he's gone schizophrenic or something, he's hearing voices, booming like the voice of God. *"Jody, come on outside and talk to us. This is Cal, you guys. Come on out."*

Then Jody understands, when Cal says, *"They want you to throw the gun out first."*

Jody pulls out of her, puts his hand over her mouth, and shakes his head. He pulls his pants on, then goes into the front room, looks through a corner of the window. There's Cal, and a lot of cops.

Cal's standing behind the police barrier, the cruiser lights flashing around him; beside him is a heavyset Chicano cop who's watching the S.W.A.T. team gearing up behind the big gray van. They're scary-looking in all that armor and with those helmets and shotguns and sniper rifles.

Jody spots Annie's dad. He's tubby, with a droopy mustache, long hair going bald at the crown, some old hippie sitting in the back of the cruiser. Jody figures someone got their license number, took them awhile to locate Annie's dad. He wasn't home at first. They waited till he came home since he owns the car, and after they talked to him they decided it was his daughter and her boyfriend they were looking for. Got the address from him. Drag Cal over here to talk to Jody because Mom wouldn't come. Yeah.

Cal speaks into the bullhorn again, same crap, sounding like someone else echoing off the houses. Jody sees people looking out their windows. Some being evacuated from the nearest houses. Now an *Action News* truck pulls up, cameramen pile out, set up incredibly fast, get right to work with the newscaster. Lots of activity just for Jody and Annie. Jody has to grin, seeing the news cameras, the guy he recognizes from TV waiting for his cue. He feels high, looking at all this. Cal says something else, but Jody isn't listening. He goes to get the gun.

"It's just us, Jody," Annie says, her face flushed, her eyes dilated as she helps him push the sofa in front of the door. "We can do anything together."

She is there, not scared at all, her voice all around him soft and warm. "It's just us," she says again, as he runs to get another piece of furniture.

He is running around like a speedfreak, pushing the desk, leaning bookshelves to block off the teargas. Leaving enough room for him to shoot through. He sees the guys start to come up the walk with the tear gas and the shotguns. Guys in helmets and some kind of bulky bulletproof shit. But maybe he can hit their necks, or their knees. He aims carefully and fires again. Someone stumbles and the others carry the wounded dude back behind the cars.

Five minutes after Jody starts shooting, he notices that Annie isn't there. At almost the same moment a couple of rifle rounds knock the bookshelves down, and something smashes through a window. In the middle of the floor, white mist gushes out of a teargas shell.

Jody runs from the tear gas, into the kitchen, coughing. "Annie!" His voice sounding like a kid's.

He looks through the kitchen window. Has she gone outside, turned traitor?

But then she appears at his elbow, like somebody switched on a screen and Annie is what's on it.

"Hey," she says, her eyes really bright and beautiful. "Guess what." She has the little TV by the handle; it's plugged in on the extension cord. In the next room, someone is breaking through the front door.

"I give up," he says, eyes tearing. "What?"

She sits the TV on the counter for him to see. "We're on TV. Right now. We're on TV . . ."

Occurrence at Owl Street Ridge

Dana could *feel* getting fired. The event had weight and density she could feel inside. It was like a jagged stone caught under her sternum making it harder to breathe as she climbed the steep driveway to the walk that led to her front door. It was late afternoon, and although the sky was glazed gray with November clouds, it was a Los Angeles sky and it wasn't even cool out. Just sort of murkily damp. Thick grey mist above, brown smog in the Valley just below. She had to tell her husband she had been fired; she had to make it seem all right for the kids. Her husband was going to be pissed off.

She paused at the top of the drive, breathing hard, wondering again if she were beginning to develop asthma herself, late in life. She turned to look down over the San Fernando Valley. Owl Street Ridge was the upper end of Owl Street, overlooking Sherman Oaks and Ventura. She could see part of Universal Studios from here. They lived ten minutes from the Universal theme park, and fortyfive minutes, with light traffic, from Disneyland; but they hadn't taken the kids in two or three years.

It was late November and Thanksgiving was looming, and Christmas hulked ominously on the horizon, and she'd lost her executive-assistant gig.

They'd bought the house when they were both working full time and Reuben was expecting to be promoted; before the beer company where he worked got bought and downsized. They were above the worst of the smog here; it was like a brown cauldron below her, boiling with cars and commerce and gangs. If they had to give up this house, they'd end up moving into the valley; Loni and Carl would be dunked headlong into all that smog. Air quality was supposed to have improved, but she couldn't see the improvement.

Reuben wanted to sell the house and buy a condo from one of the plant supervisors, two blocks from the Brewery, down in the flats. She'd been over there two or three times, to visit Reuben's work-friends. The smokestack from the brewery gushed what the plant claimed was only steam, but it was an acrid steam with a freight of acids, of sulfites, of charred hops, and the kids who lived in the neighborhood had red eyes, all the time; they seemed tired and confused.

So she'd fought moving, although they'd had the house refinanced twice already, and they could barely make the payments—and now she was fired.

She turned away from the murky Valley, and froze, for a moment, seeing something . . . someone across the yard. Thought she saw her Aunt Louise, who was twelve years dead, crouching under the fronds of the little palm tree in the garden, like one of those lawn gnomes, about the same size: smaller than a human being should be but proportional. Aunt Louise, crouching like a little girl with her arms around her knees, staring at her from the dimness, her face striped in shadow. "Louise?" The figure seemed to withdraw into the shadow like someone falling slowly away down a vertical shaft into darkness, getting smaller in a distance that couldn't be there. And then she . . . it was gone.

Stress, or maybe acid flashbacks. She'd only tripped twice, in the 70s, decades earlier, but who knew when it could come back on you? It wasn't like she never saw things that weren't there—she had visions that were part of her artwork. But they'd never intruded on the real world before.

" 'They're coming to take me away, ha-ha,' " she murmured, as she went into the house, shaking her head. An old song. How'd it go? *To the funny farm, where life is beautiful all the time* . . .

She found the kids in the family room, the two boys sucking into the Playstation. A new videogame, *Helltrucks IV*. All four kids were there, which was unusual: Sonya and Damon, the teens, the oldest, both with terrifying grillworks of braces; Carl and Loni, eleven and nine, with asthma.

Loni was watching the game listlessly from the sofa-futon, breathing shallowly, inhaler in her hand. Stretched out on the sofa, Loni was long and slender, bony and flat-chested like her Mom; but sometimes Dana thought maybe she just wasn't eating much. "Hi Mom," she said, her eyes flickering to her and back to the careening Monster Trucks on the tv screen. She wasn't really interested in the game; it was just something to keep her eyes busy while she lay still, waiting for the asthma attack to fade. She had a book beside her, closed: Amy Tan.

The oldest, Sonya, was curled up in the black leather La-Z-Boy: a chunky girl with her Dad's short, stocky proportions and round face; she had her Mom's curly brown hair and pale blue eyes. She was wearing headphones and staring into a Civics textbook.

Last night's too-brief conversation with Sonya replayed in Dana's head. "Sonya, if you think you're too fat to get dates, or whatever—I mean, it's not like you're more than pleasantly plump—"

"Oh Mom, please. God. Pleasantly . . . oh please."

"Okay, whatever. If you're really worried about it, diet."

"It doesn't matter if I lose weight. They won't like me anyway. It's just the way I am. They think I'm weird or something."

A look of accusation; then she'd gone to her room.

"Sonya—or should I say Grinch-face. You got a look on your face, like you read in that textbook your best friend died . . ." Dana said now, though she wasn't looking at the girl.

"It's giving me grief, all right, this text book," Sonya said, closing the book.

"Sonya made a *fun*-nee," Loni said.

"The whole bunch of you, it's like a funeral all the time, what a bunch of gloom buckets," Dana said.

"Gloom buckets. Is that, like, a seventies expression?" Loni asked. "Please don't teach it to us."

"*I'm* not glooming and stuff, Mom," Carl said, " 'cause Damon just died. He killed me three times but I'm not letting him cheat anymore. I'm killing his ass."

"*You're* dying," Damon said. "You're going *down*, shit-head."

"Damon—you don't use that kind of language," Dana said automatically. She didn't actually understand why it was important for her kids not to use obscenities. Or why she allowed butt-head and not shit-head. She'd cussed like a drunken sailor, herself, till she had the kids.

She sat on a sofa-arm between the La-Z-Boy, and Loni on the sofa, stroking Loni's hair. "How you feeling, Loni Maroni?"

"I'm okay. I had a little attack but it's better. I got an A on my English exam."

"Cool." The boys both glanced darkly at Loni, then returned their attention to the game. She was the only one who had the focus to get better than a C average, though they were all bright kids.

Sonya unwound from the chair, stretched, and left the room, smiling at her Mom and punching her shoulder softly as she went. When Mom had come closer and sat down, that made one body too many in the room; Sonya lately needed more personal space.

"You home early, Mom?" Carl asked, expertly thumbing the controller to make his truck jump a ramp and fire missiles at the same time.

"Am I home early? Um..." Dana found herself staring at the frenetic churning on the playstation screen. Each half of the screen had a truck with a monster's face on it that spit machine gun bullets from glowing demonic eyes and missiles from a toothy mouth; there were extra points for running over screaming pedestrians. She grimaced and looked toward the side door to the garage. Reuben might be out there working on his Vespa. He was off today. She didn't want to tell him yet.

"Yeah," she said. "I'm home early. They..." She stared at the careening, flame-belching trucks on the screen. "I got laid off."

Not true. She'd been *fired* for using a computer graphics program to design sculpture boxes on company time. She'd been warned more than once.

Damon and Carl exchanged looks; Loni looked at her Mom to see how she was taking it. They all knew what it might mean. The boys kept playing *Helltrucks IV*.

Time to find Reuben, face the music. Her husband was probably going to act like she had gotten fired on purpose, somehow. Passive aggressive, because she didn't want to work. She thought she was an *artiste* or something, he'd say again.

He'd say it all the sharper because he was only working part time himself. The brewery in Van Nuys had acted like they were doing him a favor, letting him stay on part time as a quality control inspector instead of laying him off completely.

"Your Dad in the garage?"

Damon half looked at her, then jerked his eyes back to the screen. His long stringy dishwater hair swung with the motion. He was wearing a Marilyn Manson t-shirt she hadn't seen before. He was into death-rock now. She tried to pretend it didn't worry her. After a moment, Damon said, "Yeah Mister 'That's *My* Machine' is in the garage."

She knew what that meant. It wasn't that Damon wanted to ride anything so teenage-uncool as a Vespa. He had probably offered, again, to help his Dad work on the Vespa, and he'd been turned down, and really he just wanted to work on something masculine with his Dad, to be at his side. But most of the time Reuben pushed him away.

Feeling dread dragging behind her like heavy iron chains, she went into the garage. Reuben was sitting backwards on his '65 Vespa, screwing something onto a brake light. It was a vintage machine he'd been tinkering to cherry for twenty years, on and off.

"Hi," Dana said, coming to sit on a sawhorse in the cluttered garage. It smelled like oil and paint and the catbox.

They made no move to embrace. They used to hug, she remembered, any time they'd been apart, even for a few hours. Years ago.

"So, hi," Reuben said. "You home early?"

"Um . . ."

He looked up at her. "You got fired?"

And she told him and Reuben said what she'd known he'd say and then he added, "They fired you because you did art at work when you were supposed to be transcribing a letter. Do we see a pattern here, for God's sake? Your ego-thing about your art, it keeps you from being with the kids, it keeps you from working and it gets you *nowhere*."

"It doesn't have to sell to be worthwhile. And I don't do it much—come on, it's such a small part of the day. It's usually after everyone's asleep. I mean—if I *did* work on it more I might get somewhere in the way you mean. I do a *tenth* of the art I'd like to be doing."

"Just remember," he said, walking out of the garage ahead of her. "You were the one who talked us into staying in this house we can't afford, just remember that."

Like I could ever forget that.

"Carl's doing weird stuff in the bathroom again," Loni said.

Dana was sitting at the dining room table, chin cradled on laced fingers, elbows to either side of her plate. The dirty dishes were all there, the remains of macaroni and cheese and broccoli, and empty soda cans. No one had offered to clear them. She thought about her own mother, who was from Montana, and how appalled she'd have been by dishes left on the table like this an hour after eating. Most the time they ate in the living room, on TV trays, watching the Simpsons or something, and it felt funny to be looking at each other, and not the tv, while eating. But she'd thought they needed to eat together at the table, after Reuben had gone out in his *SouCal Vespa Club* jacket to the sports bar to watch football and eat a hamburger. It was something he did when he was angry: go to the bar for dinner.

"Mo-om . . ."

"Hey, I told you, Loni, that's just boys anywhere from ten to twenty-five, and we just make them neurotic by banging on the bathroom door trying to get them to stop, you know . . ."

"No, Mom, I don't mean that, I'm used to that. Whuppa whuppa whuppa, fine, whatever. No I mean he's in there talking to the mirror and sh . . . stuff."

"He's just trying to freak you out. Why don't you help me clean this . . ."

"I've got homework to do." She pounded upstairs.

The 'help me clean up' thing always got rid of them. Dana felt like being alone. She felt, actually, like going up to her sewing room, that she really used for her internet cubbyhole, and check the postings for her graphics site.

But she went instead to stand outside the bathroom, and listen, vigorously disliking herself for it. Remembering coming home to her own bedroom to find her mother poking through her bedroom drawers. Looking for birth control pills.

"You are the soul brother from Hell, you live in a magic spell, you can't stand the demon's smell, you have to get away, away, away," Carl was chanting, in the bathroom. She knew, somehow, he was looking into the mirror as he did it.

She let her shoulders slump and gave in to her Mom impulse. She pounded on the door. "Carl—if you were in a Pentacostal family they'd call the exorcist now. Open the door."

"I'm on the . . ."

"No you're not. Open the door."

After a moment, he opened the door and stared up at her with limpid, red eyes. His hair looked mussed; he'd used lipstick to make marks around his eyes like lightning bolts. He didn't look scared. It was just his Mom, she was a weirdo anyway, she was an artist, she used to be a rock groupie, his Mom wouldn't care if he did his eyes like a rock band and made up lyrics. His Dad, though . . .

He glanced past her to see if Dad were around.

She put her arms around him. "You goof ball. I thought your brother was the Marilyn Manson fan."

"I don't like Marilyn that much. I like Trent."

But she'd hugged him as an excuse to smell his hair. And it was there, the smell was there. Pot-smoke, sharp and distinct.

It wasn't just pubescent eccentricity. He was in an altered state.

This hadn't happened before, she'd never caught one of them stoned, but she knew how it would go if she talked to him about it. He would deny it, and she'd say don't kid a kidder kiddo, tell me or I tell your Dad. Eventually he'd stop denying it. Then she'd lecture him, trying the whole time not to sound too self righteous, too much like a cop guest-lecturing on the D.A.R.E. program, trying to be understanding, and he'd agree, *You're right Mom*, and he'd be much more careful next time not to get caught or maybe he really wouldn't use the stuff again—but she'd never know for sure.

In her imagination she saw him spiraling into heavier use, and then maybe speed, there was so much speed around in his school district, there'd been two suicides because of it, in the last year. She had to talk to him.

Not tonight, she told herself. Tomorrow she'd search his room, see if he had a stash. She couldn't deal with it yet. Not yet.

Anyway, it was hopeless, wasn't it? Suddenly it all felt that way. A *quietly* dysfunctional family. Depressive, whining their way into drug abuse and suicide by slow degrees—or into lives of quiet desperation and bad marriages that were just as bad as suicide.

"Wash that stuff off, before your Dad sees it," she said. "He's coming home any minute."

Carl hastened into the bathroom, ran the water, began industriously scrubbing. Reuben never actually hit the kids but he'd sit his target down on the living room sofa and he'd pace up and down in front of the kid, yelling, gasping between bursts of syllables, stopping to jab a rigid finger sudden like a gun going off, making the kid shrink back; then back to pacing, yelling, for an hour, two hours, as longwinded as Fidel Castro. Mom as much as the kids hated Dad's living room lectures.

She sighed, seeing when she'd hugged Carl he'd pressed the outline of an eye in blurred lipstick lightning jags onto the shoulder of her white sweat-shirt.

She went to the garage for a bottle of wine; paused to look at Reuben's Vespa. He rarely rode it. The antique Italian scooter, poised rakishly on its kickstand, jeering at her. She went to the garage fridge where she kept the wine. Three bottles of white. Wait—there'd been four. Hadn't there been four? Reuben didn't like white wine. Which one of the kids . . . ? Damon, she thought. He was the one she'd caught stealing the dregs of cocktails on New Year's day.

Forget it. Not tonight.

She took out a bottle, closed the fridge—and found herself staring at that shelf, that one old stained, wooden shelf, to the right of the fridge, and the little blue can on it. She ought to throw that can away.

She thought, *I could open that with a screwdriver* . . .

She made herself go to the kitchen; she poured a large glass of chardonnay and carried it to her "sewing room". The sewing machine was gathering dust in the closet. Most of the little room was taken up by her computer, with its big screen, the racks of CD roms.

The last noisy fight they'd had, theoretically about money, Reuben had said "Why don't you sell that damn time-wasting super-graphics computer of yours?"

He'd shut up when she'd suggested they'd make a lot more selling his Vespa. That silenced him, but left a simmering resentment.

She booted up, signed on, ignored the "You've got mail!" to go immediately to her website and check the postings page. Two new ones, both, as she'd hoped, reacting to her new "cyberspace installations". One guy was from England, and the English never openly liked anything, so she was encouraged when he called it "fairly interesting"; the other was a woman she'd heard from before, in Florida, gushing about the realism, the three-dee quality of the "digital Cornell boxes", and forgetting the most important thing: the composition, the statement. "I liked Babydoll Head with Ouroborous Snakeskin best . . ."

Dana had found both the babydoll head and the shed snakeskin in the back yard; she'd arranged them into a box, with a small baby-crow skeleton she'd been saving; she'd painted the crow skeleton in four colors, then photographed the whole arrangement with a polaroid over and over till she got one that was clear enough, scanned the photo, and digitally enhanced it, adding detail.

She went to the page to look at the image. She wasn't wrong: it was beautiful. Theoretically, the images were for sale, but she'd only sold one, for 50 dollars.

An Instant Message tinkled at her. She frowned in annoyance. She hoped it wasn't the guy who'd bought the box graphic—he was always trying to drag her into cybersex. Online sex fantasies, frantically typed until exhaustion or boredom—the only consummation they offered—had lost their tang.

Your art is beautiful, the message said.

"Thanks," Dana typed. "Who am I talking to?" There was no name over the I.M. It must be some rogue software someone had—you were supposed to be able to read the screen name of the person sending the message.

You should have had the chance to live as an artist.

"Is this Rodney?" The guy who'd bought her art. Just so he could I.M. her about cybersex.

It's Louise. Honey-darlin', don't kill them.

"Louise who? Kill who?"

Everyone. You're going to kill everyone on Thanksgiving, Louise, with that little blue can of poison. You're going to put it in the marshmallow jello, of all things, because they all eat that, even Reuben, and you're going to say to yourself that maybe you'll be with your friend Alena . . .

She had to start a new IM Box.

. . . Alena who killed herself when she couldn't get off heroin . . .

"Who is this really?"

It's Louise. I'll meet you tonight at the Ferris wheel. I have been watching; I've been near; I love your kids. Especially Loni.

"I'm going to report you to AOL . . ."

But there was no one there, now. No ding came back. She was gone.

There was no one who knew about the can in the garage, and what she'd been thinking without really thinking it.

She hadn't really known herself what she'd been thinking, until the IM had prompted her.

Louise had always called her honey-darlin'.

Louise was dead. Dana had sat with her as she'd died, and she'd seen her embalmed body in the coffin.

I love those kids, she'd said.

Dana burst into tears.

Lying alone in bed, she remembered Louise, that summer in San Francisco. Dana had visited Louise for a summer, when she was a teenager, Louise in her late twenties. Louise had taken her to a show of those miniature, beautifully shaped Bonsai trees, and she'd thought it would be boring—but with Louise there, explaining how some of them were hundreds of years old, and how each one implied a whole landscape, she'd found them enthralling. That night they'd gone to the stage version of the Rocky Horror Show, and afterwards they were dancing down the street together singing the musical's ridiculous songs. Two nights later they went to a gay bar and though Dana wasn't allowed to drink, the boys let her stay in the bar and all the queens were so nice and they danced with her and Louise . . .

She drifted to sleep thinking of Louise.

It was one of those dreams that didn't quite go away, when she woke, because she didn't wake up completely. The dream of the carnival was waiting in the wings.

Reuben had wakened her, for a few moments; he'd come in, grunting as he undressed, rolled heavily into bed, smelling of Guinness. She went easily back to sleep as he curled into his usual fetus. And the dream resumed.

". . . you go on the topsy-turver, the whirly-jack, the smasher, but you won't go on the Ferris wheel!" Damon was saying, teasing his Mom. "Come on, we can drop popcorn on people."

"Well there is that consolation. Okay," Dana said, "popcorn, but no loogies." She looked up at the Ferris Wheel; for a moment it turned into a mandala, then into the Tibetan wheel of life, and then it was a Ferris wheel again, with neon tracing its spokes.

Then they were riding the Ferris wheel, and there was no transition: they had *always* been on it, they were permanently on it, and she saw that she was alone in her swinging metal seat. Her family was in the other chairs, each of them alone; Reuben was across from her, Damon below him spitting down on Carl, and the two girls, each alone in their own Ferris wheel seats. Then, her own Mom and Dad, in separate seats, Dad alive again, if that was being alive. Below Mom and Dad were here her sisters, who'd both married badly, and Reuben's boss was there too, and the guy at the bank they had to answer to about the loan, the loan officer had his own seat, and they were all of them going around and around and around and around and around: always in the distance, passing.

Around and below them was a carnival, The Carnival With A Secret Name, fulminating in neon, streaming with crowds, people holding hands and going places together, in twos and threes, taking part in the world. The booths weren't carny games, they were places to get

married, and divorced, and where children were born, and families had
their photographs taken, and the crowds ate and laughed and moved
on, and they did all this in fast-motion, like a sped-up film. The air
didn't smell like a carnival should, instead it smelled like Dana's house,
this carnival: like laundry waiting to be washed, and dish soap, and
garage oil, and cats and the sort of perfume that adolescent girls wore,
and macaroni and cheese dinners; and she went around and around.
The sun came up as Dana's side of the Ferris wheel went up, it followed
her up and it was overhead when she was at the top of the wheel, then
it went down in the west when the wheel turned her to its other side,
and it was night when she was at the bottom, and then the Ferris wheel
rotated up again and the sun rose with the turn of the wheel, with
Dana's rise upward, and it was overhead when she was at the top, and
then it began to sink as she went down the other side, seeing her
husband from behind, across from her, and it was dark at the bottom,
and then she was coming up the other side, and so was the sun, and
another day went by.

She tried shouting to her family, to the kids, to Reuben, and they
would glance at her with hollow eyes, and point at their ears and shake
their heads, they couldn't hear her. The Ferris wheel turned and she
rose, and the sun rose, and the wheel carried her up and around and
the sun came up and circled round the sky, and she sank down with
the wheel, and the sun sank into the horizon, and then there was a
pulse of night, and then the sun came up across from her, its light in
her eyes, as she rose again on the wheel and she called out to the kids
and they pointed at their ears and shook their heads, and the wheel
turned back to darkness...

After almost a year, she looked for the ride operator. No one was
there. There wasn't even a control booth. It had no controls she could
see. She took a deep breath, and stood up in the swaying car, and tried
to jump out when the car swung down low...

But there was a soft plastic transparent wall in the way. She knew
it was just in her feelings, that wall, and not there in any other way,
but it was impenetrable all the same.

So she sat back down again, and several more years passed, the sun following the course of the turning Ferris wheel, and crowds coming and going. And two more years, and three more.

"Louise," she thought, *"you said . . . you said . . ."*

Then someone dropped into the seat beside her, dropping smoothly from above, making the car rock a little as she sat back in it. Louise, smiling.

They hugged. Louise was warm; Dana could smell her perfume, some exotic flower.

Dana sat back—as the Ferris wheel continued to turn, to lift them—and looked into Louise's eyes. Rich brown eyes, like good soil with gold dust in it.

"Can you get me off this wheel?"

Louise stretched—and when she did, there was a fluttering behind her. There were opalescent wings there, weren't there? But when Dana bent to look closer at them, they weren't there.

"Yes, if you're willing, I am," Louise said. "It's just a life's worth, and only half a life at that."

"Are you really here?"

"Yes."

"Am I dreaming?"

"Yes and no. You aren't normally the kind of person who knows when they're dreaming, right?"

"No I'm not. I never say 'this is just a dream'. I always flounder about in the weird shit in the dream . . . and never realize . . ."

"But this time you know it's a dream. That's why it's not a dream. Not the way people think of dreams."

"Why did you say that, online, about the can of poison and the kids?"

"Look at that image you made again, the one under fate.jpeg in the Discarded Art directory on the C drive . . ."

"I . . . that's just a morbid fantasy image. Self indulgent bullshit."

"You believe it's a prophecy. It will be a self fulfilling prophecy in a sort of way, on Thanksgiving day. I mean, they won't look exactly like that, if they were to die on Thanksgiving of poisoning, but dead is dead. Unless I do something. We both do something. Not just for you; for the kids. I never met the kids in life, but I always loved them. I haven't been far."

"Louise . . . I don't get it."

"You're wrong about those children: they're more than just the sum total of your failings. They're in trouble, they will struggle with neurosis—but the deaths you envisioned for them, later in life, that's just a fantasy of your depression."

"So now you've warned me . . ."

Louise shook her head. "Even if you remember this dream . . . the part of you I'm talking to now is not in charge of your life. The sick, reactive, automatic part of you, that's in charge of your life, and you can say 'I won't do that thing' and mean it *now* but you, the part that means it now, you're not in charge, most of the time, the 'it' thing is in charge. And even if you remember this dream, it is too strong, when it takes you, and unless you do what you must do *here* and I do what I must do here, you will do what *it* must do. And the family will die. The children."

"What do I have to do?"

"Be willing to accept a gift even though you know it's a genuine sacrifice on someone else's part. Be willing to accept that sacrifice."

"What do you mean?"

"I'm going to take your place and set you free to live the other life you could have had . . ."

"You can do that for me?"

"It means I will remain here on the wheel—unless I can *will it* to stop. But it's hard for me alone to will it to stop because it's propelled by all the people riding it: their misguided wills keep it going . . . If I can make them hear me . . . I think I can do it, eventually."

"Oh no. I . . . I couldn't go somewhere . . . without the kids."

"Think about it. You really do deserve better. And I must pay a price myself—the price I didn't pay in my own life . . ."

"No, I . . . I can't just . . ."

"Consult yourself, honey-darlin'. What does the realest part of you want?"

Louise opened her arms, and after a moment's hesitation Dana went into her embrace, and saw the wings of shimmering white energy, stretching out vastly behind Louise, and the darkness on the horizon cracking wide, light spilling through ... and the sun rising ... And stopping.

The sun stopping in its tracks.

Then she was standing under the Ferris wheel, watching as it turned, and the sun had begun moving once more, and the wheel turned with Louise where Dana had been. It looked like Louise was praying.

Dana was swept away by the crowd.

She didn't usually remember her dreams. She remembered that one.

She didn't even go the bathroom, after she got up: she went right to her sewing room, and booted up and, though now she *really* had to pee badly, went immediately to the fate.jpeg and opened the file and the image filled itself in on the screen, line by line. Then it was all there ... Her four kids in a Cornell box: but they had grown up, all but Carl, who'd died at fourteen. And they were ...

... dead. Dead and arranged in the four corners of the boxes, each body as it had fallen in dying. Damon dead in a car accident, bloodied, with broken windshield glass around him; the year he'd flunked out of college, one of his friends would drive the car to both their deaths.

Carl dead of a drug overdose amazingly young.

Loni dead of a severe asthma attack because she'd stopped taking her medication out of sheer depression.

Sonya, huge, the last to go, dead at forty-eight years old, of obesity-related heart attack.

To save them from this, to save herself from the Ferris wheel, she would use the poison.

And that would punish Reuben, too.

Dana exited the jpeg, and deleted it, and ran to the bathroom.

It was while she was taking a shower, that she realized: *they really are better off dead, now, with the family, than dying like that later.*

The warning from Louise wouldn't stop it. It was just a dream. The reality was what was coming, in their lives; what life was like now for them: hollow. Meaningless.

Oh, God. Help me.

*   *   *

The door bell rang.

The kids had left an hour earlier, that same day. It was the last day of school before Thanksgiving vacation. Dana answered the door, feeling strange as she went; feeling that time was slowing on the way to the door, that she was moving in slow motion.

At last the door opened, and outside was a tanned, lean, white haired man in a chauffeur's uniform; his brows were heavy, his eyes hawkish, his face lined with bitterness and regret. He wore a chauffeur's uniform and cap, but very old fashioned, doublebreasted with brass buttons, something from the early twentieth century.

There was a white limo waiting in the street. "I am sent for you, madame" he said, and that seemed an odd way to put it. He had an accent that sounded Southwestern to her.

"Who . . ."

"Louise sent me. I am your driver, ma'am. I am Mr. Ambrose Bierce. Your aunt requisitioned me: her sense of humor. I would offer to take your bags, but it would be supernumerary, and might be taken for archness: for where we are to go, no baggage may be taken."

Dana's mouth was dry. Was she hallucinating this? Was this part of the insanity that would kill her and her family?

She managed to say, "I can bring nothing—and no one?"

"Precisely nothing, madame, and exactly no one, but only yourself." He took a step backward and gestured at the limo. Now its passenger door was open. It hadn't been, a moment ago.

She took a step forward and stopped—there was an invisible plasticity in the way. She shook her head.

He reached out and put his hand gently on her arm. "Now try."

She tried, and found she could now move through the door. They went to the limousine. It all felt very real, not dreamlike. She stumbled over Carl's skateboard, barking her ankle on it, and the feeling was quite real. "This really isn't a dream?"

"No ma'am," the chauffeur said. "This isn't a dream."

The limo was closer, closer. She started to look back at the house. "Do not look back, madame," Bierce said.

"Would I turn into a pillar of salt?" She stopped at the limo door; she was stalling.

"Do not joke about that. Those who flay the Bible for their advantage are fit objects for humor; but its admonitions, I have discovered, are for the most part no joking matter. I was an atheist in life, and I do not now have that privilege. No, looking back will not make of you a pillar of salt, Madame. But you'll be back where you were for good, rather *like* a pillar of salt."

She got into the limo. It smelled of old leather. There was a drink bar. She realized her clothing had vanished. She was sitting on the seat naked. There was a prescient electricity in the air, and everything looked faintly electric blue and yet it was all quite real.

The limo drove down the street, with no engine sound at all, and turned right, onto a dead end street where there was an unfinished housing development. No one was around. There was a tunnel in the hillside at the end of the street. She'd taken a walk the day before and the tunnel had not been here. Her heart was thudding as the limo ghosted through the tunnel; began pounding as she came out the other side, and she was on a sunny street in San Francisco. She looked through the back window: there was no tunnel behind them. She put her hand on the seat beside her and felt something new, and looking she found clothing folded there.

She put the clothing on. Blue jeans, painted with interesting designs. Her own designs. A blue workshirt with various counter-culture buttons pinned to it. There were no shoes.

The limousine stopped and she got out. She was in front of the old Victorian house, in San Francisco, where Louise had lived. A man and a woman walked by, smiled at her, and went onward. They both had longish hair, carefully coifed; they wore polyester bellbottom pants, and platform shoes and gold-tinted sunglasses; the woman wore a tank top with a picture of a snake artfully airbrushed on it, and the man wore a shiny green shirt with a big collar and a gold chain.

"Holy shit," Dana said.

The woman glanced at Dana over her shoulder, shrugged, and moved on.

Panicking, Dana turned to the limo, but it was driving away. She ran after it, thumping on its roof. The limo stopped; a window rolled down and the chauffeur leaned over toward the passenger side. "Yes madame?"

"What about . . . what about my kids?"

"You're taking care of them, after a fashion. Through Louise. She will be you. She's started today, when you and Reuben meet."

"Today—in the 70s? She's starting before the kids are born?"

"Just so."

"I don't think I can . . ."

"It is significantly too late, madame. Louise applied to save the children, and the decision is made. You will have the life you desired, and I have no doubt but that you will genuinely enjoy it."

The window whirred upward. She pounded on the roof, but the limo drove down the street, gathered speed, and was gone from reach.

She stood there panting on the sidewalk until, by degrees, the panic lifted from her. This was an adventure, at least, wasn't it? This was the adventure she should've had. She turned to Louise's house. The kids would be all right. They would; they will.

There were small trees on the street in full leaf; the sun shone, driving a wind that in turn drove a few luminous-white clouds. Late June, maybe. She walked across the sidewalk, feeling the sun-warmed concrete on her bare feet, and up the steep wooden steps to the Victorian's front door.

There was a key in the lock. She turned the key, opened the door, and put the key in her pocket. She stepped into the shadiness of the hall; hardwood floors and antique throw rugs. There was a letter addressed to her on the little antique table beside the hall closet. A letter from an attorney.

Miss Simmons, it said, your Aunt Louise, having died, has left you this house, and a small stipend.

The letter was dated June 23, 1974. It was a new, freshly typed letter.

Aunt Louise, yes, had left her the house in her old life, but it had been sold by her parents, and most of the money squandered on her father's idiotic investments . . .

Dana went upstairs and stood looking out the bedroom window at San Francisco. And then she saw her own reflection in the window. A young woman. She was twenty four years younger.

*   *   *

Dana lived in San Franciso, in Louise's house, for 16 years, while Louise rode the Ferris wheel, and took her place on Owl Street Ridge.

She thought about the children less often as time went on, and the memory most of the time was dreamlike, images from someone else's photo scrapbook. It wasn't as if they'd been kidnapped, or taken from her; they were there, and yet they weren't.

Dana quickly found herself drawn into the artistic life of San Francisco in the 70s. She had gay friends, and marched in Gay Pride parades; she was among the first performance artists; she was in and out of two art-punk bands; she fell in love three times; she got addicted to heroin over a summer, and kicked it in the fall, and started again in December, and kicked twice more before fighting free of it for good. She had shows of her art constructions—physical, not digital art—at community centers, and local shops, and on the sidewalk. It took six years and kick-ass luck to go the next level: a boyfriend had roomed with a guy in college who now wrote for ART FORUM and he talked the guy into seeing one of her shows. Impressed, the ex-roomie wrote it up. The SF MOMA's curator came to see for himself, and bought some pieces, and that brought buyers from New York.

She traveled to shows in New York and shared a gallery with Basquiat; she spent six months drinking wine in Paris, three months smoking hashish in Amsterdam, and almost lost her soul to absinthe one week in Barcelona.

No matter what she did, however, she always had the presence of mind, this time, to never get pregnant.

In 1982 she got an envelope in the mail; in it was a photo, dated a few weeks before. Feeling sick and disoriented she stared at the picture for ten minutes. It was a photo of herself, and Reuben, dressed for the era, and there was a baby in Reuben's arms, about a year old, and it looked like this "Dana" was a few months pregnant with another. Looking closely at the expression on this Dana's face, she could see it was really Louise.

She felt the children sometimes, when she closed her eyes—she could feel the other Dana's hands on the children's hair, feel them tugging her sleeve. Then she'd look, and they wouldn't be there. Still, the connection was real. Sometimes it was painful, sometimes it was reassuring.

She had lived the future, some of it, and she knew what was coming—but only when it came. It all seemed inchoate in her memory, when she thought about it, and she found herself unable to articulate warnings about fuel shortages, wars, and John Lennon's assassination. Often the big events took her by surprise, so caught up was she in her life.

She never forgot the children; but she knew they were taken care of; that in some way she herself was taking care of them. And she was able to let them go, most of the time. Except sometimes, late at night, when she slept alone; when the darkness is like a relentless mirror, giving back what's hidden during the day. Those times, staring into the glassless mirror, feeling the child-shaped hollowness in her, came more and more often . . .

In 1990 she could bear it no more. One warm Spring saturday she took a plane to Los Angeles, rented a limo, and found the house on Owl Street. She sat in the limo, and looked out through its one-way window, watching Dana, this other Dana, in the front yard, playing with little Carl, who was, what, around two, two and a half; and Damon, and Loni, who seemed older than Loni should be. They were playing with squirt guns; Dana had one too. Where was Sonya?

Dana watched as Reuben came out of the garage, smiling, pushing the Vespa. He had the same face, but somehow it was utterly different. His expression . . .

Reuben called to Damon, who dropped the squirt gun and ran to him. Reuben handed Damon a helmet, and the two of them got on the Vespa, Damon with great familiarity and comfort, hugging his Dad from behind. They rode off together, smiling.

The Dana in the yard was looking at the limo. She told the kids to play in the back yard, and they went without argument or question.

Dana came to the limo, and the other Dana opened the door for her. They sat inside, hidden from the world, looking at one another. Looking into this other Dana's eyes, Dana the artist burst out, "Louise!"

Louise smiled. "Hi. I've been expecting you."

"Um—where's Sonya?"

"Ballet."

"You're kidding me."

"She'll never be a prima ballerina—she's too tall, and she'll always be a bit overweight—but she enjoys it." She gazed at Dana with a trackless compassion. "How come you're crying? Miss the kids?"

"Yes. And . . . I'm just so jealous, how you. . . . Reuben never had that expression on his face when I was married to him. Not after the first two years. The kids seem different—I mean, not just that they're younger than when I last saw them . . . God that's such a strange thing to say . . . Oh, and—Loni is the wrong age, for 1990, she's too old, she looks five but . . ."

"Reuben and . . . you . . . didn't do everything the same. I . . . You had Loni sooner. And I should tell you that Reuben manages a Honda shop now."

"He used to make fun of Hondas!"

"He still does. But he prefers it to the brewery."

"Oh God—I should have . . . they . . . I didn't know how to . . ."

"I understand," Louise said tenderly. "Don't think there was anything you should have done that you didn't do, except for things you didn't know you could do. I brought something into the house you couldn't bring and only because I was able to go places you couldn't go. I brought it from the other side of death. It was given to me to bring. I brought complete acceptance to Reuben, no matter how selfish he was, and I dissolved all his resentment in it. The kids opened to me, too, when they felt it. . . . It's like Grace, like baraka, in the way it flows from the divine, but it's not something that comes as a gift, like Grace: I paid a price so that this Special Grace could be here."

"Louise—I can't come back, can I? I mean—I know it wouldn't be fair; you've taken them off the Ferris wheel and now I want to come back when you've done everything *for* me. But . . ."

"You could come back. The question is: have you had enough?"

"I don't know, I just know I . . . when I look at the kids . . ."

"Of course. But understand—if you come back, you'll have only your memories. Your skills will come with you, anything you've learned. But the events *will not have taken place*. All that's happened to you in the past sixteen years will be gone. You will not be a famous artist . . ." She smiled. "You won't have won those prizes for your art. Your constructions will no longer hang in the MOMA."

Dana found herself breathing hard. Her pounding heart seemed to move up into her head, to bang in her skull. It was so *loud*. "I . . . can't do that."

"You're identified with who you are now. Or who you seem to be. And so: Good bye, Dana."

Louise, the other Dana, got out of the limo and walked back to the house.

Pouring herself a drink, Dana told the driver to take her back to the airport.

Two years later, she found herself thinking of the children every night. Even of Reuben. She was beginning to see tedious patterns in the ebb and flow of the art scene, the avant garde. Nothing and no one seemed fresh; everywhere was irony, cynicism. Art itself was more than a consolation, but the life seemed empty. And the men she met were frustrated when she refused to commit to anything really long term. She felt it would be some kind of betrayal of the children, to marry.

The loneliness whispered to her from the corners of her bedroom, late at night, and it was at three a.m., this time, that she took a cab to the airport and caught the next plane for LAX.

She rented a limo; she went to Owl Street Ridge. Not sure what she wanted . . .

She dozed in the limo for hours, woke at 7, saw the other Dana puttering around the house, with little Carl following her around, pulling on the hose she was setting for the sprinkler. The other Dana—Louise—stood and looked at the limo.

Heart thudding, Dana, in the limo, told the driver to go.

She went to a hotel, ordered a room service breakfast, and tried to eat. And couldn't. She lay on the bed, staring out the hotel window, for hours. Then she called downstairs and ordered the limo brought around again.

Dana was waiting by the mailbox when the limo pulled up. She opened the door for the other Dana, and the other Dana, wearing a flower-print house-dress, got in beside her. "Hello, Dana."

"Hi Louise."

Dana was afraid to embrace her.

Louise asked. "Is it enough, this time? Enough of what you thought they took from you?"

Dana looked at the house.

"I *let* them take it from me. And I'd never have enough. But that doesn't matter. Something else in me . . . I can feel it, Louise. Something else in me wants to pay the price."

Louise kissed Dana on the cheek. "You should know, that not everything is great. Reuben still acts like a little boy some times. Damon imitates that. Sonya falls into fits of self pity. Loni still retreats into reading, still struggles with asthma. They're more opened now, there are more possibilities. But . . . they're not so different."

"I wouldn't care. To tell you the truth—I feel better, knowing that."

"And the things that have happened to you—all the honors, the achievements. . . ."

"I'll remember it. That'll have to be enough. And maybe I can make some of it happen . . . when I have time."

"I've tried to do some of your artwork, in case . . . in case there was a continuity. I just don't have your talent, though. All the equipment is there . . . I've been posting images online . . ."

"Will they—will they be disappointed in me? I'm no angel."

"Neither was I all the time. Do me a favor—get out of the limo, honey-darlin'."

Dana looked at her. Then she got out, closed the door behind her. Loni ran up to the limousine. "Mama?" She looked up at Dana—Dana the artist. "Where'd you get those clothes?" She was wheezing a little.

Dana looked down at the black leather jeans, the Depeche Mode t-shirt she'd worn from San Francisco. "Just trying 'em out, hon."

She picked Loni up. "Do you need your inhaler?"

"I think so."

Dana caught herself. What about Louise? She couldn't just . . .

She turned to see the white limo driving off. The passenger window whirring down and Louise was waving. Louise, not Dana, waving goodbye. Then Dana remembered that the driver at the airport had

had his back to her, most of the time. She'd been so distracted, she'd hardly looked at him. But he'd been a lean, white haired man.

Carl came running around the corner of the house; falling, laughing, getting up, running to her. She took his hand. "Carl, you look thirsty. Let's get some soda or something to drink."

"Okay," Carl said. He hung on her arm and swung from it.

"Yeah," Loni said. Her voice wheezy. "Somethin' to drink."

"First let's get your inhaler, Loni Maroni."

Loni laughed. "You never called me that before. I like that."

Reuben found her in the garage, with Loni handing her tools and looking on, and Damon helping her hold the joists together. "What the hell is all this stuff, Dana?"

She finished fitting the corners of the wooden box-frame together, then went to him and kissed him. There was eighteen years of a certain feeling accumulated in the kiss, and after a moment he stopped resisting. Then he stepped back, head cocked, trying to make her out. "That supposed to distract me from noticing you bought a work bench, what looks like two hundred dollars worth of tools..."

"Three hundred. Plus paint, sandpaper, glue, materials—with the work bench about six hundred dollars. It didn't work, that kiss?"

"It did sort of yeah but..." He tried to hide a smile as the kids laughed. "But Dana—we really can't afford—"

"I sold the computer. My graphics computer, the software. Used computers don't bring much but that one... fourteen hundred bucks. Not half what I paid but..."

"You sold your computer!"

"Yes. I'm tired of casting my pearls online. I'm going to be quitting my job, too, sweet-heart. I'll try to find something part time. We'll do all right."

"Quit your..."

"I've got a plan. See, I know of this guy at ART FORUM who'd really like my work. He's almost ready to retire from there now but I know someone in San Francisco who knows him... I have to get that guy in front of my work... I have three pieces in mind... then..."

Reuben had gone all cold. He was good at that: no one could accuse him of raising his voice but he had a coldness that cut deeper than *loud* ever could. "Dana—I don't know what bug has crawled up your . . . You just can't waste more time on this."

She was laughing at him. He was amazed, and doubly furious. "You're too much, Reuben. I'm sorry, hon, but you have no authority over me. You can act real cold, not talk to me, sleep in a far corner of the bed, and thereby consign yourself to a contented little Hell. You can threaten to divorce me and even go through with it. But this is happening. And what I think is gonna happen is, you're going to want to quit your job to be my manager. See, I don't have any doubts about what I can accomplish, not now . . ."

He did all those things except divorce her. He was nothing if not predictable. And though she found the contacts in San Francisco, and got a page (just a page, this time) in ART FORUM, it took her two years longer, after her first big exposure, to start getting the calls. Her timing wasn't right, at first. She didn't have the momentum of a career to help her past trendiness in the Scene; she had to discover what resonated in the intellectual mainstream now, for break-in art. It was politics, she discovered. She went to the ghetto, she took photos with a brownie camera, wanting them crude-quality, and worked them into the overall construction; she interviewed black men on death row and wrote the interview longhand on the end papers of old Bibles at the back of her constructions.

Once she visited the San Francisco Museum Of Modern Art. As Louise had promised—the Dana Simmons room was gone. Her art work was not there, not yet.

Then MODERN ART REVIEW did a cover story. Buyers called from New York. Reuben begged forgiveness, and quit to become her manager. The whole family took a long vacation.

The intimacy came back into their marriage—she'd had enough *good* sex—and the level of hostility dropped to nil, and the children flourished in the new atmosphere Sometimes she and Reuben still argued, a little: he complained when she didn't spend enough time on her artwork.

And everyone was wrong, when they speculated about her reasons for the inscription carved into the new monument she erected on Louise's grave. THANKS, LOUISE, FOR LETTING ME PAY.

Wings Burnt Black

Do not envy the Man
with the X-Ray Eyes...
—Blue Öyster Cult: *Heaven Forbid*

Is there really any hurry about killing me, Eric?" the Murderer asked. "I mean, wouldn't you like to draw it out? Savor it?"

And the Murderer smiled a mouthful of green teeth.

" 'Smiles form the channels of a future tear,' " the Crow replied.

"The ghost quotes Byron! And how altogether Byronic you are!"

"Mockery stalls for time," said Eric, who was called the Crow, cocking his pistol, "and that's another way of pleading."

"Don't flatter yourself. I would not plead with God himself. And don't imagine that I disbelieve in God. I know better: the villain is well-known to me."

The Murderer, the object of the Crow's vengeance this night, was half reclining on a chaise longue on the balcony of his condominium on the thirteenth story of this concrete high-rise. The Murderer was nestled in an almost believable semblance of slack calm; he had a daiquiri in one hand and a Marlboro Light in the other. The Detroit night was just beginning to burn, far below. Vaporous grime watercolored the full moon a sordid gray pink. The Murderer was a slim, sunken-eyed man in leather chaps and snakeskin boots, his face angular, just a little cocaine tremor in his fingers making the ash from his cigarette shiver into the monoxide wind; the wind carried the ashes into the sky to the wheeling, raucous crow, the bird that followed Eric every-where—and made the bird blink.

Eric was sitting on the balcony wall, rocking on the wall in a way no sane mortal would do; teetering, one leg crossed over the other, elbow propped on his knee, the gun loose in his hand but never wavering from the Murderer's forehead.

The bird settled on Eric's shoulder.

The Murderer looked at the black bird on Eric's shoulder and pulled on his cigarette, let smoke loll from his mouth and drew it back in through his nostrils, then said, "Here's another quote for you—I can't remember who said it: 'Hell is truth seen too late.' Probably is, for most people. And of course you know: the truth protects itself."

"I've heard that said." The Crow's finger tightened on the trigger ... then eased. He simply wasn't ready to fire the gun. There was something undone here, besides killing this man, but he didn't know what it was yet.

"But I have seen the truth," said the Murderer, "and I just don't care. You see, I've been ... well, not quite dead, but close. Enough to see through the veil." He pulled on the cigarette. "My parents were Santeria initiates, you know."

He paused as they both turned to look at a thudding police chopper tilting like a clumsy dragonfly, eddying flame-lit smoke with its blades, highlighting the murk of burning buildings with its downseeking spotlight, its bullhorn voice trying to warn the looters: the feeble, echoing voice of authority, its own self-mockery. *"By order of the governor, looters can be shot. This area is surrounded by police. Do not ... do not ... not ... not ..."*

"Can you imagine being cut in half by a helicopter blade?" the Murderer asked idly.

"Yes. That'd be too quick, for you," mused the Crow, just as idly. "If I drop you from up here, you might live for a while, and your bone edges, Murderer, your splinters, would break through your skin and then I could tap them with the muzzle of my gun."

"I doubt I'd be conscious at that point. You'd be better off breaking my bones up here. I understand you're strong enough. I know I can't kill you. And you can kill me. But you cannot kill the ones who are really responsible for Shelly's death."

"Liar!" The word banged from Eric and rebounded from the concrete face of the building to pierce even the cacophony of the burning city: LIAR!

And then the Crow, in a single motion, had moved to straddle the Murderer's legs with one boot planted to either side; lividly painted face catching the fire truck's cherry-top glare, flickering in and out of shadow, his premonitory eyes black as the Pit, his gun the unyielding blue of gunmetal, its muzzle now pressed to the Murderer's mouth. "If I shoot at a down angle, and miss your heart, Murderer, your jaw flies apart, and you will live to suffer, for a while, but you'll keep your foul mouth shut." His voice was like a brush-stick dragged over a snare drum. *Mouth shuhhhhhhhhhhh . . .*

But the Murderer spoke, even with a gun muzzle denting his nicotine-yellowed lips; his sunken eyes meeting Eric's, both their gazes as unwavering as the gun.

"You think you have found in me the one who ordered the attack on you; the one responsible for Shelly's death. You think you pull a trigger and the deed is done. But think—and heed and check it out and I'll tell you the motherfuckin' truth!"

The Crow took a step back and said, "Raise your drinking glass."

The Murderer obeyed and the Crow quoted Byron once more, " 'Here's a sigh to those who love me, and a smile to those who hate; and whatever sky's above me, here's a heart for every fate.' " He fired the gun—fired it at the glass in the Murderer's hand, with marvelous precision, so that the shattered glass was driven into the crime lord's tendons along with the bullet.

The bird, the black crow that was Eric's familiar, settled to the concrete and began to peck at bits of flesh and spots of cocktail spattered behind the Murderer.

The Murderer managed not to scream, but a gurgling growl escaped him as he clutched the shattered, riven hand to him, sitting up, eyes hot. He didn't drop his cigarette; but drew on it deeply, shaking.

But he smiled. Green teeth.

" 'Pain is the father of truth,' " said Eric. "Now don't fucking lie to me again. I'm sure I'd already know if there were others . . ."

"There is another," said the Murderer, in a triumphant, pain-shivered growl. "The one truly responsible for Shelly's death. Listen now . . . I ordered you and your love 'done,' yes—but who am I? I am a consequence. I was raised by a man whose greatest joy was in raping very small boys, taking them from behind first and then the mouth; my earliest sharply remembered taste is of my own blood and shit. My mother was a Santeria priestess until junk made her a whore. My parents made me what I am, you see. I could have been nothing else! And if there was any margin for transcending my making, it was taken up by my genetics. My father was chromosomally a killer; my mother chromosomally an addict. *But who made them?* Their parents were at least as bad—and my father was raised in a nasty bitch of a slum. And on it goes back into the blur of time." Grimacing with pain, he paused to suck on his cigarette. "So . . . so who is to blame? I have never had the faintest inkling of a choice in the things I do. Not the faintest. None, my friend! I am a psychopath and I know it. Was Jeffrey Dahmer really given a choice? Or did he have to be what he was? He was damned from birth. So who decided his damnation? Random chance? But you are here, and you know there is a spiritual world: you are part of it. Which means that there is a spiritual agenda, a cosmic purpose—a hated purpose, to my mind, but a purpose all the same. Does that purpose stint on brutality? Does it hesitate to create Inquisitions and the Holocaust? And doesn't it just fuckin' adore creating Aztecs and Celts who butcher children for their gods? Who was it who made life brutish—and short? Who jacked up the suffering? Who made de Sade and Lizzy of Bathory? Who made Eichmann? Who decided that two-year-olds should die of AIDS and four-year-olds of cancer?" Suddenly the Murderer sprang up and flicked his cigarette at Eric, and pointed a trembling finger at him with the cigarette hand, and quoted from the Book of Job: " 'Where wast thou when I laid the foundations of the earth? . . . Who hath laid the measures thereof, if thou knowest? Or who hath stretched the line upon it? Whereupon are the foundations thereof fastened? Or who laid the cornerstone thereof . . .' "

The Crow's normal supernaturally rectified implacability was set ak-ilter; for the first time he was unsure and his voice showed it. "It's not for me to punish blasphemy; that, others punish, later."

But the Murderer was thundering on, still quoting the Bible: " 'Hast thou entered into the springs of the sea? Or has thou walked in the search of the depth? HAVE THE GATES OF DEATH BEEN OPENED UNTO THEE?' "

"Ah," said Eric, "it was you who opened them for me." And once more he leveled the gun.

"No," said the Murderer, with a lethal quiet, dropping his hand. "He put me, like a bullet, in His gun. And He pulled the trigger, He killed you, and Shelly—I was just the instrument. I was made as I am, a murderer, and fate brought us together, you and I, and *who loads the guns of fate?*"

Eric looked at the gun in his hand, and it drooped. He looked out at the night sky: black construction paper with cheap acrylics slurred by an uncertain hand.

"I am going to inquire," Eric said. "You can run if you like, but you know it doesn't matter where you go, or how. You can go to South Africa and lock yourself in a bunker a thousand feet down a diamond mine, and I would come to you. You know that—don't you?"

"Yes." There was no guile in the Murderer now.

"Or you can stay here, and take drugs for the pain, and wrap your hand, and wait for me to answer you."

"Yes. But just remember: your mission is one of final vengeance. Don't lose sight of your goal."

The Crow stepped up onto the ledge—he spread his arms like the wings of the bird that rose to flap beside him, and dove off the ledge. He fell. He turned end over end, never changing pose as he fell spread-eagled, and when he struck the crow-black street facedown he seemed to fall through it as if it were water; the bird followed him down; and they'd vanished into the street itself. Then steam rose from a manhole cover, and there was nothing unusual in that, but this steam moved consciously, and took shape: the shape of a crow, and then another crow, these shapes becoming as real as anything is, two birds, street-black and flapping into the sky, up and up through the smoke and columns of rising heat, spiraling ever higher, to heights where no earthly bird could find air for purchase or breath to draw, and higher yet, the two of them rising like ash above the flue of the whole burning world.

And then vanishing from this world; for heaven is not above and hell is not below.

Shaped once more like a man, Eric passed into a muttering void, and he saw that his familiar was still with him, though now in the shape of . . . a conquistador.

"Is that the shape you had when you were a mortal man?" Eric asked the wraith, the dark little man with sharp beard and dull armor.

"Yes. We killed the Indians, all the Indians in the village, trying to force from them the whereabouts of El Dorado, but they didn't know, and the last to die touched me with the feather of a Crow, and said something I did not understand; thus he cursed me. Soon after, I died of typhoid; and became sometimes a man-wraith, and sometimes the bird, when I am needed. Someday perhaps I will have worked off my penance."

"And what was *my* penance? To be murdered? To have my true love murdered before my eyes? What crime was this penance for?"

"I do not know. I only know what I am commanded to do; not the why of it; never the wherefore." He drew his hand over his body, and his wraith-garment transformed, armor became soft gray cloth, and he was then clothed as a monk. "Best to dress for humility, in the higher planes . . ."

Eric shrugged and remained as he was: in black leather, face painted a livid mockery.

Still they ascended, through veils of almost-being, passing, on the way, this and that consensual fantasy of the afterlife, some decaying and some, for a time, holding fast: a glittery, musical Protestant heaven; a dour Hasidic afterlife; a roseate Hindu afterlife gyrating with blue-skinned idols; an Amerind forest of plenty; and on it went, until they'd passed from the realm of expectations and into the brighter lights, where reality became impatient and asserted itself.

Here Eric looked about for someone in authority.

The looking was a summoning: and the Guardian Entity faded up, sank upward into being: was suddenly there. To Eric in that moment the Entity looked like an emblem, like a playing-card king, almost: it had austere faces duplicated above and below, in mirror opposite; if he looked into the Entity's middle it was like looking down a reflecting corridor of mirrors into a sentient infinity. If he tried to hold the whole thing in his mind it came across like an intricately calligraphed Hebrew letter; a letter that looked back at you. Eric found that staring into the Entity was too vertiginous. He focused on the upper set of apparent "eyes" as he waited for the Entity's challenge.

The crow familiar hung about in the background, hooded head humbly inclined as the Guardian Entity spoke. Eric stood his ground in this groundless place; he consciously remained the Crow archetype head to toe, leathers and makeup and gun; hovering in this gray but sparkling violet place, where, just on the edge of one's peripheral attention, paisley became swastikas became crucifixes became pentagrams became Stars of David became leering goat heads became enneagrams became serpents became angels . . .

"Well?" the Guardian Entity said, by way of acknowledgment. This was how Eric heard it, anyway.

"I've come to speak to God, to demand the truth."

"You truly think you can make demands of God?"

"I was murdered; more important, my true love was murdered; it happened on the day of our wedding."

"Sounds like—you're from Earth, no?—sounds like a Scottish folk song. I'm sorry, I don't mean to jeer at you: you produce that in me yourself; I give back your own doubts. And I do know that, subjectively, suffering is its own dimension, and goes on forever; or seems to. But, as you're from Earth, have you read C. S. Lewis's *The Screwtape Letters*? 'All horrors have followed the same course, getting worse and worse and forcing you into a kind of bottleneck till, at the very moment when you thought you must be crushed, behold! you were out of the narrows and all was suddenly well. The extraction hurt more and more, then the tooth was out. The dream became a nightmare and then you woke. You die and die and then you are beyond death.' "

"Where is Shelly?" Eric suddenly felt a dizzy need to see her.

"I thought you wanted to interview God—now it's the lost love you want to see? Not that they aren't identical. But not to you, not yet. You really ought to keep your mind on your aim. Spirits quickly disintegrate, here, who flicker from one mental fantasy to another. To answer your question, Shelly is in another realm. She is caught up in her expectations. If you go there, you'll get caught up, too, and your aim will be left undone. You do intend to wreak justice, no? A reckoning?" A ripple ran through the Guardian Entity's living iconography . . .

"Yes," Eric replied. "A reckoning."

"And you know, of course, that inflicting suffering on the Bad Boys, will not really balance the scales very well."

"Yes, but it's better than nothing."

" 'It's better than nothing'—which is just exactly what God said . . ."

"It could be that you're not the servant of heaven you seem; perhaps you're a demon, sent to endlessly stall me. The way the Murderer stalled me."

"I contain shadows of course, Eric, but I am not a shadow, no. You're more shadow than I am, my boy. I see you have a gun with you."

"Yes," put in the crow familiar, "he has it. His will is in the form of a gun."

There was a shade of warning in the monkish crow's comment.

"I see it. Most impressive." His "voice" was surprisingly lacking in derision. "Quite a piece you have there. What caliber? Forty-five? A Colt, is it?"

Only then did Eric understand his own gun: it was, especially on this plane, not a mechanism of steel, except in shape; here the gun was the *embodiment of his will.*

The gun was an expression of him, as all guns will be for the user, anywhere, but on a deeper level: literally, the bullet was fashioned from his will, was compressed will itself.

As such, it was not without meaning here; it could destroy, in the higher realms.

"I will see Shelly," said Eric, "after the reckoning. Now: I have come to demand: *Who is at fault?* The Murderer has convinced me, at least to the point of reasonable doubt, that the Murderer could never have been in command of himself, really, that he was a cog moved by other cogs. Some seem to have choice in their lives—others have no choice, because of the absoluteness of their nature and, I guess, nurture. Seems like he's one of those. Unless he's lying, and I can detect lies, and he wasn't. And then there are those born demented; bad seeds, and all that: how much choice have they got in what they are? None. So who's really to blame for what they do?"

"So you're saying you should forgive everyone with equal compassion because they cannot help themselves. 'Father forgive them they know not what they do'?"

"Now you *are* mocking me. No. I exist, post death, purely to effect a reckoning; to thereby ease my suffering, and Shelly's. So our spirits can rest. There *must* be a reckoning. This is, after all, a universe in which math is king, no?"

"No, mathematics is a chancellor, merely."

"Deny it: that the Murderer is, ultimately, not responsible for his actions."

"Do you know Shakespeare? *''Tis true 'tis pity; And pity 'tis 'tis true.'* "

"I see."

Eric drew his gun.

"Then . . . ," said Eric, ". . . who do I kill?"

"In the land of death? Be serious."

"I'm not obtuse. This place has as much to do with being as with non-being and even in the land of death one can be made not to be. Who, then? Is it God?"

The Entity did not reply.

Eric thundered his demand: "Who do I kill? Who, finally, is responsible for Shelly's death? *MUST I KILL GOD?*"

Must I kill God . . . Must I kill God . . . Must I . . .

They weren't echoes, in the sonic sense, but somehow the words reverberated all through the various heavens . . .

Must I kill God . . .

He remembered the Zen saying that went: *Kill the Buddha! Kill the Buddha!*

The Guardian Entity's signatory substance opened, like a gate, and the Crow walked through it; the monkish crow familiar following. Walking through the gate of the Entity's body.

They ascended stairs that were in that moment created for him, and they passed through all spectra, from red-shift to yellow to blue to the place where waves move so frequently they mesh one into another and come to a stop, outside of time. A place where you could, if you could go there, strap galaxies onto your shoes for Roller Blades. The place that is the Sum of Suns and the Sum of Sums, at the pinpoint of the pinpoint, atop the Ray of Creation.

Here, somehow, the monk had become more his own signification; more living symbol: and glancing at him Eric saw that he had the head of a crow, big as a man's head, within a monk's robe. *Something like Horus*, Eric thought.

He was a little surprised at his ability to think at all here; surprised that this place didn't destroy his mind, as it was quite beyond human capability. But he knew, then, what protected him:

The gun.

The gun in his hand was the focal point of his will; so long as he kept the greater part of his intentionality focused there, it parted the walls of wonder for him, and kept him sane.

At length, they came to a realm where all music accorded into one recurring chord that was always the same and yet never repeated. Here an angel stood in their path, towering over them; a manlike figure of light, complete with magnificent iridescent-white wings, a tarot image that moved and spoke and carried a sword, clutched in both hands and angled downward, that seemed to stretch on forever and yet held the proportions of a sword. Eric had a sense that the sword was in relation to the subjective universe the way that a laser is in relation to a compact disc; or perhaps the way a threaded needle is in relation to the tapestry in elaborates.

"Are you the one?" Eric asked.

"Could you be more specific?" Its voice was at one with the endless chord that reverberated here. Each of its words had infinite implications. Eric focused on those that were relevant to him.

"The forger of destinies," Eric went on, with no hint of fear. "The one who decides—to be more *specific*—who is to be murdered, on my world. The one who decided that Shelly would be tortured to death. That one, I would destroy."

"Even if, in consequence, the universe tumbles apart?"

"Even if the universe tumbles apart," Eric replied, without hesitation. "Shelly *was* my world. All that was good in it."

"How did one so selfish come so far? But now I perceive: the gun. You are a kind of magician, and this gun is a kind of magical staff."

"It is the instrument of my will, which is at one with my vengeance. Who is responsible for what happened to me and Shelly? Never mind my murder: who caused Shelly to suffer as she did before she died? Was it the Devil? Is there a Satan who frustrates God's designs and takes away choice and makes a joke out of justice? Is that the deal?"

"Satan, Iblis, Shaitan, Set, whatever you care to call him, is incorporated within the total being, and is a minor functionary. Another kind of gatekeeper; a filter. A shadow. He is not responsible."

"Then who do I kill? Well? Let's have it, dammit! *MUST I KILL GOD?*"

Eric half expected the angel to make a remark about monumental, cosmic hubris; but the angel didn't. The angel knew well the power of totality of belief; of focusing absolute attention on one's Aim. How else had the created part of the universe been created in the first place?

"Yes," said the angel, not exactly lying, "I am the one responsible."

So Eric raised the gun to the place where the angel's eyes should be, to the two beacons of chaotic light set side by side, and aimed it between those fulminations, and with all that he was, made the bullet of his absolute dedication to vengeance "fire" from the "gun" and—

The angel's wings folded about him, and the bullet struck a wingtip, which exploded in white flame, and burned like the tip of a welding torch and a burned feather fell, down past the sword and into creation, and then the angel opened himself, as if he were a gate, and Eric stepped through that gate, and into the Place where God, in our terminology, can be seen.

Something like Ezekiel's Wheel turned there; something like a mandala of evanescent configuration; but Eric knew these appearances for semblance, too, and he passed through them also, with a shudder, keeping all his attention focused in his gun, and he found himself . . . strange expression, that: 'he found himself' . . . in the Presence which, to the best of Eric's capacity to see, was something like . . .

   . . . *the place where plus and minus meet and incorporate one another; where positive and negative, active and passive neutralize; where two needles meet point to infinitely sharp point, their unconditionally sharp points exactly poised one on the other; the needles—widening past the junctured points to infinitely expanding cones—turning each in the direction relatively opposite the other. And pinned between these points is consciousness, present tense: the first circle of consciousness, the stone dropped in the pond; between these point-on-point spikes is crucified this: the unspeakable suffering of God.*

   And radiating from this suffering: the ineffable mercy of God.

   An Eye. There was, to the best of his capacity for seeing it, an Eye there, an Eye that spoke . . .

   The lame and inadequate phrase "the best of all possible worlds" came into Eric's mind. The word "possible" was like a key opening up a Pandora's box of answers to his spoken and unspoken questions. The Eye spoke to Eric and he heard it this way: *"I am an outgrowth of the necessity of Being. I create, and am myself created by the Must Be. I am trying to retrieve Time and thus end suffering; I can do only that which I can do. Pull your trigger, and complete my crucifixion."*

   Eric pulled the trigger, with a despairing sense of inevitability.

   The bullet struck where the two infinite needles met and a void opened there and inexorably Eric was drawn into the void, and was *not*: he no longer existed: and then he was and . . .

   . . . and found himself . . .

   . . . spinning there, between the needles, in all possible directions, looking out at looking in . . .

   Shelly . . .

   Remembering her directed the part of God that had always been Eric to an interior orientation, back to the grip of time, and he was, then, back on the Earth . . .

   The mortal world. Standing on the rim of a balcony. In Detroit, Michigan, on a certain October 31.

   "Oh," he said, sighing. "I see."

   "You really went?" the Murderer asked, with real curiosity, as he whoofed up another hit of cocaine from a little metal bottle, so as to blur the pain in his shattered hand.

"Yes."

"Did you find out who's really responsible for your—no, screw that, I sure as hell would like to know: who's responsible for *me being the way I am*? I mean, I killed my old man and my mom, 'cause I blamed them, but that didn't seem to do it, you know? I mean—"

"Shut up. You're tweaking. Yes, I put a bullet into God. Was in consequence reminded that I am you and I am God, and Justice is doing the best. It can, and I myself am the one impossibly responsible, and . . . and the truth is often paradoxical."

"I see. So there's no point in killing me!"

Eric hesitated; and then a burnt feather drifted down from above. His familiar gave a raucous cry and plucked the feather up in its beak and flew to Eric's shoulder. He took the charred feather from his friend's shiny black beak, the gun-burnt feather that had fallen from the final angel, and he twined it into his hair as the Murderer waited for his answer.

Would he let the Murderer go?

The Murderer made another stab at persuasion. "If I am you, and you me, and we're all contained in God, then, eventually, if you shot me—you'd be shooting yourself, right? So you've gotta cop to it: there's really no point in shooting me."

"Wrong. There's a thing called *consolation*." Eric smiled. "It's better than nothing. Shooting you—is the consolation prize."

Then things went as they did in the tale of the Crow, and justice was served, insofar as it could ever be, and the Murderer was shot dead by Eric's will and with metal-jacketed .45 slugs, and Eric's spirit in due course found its way to Shelly and, there, after the human presumptions melted away and Eric and Shelly came out of expectation into the light that is divine attention, Eric found more than consolation, he found completion: in her.

Tighter

It occurred to Janet that one notch tighter would kill him.

They were in Bedroom One of the two-bedroom apartment that her and Prissy rented on West 12th, just off Broadway in Manhattan. It was their crib, they didn't live here, so it was pretty minimal. A bed, with a mirror headboard, red satin sheets, no blankets. A blue carpet that they kept vacuumed, a dial-control light turned low, and a radio. The radio on the floor. The tricks only cared about clean sheets, and things not smelling bad, no used condoms lying around, the girls keeping themselves pretty fresh. They cared about that, they cared about the right kind of service, and they cared about not being here during a raid. Anonymity is golden, the guy who taught English at PS 102 told her, as he paid her the hundred.

Harry, the trick she was straddling and strangling, was about fifty, mat of black hair on his flat chest going white at the tips, like the oily hair on his head, his streaked widow's peak. He had a bulbous belly, powerful short legs, long arms, a fading Navy-type tattoo on one wrist of two dice rolled to snake eyes. He wore thick glasses, even while they were doing it—so he could see her sitting on him naked, he said. See it clear. The cokebottle glasses made his eyes seem like big glossy-brown blobs; the glasses usually got steamed up, after awhile. *You're so full of shit your glasses are steaming up*, she thought. He had a long narrow

nose, with little black hairs growing out of it; same kind of hair in his
ears. She was straddling him and she was strangling him, and that's
what he'd paid her to do. Erotic strangulation. She was supposed to
tighten the narrow black leather strap, crossed in an unfinished knot,
until he came near to blacking out; and then she was supposed to loosen
it so he could breathe, gulp big draughts of life, she pumping up and
down on his thing while he was sucking in the air. His thing had a
metal cock-ring around the base of it, keeping the blood in, almost like
it was being strangled too. He paid her triple rate for this, something
kinky and risky. Three hundred an hour. "Just try saying no to that
much money," she'd told Prissy.

"I would and I fucking could say no," Prissy said, when they'd sat
around the living room of the crib eating Chinese food from cartons.
"If the guy gets a heart attack or something . . . Sure I'd say no to
that . . ."

But, Harry gave two hundred dollar tips sometimes. He took the
bills out of that paper bag he came here with . . . And she had seven
thousand dollars put away in her money market account. Another thirteen grand or so, she would get matching funds from the Small Business Administration, open her own business. Hair cutting and nails
parlor. Her own nails were an inch and a half long, beginning to curl,
and they had cat-eyes in sequins on them. It was really well lacquered
and shaped, really well done. She and Prissy did each other's nails after
work. They were a good team. Prissy was the blond, you needed a
blond, and Janet was the brunette, her hair cut like Betty Page. With
the bangs and all. She was half Puerto Rican and half Russian, which
was all she knew about her real parents. Her adoptive Dad had tracked
her down once. *"I can't believe we invested all that effort and time and
money in adopting your little brown ass and raising you up and you just
become a whore. A human waste."*

Harry was thrashing under her. He still didn't give the signal.

She didn't take drugs anymore. She saved her money so she could
get out. She didn't like the business now, though some of the guys were
pretty nice, and she'd never more than sort-of-liked this business.
Where could it take you? She wanted to be going somewhere. And
who was going to marry her, except some pimp asshole, and she hated

pimps, fucking hated them. And she did want to get married, and not to a loser like Amil, and have kids: she'd made up her mind on that when she'd turned 29. One more year, she'd be thirty . . .

If she tightened it another notch and just held on, she could take the money in that paper bag. It was Harry's job to collect money from bookies in the area, for the Pasta Potentates, as her ex-boyfriend Amil had called the mafia, and he always just stuffed the money in a paper bag. He said if he put it in a briefcase or even a duffel it'd look like he was carrying money. He was skimming from the That Thing Of Theirs, and one of these days, if he didn't die right here, they'd finish the job for her anyway. That was something to consider . . . He was headed for an early grave any way you looked at it . . . They'd kill him sure . . . And she was pretty sure he was careful to let no one know he came here. He was married, for one thing, for another you stop at a whore after you're collecting people's money, those people will suspect you of using their money on that whore. So you don't tell them about stopping at the neighborhood crib on your dinner hour.

Harry was clutching the side of the bed, his knuckles white, his fingers clenching on the fabric, loosening a little, clenching. His face was swollen, patchy-red. He was making noises like that rabbit had made . . .

When she was a little girl, about 12, her adoptive Aunt had brought her a rabbit for Easter, the French kind with the floppy ears. Later that year she'd caught it humping her stuffed toys. It'd made hissing sounds, which sounded weird from a rabbit, as it humped her teddy bear, and she'd slapped it away from the bear in sheer disgust and it *jumped* onto her hand and clamped onto her wrist, the way a dog will clamp onto your leg, and the rabbit *began to fuck her hand*, it was a little fuck-animal, now, and not a rabbit anymore, and it was fucking her hand with its little pencilly thing, making those hissing sounds, and as she tried to claw it away from her—Prissy hadn't believed it when she'd told this to her, but it was true—it came in her palm, wet warm gunk splashing down her wrist and she'd screamed and flung the rabbit away so it smacked against the wall over her bed and it's neck broke and it died. She burst into tears and Amy her adoptive Mom came in and found her with a dead rabbit on the bed and cum on her hands and she decided in her illin' red-haired head that Janet had *done it on purpose*. Just like Amy had said Janet got pregnant on her own when really Doug had date-raped her, when she was fourteen, though back then no one used that term. And she'd run away to have the abortion they wouldn't let her have, because they were Catholic...

(Harry's eyes were going pinpoint, his tongue was sticking out).

And Janet had never gone back ... And she'd followed a rock band around for a couple of years, and worked in different places and started taking money, when she was seventeen, for having sex, and then she gave it up for a few years when she got the grant to go to community college but then the legislature took that money away and she started turning tricks again...

The radio was playing the *Sounds of Silence* by Simon and Garfunkel. "Hello darkness, my old friend." It sounded like Paul Simon was singing from under the bed. *Are you under there, Paul?*

Harry, the trick, was convulsing, but he hadn't given the loosen signal. If he failed to give it to her and he got all blue, she was supposed to stop on her own. His thing thrashed inside her, not big enough to fill her, or any woman; it was almost like a clapper in a bell.

Ding dong, Harry, she thought.

He was changing colors...

She heard a guy moan from Room Two. That albino black guy Jediah that Prissy did. *He's pretty weird, but he's no weirder than Strangle-Me Harry, and Jediah pays cold cash in advance*, was all she'd say about him. Prissy'd gotten him to come in just about twelve minutes. Her and Prissy, what a team. Prissy'd paid her home phone bill, once, when she'd had that infection and couldn't work for a month. "I could have taken it out of my savings," she'd told her, when she'd figured it out.

"Don't you ever touch those savings, Janet, you dumb bunny," Prissy said. If she liked you, she called you dumb bunny.

He was making that hiss as he fucked at her (you couldn't call it fucking, it was more like fucking at), hissing with the itty bitty increments of air he could get ... less and less air ... An unfamiliar feeling came over her as she looked at him; as she looked at her hands, aching but not really tired, and her strong forearms. She worked out. And her strong thighs straddling him, pinioning him.

She didn't feel like she was serving him, any more, in that moment. She felt a kind of current in her, a hot good current, and it gave her the feeling of *being in control* and it was something she hadn't felt quite like that before.

I mean, in a way you were always in control of tricks, if you knew what you were doing. You had strict rules, you led them around by the dick in a way; you politely make them take a shower first, make them state categorically they are not undercover police, no entrapment please, and most of all you made them cum in under the time they had paid for so you could get rid of them and bring in the next guy or take a break if you didn't have another guy right then. Breaks were important.

He was turning seriously blue now.

Well. Let's think about this. There might be as much as $20,000 in that paper bag of his.

That Thing Of Theirs, the Pasta Potentates, they wouldn't know where he was. Prissy would get her back on this, and the two of them could wait till two in the morning, take him up to the roof, carry his body over two or three building roofs, drop him into the alley, dressed, make it look like he was taken up to the roof and robbed. Leave some gang sign on him or something.

He was shaking, really shaking now, his glasses half flopped off— he was making the sign—

So she stood a good chance of getting away with it, if she did it right. But then, she'd have to live with it. Because, like Amil used to say, where ever you go, hey, there you are.

That was really not too easy for Janet to imagine, living with something . . .

With strangling this ugly bastard to death.

But it was a good feeling, this sensation in her arms, her whole body. All of her connected together in one purpose. It was a feeling like Amil had described to her; he was into black magic, and he said it was that kind of feeling when it worked. But if it worked for him, why was his magic ass in jail?

Harry was clutching at her wrists now. She'd never killed anyone before—was she really going to do it now?—though once in a while she'd felt like it. She hadn't felt it was genuinely in her to really go through with killing, though, except in self defense. But now she felt she could do it. She wasn't sure if she *would* do it—but *she knew she could*.

She was really capable of killing him. It was amazing to her. Her hands trembled, pulling the taut cords tighter.

If she didn't let him go right away, and if she didn't have the nerve to go through with it, he'd know she had thought about killing him, and who knew what he'd do? He had always been kind of sweet, really, never the faintest sign of violence, and he'd sounded sort of pathetic and sad when he'd told her that his mother had punished him by sitting on him and strangling him and it was the only kind of embrace he'd ever got from her. I mean, you hear something like that, you feel like you're a step too far into somebody's life, and like it or not you feel what they feel a little, if you can feel anything at all. Maybe because it was something that had happened when he was a kid.

And if you thought of him *as a kid* it was harder to hold him at a distance; harder to kill him.

But it was almost done. One notch tighter. Then it'd be all over.

Paul Simon was just finishing singing the "Sound of Silence."

Harry had a look in his eyes like he was fighting his own ecstasy . . . Like he was only half resisting . . . She could almost see the specks in front of his eyes that he must be seeing, the pretty starbursts . . .

He wasn't fighting all that hard. See there? Part of him wanted it. Wanted her to go all the way. It might be the ultimate high for him, dying this way, like that guy in the band INXS (and what a waste *that* had been compared to this jerk-wad Harry), like Vaughan Bode whose comix Amil had liked so much, a legendary way to go, and he was digging it: even as he thrashed under her, his dick was ding-donging in her, and she thought she felt cum squirt—she felt it in his dick's spasm, not through the condom—and in her mind what she saw jetting was blood and not sperm, he was cumming blood as she strangled him—the straps almost cutting into his throat, making the veins on his neck stand out purple like on a hard dick.

Wanting it, she could see it in his eyes; he was wanting it, if not completely—but hell, if deep down he wanted it, well then, that was something she could live with. And eventually she'd learn to put it out of her mind no matter what.

Yeah. Hell it'd make him happy.

He was flapping at her with his hands, weakly, now, and there was something babyish about the motion, and that thought brought an image to her mind . . .

She tried not to see it, but an image of this jerk-wad as a small boy, being choked by his mother, came into her mind's eye, and Janet's will stammered and her hands relaxed a little—and, using that hesitation he thrashed like a bronc and threw her off him, and she fell onto her side, off the bed, and he clawed the straps away from his throat where they'd dug in deep red marks, and encircling rings of purple were forming, and he choked and sputtered, "You bitch, you fucking bitch," at least that's what she thought he was saying. "You failed, you stopped." That she heard clearly, though it came out in a squeak, and she stared at him in surprise, thinking she ought to yell for Prissy but feeling disoriented, stumbling on some inner ledge.

"You failed, bitch," he said and lunged at her, throwing himself down onto her, pinning her to the floor by her throat, banging her head on the wood under the carpet. She tried to yell but he'd cut off her wind, his arm straight, his strong hand and the weight of his upper body squeezing her throat. She flailed her legs, trying to bang the radio or something, make enough noise to summon help. Couldn't hit anything but the floor, thumps that just weren't very loud.

He was still coughing and choking, himself, as he tried to choke her air out, and he was drooling a little, blood mixed with drool dripping on her face as he squeezed some and then squeezed harder.

Maybe it would be enough for him to punish her, and he'd let her go . . .

But now he was saying something that gushed icewater through her. "We did it four times, that's longer'n I let the others go. I usually punish them after three. Mama got away from me, I went to do her and she was already dead, but here you girls are, I done three like this, and I pay a guy in the Outfit—" He stopped to cough some more and spat blood at her. "And he takes care of the bodies with beautiful profess—" Choke. Spit. "Professionalism."

By now Prissy was across the apartment in the living room, watching TV while she waited for her next appointment, and even if she did hear the noise she'd ignore it because they always thrashed and banged in here, during Harry's appointment, it was part of Harry's thing to thrash around and there was always some noise. Prissy wouldn't be coming.

You're going to have to survive this on your own, girl.

Janet rallied her strength and loosed it through her in one whiplash, her whole body whipping, and he lost his grip and rocked back, flailing for balance. She lurched and twisted left, and she scrambled to her feet and grabbed the leather strap and twisted it around his neck from the side, while he was in profile to her trying to get his balance, and she tightened, and tried to yell for Prissy, but her throat was still tight and gummy and wouldn't make more than a squeak.

The two of them were on their knees, him facing to her left, she facing him, and he tried to slug at her but couldn't hit her directly at this angle. She'd gotten the straps in the ruts she'd made earlier and with just another notch tighter she could—

He jabbed an elbow hard into her gut just below her ribcage, and all the air burst from her mouth like from a gashed bicycle tire, and her grip loosened and he wrenched free and slugged her in the side of the face, and she fell over, still not able to make a sound, and the strap—*the strap!*—was around her this time and she could feel the taut, concentrated finality of the grip as he tightened it. He was taking no chances, he was focused this time. She tried to kick but she had no air in her at all after having it knocked out of her and she was already dizzy and weak ... Starbursts in front of her eyes, prickles in her hands and feet, paths of prickling nothingness traveling from her extremities to meet in her heart ... His glasses were hanging from one ear and she saw his gaping face, white and blotchy red, filling her vision, and she *thought oh no, it's the last thing I'll ever see, oh no, into eternity with his fucking ugly pan* ... She tried to claw at his face but her hands were like the hands of blow-up dolls, soft clubs without pith, without strength ... The darkness closed in like a tightening circle, the dark circle getting smaller and smaller, making her smaller inside it ... the last thing she'd see would be the sparkles, the flashes ... She heard a man's voice on a radio commercial saying, "WE'VE GOT FIVE HUNDRED, RIGHT THAT'S FIVE HUNDRED GUITARS TO GET RID OF, GREAT BRAND NAME GUITARS AT GUITARLAND DISCOUNT CENTER! WE'VE GOT AMPS, WE'VE GOT DRUMS, WE'VE GOT EVERYTHING YOU NEED TO WALK IT INSTEAD OF TALK IT! THIS IS ONE CHANCE AND ONE CHANCE ONLY CAUSE THERE'LL NEVER BE A SALE LIKE THIS ONE ..." The voice was getting smaller. "At Guitarland In Jersey City ... take the ... expressway to ... exit to ... but ... now because ... again ... not again ..." The radio was gone. White noise took its place. Something was about to pop ...

Then there was a roaring in her ears and air burst painfully into her lungs and he was like that movie when they turn Robocop back on, there was a fluttering in the darkness and the fluttering became light and shapes and she could see again.

She saw Prissy standing over Harry, who was on his knees, digging with weakening fingers at the radio cord she was tightening around his neck. Prissy worked out too, and her muscular forearms trembled but held on firm, and she'd got the strap in the same ruts and there was blood coming out his mouth and he almost smiled but couldn't ...

He died all of a sudden, just going limp, and he wasn't faking either, it was so real, you could just see the life fly away out of him. Maybe something burst in his brain.

Prissy let him drop and kicked him once, not very hard.

"Asshole." She was breathing hard but seemed calm. "Janet? You okay, ya dumb bunny?"

She came over to help Janet stand. Janet could only croak the words out, but at least she could breathe. "I'm ... okay. Be all right."

" 'kay." Prissy was looking around for something. She found the brown paper bag wrapped in Harry's coat, jammed into one sleeve. She pulled it out, dumped the money on the bed.

"Well all right. We open a business. What you want to do with his body?"

Your Servants in Hell

Twenty-five whores in the room next door
twenty-five floors and I need more . . .
                    —Sisters of Mercy (Vision Thing)

W hat bothers me, Roland," said Frater Butterwick, Third Level Satanic Magus, as he ate another cinnamon swirl, "is the lack of concrete results."

Roland didn't answer for a long time. He drew his long lean length back for a stretch that screeched his chair across the floor of the quiet coffee house, prompting a scowl from the would-be poet with the soul patch and powder-yellow glasses sitting a table away from them. Roland smiled complacently at the poet, who looked away, went back to scribbling in his notebook as he sat under the poster photo of William Burroughs reluctantly letting Allen Ginsberg hug him.

Roland was almost six foot five, shaved bald, black goatee, razor inflected eyebrows accenting his Satanic appearance. If you're going to be the High Priest of a Satanic Church, you don't want to disappoint people: half the reason the acolytes come is for the Satanic mystique. Roland's face was almost ageless, though his sister—and sex-magick partner—had confided to Butterwick that Roland was almost fifty-five. She had hinted that his youthful appearance was due to magickal rejuvenation; but one of Roland's oldest acolytes just happened to be a plastic surgeon. Roland wore a black suit, vest, silvery tie, storm trooper boots; his nails were just long enough to be pointed: a good touch.

Butterwick wore a long black coat, a shapeless sweater to hide his roundness, though it made him too warm in here. Unlike Roland, he didn't sport his baldness: hair was combed over to hide it; he was chubby and blurring into real obesity; spectacled, small eyes, small dark-red lips like pie cherries showing through the crust of his pie face.

A slim, sexily petite brunette in a beret came in, asking the bored spike-haired kid at the counter for a double latte, nonfat milk; a Betty Boop of a girl, with a kelly-green body stocking, short black leather skirt, boots. Both Roland and Butterwick stared at her with thinly disguised lust. "Should have sat outside, where I could smoke," Roland said, staring at the girl's finely turned, almost miniature rump. Butterwick had a sudden, invasive memory of lifting up the skirts of his sister's Barbie doll to see the creased pink-plastic ass; the disappointing absence of twat.

Still, Roland didn't respond to Butterwick's implied question: Is there a way to get concrete magical results? Cool reticence was one of many ways Roland kept the Temple Brethren in line, and Butterwick knew it. Roland even taught something of the sort to Priest Initiates like Butterwick: " 'Magick is 98 % psychological; hence you must with every posture and every syllable be conscious of your impact on followers."

At last, watching the girl walk over her to her table and take the inevitable notebook out of her bag, Roland said, "You know better than that, Butterwick. 'Concrete results!' You get concrete results, from magick, exactly when you get concrete results. There are, generally, no guarantees. Not from here. We're skating the edge of oblivion, and that's how we like it, Butterwick. On the edge—not over the edge." Roland's wolfish smile flashed; his black eyes shone. "It's what keeps us alive, that balancing act. Slide too far in, and you're out of your depth; move too far from the abyss and you're asleep and powerless. Skate the edge, Butterwick. Know thyself; increase your being, your Will. Embrace synchronicity. Do the assigned rituals. Incorporate Chaos. And may I point out: You won a thousand dollars in the lottery. Had you ever done that before your work with Ritual magick? I think not. A pleasing synchronicity; less than Pure Will but more than accident."

Butterwick squirmed on his chair, thinking: A thousand dollars? He'd conjured for a million. A thousand was a bitter disappointment.

He mashed crumbs of cinnamon swirl, licked them off his thumb, and leaned back enough to circumspectly see up the girl's skirt, all the while thinking over every word Roland had said.

"Nothing but green fabric visible that way," Roland said softly. "If you want to see her stuff, you have to get her alone, and rip the fabric off with your teeth." He grinned; his own teeth were filed. "She'd go for it bigtime, too."

"No doubt. It's the getting alone that's the hard part," Butterwick murmured.

"Is it?" The smile was coiled like a snake, now.

Butterwick could feel his cheeks flush. Roland was implying that he, Roland, got plenty—and Butterwick got none. And Roland's willie-wetting was not just off his sister. Only during occasional special acts of sex magick in Solstice Celebrations, when the planets were aligned just so, did the priestesses of the Temple sigh, and give it up to Butterwick. And in the atmosphere of ritual, it was all so . . . confining. At least at Butterwick's level of tantric initiation. Orgy magic was something only Roland and his sister and a few others were consecrated for.

Roland enjoyed humiliating him this way, rubbing Butterwick's nose in his sexual inferiority, and that was absolutely appropriate; it was right that Roland should humiliate him: that was one of the downsides of the Church of Eternal Satan (that slightly awkward name was to distinguish it from a rival and more powerful church—the "C of S": Church of Satan). The whole philosophy of diabolism revolved around self-assertion, self deification, and if you weren't more powerful than your peers, you weren't asserting your Self, then you weren't, in that degree, deified. "Dominance verifies accomplishment", in Roland's phrase. He didn't demand literal boot-licking; the acolytes would have rebelled. He kept it subtle.

It didn't matter; Butterwick would, he silently vowed, by hook or crook, find out what he needed to find out; would destroy those who stood in his way, who tried to trip up his climb to High Priesthood; would quit his dreary office job as a paralegal, become a dues-collecting High Priest who didn't have to work, like Roland. It was his duty, ultimately, to overthrow Roland. All the priests aspired to it. Roland, like all Satanists, relished competition, or claimed to.

And since Butterwick was discussing a coup, with Marchmain and Strensis, to push Roland out of power—or, failing that, to kill him, well ... it was a duty he had every intention of fulfilling. And he thought, ultimately, it would come to killing. Perhaps poisoning one of those bottles of expensive red wine Roland loved to drink. If he, Butterwick, had the will, the True Will, to go as far as killing—not some doomed-to-fail kill-from-afar ritual, but actual personal killing—then the others would see that he was the High Priest by a *fait accompli* of true Will.

And before he quit his paralegal job, he decided, he would come into the office and put a Spell of Submission on Sandy, the receptionist who literally wouldn't look at him. He would ...

Stop letting your mind wander, he told himself. Focus! It's all about focus, concentration on the object, doggedly following through. Make Roland talk.

"I notice," Butterwick said, "you use the qualifier 'generally'. You said, um, 'There are *generally* no guarantees. Not from here.' What do you mean, not from here. And this talk of being out of one's depth ..."

"Well. There are highly risky forms of ... commitment. Things I myself have not attempted. I suppose a very brave, very committed priest might ..." He shook his head. "No, that would be like randomly pouring chemicals together in an explosives lab."

"What sort of ... forms of commitment? We've already given over our false souls to the angel of Light, so that we can create Diabolic Bodies of Light; we've signed in blood; we've carried out rituals of commitment twice a year for—"

"Those are rituals of commitment. There is a kind of real commitment, realer than ritual alone. But it is something not even I am ready for—and if you repeat that to anyone ..." He turned to look directly at Butterwick, leaned over and whispered in his most reptilian voice, "If you repeat what I tell you, I will kill you. And all your machinations with that oaf Strensis will avail you not."

Butterwick went cold. How much did Roland know? Was he probing, guessing? Probably.

"There are no machinations. I am your priest—I am sworn to you and would not—"

"See that you don't." Roland waved a limp, dismissive hand, sublimely unconcerned. "So you want concrete results? Then go to this address . . ." Muscles bunched in the corners of his jaw, Roland scribbled on the back of his cafe receipt. "You'll see what appears to be a derelict building there . . . something you'd never go into, normally. But do it. Go in. Ask for Cinch."

"Cinch?"

"Yes. Tell him you want the *Book of Commitment*. In that place . . . if I were you, I'd take a gun."

"But who is Cinch? I know all the—"

"You don't know, as the man says, dick. Now trouble me no further." Roland stood, and walked across the room, gazing at the girl in the beret. He spoke to her softly, keeping his gaze fixed on her, and to Butterwick's amazement she left with Roland ten minutes later.

Butterwick walked through a pleasant urban garden, a place of brick edged planters and fountains that fed sculptured streams, and little Japanese bridges; a tableau set between two skyscrapers at this frontier between Downtown San Francisco and the Tenderloin.

Red-rimmed shadows slid across the faux-marble wall enclosing the garden, and he turned to see the sun setting; racing clouds throwing the shadows. A young couple with a baby stroller sat on a redwood bench looking at a fountain. The baby sat up to stare at the burbling waterfall and the couple made nonsense syllables at the little girl, and held hands and smiled at one another and suddenly Butterwick was very lonely. These people seemed so content, so in place here; and he was from a different world, where there was no contentment, only the hope of satiation.

He wondered, for a moment, if he had taken a wrong turn somewhere in life . . .

He shook the thought away, and continued into the walkway between the buildings, through a parking lot, past a closed deli, a closed boutique and, a block further, along a vacant lot to the corner Roland had told him about.

There was nothing here—except the foundations of a building that had been torn down, a wound, a socket in the jaw of the city, oozing mud and trash, edged with the crusts of old walls sprayed with palimpsests of graffiti. Some of the graffiti was remarkably artful; there was a lifesize spray painting of a Vaughan Bode girl, cartoonvoluptuous, rising up out a conflagration of layered street tags, her thought balloon reading: THAY TOLD ME THAY'D TAKE CARE OF ME BUT I'M SO LOST.

Butterwick walked around the corner where he could look into the foundations from another angle; there were raw concrete galleries; the containing wall under the lot-side of the sidewalk had been broken away, except for a ragged rim along the bottom, creating a dark gallery within, slathered with graffiti, its concrete floor lumpy with wet trash, homeless men wrapped in filthy blankets; to Butterwick's eye the trash and the homeless blending seamlessly. Failure of Will makes trash of men, he thought. *Ave Satanis.*

He found the way down through a bent lower corner of a hurricane fence, and crossed to the dim gallery, feeling in his coat for the snub nosed .38. He was not particularly afraid, here; he was a habitué of the dark side of the city, and most of the time the street element left you alone—if you looked like you were going to shoot them if they fucked with you. And of course you had to avoid certain gangster areas. But the .38 was a comfort.

He walked through the mud and grass—it seemed cleaner than the concrete—ignoring the muttering squatters. *Hey what you lookin to get. I can get it, yo, roundboy, hey, what up, you got a dollar . . .*

. . . Along the improvised portico, and heading for the hole in the wall at the corner: a peanutshell-shaped hole, busted-through by squatters with stolen tools.

He heard someone behind him laugh as he went through.

Inside, there was another narrow, trash choked hallway, and a stench as layered as the graffiti, and, in the shadows to the right: a hole in the floor. Wires ran across the floor and down into the hole, where the squatters ran stolen-current lines to underground warrens. He took a flashlight from his left-hand pocket, kept his grip firmly on the gun in his right, and approached the hole, his nose wrinkling at the deepening smell. How did they get farther down? But there: a crooked aluminum ladder, scavenged from some construction site, just high enough to lean against the inner rim of the hole. No one visible below.

To steady his nerves, he took a deep breath—and regretted it. The smell was worse than he'd thought. Feces, rotting garbage, urine, kerosene, body-stench.

He stuck the little flashlight between his teeth and descended the ladder. He looked down this lower hallway—and someone at the other end, lit by a portable, metal-caged light clipped to a rusty nail in the ceiling, turned to glare at him: A shapeless figure with long matted grey hair. Butterwick pointed the flashlight and the gun both, and the old man fled, down to the left.

What if Roland is playing a joke on me? Butterwick thought.

But he went down the hall, turned a corner, found himself in a room about fifty yards by thirty, some sort of furnace room once, a boiler remaining in one corner, the floor mostly hidden by yellowgrey layers of old newspapers, melded together by urine and time. The occasional headline underfoot: JFK SHOT . . . TET OFFENSIVE . . . There was only one of the caged lights, near the door; the farther half of the room was in shadow broken only by a blueness licking up from cans of Sterno, and a scrapwood fire in a trashcan; vapors rose to gaps in the ceiling.

Shapes in the corner he'd taken to be bundles of baglady junk . . . began to move. He saw that they were people, mostly, deeply swathed in grime-colored clothing; there were beards and matted hair; one of the bearded faces was surely a woman, because he could see her breasts all but bare where her buttonless plaid shirt hung open: some mad dyke taken refuge here; like the woman who'd shot Warhol, he supposed. Her beard was thin, like an ancient Chinaman's, but long and filthy.

She emerged from the shapes in the corner as if squeezed out from a valve of greasy rags; as if *expressed* toward him. She stopped five paces away. "Yewacop?"

"No. Passing through. Looking for Cinch. You know a Cinch?"

She stared at him and her mouth dropped open; her teeth surprisingly sound. "You're shittin."

"No."

"You go down there you probably use all your bullets in that little gun and still never come up, dumbshit."

The others laughed.

"I've got a lot of bullets. I'm not afraid of a lot of homeless, spineless parasites."

"Homeless? You think they all 'the homeless'? Man around here people wish they was just fuckin homeless. Homeless!" The others laughed at that, too. She was their spokes-model.

It had struck him that the specimens he could see here, huddled against the wall, were not just homeless people; even a Satanist knew the homeless to be mostly the unlucky, the disenfranchised, and the unmedicated insane; no, this was some other order of human desperation. Drug addicts and . . . something else.

"Where's Cinch?"

She tugged at her beard, pulled several times hard, making her lower jaw clack. "Just—down. Seven more down."

She pointed at the deepest shadow, in the corner opposite him. He was glad he'd worn boots as he crossed the floor. He stepped over something—someone—and followed his thin flashlight beam into the big crack in the wall.

Another blackened concrete hallway, in there, dust-caked pipes along the ceiling.

Butterwick heard a wordless voice quite clearly, inside him somewhere; it was a voice that had always been there; was there in everyone. He'd never heard it so clearly before.

It was telling him not to go on.

He went on. He always did.

On the third floor down, filthy men and women were fucking, in listless couples and stinking heaps, except for a white guy busily sucking a crack pipe; guy wore what looked like the remnants of a very expensive Armani suit; his limp grey dick was hanging out of his open fly and he was watching the others in their sluggish fucking; one man was fucking an unconscious boy in the ass. The scene made Butterwick's stomach try to crawl out his mouth.

He picked his way across people on the floor; through a litter of syringes.

If one of those needles goes through the sole of your boot, you get HIV, he thought. Fuck Roland, goddamn Roland.

But he went on.

The fourth floor down seemed to be a general latrine; he had to pick his way through piles of shit; over puddles of vomit and urine; and two stained, desiccated corpses. They were dead, weren't they? Or did he see them twitch?

The fifth floor down. Two clean, crop-haired women, one black and one white, neatly dressed in workshirts and white shorts, were sitting on a picnic blanket in the middle of a big empty room, in a single patch of light from a silver candelabrum set on the floor. There was a wicker picnic basket and there were china plates and there was a bottle of white wine chilling in a silver bucket and their silver clicked against the plates as they ate what looked like the private parts of a man, barbecued; it looked like that, but might not have been.

It was cold there, and their breaths steamed, and the platter steamed too. They didn't even look up, though he stood only fifty feet away.

Once he was certain he was not dreaming, Butterwick went on, down the next ladder.

The sixth floor down was black, there was no light here, and his flashlight only seemed to penetrate two feet in front of him. He heard a smacking, chewing sound, and a wet slapping sound, every so often a voice from television. That blond woman with the daytime talk show. "...Judy isn't sure why she feels she has to do these things and we have a psychiatrist today who..."

He hurried on...he thought the voice said, "Butterwick, when he..." as he passed through the hole in the wall, found the ladder down to...

*   *   *

... the seventh floor down was a forest of bodies, most of them dead, hanging from the ceiling by the neck, on runners, and they moved around and around on the runners like clothing in a dry cleaner's. Some were mummified, some were fresh, some not quite dead, but what bothered him most was that they all hung off center, as if the room was tilted somehow; they pointed at some other center of gravity. One man, hanging, twitching, was trying to fuck a body in front of him. "Butter . . ."

". . . wick."

The eighth floor down was well lit by fluorescent lights in the tiled ceiling; the room was clean as a whistle. Butterwick seemed to see men in spotless suits and uniforms standing at chromium tables, pointing at maps, talking of allocations, clicking at calculators, laptops, and using long jointed aluminum instruments he couldn't identify. But he couldn't be seeing these men; he couldn't have seen the women with the picnic blanket. There must be something in the mist, the oily vapor that hung in the air with a smell of burnt plastic; something that was making him see these anomalies, and he firmly looked away from the men, though he heard them start to move toward him; he heard the clicking of the instruments in their hands, cryptic metal instruments of some sort, and he ran to a gap in the wall shaped like a skewed triangle, ducked through—then stopped, and turned, and looked back. It was darkness back there, just darkness, and smoke.

He went down the hall and down the ladder—this one a rope ladder, made of old wire and clothing—and stepped off it onto the ninth floor down, and went down the hall and found a small room, just ten yards by seven, and in it saw . . .

A pile of ancient paper trash.

The room was a bit of a relief, and also a disappointment: there was nothing here—that he could see—to be afraid of. There was a light in the far corner, clipped to a pipe in the ceiling. There was a dented filebox, against the nearer wall to his right.

And in the farther corner, the heap of trash, about three feet high, sloping down to his feet with scatterings that papered the bottom of the floor. Just a pile of paper, most of it yellowed, rotting; on the pages were words, in dozens of languages and glyphs; there were hermetic symbols and mathematical figures and hieroglyphs and a great many words in Latin. He moved toward the higher end of the heap and called, "Cinch?"

No reply, except perhaps a rustling from under the paper. A nesting rat or a big termite feasting on the pulp, he thought.

He mulled over what he'd seen on the previous floor. This was a place of magick, indeed; if he hadn't been only hallucinating. "Cinch" could be here.

He took a step toward the heap of paper. "Cinch?"

"Quis turbat quietem ei qui quiescere nequit?" came a thin, old man's voice, whimsical and contemptuous.

The voice came from the heap of paper. He recognized some of the Latin but . . .

"I'm afraid," Butterwick said, "that, um, my Latin is rusty. Do you speak English?" He licked his lips; it was like dragging a dry washcloth over sunburnt skin. "I . . . Roland sent me . . . He said I could ask for the *Book of Commitment* . . ."

"Who will you give yourself to, tiny one?"

"To . . . Lucifer the Light; to He who is called by many names."

"No other names need be said, once here. You may call him Arthur or Chang or Beatrice if you like. Anything at all."

The paper began to flutter . . .

Butterwick stepped closer and saw that the heap was made up of every sort of paper; some of it looked like papyrus; some like parchment, scribbled on by goosequill; others were brushed in a delicate Oriental hand, lettered in Chinese; there were illustrations, pages ripped from antique illuminated manuscripts; there were modern pages. No two sequential pages lay together, each one was an orphan, lost from its parent book. And they moved, shuffled themselves, they seemed to be reordering within, faster and faster, rustling furiously, blurring, sorting a sheaf of papers, as if the pile of trash paper were printing, organizing, some portion of itself into . . .

A book lay at his feet. The book cover did not say *The Book of Commitment*; neither was its title in Latin or Greek or in some cypher, as was usual for grimoires.

The title, red on brown leather, in English, was:

YOUR SERVANTS IN HELL

This, he thought, bending, hands shaking to pick the book up, was real magick. Roland could not have arranged this. Anything was possible now.

He took the book, and stood, and saw a little man in a monk's robe, standing knee deep in the remaining heap of paper. On the front of his robe was an old, old brown stain which Butterwick knew, somehow, was blood. The man's face was thin; his nose long, chin slight, eyes . . .

There was nothing unusual about his face, his hands.

His eyes . . .

He was perfectly normal really.

His . . .

Butterwick turned and fled the room, reeled on a wire of definitionless panic. He went up the ladders and down hallways without looking at what was in the rooms; he looked only at what he had to step over, and he ran on, carrying the book and the flashlight and gun. And kept climbing, until he reached the open air.

But all day, and all that night, the air, wherever he went, smelled of sewage, no matter how he bathed and changed, and no one could smell it but him.

It was night time, in Butterwick's apartment, and he was making ready.

It was a simple failure of will, on Roland's part, Butterwick decided, as he cleaned off his desk in his studio apartment, closed the curtains, made ready to conjure from the book. Roland knew about Cinch, the place; he must have been there, must have tried to get the book at some point. And had lost heart. Some of those dark rooms beneath rooms, under that gallery of trash, had called for all Butterwick's courage. Roland had failed to give up every last ounce of nerve; had entirely lost his nerve. Perhaps on seeing the old man, an ordinary old man with an ordinary little smile and ordinary eyes, Roland had panicked and run, and Butterwick could understand that: for quite without reason the harmless, quiet old man, Cinch, was the most terrifying thing Butterwick had seen, under the city, nine levels down.

Still—strange that Roland had quailed. But there was a difference, perhaps: Roland had so much, already. He had control over others; had women and didn't have to work. He wasn't motivated enough. But Butterwick, on the other hand, had nothing to lose.

Nothing to lose . . .

He turned to the desk, switched on the desk lamp, and opened the book.

The desk lamp went out. Darkness spilled over the desk.

"Shit!" Shivering at the coincidence, he went and got another light bulb. Replaced the bulb, the lamp lit—and blew out.

He could hear his heart in his ears. "Magick obtains from True Will; which obtains from courage," he reminded himself, aloud.

He was out of light bulbs. He went to the mantle, found a black candle in a sconce, lit it, brought it over—and the book tolerated it. The flame fluttered, but remained lit.

The book is real! he told himself. Already: concrete results. Here is power!

He read the first page of the *Book of Commitment*:

YOU HAVE PASSED THROUGH NINE DARK PLACES TO FIND THIS LOGOS. YOU HAVE ACHIEVED WHAT YOU HAVE ACHIEVED. YOU ARE WITH US. WE ARE WITH YOU. WE ARE YOUR SERVANTS: IS THAT NOT THE PROMISE? IN OTHER TIMES THIS BOOK WAS WRITTEN ON SKIN, ON SCROLL, ONE PAGE AT A TIME IT WAS MADE. IT WAS FOUND, ONCE, BELOW EIGHT CAVES: A LATER TIME BELOW EIGHT GROTTOES. ARE WE NOT YOUR SERVANTS? HAVE YOU NOT ACHIEVED WHAT YOU HAVE ACHIEVED? SAY THESE NAMES: CYROS, ZAYROS, KALLOS, AND FEEL WITH ALL OF YOUR BEING THE DOMINATION YOU CHOOSE, WHILE SEEING THESE SIGNS: . . . FOR THIS IS THE SPELL OF DOMINATING WOMEN. IS THIS NOT YOUR FIRST DESIRE?

*   *   *

"Like it's readin' my mind," Butterwick muttered, with a chuckle. Then he thought: How does it know I'm male, wanting to dominate women? The book must be only for male initiates . . . He turned the page, many pages, reading ahead. Seeing THIS IS THE SPELL OF DOMINATING MEN IN WAR . . . THIS IS THE SPELL OF DOMINATING ALL PRIESTS WHO NOW SERVE ABOVE YOU . . . THIS IS THE SPELL OF DESTRUCTION . . . THIS IS THE SPELL OF SELF HEALING . . . THIS IS THE SPELL OF LIVING FOREVER . . . THIS IS THE SPELL OF TRANSFIGURATION . . .

Butterwick went back a few pages—had he seen rightly? The spell of living forever? And again it was just a few words, and a visualizing, some symbols to make clear in the mind. Usually, for any conjuration, one had to work oneself up into a fit of concentration, picking the astrologically useful days, consecrating everything precisely, using exactly the right sort of wood in the wand, the right incense burning on the right sort of altar turned just the right direction. But this magicking seemed an impossible simplicity. And if this sort of thing really worked, why had he never seen it before?

But then the real thing would have to be rare . . .

Well, naturally he'd perform the spell of living forever first . . .

But, coincidentally or not, at that moment he read a line in the book he hadn't noticed before:

WORKINGS MUST BE PERFORMED IN ORDER: THIS IS YOUR ASCENDANCY. NO WORKING MAY BE OVERLOOKED. EACH IN SEQUENCE . . . Well then. He must go back to the beginning—and magick his way up through the workings, in order, one by one. Starting with his unbridled lust—Praise Satan!— for Sandy Oswald.

Butterwick stared down at Sandy in amazement, as her head bobbed over his crotch. His pleasure itself seemed amazed, so that she had to work with surprising energy to maintain his firmness. The Working had shaken him. He'd assumed that the first run-through would be just that, and he'd have to take the book with him to work, use it in the storeroom near her, or follow her home and perform the rite on the roof of her building or . . .

But half an hour after he'd spoken the words, and was busy copying the spell into his journal (what if the book were somehow destroyed?), there came a knock at the door.

Amazement upon amazement: She'd been there, standing in his doorway, and she'd begun undressing the instant she'd come in, with the air of a woman preparing for the gynecologist. Now, her golden brown hair whisked her bare shoulders with the motion of her head; her firm, upturned breasts bounced; breasts pleasantly mottled with freckles. She wasn't particularly good at giving head. He jammed himself into her cruelly, seeking deeper sensation, and she didn't object, made scarcely a sound. She hadn't spoken since coming in except to say, "Fuck me. Fuck me, please." Said with no real passion, but with something like urgency.

He pushed aside the amazement and the residue of fear at the unnaturalness of it all, and focused on sensation, on having her, and the excitement mounted in him, and he soon gave up a sparse, discouraged spurt.

She shivered, and fell unconscious at his feet.

"Sandy?" Butterwick knelt, and lifted her head. She was breathing. Just unconscious. When she woke, would the spell be broken? Would she scream for the police?

He left her on the braided rug and went to pour himself a glass of wine; to sit on the couch and think. He looked at the girl lying on her side, snoring softly, knees drawn up; he looked at the book; he looked at the girl; he looked at the book . . .

He heard, almost, that wordless voice again, and pushed it back down, inside himself.

He drank off the wine, poured two more glasses, drank them off too. Then he knelt beside her, and toyed with her body. Excitement came to him again—but he wanted her responsive.

He went back to the book and, with a mounting fever of desire, read once more the Names of Power:

CRYOS, KARNOS, SUMBOS—

Wait.

This was the first page, wasn't it? But those weren't the Sacred Names he'd read before.

He went to his journal, where he'd written the spell down.

CYROS, ZAROS, KALLOS. Different.

He went back to the book. Was he on the right page? He was. He must have written it down wrongly. But his memory, too, seemed wrong.

No matter. The wine, the late hour. Rely on the book.

YOU HAVE PASSED THROUGH NINE DARK PLACES TO FIND THIS LOGOS. YOU HAVE ACHIEVED WHAT YOU HAVE ACHIEVED. YOU ARE WITH US. WE ARE WITH YOU. WE WERE YOUR SERVANTS: IS THAT NOT THE PREMISE?

—and farther down—

...ARE WE YOUR SERVANTS? HAVE YOU ACHIEVED ANYTHING? SAY THESE NAMES, CRYOS, KARNOS, SUMBOS...

No. Most of that was different—wasn't it?

He brought his journal over close beside the book. In the journal it read WE ARE YOUR SERVANTS. IS THAT NOT THE PROMISE?

In the book it read WE WERE YOUR SERVANTS. IS THAT NOT THE PREMISE...

Were? Premise?

How could it ever have said were? Surely he would have noticed that—because it made no sense. Unless it referred to some ancient, Atlantean time; some previous incarnation any great magician might be expected to have. That must be it.

He looked again at the text in the book's first page.

YOU HAVE BEEN PASSED FROM HAND TO HAND THROUGH NINE DARK PLACES TO FIND THIS LOGOS. YOU HAVE BEEN ACCUSED. YOU ARE WITH US. WE ARE WITH YOU. WE WEREN'T YOUR SERVANTS: IS THAT NOT THE PROLOGUE? IN OTHER TIMES THIS BOOK WAS WRITTEN ON SKIN...

Oh no. It had changed again—hadn't it?

It must have. It's tone had been almost obsequious, the first time; he

had noticed it. Now it was almost dismissive. Yet, here yet were the
magickal words, so it said, for dominating any woman. For having her.

It must be a test of his Will, he supposed. And more testimony of
the magickal nature of this grimoire.

He spoke the words now written on the book before him; he visualized; he concentrated . . .

There was a knock on the door.

He looked at Sandy; then at the door; then at the book; then back
at the door. Another knock. Harder.

"Who, um, who is it?"

No answer. Another woman perhaps. Perhaps the bitch from the
cafe he'd desired. And why not? Eagerly he crossed to the door and
unlocked it and—three men shoved inward.

They were pale men, even though one of them was a black man.
They wore mostly rags; he recognized one of them as the white man
who'd been sucking on the crack pipe, in the filthy, ragged suit under
the city. They pushed past him, slamming the door behind them. All
three with matted hair; with a great stink and hot, inhabited eyes. Two
white men and one black, kneeling beside Sandy, gripping her. They
spoke nothing except aggrieved-sounding nonsense syllables. "Mngh!
Zzz-eb-bububuh . . ." Whining.

He backed to his desk, opened the drawer, pulled out his gun, said
hoarsely, hands shaking: "Get away from her. She's mine. I'll shoot."

"Mngh . . . puh-oofffff . . ." They were raping her still-unconscious
body. Putting their filth-crusted members into her mouth, her anus,
her vagina, turning her like a blow-up sex toy to get the angle, none
of the three bothering to take off their pants. Opened flies. Stench. Soft
gruntings. Heavy-lidded, febrile eyes. Ignoring him.

He raised the gun—then thought: Somehow, if the girl doesn't re-
cover, if they go mad when I begin to fire and they kill her, I can be
blamed. The police would be called, they'd be here quickly, and shooting one of these creatures—and he knew them to be creatures—or
even two of them would probably not stop the third from getting to
him . . .

He lowered the gun, hyperventilating. He drank off the last of his
wine, sank into the couch, watched them. His gorge rising.

They were once men; they were now demonic: that was clear. They were possessed, and beyond possessed. Evidently the second working had turned the girl over to them. A sort of sacrifice. But why?

"I know what it is," he said aloud, with sudden inspiration. "I'm a fool." Of course! He was supposed to do the spells in non-repeating sequence! He could only do the first one again when he'd done all the others—and anyway, once he'd achieved the power of the Over Magus, the True Will, through the workings in the book, he'd not need the spells of domination. To desire a woman, at that level, was to have her.

The men were still grinding almost soundlessly, tirelessly at the girl, murky pumping shapes in the dim room. Their reek choked the air. He lit two sticks of incense, and turned his desk so it was between him and them, and he could face them while doing his working. Keep an eye on them without having to look at them; he couldn't bear to look at them directly. He had seen Sandy's face in that glance; unconscious and yet feeling—and he had, all in a flash, seen her as she must have been as a little girl. Someone's daughter. And he was amazed at his own depth of feeling: more than he could bear. With long practice, with polished skill, he withdrew from caring.

He must focus on asserting real command over the night's Magick. He felt that his next effort would banish these three even as it destroyed Roland...

Oh yes, Roland must die, and right away. It was obvious what Roland had been up to—but it would backfire on him...

Excitedly he turned to the next working. THIS IS THE SPELL OF DOMINATING MEN IN WAR. It read:

THIS CONJURATION READ ALOUD TIMES THRICE. THREE TIMES READ IT, AND THE THIRD TIME ITS BUSINESS IS DONE.

I ADJURE AND COMMAND ALL SERVANTS IN HELL IN THE NAME OF HE WHO POSSESSES THEM [here visualize the symbols scribed in the margin] AND COMMAND IN THE NAMES MERRINUS, ERIN, JAYARR DOBBSUS WHO IS THE HARVESTER OF EYES, ZELOS CORINMECH—NOW STRIKE DOWN MY ENEMY, HE WHOSE NAME I NOW UTTER— WHOSE VISAGE I VISION—

Here Butterwick visualized Roland and spoke his name.

—AND WITH THE SUBMISSIVE OBEDIENCE OF MY SER-
VANTS IN HELL, WITH THEIR CLAWS AND LASHING
TAILS I SMITE HIM—WITH THEIR FIRES AND FURIES—
AND WITH A VAST SUFFERING I SMITE HIM AND I COM-
MAND HIM TO COME BEFORE ME AND TO BE DESTROYED
AS ORDAINED—THIS I REPEAT, TWICE MORE.

Butterwick saw that the three men, if that's what they were, had
ceased their brutalities, had left Sandy, barely alive, to bleed quietly into
his rug, as they knelt facing him, arms dangling, their heads jerking
with his words; they seemed caught up in silent agony, as if the words
were a lash, as if the imprecations hit them too; or perhaps it was silent
laughter.

Butterwick began the second repetition, reading from the book:

I ADJURE AND CORRUPT ALL SERVANTS IN HELL IN
THE NAME OF HE WHO POSSESSES THEM . . . AND
DAMNED IN THE NAMES MERRACK, ERUS, STANGIVANN
WHO IS THE SCISSORER OF TONGUES, ZELOUS CORMAC—

Butterwick's voice trembled, almost failed here. Corrupt? Merrack?
The words and names were changing and he was compelled to read
them anyway; he dared not cease halfway.

NOW STRIKE DOWN MY INANITY, HE WHOSE NAME IS
AN UDDER, WHOSE VISAGE I PISS ON—

(Udder? Piss on?)

Butterwick tried to visualize Roland but found himself staring at his
own image—a photo of himself on the wall in his acolyte's robes, from
his first initiation, as he read on, impossibly the same page he'd read
moments before:

—AND WITH THE SUBJECTIVE OBEDIENCE OF NO SER-
VANTS IN HELL, WITH THEIR CLAWS AND LASHING
TAILS I SMITE—WITH THEIR FIRES AND PUERILITIES—
AND WITH A VAST SUFFERING I SMITE HIM AND I COM-
MAND HIM TO COME BEFORE ME AND TO BE DESTROYED
AS ALWAYS IN VAIN—

There was a knock on the door.

The black man with the gray face got up, and crossed to the door and opened it—and Roland strode in, smiling.

He looked at the three men, and the woman, and laughed, and closed the door behind him. The lost black man backed away from him and rejoined the others.

Roland drew his gun, a .45 automatic, and calmly checked the load. "Yes, it appears to be loaded," Roland murmured.

Butterwick visualized Roland turning it on himself; committing suicide.

Roland switched on an overhead light, and pointed the gun at Butterwick. "I heard you summoning me. I've come. But I know about that book. If need be, I'll kill you, then I'll give the gun to one of these braindead vermin—it's not my gun of course—and they'll play with it till the police come, and they'll take the blame . . . You really shouldn't have plotted with those two fools . . ."

Furiously, Butterwick began the working the third time.

I ADJOURN TO YOUR SERVICE IN HELL IN THE NAME OF HE WHO . . .

Butterwick stared at the book. The text had changed again.

IN THE NAMES MERRILYN, ANNIE, ZELDA—

"Terrifying names, Butterwick," Roland sniggered.

Butterwick had stopped reading aloud. But his eyes took the rest of it in as his stomach lurched with each syllable.

. . . AND WITH THE SUBMISSIVE OBEDIENCE OF THE LOWLIEST OF SERVANTS I BEGIN MY SERVICE IN HELL— THAT SERVICE, WITH DROOPING LIPS, WITH BONELESS SHAKING HANDS, WITH SPINELESS QUIVERINGS, TO WHICH I HAVE RUSHED HEADLONG MY WHOLE STUPID, EMPTY, COARSE, SELFISH LIFE—THAT SERVICE IN HELL WHICH COMMANDS ME TO DESTROY MYSELF ETER- NALLY AS ORDAINED, THIS I REPEAT FOREVER, LIKE THE SORDID, MINDLESS, GIBBERING SLAVE I HAVE BECOME IN THE DEIFICATION OF MY PERSONAL GOD, THAT VANITY THAT IN DESIRING EVERYTHING ERADICATES ALL AU- THENTIC POSSIBILITY. I AM A DOG CHASING HIS OWN

TAIL AND CHEWING IT OFF AND THEN CHEWING AWAY
HIS OWN HINDQUARTERS, I AM—

Sandy screamed. Roland looked at her—and Butterwick looked at
her and saw something that disoriented him to his roots: he saw four
men now tearing at Sandy, ripping away strips of her—killing her,
most definitely killing her—with hands and teeth, like a pack of feral
dogs worrying her flesh apart, the four men thrashing in a spreading
stain—

And one of them was himself.

A doppleganger, he thought. A mocking demonic reproduction of
himself.

Roland too was staring at the four men—and not without real loath-
ing, real repugnance. Roland stuck his .45 in his waist band. "I don't
think it'll be necessary to shoot you after all, Butterwick . . ." He muttered, grimacing.

Butterwick, the real Butterwick, turned and grabbed at the drawer
in which he kept his gun. He would kill Roland, kill the three men,
kill the doppelganger, put Sandy out of her misery, run for a border,
any border—

The drawer wouldn't open. No, his fingers couldn't find the handle.
No, no, that wasn't it (Sandy made a bubbling sound and thrashed with
a kind of finality), he was touching the handle but it was too slippery
or . . . No. He couldn't feel the handle. He realized, then, that he could
no longer see his hands on the drawer handle.

He couldn't touch the metal, the wood. He looked down at himself—he wasn't there. No feet. He raised his hands—and couldn't see
them. Couldn't feel himself physically. He was . . . just a viewpoint. Sep-
arated from his body.

Physically . . . Physically, he was across the room. His body kneeling
by the girl.

Across the room, rending Sandy. Distantly, very distantly, he could
feel her flesh wet under his body's hands.

"Roland—Roland!" Butterwick called. Not quite hearing his own
voice.

Roland shook his head—but not in response to Butterwick. Roland couldn't hear him. "God you're a loathsome bugger, revealed this way, Butterwick."

Sandy died. The four men lost interest, when she became completely lifeless. They got slowly to their feet, and stood a moment, as if waiting for a command.

Butterwick saw another Sandy, standing by the bay windows overlooking the street—a transparent Sandy; mostly just her head, and a sketchy suggestion of body. Her spirit. She seemed so much more substantial than he was. She was looking toward his viewpoint; seemed to sense him there. "I'm glad it's over," she said. "For me, it's over. It's funny the things that mattered, before. Like pinwheels. Everything was pinwheels. Now they've stopped turning. I can forgive you, Butterwick. But I don't think that will help you."

Then the light shifted, and she was gone; there was only her torn and flayed remains on the floor.

The Butterwick who stood beside her body looked toward the door; and so did the other three, like a pack of trained dogs hearing their master's call. They walked to the door, and out the door.

Abruptly, Butterwick was in the hall. He was floating down the hall to the stairs, and down the stairs, following the four men whose hands dripped red on the carpet. Butterwick's ambulatory body and the three intruders . . . Mr Fuller, the owner, would shout at him for that dripping, surely . . .

Turn back. Don't go with them.

He tried to hold back—but continued to float after them; a viewpoint, a watching: a step, just a step, behind the Butterwick body, as it followed the other three down the stairs. He followed his body to the street, and down the street, and another street, and another, trying to leave, to turn back, never able to stop, drawn on an unbreakable tether, as he always would be.

Down through the hurricane fence, across the vacant lot, into the gap in the wall, down the stinking hallway. He could feel nothing—but he could smell everything.

He followed his body down through the hole in the floor.

*   *   *

Roland watched them go out the door. He closed it behind them. Wondered if there was anything here to connect him to the girl. He was wearing gloves, so, no prints. He started for the door. Then he stopped, and turned, and looked at the book. He shrugged, and crossed the room. The book now lay closed, though he hadn't seen Butterwick close it. It's title read:

YOUR SERVANTS IN HELL

He opened it.

YOU HAVE PASSED THROUGH NINE DARK PLACES TO FIND THIS LOGOS. YOU HAVE ACHIEVED WHAT YOU HAVE ACHIEVED.

He chuckled. He knew how it worked. The oaf Butterwick was not the first one he had fed to Cinch.

He closed the book—and saw the inevitable new title.

YOUR SERVICE IN HELL

Roland smiled. He really should get out of here. But he couldn't resist one look inside—opened it to a random page, near the end. Read a passage. Paled.

Roland closed the book, quickly. And before the cover had quite clapped shut, its pages began to tremble, to shuffle like a deck of cards in the hands of a spastic, and exploded up into the air, a flurry of paper making him backpedal. The disintegrated book, the cloud of pages, swirled through the air in spirals to the disused fireplace; went up the flue, and was gone.

And Roland went out, laughing nervously. Thinking about what he'd read in the book, moments before. The more powerful demons loved to frighten magicians. It was just demonic banter, nothing to worry about. Nothing real.

But he would never quite forget what he'd read there...

YOU WHO ARE FAR TOO CLEVER TO TAKE PART IN THIS BOOK; TO READ ITS NAMES ALOUD; TO CROSS THE BARRIER INTO REAL COMMITMENT TO HE WHO POSSESSES THE SERVANTS OF HELL: YOU.

YOU, ROLAND. WE'RE WAITING FOR YOUR SERVICE IN HELL.

YOU PLAY IT TOO SAFE TO SUBMIT TO US. BUT IT

MAKES NO DIFFERENCE AT ALL. YOU CAN'T LIVE FOR-
EVER.

YOU HAVE TO DIE SOME TIME, YOU DUMB SON OF A
BITCH.

Whisperers

Can an angel be desperate? Nothing else could explain his choice of interlocutor. What a poor confidant of divinity I make! I did not even make a "doctor" of divinity; I left the university two years short of a doctorate. I might vaingloriously style myself a lay theologian— but a lay theologian of no great gifts. A haphazard scholar merely. Of course, on that day, in 1953, when I met the angel, I was on my way to see the Bishop of L——————— in Lower Saxony, in the northwest of Germany, and that was surely some of it...

The train to Oldenburg swayed and rattled through a dull winter afternoon, stopping only once, since morning, in dour little Wildeshausen, the diesel train's course paralleling the Hunte River, swollen now with the first easing of the ice. I had a window seat; to my right the river; beyond it, sodden fields, the stubs of dormant crops browned and beaten by repeated hailstorms, piercing winds, fits of snow, until one couldn't be sure turnips were not wheat, grape vines were not string beans. The closer we got to Oldenburg, the more industry began to assert itself, factories like castles designed by dullards—they did nothing to alleviate the sternness of the landscape, but seemed its culmination. And the sky had the semblance of an aluminum lid, clamping all beneath it.

The chilly second-class car contained myself, and four other passengers. There was an old woman to my left, a young couple, silently holding hands, and a man of about my own age, all swaying in counterpoint to the swaying of the coach, each gazing at some inward stream of associations. Four people in the same car but each in their own world. Certainly no one took undue notice of me: a graying middle aged man in a threadbare suit; a scholar on a stipend. A man who would not be met at the other end of the train trip; who arrived at train stations and ship's docks expecting no one to be there waiting for him. Whose only friends were books, the occasional opera seat, and schnapps.

It was the sort of day, and the sort of company, that gave every little distraction the glamour of novelty: an old fashioned horse drawn wagon, carrying hay to cattle, in an era of trucks; the welcome thought that soon the afternoon tea cart would clatter down the hall, bringing us dry little cakes and weak tea; the man who'd come in without my noticing him, seated across from me.

When I think back now to record his clothing, I find myself at a loss. It seems to me he wore a three piece suit; perhaps there was a yellow woolen scarf, loose about his neck; but I can just as easily remember him wearing a gray, coarse robe; and then again he seemed to be wearing a silver breastplate and a great coat of golden fur, and fur covered boots, like a sort of Viking. But that cannot be—who dresses with such Teutonic excess, now? And which garment was he in fact wearing?

I remember his face, clearly enough—the oddly long chin, almost like something elongated by some expressionist painter; his gray eyes, slanted down at corners, the color of the sea at dawn; his hair . . .

But he had no hair, did he? Was he not bald, his head magnificently round and sun-blushed?

Yes. Yet I also remember his long, shiny, wavy black hair, almost like a woman's.

He looked at me; that gray, oceanic gaze dismayed me. When had he come in? The car was heated, but the hallways were drafty, and rackety with the sound of the train; if the door had opened I'd have heard it, and felt the metal-cold draft. On so monotonous a journey every face would have looked toward the door when it opened. I'd certainly have noticed.

Embarrassed by his steady gaze, I besought my satchel, and drew out my notes for the Bishop. The good Bishop was a minor expert on the Bogomilian heresies, and the controversy over the alleged connection between the Cathars and the Templars. He was an apologist for medieval persecutors of heretics, but he was a genial man, and I looked forward to clarification on a Jesuit's thinking on Courtly Love—this, I reflected, I would have to come at indirectly; seduce him into exposing his opinion, as it were, since the subject of erotic sublimation in Christian mysticism was but dimly regarded . . .

"They were all fools, those visionaries of Courtly Love," said the man with the gray eyes. The syllables of his voice . . . At the time I knew there was something odd about them, but could not identify it. Now, I recall a quality of what I can only call "unbeginning" and "unending" about the sound of the words—prosaic as they were, in many respects. The literal content was rarely impressive. But each syllable seemed to start out from some great distance, as if it had been first spoken on the far side of the universe, and it only came to me at the end of some great journey. Then too, the end of each syllable seemed to fade off again, to taper infinitely without quite tapering off. Yet there was no difficulty in hearing him: the words were not blurred or "lost in the distance". The voice itself was soft, but quite masculine.

I responded with a vague, "I beg your pardon?"

"You were reading about the concept of Courtly Love, I believe. This idea of communing through sublimation is all backwards, *Dolce Stil Novo* regardless. But it is, of course, a matter of no significance; the history of the human race in itself, in particular or via macroscopia . . ." He made a gesture that I took for a kind of shrug. It was a hand motion that was also the tracing of an unknown shape on the air. An exquisite dismissal.

"I see," I muttered, not seeing at all. Thinking what sharp eyes he had, to see what I was reading across the car, and to read it upside-down at such a distance.

"I wonder if you could help me . . ." he began.

I glanced at the other people in the car; they seemed indifferent to the man, and to my conversation; no one seemed to be eavesdropping, which was strange in itself.

"You are, I believe," he went on, "on your way to see a bishop."

I must have looked startled.

He smiled (it was all existing smiles, and none of them), and inclined his head; made another hand gesture which might have had something to do with "a dismissal of anxiety"—yet it was a gesture alien to my experience; like deaf signing, but in a vocabulary no deaf person would recognize, though any human might inexplicably understand.

"I am unable to leave the one you see here, to my left, and the ones you do not see, who are also attached to that gentleman, or I would speak to some mortal spiritual authority myself. I had an opportunity to speak to a Lama on a dock in South East Asia, when this gentleman traveled there, but the Lama refused to converse. He took me for something diabolic. Perhaps because of the peculiar work I have been assigned, I am beginning to resemble something diabolic; or perhaps he was too superstitious."

(These are, are they not, the words he spoke? I'm usually quite good at remembering details of appearance, of colloquy, having nearly a photographic memory. But I seem to be making marginal approximations of his words. It is distressing.)

"I am not sure I understand," I said. "But—how is it that you know my precise destination? I have not spoken of it aloud since early yesterday."

I was becoming distinctly afraid; I began to suspect he was a madman who'd followed me here; who'd broken into my mailbox, perhaps, and read my correspondence. How long had he been spying on me?

I shivered, thinking: months? Years?

"I have a need," he said, "to communicate with my superiors—my absolute superiors, not my immediate superiors. I wish to 'go over the heads' of my immediate superiors. But I should first explain: I am what you would call an 'angel'. A 'supernatural' being. Nothing could be more natural, than being what I am, but that is all aside, I must try to use your terminology. Sub-eternal linguistics is, after all, a specialty of mine: one reason I was chosen for this job . . ."

I eyed the door, thinking to rush past him and howl for the conductor. But then I thought: What if he is not a madman—but, instead, a madman's hallucination?

I had been having many restless nights, lately, and the days seemed empty. The days seemed like pearls that had been broken from their string, and lost their lustre, gone colorless; each disconnected from any larger design; each with a shadow within, its own core of grit. I had begun to read Sartre's *Nausea* repeatedly, and with too much sympathy.

Perhaps the stranger read my expression. "No, you are neither mad nor beset by the mad. I apologize: I should have extended some knowledge."

He made another slight, arcane gesture—not a magical "pass", but, instead, a mode of expression—and suddenly I knew that he was what he said he was.

How I knew truly cannot be expressed. I had heard it averred that there are forms of knowing, of unmitigated certainty, which are non-rational but also non-pathological. I had always assumed that they were a product of some primeval faculty of the mind that nature found it useful to encourage in humanity: a capacity for experiencing the imagination as real, so as to make the creation of religion possible, religion having a sociobiological function as being one of the great stabilizers of society. That is, religion as a useful fantasy. My own interest in it was that of an antiquarian, a collector of the more exotic by-products of human folly. I saw religion as an anthropological study, as a wonderful curiosity; a construct like architecture, but less real.

But now I knew that he was an angel as certainly as I knew I was in a train, that it was winter, that my name was Johannes, that I was born in Switzerland and moved to Cologne when I was seven. I knew I had gone to grammar school in Cologne, and I knew that this man was an angel.

He emanated no special air of benevolence, or holiness; he was, in his appearance, of uncertain definition. But there was a sense of "connectedness to the infinite" about him. He was quite definitely an angel.

I made a small sound in my throat, and the old woman beside me glanced at me then looked quickly away.

"That noise you made, which comes from some other center in you than the one I have been in conversation with," the angel said, "is the only sound they have heard from us, this while. The others in the car are unaware of me; they cannot hear our discussion. Now, if I may continue—I need to speak to the superior of my superiors. It is quite mistaken to suppose an angel in constant communication with the Absolute, at least when we are 'here'. In this 'here' we are projected into time; if we were not, we could not empathize with human affairs at all. The root of my being remains eternal; but my consciousness is trapped in the temporal, at least to the extent that I cannot know God's will as directly as I might outside of Time. So you see, this projection from the eternal into the subjective flow of time lawfully prevents direct communication with the Absolute. However some mortals—perhaps because all mortal destinies are intertwined with Death—are able to pray directly into eternity. Small children do it best; then certain people who open certain parts of themselves to the eternal; the occasional persevering cleric can do it. But I cannot do it. This will seem a paradox but you may consider that paradox makes the universe go 'round. So you see: I wish to transmit my petition through someone who can pray into eternity, and thence to the 'ear' of the Absolute."

I found my voice, though it came with difficulty. "Why . . . why not . . . simply take yourself to a church . . ."

"Because the man I am assigned to will not go to a church. Nor to a cleric. It would be the last place he would go."

"The man you're are assigned to . . . Oh I see . . ."

It had been some years since I'd read Mr Clive Staples Lewis' amusing, psychologically penetrating volume, *The Screwtape Letters*. A demon's letters to an apprentice demon, advising as to what to whisper to humanity, how to destroy his charges. The book asserted that for every demon whisperer there was also an angel. An idea so familiar it appeared in comedic cinema and animated cartoons. It was too simple, too folkloric, to be literally true, wasn't it?

"Are there then angels whispering to all men and women? Angels and demons?"

I thought his eyes flicked to the empty place on the seat between myself and the old woman; or perhaps the recollection, now, is but wishful thinking. "Not to all men and women. Only to those with souls."

A disquieting concept. "Not everyone has a soul?"

"Everyone has within them some expression of *spirit*—as a wave expresses sea before sinking back into it, obliterated; not everyone has something more permanently defined. Not everyone has *soul*, though anyone might develop one. But I cannot discuss this with you; I cannot give out such gifts, nor such miseries. I can also promise you no benefit for carrying a message for me. I only ask that you do it; it is entirely up to you. You will not be punished if you choose not to cooperate."

"What exactly is the content of this message?"

"I wish you to say . . . Wait. Wait a moment."

He had broken off to turn to the man next to him—I had thought he was going to whisper to that man. But that's when the room telescoped . . .

I don't know how else to describe it. Unless—

That morning, when I'd first entered the train, it was still dark outside. At times, the interior of the car was reflected on the window, against a backdrop of the dimness of nascent morning. I often stared in fascination at such reflections—they were something like photo negatives, but without the reversal of a negative. The image that morning had showed the travelers—three at the time—reflected in all their solid banality, and then telescoped out, a fainter reflection beyond the one in the foreground, the three travelers reflected again, a kind of lost hall-of-mirrors effect, beyond, so that three became six. The extra three seemed like mockeries of the sad, unfinished souls of the reflectors.

Now, the train car around me—not in reflection, but the car itself—seemed to stretch out, to telescope, repeating itself, so that I saw attenuated echoes of the people in the car—visual echoes, sitting beside them. To either side of the stout, bearded, bowlerhatted man across and to my left, sat two alternates of the same fellow: to his left was a hollow-eyed, sullen, demonic version; to his right was a bright eyed, cherubic, slightly amused variant. The latter his angel; the former presumably his devil. Both were whispering, in turn, one in each ear. They seemed to take turns, neither speaking more than a statement or two. The

man's face showed me expressions that I'd been unable to discern before—these expressions passed, normally, too subtly and too quickly:
his reactions to the whisperers. There were other, equally caricaturish
whisperers beside the old woman and the young couple and the bowler-
hatted man. They did not whisper incessantly; they sometimes sat gazing thoughtfully into space, swaying with the train—transparent figures
though they were—not quite in sync with the swaying of their pri-
maries.

But the angel who'd addressed me did not resemble the bowler-
hatted man, nor anyone else in the car; nor did he whisper to the
mortals in the car.

He was whispering to the demon. The stout man's demon.

What would an angel whisper to a demon? If only I could overhear!
I thought to make out some of it—but it was not in any language I
recognized.

I shrank in on myself, hugged into my corner, as if to squirm away
from the mercurial faces beside the mortal ones; I glanced at them, and
looked away, glanced and looked away. I was afraid of the hollow-eyed
ones. I was afraid my regard would call theirs to me.

Then the angel turned back to me, and the telescope shut itself, as
if tied to the motion of his head. We were once more but six in the
room, counting the angel.

"There, that's done, I've planted a doubt," he said.

"I don't . . . I thought that . . ." I couldn't quite articulate it. And my
mouth was so dry.

"No, you see—I am . . . specialized. Most people have but two whisperers—only a few have three. And the third does not whisper to them!
I am not an expression of the higher and lower selves of these others;
I am sent on a particular mission. And not my first. This is the terrible
thing: I am an angel who must, at times, speak evil. I am not 'good'
or 'evil' as you understand these things, but neither does carnality taste
sweet in my mouth. You look confused; some examples perhaps. Some
centuries past, a certain potentate in North Africa discovered a weapon
somewhat in advance of the rest of the world; this weapon of destruction he would have used to conquer Europe. We were working on
encouraging the Renaissance, and sewing the seeds of the rights of Man,

at that time; this potentate despised European and Arabic civilization—
he was a barbarian, a sort of nihilist, and would have destroyed both
Moorish and Christian cultures, and set back the timetable by centuries.
He was naturally encouraged in this course by his dark whisperer; his
whisperer of the light was unable to dissuade him. So it was necessary
to allow him to play out his fantasies—to seem to encourage him, but
in a way that would at the same time diminish him. I whispered to his
demon that the potentate need not reserve his destruction for the Eur-
opeans—why not foment slaughter close at hand, so best to perfect the
weapon and destroy those who would undercut his throne in his absence? So he used this weapon—a cannonshell filled with noxious gases
designed to paralyze the nervous system—on thousands of his own
countrymen. This, as we had foreseen, turned his own soldiers against
him, and so he was assassinated. He himself was the inventor of the
weapon, and the secret was lost with him. More recently, I have twice
used the same sort of whisper to deter tyranny—and Hell's Dullards
have not caught on yet. I may use it a third time on the Chinese . . .
The scenrio I'm referring to is the judicious use of Russian winters.
Napoleon had gone mad; his civilizing impulses were sublimated to his
venality, and we foresaw a holocaust if he was not stopped; I whispered
to the demon who whispers to Napoleon. 'Why stop with Western
Europe . . . Why not Russia?' I made the same suggestion to Hitler's
demon. A very suggestible fellow he was, too, reflecting Hitler's own
tendencies. And off Hitler went, like Napoleon, spending his energy,
spilling his seed, on the frozen steppes of Russia. And now? This oafish-
seeming fellow in the bowler hat you see before you is a Soviet scientist
who has discovered something he was supposed to have given to the
Kremlin. But he made contact with British intelligence, and defected;
and he plans to sell it to the highest bidder. His weapon is a nuclear
device that can be carried in a soup can and made from ordinary silver,
with minimal effort. I will whisper to this scientist's demon—who cannot hear me now, of course—that first the weapon should be demonstrated in the laboratory. The laboratory in question has made
insufficient safety considerations . . . All will die, including our scientist,
and his secret will fall through the cracks. Perhaps. Or I will fail: I
will fail to persuade the demon to persuade the scientist, and the

weapon will go into sporadic development until the year 2006, by your reckoning, at which time it will be stolen and used to destroy large parts of the Eastern United States, with radioactive consequences that will make North America a wasteland for centuries to come, and shifting the balance of power to those who listen to the wrong whisperers ...I am not sure I will succeed, and feel more and more unsure of that success each day..."

"I see—and you wish to inform the...the Absolute as you call it ...that you don't anticipate success and that the consequences would be dire for—?"

"No, no not all! My superiors are aware of my misgivings in that regard. They are only mildly concerned—the United States is regarded as an experiment that went wrong, after all. No, the message I would have you take to the bishop for me is a request for a transfer. It's something I cannot offer up through the usual channels; it must go straight to the top."

"What?"

"A transfer to another specialty. Anything else so long as it is away from humanity. One gets used to the smell, psychic and otherwise—but it is so cold in the shadows they cast...So cold in the shadow of their demons. And I must spend my life in that shadow, in that chill. Remember that my work requires me to be 'in Time'. So, though I am not mortal, I am subject to other effects of Time: tedium! Ennui! Worse—I am slowly sickening, within myself, with this task of whispering evil to evil. To do it, one must contemplate evil—one must spend one's energy speaking the vocabulary of evil. If there were some open conflict—if the demons could turn and rend me, engage me in combat, what a refreshment that would be! But though I can affect them—as when I hide from them my conversation with you—I cannot come into open conflict with them. And it is like being a tick in the fur of the most scabrous of sewer rats. But you see how it goes? I begin to think of myself as 'a tick', a bloodsucking thing. You see how this employment sickens me? A pervasive entropy threatens to make the spinning atoms in the inner works of my being creak to a halt. How I long for a transfer..."

"I think I understand," I said, as the train pulled into Oldenburg. "But oh please—speak to me of heaven and hell, do they exist?"

"Yes and no."

"What of life after death?"

"Yes and no."

"Can you not be more specific?"

"Yes and no."

"Won't you tell me, at least—does humanity have an ultimate purpose? Is life meaningful? Is all suffering in some way meaningful?"

"Yes and no."

"Please—could you give me a little more, ah . . ."

The train rocked to a stop. The stout man stretched, and stood; the angel stood up too. "Will you speak to the bishop for me? And if he does not respond—someone else?"

"I will speak to him. Before you go, please tell me . . ."

But I was alone in the car, then, the others had all left, except for the old woman, who was standing in the doorway staring at me. I realized, then, that there were tears of frustration and loneliness on my face, and that I was weeping, and that was what made her stare so.

At my look, she hurried away, and I was left alone, to listen to the warning hiss of the train's engine, and the murmur of people who had someone to greet them on the station platform.

The Bishop of L_____ was as stout as the bowler-hatted man on the train, and more red-faced; though clean shaven, he rather resembled him.

I knew what the bishop's response would be. But I had promised that much, so, before the interview, I told him of my encounter on the train. His former mild bonhomie instantly dissipated. He took the coffee cup from my hands, put it down on the tray, and told me that he disliked practical jokers, and if I was not one of those, then he could be of no use to me, since I was in need of a physician. He asked his secretary to escort me from the church residence. I had not even gotten my interview.

I knew, though, that if I wrote to Fr. H_____ he at least would take me seriously—and would undertake the requested prayer for the unhappily assigned angel. I wrote the letter—and did not send it. Instead, I burned it.

Though more than human, the angel had seemed to embody less than divine perfection. Presumably a system, a bureaucracy if you like, of such creatures could well be fallible, would sometimes make mistakes. Perhaps initiating such a "transfer" would leave an opening for a mistake; would make room for a lapse of attention. Suppose the whisperer's whisperer were not there to whisper—at some critical juncture?

The United States is a brash, unwholesome nation but it seems to have its place in the game of power. And dead children in America are as sad a sight as dead children anywhere.

No. I could not write the letter.

I was tempted to—of that you may be certain. Late at night, something whispered to me: write the letter. Lines of security had been breached, and word had gotten out.

But I hear the other whisperer too. Once you know they're there—there for some of us—you begin to hear them. First one, then the other. And if you listen unusually hard—sometimes a third.

Perhaps it's the third who suggests that I might for the first time do something of importance—I might carry out an assassination. I know just who it will be.

Learn at Home!
Your Career in Evil!

It was while his wife slept: that's when it was easiest to think about killing her. Just the fact of her being awake, Elias Kander had learned, troubled him with doubts about the project. It was as if her movements about the house, her prattle, spoke of her as a living, suffering reality, and underlined the deepest meanings in the word murder.

But as she slept...

On those nights when he'd been working late in the lab, he would come home to find her soundly asleep, resentfully dosed with sedatives. Sedated, she was reduced to something like a hapless infant, clutching the quilt her grandmother had made. A time when, he supposed, he should feel pangs of conscience at her profound vulnerability, was just the time he felt safest thinking about her annihilation. Vistas of freedom opened up, in her hypothetical absence...

But what if there really were hell to pay?

What if evil were objectively real and not relative? And what about the thing in the lab?

A sleepy Tuesday night, the city hugging itself against moody Chicago winds off the Lake; but it was warm by the gas fire in the steak house.

Kander and Berryman came here after an afternoon's research, as it was across the street from the university's library.

Waiting for Kander to return from the men's room, Berryman sipped his merlot and looked at his companion's empty place across the table. How thoroughly Kander ate everything; not a shred of beef left, every pea vanished.

Berryman considered his own peculiar ambivalence to their monthly dinners; their boys' nights out. He'd felt the usual *frisson* on seeing Kander's almost piratical grin, the glitter in his eyes that presaged the ideas, in every philosophical menu, they'd feast on along with the prime rib; and a moment later, also as usual, a kind of chill dread took him. Kander had a gift for taking him to the frontiers of the thinkable, and into the wilderness beyond. But maybe that was the natural consequence of a humanistic journalist locking horns with a scientist. And sometimes Berryman thought Kander was more a scientist than a human being.

"I've been thinking about journalists, Larry," Kander said, sitting down. He was a stocky, bulletheaded man with amazingly thick forearms, blunt fingers; more like a football coach than a physicist who'd minored in behavioral science. He wore the same threadbare sweater the last time they'd suppered together, and the time before that; his greying black hair—an inch past the collar only because he rarely remembered the barber—brushed straight back from his forehead. Berryman was constrastingly tall, gangly, had trouble folding his long legs under the restaurant's elegantly minute tables. Long hair on purpose, tied in a greying ponytail. They'd been roommates at the university across the street where Kander had research tenure.

Berryman scratched in his short, curly brown beard. "You're thinking about journalists? I'm thinking about leaving, then. You'll be doing experiments on me next."

"How do you know for sure I haven't been?" Kander grinned and patted his coat for a cigarette.

"Amy made you give up the cigarettes, Kander, remember? Or have you started again?"

"Oh that's right, damn her, no smokes, well—anyway..." He poured some more red wine, drank half the glass off in one gulp and said, "My thinking is that journalists are by nature dilettantes. They have to be. I don't mean a scholar who writes a ten volume biography of Jefferson. I mean—"

"Guys like me who write for *Rolling Stone* and the *Trib* and, on a good day, *The New Yorker*. Yes, I'm well aware of your contempt for—"

"No, not at all, not at all. I'm not contemptuous of your trade, merely indifferent. But you must admit—journalists can't get into a thing too deeply because the next piece is always calling, and the next paycheck."

"Often the case, yes. But some specialize. And you get a feel for what's under the surface, though you can't spend long looking for it. Sometimes, though, you're with it longer than you'd like..."

"Yes: your war correspondence. I daresay you learned a great deal about South America. Peru, and, oh my yes, Chile..."

"Sometimes more than I'd like to know. What's your point, implying that journalists are shallow? You going to have a bumper sticker made up—'physicists do it deeper'?"

"Given the chance, we do! Unless we make the mistake of getting married. But my dear fellow—" Kander was American, but he'd gone to a boarding school in England for eight years, as a boy, and it had left its mark. "—I'm talking about getting to essences. What are the essences of things? Of human events? To get to them you must first wade through all the details of a study. Now, journalists think they dabble, and knock off an essence. But they can't; more often than not they get it wrong. A scientist though—he may work through mountains of detail, rivers of i-dotting and oceans of calculation, but ultimately he is after essences—the big picture and the defining laws that underline things. Now take your upsetting sojourn in what was it, Peru or Chile? Where you discovered that during 'the dirty war' whole families of dissidents were disappeared—"

"It doesn't seem to matter to you what country it was, Kander... Sometimes they weren't even really dissidents. They seem to pick them at random, some sort of quota."

"Just so. And they murdered the men, used some of the women for sex slaves, and when they abducted women who were pregnant, they often kept them alive just long enough to bear the children, whereupon the children were taken from them, for sale to childless officers—"

"And the women were then thrown alive out of airplanes over the Pacific. What's your point?" Berryman knew he was being snappish, but Kander was being altogether too gleeful over a recollection that never failed to make Berryman's guts churn.

"When you write about it, you write—and very well, yes—about the political and social histories that made such brutality possible. As if it were explainable with mere history! There's where you made your error. It wasn't history, my boy. It wasn't a shattering of modern ethics with a loss of faith in the rules of the Holy Roman Empire; it wasn't brutalizing by military juntas and a century of crushing the Indios'."

"You're not going to say Eugenics, are you? Korzybskiism? Because if you are—"

"Not at all! I'm no crypto-Nazi, my friend. No—if you look at the essence of the thing, it was as if a sort of disease was passed from one man to another. A disease that killed empathy, that allowed dehumanization—and extreme brutality."

"It is a kind of disease—but it has a social ontology."

"Not as you mean it. That kind of brutality goes deeper. It is contrary to the human spirit—and yet it was very widespread, in that South American hell-hole, just as it was among the Germans in World War Two. And the secret? It may be . . . that evil is *communicable*. That evil is communicable almost like a virus."

"You mean . . . there's some unknown physical factor, a microorganism that passes from one man to another, affecting the brain and—"

"No! That is just what I don't mean. I mean that evil as a thing in itself is passed from one man to the next. Not through a virus, or the example of brutality, or through coarsening from abuse—but as a kind of living, sentient substance—and this is what underlies such things. This is the essence that a journalist does not look deep enough to see."

Berryman stared at him; then he laughed. "You're fucking with me again. You had me going there . . ."

"Am I?" Shutters closed in Kander's face; suddenly he seemed remote. "Well. We'll talk about it another time. Perhaps."

Just then the Mexican busboy came along. "You feenish?" he asked.

"Yes, yes," Kander muttered impatiently. And he could not be induced to say much more that night, except to ask what Berryman, an associate at the university, thought of the new coeds, especially the latest crop of blondes.

It took only six weeks for the toxic-metals compound to do its work on Kander's wife. It was not a poison that killed, not directly: at this dosage it was a poison no one could see, or even infer: it was just despair. A little lead, a little mercury, a few select trace elements, a compound selected for its effect on the nervous system.

They were watching *The Wonderful World of Disney* when he became sure it was working on her.

It was a repeat of the Disney adaptation of *The Ransom of Red Chief*. She liked O. Henry stories. He had found that watching TV with her was often enough to satisfy her need for him to act like a husband. It was close enough to their "doing something together." It wasn't really necessary for him to watch the television, it was sufficient for him to rest his gaze on the screen. Now and then he would focus on it, mutter a comment, and then go back into his ruminations again. She didn't seem to mind if he kept a pad by the chair and scribbled the occasional note to himself; a patching equation, some new slant to the miniature particle accelerator he'd designed. How the world would beat a path to his door, he thought, as the little boy on Disney yowled and chased Christopher . . . what was his name, the guy who'd played the professor on *Back to the Future* . . . Christopher Lloyd? How the world of physics would genuflect to him when he unveiled his micro-accelerator. A twenty-foot machine that could do what miles of tunnel in Texas only approached. The excellences of quantum computing—only he had tapped them. The implications . . .

But it was best that *she* disappear before all that take place. If he were to get rid of her when the cold light of fame shone on him—well, someone would look too close at her death. And if he divorced her . . . her lawyer would turn up the funds he'd misappropriated from

her senile mother's bank account'; an account only his wife was supposed to be able to access ... never caring that those funds had paid for
his work after the grant had run out ...

He glanced at her appraisingly. Was it working? She was a short
Austrian woman, his wife, with thick ankles, narrow shoulders; she
was curled, now, in the other easy chair, wearing only her nightgown.
She'd complained of feeling weak and tired for days but it was the
psychological sickness he needed from her ...

"You know," she said, her voice curiously flat, "we shouldn't have
... I mean, it seemed right, philosophically, for you to get a vasectomy.
But we could have had one child without adding to the overpopulation
problem much, to any, you know, real ..."

"It was your health too, my dear. Your tipped uterus. The risk."

"We could have adopted—we still could. But ..." She shook her
head. Her eyes glistened with unshed tears and the image of the running child on the TV screen duplicated twistedly in them. "This world
is ... it seems so hopeless. There'll be 12 billion people in a few decades.
Terrorism, global warming, famine, the privileged part of the world
all ... all one ugly mall ... the cruelty, the mindless mindless cruelty
... and then what happens? You begin to age terribly and it's as if the
sickness in the world goes right into your body ... like your body ...
with its sagging and decay and senility ... it is like it is mocking the
world's sickness and ..."

It's working, he thought. The medical journals were right on target.
She was deeply, profoundly depressed.

"I know exactly what you mean," he said.

"It wouldn't matter so much if I had ... something. Anything in my
life besides ... But I'm just ... I mean I'm not creative, and I'm not a
scientist like you, I'm not ... if I had a child. That'd be meaning. But
it's too late for that."

"I'm surprised that watching *The Ransom of Red Chief* makes you
want a child. Considering how the child behaves ... They're all Red
Chief a lot of the time ..."

"Oh I don't mind that—wanting a child without that is like wanting
wild animals all to be tame. They *should be* wild ... But my life is
already ... it's caged."

"Yes. I feel that way too. For both of us."

She looked at him, a little disappointed. She'd had some faint hope he might rescue her from this down-spiraling pit.

For a moment, it occurred to him that he could. He could stop putting the incremental doses of toxins in her food. He could take her to a toxicologist. They'd assume she'd gotten some bad water somewhere . . .

But he heard himself say—almost as if it were someone else saying it—

"I'm a failure as a scientist. And I don't want to live in this world . . . if you don't."

It took five more tedious, wheedling days to break her down completely. He upped the dose, and he deprived her of sleep when he could, pretending migraines that made him howl in the night. He drove her closer and closer to the reach of that depression that had its own mind, its own will, its own agenda.

At last, at three-thirty in the morning, after insisting that she watch the Shopping Channel with him for hours—a channel anyone not stupid, stupefied, or mad would find nightmarish, after a few minutes— she said, "Yes, let's do it." Her voice dry as a desert skull. "Yes."

He wasted no time. He got the capsules, long since prepared. Hers the powerful sleeping agent she sometimes used. His appearing to be exactly the same—except that he'd secretly emptied out each pill in his own bottle, and put flour in his capsules. They each took a whole bottle of the prescription sedative; his would produce nothing but constipation.

She was asleep in ten minutes, holding his hand. He nearly fell asleep himself, waiting beside her. What woke him was something cold, touching him. The coldness of her fingers, gripping his. Fingers cold as death.

"I said, I've come to . . . to give you condolences," Berryman said, grimacing. "What a stupid phrase that is. I never know what to say when someone dies and I have to . . . but you know how I feel."

"Yes, yes I do." Kander said. Wanting Berryman to go away. He stood in front of his microaccelerator, blinking at Berryman. How had the man gotten in?

But he'd been sleeping so badly, drinking so much, he'd probably forgotten to lock the lab door. Probably hadn't heard the knocking over the whine of the machinery.

"If there's anything I can do . . ."

"No, no my friend she's . . . well, I almost feel her with me, you know. I used to make fun of such sentiments but, ah . . ."

It occurred to him—why not Berryman? Why not let Berryman be the one to break it to the world? Why wait till the papers were published, the results duplicated? There would be scoffing at first—a particle accelerator that could do more than the big ones could do, that could unlock the secrets of the subatomic universe, the unknown essences, consciousness itself—in a small university laboratory? They wouldn't condescend to jeering. They'd merely quirk their mouths and arch a brow. But let them—he'd demonstrate it first hand, once the public's interest was aroused. Let them come and see for themselves. The government boys would come around because the possibilities for applying this technology to a particle beam weapon were obvious . . . yes, yes, he'd mention it during the interview . . .

"Where would you like to do the interview, Berryman?"

"What?"

"Oh, I'm sorry—I'm getting to be an eccentric professor here, getting ahead of myself. Not enough sleep you know—ah, I want you to be the one to . . . to break the news . . ."

"Still, it's all theoretical," Berryman was saying, so *very* annoyingly, "at least to the public—unless there's something you can demonstrate . . ."

They were drinking Irish whisky, tasting of smoke and peat, in Kander's little cubicle of an office.

"I mean, Kander, I'll write it up, but if you want to get all the government agencies and the big corporations pounding on your door . . ."

"Well then. Well now," Kander took another long pull and suddenly it seemed plausible. "Why not? Come along then . . ."

They went weaving into the laboratory, Berryman knocking over a beaker as he went. "Oh, hell—"

"Never mind, forget it, it's just sulfuric acid, it's nothing." He had brought the whisky with him and he drank from it as he went through the door to the inner lab, amber liquid curling from the corners of his mouth, spattering the floor. "Ahhh yes. Come along, come along . . . Now . . . look through here, through this smoked glass viewer . . . while I fire 'er up here . . . and consider . . . consider that there is a recogniz- ably conscious component to quantum measurements: what is con- sciously perceived is thereby changed only by the perception. There's argument about how literally this should be taken—but I've taken it very literally, I've taken that plunge, and I've found something won- derful. Quantum computing makes possible fine adjustments of a scan- ning tunneling microscope, turning it into, well, a powerful particle accelerator, effectively . . . and since we're passing through this lens of sheer quantum consciousness in effecting this penetration, we open a door into the possibilities for consciousness to be found in so-called 'matter' itself."

"I see nothing through this window, Kander, except, uh, a kind of squirming smoke . . ."

"It's a *living* 'smoke' my friend. Listen—look at me now and listen— What characterizes raw consciousness? Not just awareness—but reac- tion. Response. Feeling. Yes, yes it turns out that suffering is something inherent in consciousness, along with pleasurable feelings—and that it's there even in the consciousness found in raw inorganic matter . . ."

"You're saying a brick can feel?"

"Not at all . . . not at all . . . but within a brick, or anything else, is the *potential* for feeling . . . now, this can be used, enslaved so to speak, to investigate matter from within and report to us it truest nature; can even be sent on waves of light to other solar systems and report to us what it finds there—this process of enslavement you see, that's the difficulty, so, ah, you've got to get involved in the training of this background consciousness once you've quantified a bit of it—bottled up a workable unit of it as I have—and that training is done with suffering . . . But how to make it suffer? It turns out, my friend, that while evil is, yes, relative, it is also, from the *point of view of any given entity or aligned group of entities*, a real essence. And this so-called 'evil' can be extracted from quantum sub-probability essences and used to train this consciousness to obey us—"

"You're . . . you're torturing raw consciousness to make it your slave?"

"Oh stop with the theatrical tone of horrified judgment. Do you eat animals? They have some smattering of consciousness. And would you train a horse to carry you over a wasteland? And how? You whip it, you force it to your will. Don't be childish about this . . . clamp down on your journalistic shallowness and look deep into the truths of life! For, my friend, life is comprised of intertwined essences! And once liberated those heretofore unknown essence are unbelievably powerful! The essence of evil . . . in order to use it I had to isolate it . . ."

"You've got the essence of evil in there?"

"Yes . . . well it's what people think of as evil . . . I envision a day when it's but a pure tool in our hands . . . just a tool, completely in our command and therefore never again our master . . . and we'll train peo-ple . . . train them in schools to use evil to—"

Berryman vaguely remembered an old Blue Öyster Cult lyric: *I'll make it a career of Evil . . .*

He chuckled, "I think this is where I say, 'You're mad, professor'. Only I don't think you're mad, I think you're drunk."

"Am I now. Listen . . . the stuff . . . just looking at it for awhile—it affects you. I spent an hour one night looking into that squirming mass and I . . ."

He almost said, and *I decided, when I stepped away from the instru-ment, to murder my wife.* "And I'd rather not discuss it! Well . . . Ber-ryman . . . did it not affect you, just now? No odd thoughts entered your head?"

"Um—perhaps." He blushed. Sex. Forbidden sex. "But—it could be just psychological suggestion, it could be a microwave or something hitting some part of my brain—to say it's the essence of evil . . ."

"Have another drink. You're going to need it. I'm going to open this chamber, and I'm going to introduce one of these . . . one of these cats here . . . And you'll see it transformed, remarkably changed, into pure energy, an energy that is pure catness, you see . . . Come here, cat, dammit ... You know we hire people to steal cats from the suburbs, for the lab ... we often have to take off their collars ... Muffy here hasn't had her collar taken off ... Ow! The little bitch! Scratched me!"

"Out-smarted you. You should be ashamed, stealing people's cats, Kander. There she goes, she's run under the ... You left the little door ... the hatch on that thing ... you left it open ... the smoke ... oh God, Kander. Oh God."

It wasn't Kander he was running from. The sight of Kander on all fours, clothes in tatters, knees bloody from the broken glass, running in circles on hands and knees chasing an imaginary tail, like a maddened cat ... Kander howling like a cat ...

Nor was it the fact that Muffy the cat was watching Kander do this from under the table and *was laughing in Kander's own voice* ...

No it was the squirming smoke, and what Berryman saw in it: An infinite spiral of despair, a hungry, predatory despair. Berryman saw the bloody drain in the floor of that South American prison where all those women had been tortured, tortured for no political reason, no practical application, to no purpose at all ...

He felt the thing that had escaped from Kander's lab—felt it sniff the back of his neck as he ran out into the partly-cloudy campus afternoon ...

But its inverted joy was so fulsome, so thunderously resonant, it could not be satisfied with merely Berryman. It reared up like a swollen genii. It married the clouds overhead and joined them, crushed them to it, so that electricity sizzled free of them and communicated with the ground in a forest of quivering arcs and darkness fell over all like the end smells of a concentration camp, and students, between classes, wailed in a chorus of despondency so uniform it could almost have come from a single throat; and yet some of them gave out, immediately afterward, a yell of unbridled exultation, free at last from the cruelty of self respect, and they set about fulfilling all that they'd held so long in quivering check ...

... the very bricks ...

The very bricks had gone soft, like blocks of cheese, and softer yet, and they ground unctuously together, the bricks of the building humping one another . . .

And the buildings sagged in on themselves, top floor falling lumpishly onto the next down, and those two on the next, and the whole thing spreading, wallowing, and people crushed, some of them, but others crawling to one another in the glutinous debris . . .

But it wasn't these he was drawn to. It was just one girl.

He was long past resisting; the thing was on them like a hurricane-force Santa Ana wind, parching out all strength for restraint, leaving only the unstoppable drive to merge and to bang, one on the other, like two people on the opposite sides of a door, each banging on it at the same time, loud as they could, each demanding that the other open it—

That's how they fucked.

He had seen the girl, no more than twenty years old, earlier that morning, in the cafeteria when he'd stopped in, on the way to see Kander, for a bagel and coffee, her hair in raven ringlets falling with springy lushness over bared shoulders; one of those clinging tank tops that cupped her just under the shoulders; tight jeans; sandals that showed small feet, scarlet nails; when she'd turned, feeling his hot gaze, her face amazingly open, full of maybes, possibilities in her full lips and Amer-Asian eyes. Golden skin. Part Japanese, part black, part Caucasian, and something else—Indian? Her cheekbones were high. They led to her eyes and down to her lips.

Her smile had been impossibly open. Not an invitation, just . . . open.

But, panicky with his rapture, he had said nothing, his heart in his throat; and she had turned away, and picked out a chocolate pudding.

Now . . . the center of the quad, under the sky . . .

The very center of the campus quadrangle. Brick, it was, with pebble paths from the four corners meeting at a concrete star in the middle. But the bricks and pebbles and concrete had all gone soft, and were alive: he could feel them returning his touch as he and the girl rolled on them, as he banged himself into her . . .

Some part of him struggled for objectivity, struggled for freedom from the overwhelming energies boiling around him . . . Boiling around the hundreds and hundreds of copulating couples and threesomes and foursomes across the campus square . . .

He had been running from the lab, he'd seen her, and she had shouted something joyfully to him as she ran up to him, tearing off her top, and he hadn't been able to make it out because of the thudding, inarticulate music coming from everywhere and nowhere, sounding like five radio stations turned on full blast over loudspeakers, five different rock-songs all played at once, a chaos of conflicting sounds merging into a mass of exuberant noise—except for no clear reason all the songs had the same percussion, the same beat . . . THUD THUD THUD THUD . . . maybe just his pulse . . . THUD THUD THUD THUD . . . White noise, red noise and black . . .

And he hadn't been able to hear her over this but she'd grabbed his hands and pressed them to her breasts—

Her breasts were songs of Solomon, were each like a dove, fitting perfectly under his hands, each one upturned and nuzzling his palm with a stiff nipple.

Run, he told himself. Get away from here.

Her belly was soft but muscular, moving in a bellydance she'd never learned in life, and he was peeling off her jeans . . . and their clothes, they found, fell away from them like wet ashes, in the magic that was rampant about them, and you could scrape them away with your nails. In moments they were nude and rolling on the impossibly soft bricks, with the white noise, the red noise, the black noise; rolled by the golden waves of godsized sound and he had only a few glimpses of the others, copulating ludicrously to all sides and with frenetic energy. The obese, unpleasantly naked sixty year old Dean of Mathematical Studies was slamming it to the rippling-buff thirty year old lesbian volleyball coach, and the fifty-five year old lady with the mustache who was in charge of the cafeteria had stripped away most of her white uniform and was straddling the quarterback of the football team and he was digging at her flapping breasts till they bled and mouthing *I love you baby* at her; and the Gay Men's Glee Club was copulating not only with one another but with the girls from the Young Republican Women's Sorority Association, and the black campus mailman was fucking wildly with the blond woman who taught jazz dancing—but it wasn't the first time; and biology classes were copulating with physics classes . . .

And they fucked faster, him and the golden skinned raven haired girl, her eyes flashing like onyx under a laser, and he could feel the spongy tissue of the inner vagina with almost unbearable detail as she chewed at his tongue, only making it bleed a little, and too close to his ear the president of the Students for Christ screamed "FUCK ME PLEASE UNTIL IT KILLS ME!" to the wrestling coach until the doddering head of the philosophy department shoved his improbably engorged dick so deep into the student's throat he gagged and choked, the old man, his wattles shimmering with his humping, singing "I GOT MY COCK IN MY POCKET AND IT'S SHOVIN' OUT THROUGH MY PANTS, JUST WANNA FUCK, DON'T WANT NO ROMANCE!" Or *was* he singing that? Was that in Berryman's mind? Some part of Berryman was becoming increasingly detached as he fucked harder, driving bleedingly hard into the gorgeous Asian student; something in him trying to crawl out from under this slavery... The old man jamming himself into the student's throat clawed at the air and fell over the other two in the threesome, shaking in death... Others, mostly the older ones, were beginning to die but even those not breaking under the strain were showing haunted eyes, amping desperation, and the Dean of Comparative Religions grabbed a gun from the fallen holster of a cop and blew out his own brains and the man next to him took the gun from the Dean's limp hand and shot himself in the throat and the woman beside *him* took up the gun...

While overhead the black thunderclouds still shed their lightnings, sent eager arcs into the receptive cunt of the Earth itself...

For a while now Berryman had been coming, ejaculating in the girl but the coming wouldn't stop, went achingly on and on and on, he was quite empty but still his urethra convulsed as it tried to pump something into her, and all that came up now was blood in place of cum, and he screamed with the pain and she tried to push away from him with her hands but her legs, locked behind his back, disobeyed her, pulled him closer to her yet—

Berryman made a supreme internal effort—something he'd learned from an old man in the Andes...

And never before had he really succeeded in it; never before had it quite crystallized in him. But now under these unspeakable pressures it came together and he was whole, and he was free—

His body was still caught, but some essence . . .

An essence! Another essence . . .

Some essence was hovering over the humping, screaming figures, and calling out . . . Calling out like to like. To another essence, its own kind. . . .

Then the other essence came; the other end of the spectrum, closing the circuit, closing the gap: the blue light, and the silence . . .

How Screwtape hated silence . . .

The silence came rolling across them in a wave of release, of icy purity, of relaxing, of forgiving, and they fell away from one another, those who'd survived, and lay gasping, falling into a deep state of rest, and the lightnings stopped, the squirming smoke dissipated in the sudden drenching downpour of rain . . . The bricks became hard and his dick became soft and . . .

And the cat, Muffy, ran past him, carrying one of Kander's eyes in its jaws.

Sweetbite Point

It was routine, his taking Danella home, and there was no reason it should turn out the way it did. He'd never felt like that before. Once or twice the uneasiness, that was all. But normally . . .

Nearly every Saturday night in the Spring, when Jeff Twilley and Latesha Twilley got home from Sweetbite Point Coastal Bowling League's "Late Night Seasonals," Danella would already have her coat on as they were still taking theirs off; ready, very ready, to go after five hours babysitting twin seven-year-old boys. The boys were usually asleep, and Danella would be yawning. Jeff would be a little tipsy but not enough for it to have much effect on his driving since, tipsy or not, he was always slow and careful and methodical, never over the speed limit. He was the kind of guy who stopped at the stop sign and looked carefully both ways for a full five seconds before moving on. It sometimes irritated Latesha, who had a lead foot, but she was glad of it when he'd had a drink.

They were an interracial couple, Jeff and Latesha. He was a chunky white guy with thinning hair and a stable supervisory gig at the lumber mill; she was a chunky black lady with corn-rowed hair and a gift for batik and tie dye that sold a fair number of Sweetbite t-shirts to tourists. He'd met her in the bowling league, and they were both in their late thirties when they got married. "Married first time and last time," he always said, and she'd say, "What exactly you mean by that, dammit, that you wouldn't never leave me, . . . or I put you off women?" But that was a joke, she knew what he meant, and she'd squeeze his hand.

He'd felt the uneasiness descend on him, that night, as he looked at Danella buttoning up her coat; and descend on him was exactly how it was, almost like uneasiness was a thing, "like a cold, cold silk scarf" he thought, later, "settling over my head." For the first time, then, as she buttoned the coat, he noticed how full her breasts were now. How her legs were longer than his wife's; how long and slim and fine they were. The same uneasiness he'd felt before, only now it was different— like the uneasiness had eyes.

That night . . .

That night Twilley was walking to the car, feeling a cool wind on his cheeks, the chill breath of the sea smelling of brine and of petroleum from the leak at the rig that the oil company claimed wasn't a leak at all, and already something was different than usual: He took the video camera from the car trunk. There wasn't really any reason to get the camera out, at a time when he was taking Danella home from baby-sitting. He almost never used the camera, and his wife gave him hell for having wasted the money on it.

Danella glanced at it when he put it in the back seat, but she didn't say anything.

"Sure cold for April," she said, instead, as he started the car and drove past the wind-streamed pines, down the dirt road to Highway 1. "I come out here from Chicago, I thought California was going to be warm."

He felt the wind buffet the Volkswagen as they turned onto the main road. "On the Northern Cal coast, you never know," he heard himself say. It was really like someone else was saying it, though it was something he might've said. "Now where I lived on Long Island, years ago, we had that warm current, you knew you could count on that, but here, boom, the *cold* . . ."

It was so distant, his own voice, he could almost hear an echo. Like it was echoing to him from a ways off, in the big cavern of the night sky.

"I think it's those weird weather patterns," Danella said. She was nineteen, a pretty girl with skin the color of cocoa—three tablespoons of cocoa in that cup. She was in community college, doing two years of general courses and then maybe going to veterinary college, if she could swing the tuition. "You know, from that global warming, all that."

"Oh yeah." The stars peered at them through breaks in the clouds, over the inky sea. "You going to be a vet, huh?"

"I hope, I hella hope. I love animals. I'd love to do that. You ever read that book, *All Things Bright And Beautiful?*"

"No." He was trying to feel his hands on the steering wheel. He felt so disconnected. He was changing lanes to pass a car, and he rarely passed moving cars at night. This was a two-lane road, it was night, and he was just never in that kind of a hurry. Plus he'd had a few beers. No reason to pass cars. No reason to be in a hurry.

He passed another car and increased his speed to fifty.

"That made me want to become a vet," she was saying. "That . . . that book." She was glancing discreetly at the speedometer.

The car fishtailed slightly on the curve.

"You like these new Beetles, huh?" she asked. "Still playin' with the new car?" An indirect way to ask why he was speeding. This was a winding coast road. Fifty was too fast for it.

But he didn't slow down. *55. 60.*

"Whoa-oh," she said, under her breath, as they shivered around a turn.

Twilley was watching for the entrance to the Sweetbite Point Arboretum. There: just ahead. He felt himself slow the car as he came to the arboretum driveway. Why? Why slow *here?* Why the arboretum?

There was no reason to turn into the parking lot.

There was no reason to pull up to the utility road the gardener's trucks used.

"Something wrong with the car?" Danella was asking.

He tried to answer, but nothing came out of his mouth. He pulled the car up to the chain closing off the dirt road, south of the main complex of the Arboretum entrance, and switched off the headlights. Then he turned the car off, took the keys with him as he got out and unhooked the chain from the metal post, and got back in the car. Danella was staring at him.

"Something I want to show you," he heard himself say, as he started the car and drove down the dirt road. "It's something. You won't believe this." Then he heard himself add, "You're interested in animals, right?"

He heard himself laugh, but he wasn't sure it was out loud.

"Sure," she said, relaxing a little. "Duh." Maybe he'd found a black bear's den in the arboretum. "But—we going to get in trouble, trespassing like this? Arboretum's closed."

"No, they're friends of mine," he said, lying with complete equanimity. "I got permission."

They bumped along the road in a darkness blotted with deeper darkness where the shadows of the trees crossed the dirt road.

"How come no car lights?" she asked. Her voice sounded casual.

"Don't want to scare the animals off," he heard himself say.

Then he found a good spot and he pulled over, and turned off the car. He got out, then reached into the back seat and took out the video camera. She got out of the car, looking around, as he took the camera out of its case.

"Is it near here?" she asked, hugging herself. "The bear or whatever?"

There was no reason to take the camera out of its case, he thought, checking to see the battery was providing juice. The little green light came on; the camera was working. There was no reason . . .

She stared at him when he switched on the car's headlights, and she watched him as he walked around the front of the car toward her.

Bragonier smiled at his own childlike eagerness as he tore open the manila envelope. The envelope had been left under the abandoned, overturned row boat, on Sweetbite beach, near the arboretum. The drop was working out fine.

Bragonier took out the videotape, padded across the Persian rug to the basement's entertainment center. He immediately put the tape into the VCR, hit *play,* and sank into the easy chair he'd pulled up close to the screen. He glanced at the basement windows, out of habit, though there was no need to check them: they were painted black from the inside. He had painted them himself when he'd bought the house, two months before. No one could see in. It was bright noon outside, but it could be any hour of the day in here, and as far as Bragonier was concerned, it was always 1:23 A.M..

Bragonier was a compact, slender man with greasy, forgotten black hair; he wore black silk Japanese pajamas figured with runes he had stitched there himself; silk slippers on his small feet. His large brown-black eyes had striking astigmatism—the telltale skewing seen on many who'd mastered certain disciplines, on both sides of the metaphysical fence.

Pixel snow, on the TV screen, and then an image: a white hand on a cocoa-colored throat. The automatic focus shifted back and forth, and the angle was a little awkward, and the camera jiggled, but there it was now, he could make it out. A big man's hand on a slim black girl's throat, seen from above, one hand presumably propping the camera on the man's shoulder, the other pinning the girl, the man straddling the wild-eyed girl, holding her down with his weight, with the strength of his legs. A little red foam at the corner of her mouth, her eyes tracking desperately through emptiness as oxygen loss shut down her vision. Her thrashing arms, batting weakly at him. The camera joggling at this, the image swiveling, jerking queasily, then stabilizing.

Bragonier watched, enraptured, as the girl died, as Twilley set the camera on the hood of the car, angled down just right, and then, in the harsh headlight, raped her warm corpse on the dirt road.

Bragonier re-lived it, as it had happened that night. He had been there, of course, but this brought it all back. And this was only the first time he would savor the tape.

He was only sorry that Twilley could not have been brought to ejaculation; they never could. It was difficult enough to maintain the erection.

Now, the tape done, Bragonier labeled it #74. *Sweetbite CA*, and carried it to the eight-foot-high coffin-shaped mahogany cabinet in the closet he'd hidden behind the plasterboard wall; the moveable wall now stood open, the coffin, standing on end, was also open, showing rows of videotapes, the short wave radio he used for the real-time transmissions, when those were possible, the drawer containing the old film footage and sound recordings from earlier encounters, and a few odd souvenirs. Most of the sound recordings were from his time with the More Man, during the study of the Akishras, in Los Angeles—he had barely escaped the Wetbones debacle . . . There were a few eight millimeter films from his time in the service of the Head Underneath, in New York. Another narrow escape. His mentor hadn't been so lucky . . .

But now, his mastery of the Method made anything possible and preserved him in safety, forever, forever.

Twilley was as surprised as Latesha when the deputy sheriff came to the door the next morning, asking when he'd seen Danella last.

He said, "I don't know. I guess when I took her home. I don't remember exactly," he said, blinking in the sunlight. It was 8 A.M. on a Sunday morning and he had a mild hangover.

"Is Danella all right?" Latesha asked, her voice rising half an octave on the last syllable.

"I'm sorry ma'am. She was found on the beach this morning. She's dead. We're . . ." He looked at Twilley, then back at her. "Still looking into the cause of death."

Twilley stared at the young cop, trying to take it in. The cop had a round red "babyface" and flat-top haircut. Under the cop's badge was a nametag that said *FISHER*. The cop was looking back at him, steadily this time.

"Oh my god," Latesha was saying. "Danella. Oh my God."

"It's all right, baby," Twilley said, putting his arm around his wife's shoulders, "We'll find out what . . ."

" 'Mr Twilley'?" officer Fisher said. "I need you to come down to the station with me, please."

The deputy had one hand resting on the butt of his holstered gun.

The first time Coach Barris felt the uneasiness was at the Sweetbite Point "Friends of the Pioneers" pancake breakfast. He was carrying a platter of pancakes past all those familiar faces gathered for the fundraiser; there was Hank from the Safeway, Louella from the gift shop on the corner of Main and Wilson, Rupert from the Cajun food place— Barris had always felt Cajun food was a bad risk for the northern California coast, where tourists wanted Mexican or seafood, but hey the guy was hanging in there—and there were all the familiar faces from the PTA, and all those kids, chattering or profoundly bored. Just lots of familiar faces streaming past on the right and on the left, and then that one face he didn't know, that little man with the crooked black eyes, staring at him, the guy's mouth moving like he was talking to himself, one hand on a little white hand towel on his lap, and then he lost sight of the guy as chubby Mrs Claremont stepped into his path, Mrs Claremont beaming at him, saying she'd seen the Sweetbite Swatters play a game last fall and he must be very proud because even though they'd only won three the whole season they'd played with such heart, and him trying to answer politely as *that feeling* settled over him . . .

And for a few moments there was a look of uncertainty in Mrs Claremont's face, like she was wondering what she'd said wrong, while Barris tried to get back in touch with what he was doing here. Everyone looked strange, faintly hostile; their purpose alien to him. He almost dropped the platter of pancakes.

Then the disorientation left him, and it was as if the volume knob on the sound in the place had been flipped down and back up, and there was a rush of noise and reassuring familiarity and he smiled and said, "Thank you, Mrs. Claremont—you ready for some more pancakes?" And he was all right, for the rest of that day. The next night Barris was working late over grades in his office, and he looked up to see one of the senior girls, in her gym shorts and T-shirt, walk past to go to the girls' showers. First there was the uneasiness, settling over him like that feeling you get just before you come down with the flu, and then a feeling like when the optometrist is testing your eyes with that machine and he clicks those different lenses down, how's this one, how's this, and till he gets it right each lens makes things look a little blurrier, or more distant. Click, some strange lens came down between him and the girl, Jonquil. She'd been using the Nautilus machines those people from San Diego had donated when they'd moved back to Southern California. She wanted to flatten her stomach, and firm her pecs—so to lift her breasts, he supposed—and he'd said she could use the machine after school, and here Jonquil was, at six o'clock, when most everyone else had gone home; a plump girl with honey-brown hair and bright red lipstick and bright red fingernails and bright blue eyes. And it was like he was riding along in the back seat of a car, and someone else was driving, and he was dreaming the whole ride, as he followed her into the showers, and turned off the water, and switched on the little tape recorder he'd bought that afternoon (wondering why as he bought it) and clamped his hand over her startled mouth, feeling the red, red lipstick greasy on his palm, and forced her down onto the tiles.

The Reverend Garner was working in his gardenless garden. His front yard contained only sand and some large rocks and a conch and a few lonesome shrubs. He used a wide-toothed metal rake to make neat, curving rows of lines around and between them.

He was a lean middle aged man with a close-clipped beard, streaked with grey like his thinning hair, which was long in the back and tied with a strip of black leather; on his tanned arms were a few fading tattoos from his youth. He wore a T-shirt of nearly twenty-five years vintage with a faded picture of Alan Watts on it, frayed jeans, and sneakers.

He straightened up from his raking, and realized that his daughter Constance was going to call him from London. He could feel it quite distinctly.

Garner began walking toward the house, feeling the sun on his back. Inside the house, the phone rang. He leaned the rake up against the wooden railing of his beach house, and went in to answer the phone.

"Hello."

"Daddy?"

"Hi baby. How're those finals coming?"

"Not a problem. It's so easy to think about school, compared to some other stuff, now. It used to be the opposite." She meant: before.

Before the abduction, before the way she'd been used and violated, in her early teens. She'd been happily empty-headed then, and now everything was, forever, so serious for her. Though she had a dorm room to herself in London, part of her scholarship, she had to share her body, her mind, with other, coarser room-mates: her memories of the abduction.

"You get out and have some fun sometimes?" he asked. "London has some fun in it, somewheres I hear."

"Sure, Daddy, of course."

"Good." But he could feel she was just saying it so he wouldn't worry. She avoided socializing. Someday, with God's grace, she'd heal fully.

She had given her life to God, because of what she'd been through. She felt safe only in constant inward prayer, in the Prayer of the Heart. And he knew that now it was more than just "feeling safe"; that she'd realized it was what she was here for.

They spoke for a while of the school of comparative religion she attended, of her professors, of a mouse that'd invaded her room (she was afraid of mice but she'd caught it in a cup and taken it outside); of a book on Meister Eckhart she'd been reading; of women friends of hers who were Roman Catholics, and how they'd invited her to an unauthorized mass with an unauthorized woman priest—part of the "Critical Mass" movement among Catholic women—and of a dream she'd had when she'd awakened to sense him invisibly, nearby, and they both knew that'd been more than a dream, so not much needed be said about it. They spoke of his work as a spiritual counselor—a minister, but not working out of a church anymore; of the grant he'd gotten for his pastoral work with people dying in Mendocino County's hospices and hospitals: it had been renewed for another year. They chatted of other work he did as a drug counselor—the sort of drug counselor who was an ex-addict, though he'd been clean for many years. Then she had to go, it was late there, she had studying to do before she slept.

"I love you, Daddy."

"I love you too, Constance, always. Call me collect in a day or two after finals and tell me how they went, okay?"

She said okay, they said goodbye, and hung up. Garner looked at his watch. He was due at a hospital in about an hour, but it was only ten minutes down the road. He thought about making himself lunch, but he wasn't really hungry. He looked out the window at the sea. The ocean was cerulean, and it rose and fell within itself like an old song. He felt a subtle hunger for meditation: he'd go back to raking for half an hour.

He went outside to his rake and set to work. He wished his Master were still alive. Still physically alive. He'd died on Mt Athos three years before. But sometimes . . .

Garner sensed something, and looked up to see a stranger walking along the rocky verge marked by the tired old fence, between his front yard and the beach. The man was running one hand, tap tap tap, along a still-standing section of the weathered, grey, sagging picket-fence that was, now, so fallen and sand-buried it was more a reference than a fence. The stranger was a small man wearing sunglasses that didn't hide the pronounced cast in his eye; he wore a brown leather overcoat that was too warm for the day. He paused, one hand on a crooked fence post, to watch Garner rake the sand in his yard into smooth patterns around the stones and shrubs.

Garner's full attention was invested in the work; in his body, in the moment. He centered in the moment with long experience, and placed himself, in some sense, in the axis of that moment's connection to eternity; and the next moment's connection, and the next. He was often amazed at how *new* eternity was if you gave it your full attention.

Just now, he was simply raking. He felt the sun, the breeze, the rake in his hands, his body within itself and in relationship to the Earth: his axis to its axis. This moment, this moment, this moment . . . walk to the other side of the little purple scrub bush . . . rake the sand carefully into patterns like musical bars around the bush . . . This moment, this moment, just this, all this, himself and not himself, all things and nothing, the light that emerged from the void, from this moment . . .

But a distraction almost tugged him out of it. The man watching.

It was not an ordinary distraction; for Garner, at this time in his life, ordinary distractions were no distraction at all. No, it was as if Garner was a planet circling the sun of his contemplation and this other man, this stranger, was another planet from a wayward system, entering Garner's orbital plane like the marauding planetoid in *When Worlds*

Collide, the stranger imposing another gravitational field, pulling Garner out of his original orbit of contemplation.

"Zen gardening?" the man asked suddenly.

"It's an affectation," Garner answered, after a moment. "I'm no Japanese gardener. If I had grass and flowers I'd be using a lawn mower and weeding."

"The wind must blot out your work quite quickly," the man said, in a voice that seemed too deep for his slight frame.

"Sure. There, as they say, is the rub." He continued raking, though not as fully consonant with the act of raking as he had been before.

"I suppose that symbolizes something to you, too," the stranger said. "The world's transience; a means of practicing non-identification."

Garner straightened up and looked mildly at the man. He extended the field of attention he kept within himself, and felt a palpable field around the stranger. The character of that field gave him a chill.

The stranger took a step backwards. "Well. Good afternoon."

Garner nodded. The stranger walked onward, following what remained of the fence. As he went, the sound of the sea came back to Garner with a roar. It had never been gone, but for a few moments it had seemed muted.

Garner watched the man walk down the beach, toward a cove where hundreds of driftwood logs and big burls and snags had been deposited, over the years, and among them an old, overturned, broken-open rowboat. For the first time, it occurred to Garner that there was something about the beach mazed with driftwood that resembled an old cemetery; the twisted naked wood like time-bent grave-markers.

As Garner watched, the stranger stopped in his tracks, and turned, slowly, to look back. Garner lifted a hand in a casual "hi neighbor" greeting.

A long blank look back at Garner, then the stranger walked on, wending his way slowly between the interrupted flowings of driftwood, toward the sand-embedded rowboat. For some reason, Garner found himself staring at the rowboat. Then he looked at his watch, and decided he'd better put on a clean shirt and shave, and go to the hospital.

*   *   *

Garner sat in a chair beside Mr Send, while Mr Send died. He had been dying for a couple of months; Garner thought it might be over today. The blinds were shut, because the light hurt Mr Send's eyes, some side effect of the radiation treatments, and the room smelled faintly of rot and more strongly of the alcohol they'd used for a disinfectant when they'd given him three more intramuscular injections. There was an IV in his arm, running up to a bottle on a T-stand beside the bed, and there were oxygen tubes in his nose. Mr Send, who had made a fair amount of money in the software industry, had a private room.

There was a TV, on a rack near the ceiling, but it was switched off—people very close to dying, Garner had noticed, rarely watched television. The dying felt as if everything on TV was saying: *We're all going merrily on, in our mocking, self referential, self important, youth-oriented denial-happy way, and we're indifferent to you and your dying.*

Send was fifty, an Iranian, thirty years in America. A short, thick-bodied man before the cancer—now he was fragile, his skull showing through the skin on his face as if impatient.

His bony hands lay across his middle; the right one curled and un-curled restlessly.

Garner had been coming here a few times a week, for two months. Early on, Send had gone through periods of peevishness and feeble, smoldering rage, and had sent him away . . . And, not long after, asked for him to return.

Sometimes Send had cursed him in Farsi and in English; Garner had pretended to be a mildly offended and irritated, though he wasn't really: it made them feel frustrated and powerless if they couldn't hurt you a little. Sometimes Send let Garner read to him.

After awhile, Garner asked, "Like me to read to you, Mr Send? I have several books with me. *The Wind in the Willows.* A book of poems by Rumi. Sherlock Holmes. Perhaps the Qu'ran."

"I . . . am not Muslim." His voice was cracked. "My parents. But . . . not me."

"Perhaps something entertaining . . ."

"No reading now."

A long pause. Then Garner asked, "Would you like some water?"
"Yes."

Garner got him a half a glass of water, lifted his head, and held it
as he sipped. He weighed so little.

A little later, Send said, "In computers . . ." He fell silent, struggling
to swallow.

"Yes?"

". . . is a thing . . . you know what it is . . . you have a program, and
it gets scrambled, it gets . . . trashed. And then it's all . . . nonsense, a lot
of random numbers and words and code and it looks like . . ."

"Like it should mean something . . ."

"Yes. But it does not. Does not mean something. My life. This is my
life. Like this file that is . . . trash. Random . . . Meaningless . . ."

"Yes. I know just how you feel. I've had that feeling about my life.
And it's also something people feel when they're dying sometimes."
They had long since acknowledged to one another that Mr Send was
dying. "But . . ." He paused to see if Mr Send wanted to say anything
else. There was only the labored breathing. Garner went on, "There's
a sort of classic way to look at it differently, if you choose to. In the
Jewish tradition they talk about this . . ." He got up, slowly, and crossed
the room and took a painting off the wall, a cheap mass-marketed
seascape. "This painting is something people put up to break up the
monotony of the wall, not something really intended for a long look.
It'll have to do. Let's just do this . . ." He took an extra hospital gown
folded over the end of the bed, and draped it over the painting, so it
covered up most of it. Only a small corner of the painting was visible
now. The visible corner looked like a random splash of lines. "You see
this corner, when you see it out of the context of the whole painting—
just this little corner, without the big perspective . . . it's just a little bit
of chaos, really." He drew back the cloth, slowly, revealing the rest of
the painting to Send, and now the chaotic little corner took shape as it
was revealed to be part of the whole. "Hidden before—and now . . .
well you see."

"Yes." A faint smile. "But—that's still . . . just faith, to believe it's
part of something . . . bigger. Something that means . . . something. We
have no . . . painting for my life."

"I know what you mean." Garner kept talking as he slowly hung the painting back up and straightened it and replaced the extra gown. "But when we observe the world, we see chaos in the small perspective and order in the big perspective—why shouldn't it be that way with our lives, our souls? Anyway, when I think of myself as 'this guy Garner who has lived this life' then it's pretty easy to see nothing very lasting there. It may be meaningful but it's not permanent—it's just a pattern on the waves as the waves go by . . ." Now as he spoke he returned to the chair by the bed and put his hand over one of Send's. Words, most of the time, weren't enough. There was something else, some other way of communicating. It was possible for Garner to share his experience of eternity through the finely-energized spiritual body he had created for himself.

Now, he extended the borders of this other body to overlap with Send's consciousness, as he spoke; extending it through his hand, his voice, his field. "But there is an underlying Self that is a truer identity . . . something that may take part in our suffering but doesn't suffer, that takes part in time but is not 'in time,' something eternal, something alive, something . . . that you are connected with, if you look for it, if you look and listen . . . search very very gently and persistently and openly . . . opening your heart to it . . ."

Mr. Send gasped, and his fingers tightened on Garner's. And then the dying man began to sob with understanding. An empirical, personal understanding that unified all that had been broken.

A little while later, Send went to sleep. Garner didn't think Send would wake from the sleep.

Garner got up, murmured some words to the air, and left the room, looking at his watch. He had to go to a hospice in Fort Bragg—

"Reverend . . . um, Reverend Garner?"

Garner was passing through the main hospital waiting room, and turned to see Mrs. Twilley, a black lady he knew from the bowling league. Garner was a pretty good bowler.

"Yes, hi, Mrs. Twilley! How are you?" He saw that her eyes were red, swollen, she was twisting the straps of her brown leather purse in her fingers. "You okay?"

"No, I ... I needed to talk to someone, and, um, my minister's on a
retreat ... I could pay you something."

"Don't be silly. Shall we sit down over here?"

They found a quiet corner and she told him about her niece's death,
and her husband's arrest, and her utter confoundment. Garner, who
knew Twilley a little, was puzzled himself. She tried not to sob as she
said, "It really looks like he did it. He can't remember it but ... But
then there's the coach—he was arrested too. For that other girl."

"Another girl was killed ... Did you say the coach? You mean at
the high school?"

"Yes. Yes to both—I'm surprised you didn't hear anything about
it ..."

"Is there any evidence to ... to tie Mr. Twilley in?"

"I guess he's got some mud from the place on his car ... Now that
ain't definite right there, but—he can't remember *not* doing ... doing
it. And the coach claims *he* doesn't remember either ..."

"Really. They don't remember ..." He felt that chill again, and a
sense of recognition.

He held Mrs. Twilley as she wept.

Perhaps, Bragonier thought, as he sat in the easy chair in his basement,
listening to the tape, *I shouldn't have done those two so close together, so
soon after my coming here. They may interfere with one another, in terms
of police misdirection.*

But he'd felt such a *need* lately, and there was something wonderful
about this cassette, the one the Barris man had made. The sound quality
was echoey, but you could hear her muffled cries bouncing off the tiles
in the shower room, and the man's grunts and the mysterious noises—
clackings, maybe a belt buckle on the floor? It brought it all back, he
was almost there again.

He listened, and squirmed in his seat with an exquisitely refined
delight.

Garner drove his beat-up old Honda Civic along the bumpy road to
the place marked out by the yellow police tape. The afternoon light
slanted through the pines and the wind from the sea, making the pine

branches toss, jittered the sun's spot-lighting, as if searching for the truth in the squared-off yellowtaped area. He got out of the car, and stood there listening with all of his being. With his ears, he heard the high, swaying trees cracking their limbs against one another; the sea growling from the cliffs on the other side of the arboretum.

Perhaps, Garner thought, *I'm wrong about all this.* Then he thought, *It isn't right to have to face one of them again. Not after what they did to Constance. Her innocence crushed . . .*

Some coincidences are coincidences. Some coincidences are not coincidences.

He smiled sadly at the flicker of self pity. He saw that he was afraid. He raised his hands and saw they were shaking. He let it happen in him. The organism needed to be afraid, sometimes. He opened consciously to that flow of energy that allowed him to suffer fear without succumbing to it. Still his hands trembled. He took a deep breath, and thought: *One foot in front of the other. Let's go.*

He knelt by the yellow tape, and listened; then he listened with another part of himself. The trees creaked, the sea boomed, the leaves rattled.

Garner suddenly straightened up, and turned, to look back toward town.

Bragonier was thinking that since the coach was out on bail, it was time to firm things up.

Later, do it later. He hit play on the cassette deck, to listen to the tape a fifth time.

Then he straightened in his chair, feeling something . . . something that . . .

He turned and looked at the blacked out windows, in the direction of the arboretum.

Bragonier switched off the tape, and listened, with all his being. He felt a chill, and a sense of recognition.

The coach, Garner thought. *I really need to go and . . .*

And what? *And be there for him. In some way.*

Garner turned and started back to his car—then he stopped, nostrils and eyes dilating, his head lifting to listen once more. He turned and looked through the piney woods. The arboretum's rhododendron had just started to bloom . . .

Something like a wisp of spun glass twisted between the trees, drifting from one grey-brown bole to another. When it passed through a shaft of sunlight, it filled out into a translucent outline, the way a cloud of dust will; and what was cloudy became a definite shape . . .

He was a little surprised at how substantial it was. It was not one of those psychic graffitis on the air that people called ghosts.

"Danella?" he said aloud, gently.

The drifting form slowed and he felt the shape respond with an anguished moan that couldn't be heard, though every animal in the woods stopped to listen to it.

"You were attacked by a predator, Danella," Garner explained. "But you're going to be all right now. I'm going to send you to another sea, a sea of light, and you'll find your grandmother there. I remember you talking about how you liked your grandmother . . ."

He spoke in this way for a while, and only a small part of the speaking was aloud, and then he went to his knees and prayed, one hand touching the ground where she'd died, and after a minute he felt the weight lift from the place. And a quiet confidence returned to him . . .

He got up, and returned to his car and drove home.

Coach Barris left his lawyer's office feeling drained, and unreal. He walked down Main Street, which was also Highway 1, smelling the sea, watching a lumber truck rumble by, and tried to understand how these things connected to what had happened to him.

People passed him on the street, as he walked to his car, and he expected them to glare at him accusingly, but no one looked at him at all.

God but he was glad Marilee was out of town. A wife would have had to stick by him, but a fiancee just might jump ship . . .

He was hungry; he hadn't eaten since yesterday. He wanted to buy some hamburger, make himself up some barbecue burgers, watch a

game, get his mind off it all for awhile. But he was afraid to go into
Safeway. People there had probably heard.

Maybe drive up the road a ways, to some place they didn't know
him, order dinner.

He fumbled with the car keys at the Toyota, dropped them, said,
"Shit!", picked them up, fumbled some more. He'd turned all fumble-
fingers.

Could he have done it? He couldn't remember *not* being there, in
the girls' dressing rooms, in the showers. And it wasn't like he'd never
had sick thoughts about some of the girls. But he'd never so much as
breathed heavy around them. And to *kill* . . . he couldn't even imagine
it.

He finally got the car open, got in, closed the car door . . . and felt
the uneasiness settle over him. That odd feeling . . .

Then he saw Corinne Valdez crossing the street, walking toward
the beach, carrying her little red back pack over one shoulder. It was
sunny, and she was going to read her homework on the beach, behind
the shelter of the driftwood, out of the wind. He'd seen her do it before,
once or twice, when he'd been out jogging on the beach.

He saw himself start the car and drive to the corner, and turn the
car to follow her. Saw it as if he were watching from the back seat. As
if someone else were driving.

Garner knew, as soon as he went into his house, that someone had
been here. Nothing was disturbed, not that he could see. There wasn't
much to disturb: he had one battered colorless sofa, one kitchen table
and two chairs, an RCA Victor record player circa 1971, a rack of
records, several shelves of books, an old FM radio, some stationery,
exactly seven changes of clothing, one wicker clothes basket, some
dishes and pots and cutlery, a calendar from the hardware store, and
four towels. That was the sum total of his possessions. It saved him a
lot of misery and energy waste, keeping things simple.

He went to the dirty clothes basket, he wasn't sure why. Then he
bent down and poked through it. His Alan Watts t-shirt was gone.

Someone had taken it. Only that: a T-shirt, still dirty, that he'd worn
just this morning.

*   *   *

Coach Barris was walking on the sand, under cliffs where springs made shiny snailtracks down the stone and the wind hummed, ticking sand.

Corinne was stretched out in a patch of sunlight, sheltered by a half-buried grey white treetrunk, stripped of its bark by years grinding on tide-submerged sand. The driftwood treetrunk looked like some strange sea creature itself, its broken-off branches like seeking stubs of tentacles, about to roll over onto her . . .

She was wearing a tank top and shorts. Her skin was golden, her hair long and straight and shiny-black.

The sun was behind him as he stood over her; she rolled onto her back and tried to shade her eyes with one hand, squinting to see who it was.

What am I doing? he wondered.

But it was so distant, that question. So distant from what he was saying and doing.

"Hi, Corinne," he said. "Aren't you cold?"

"No, the log's protecting me from the wind. Do I know you? I can't see who you are . . ."

He put his hand on the little tape recorder in his coat pocket.

Garner stood on his porch, listening. Listening and feeling.

Way down the beach, a man stood half hidden by driftwood, looking downward. Garner couldn't see who it was.

Something moved closer by, making him start a little. But it was only a cat. A Siamese cat moving sinuously along the line of the old fence. The cat stopped to look at him. Its white-tan body almost disappeared against the sand so that the black mask of its Siamese face seemed to hang suspended in space, gazing enigmatically at him.

Garner said, "Shoo!" and waved his hands sharply and the cat ran way. Then he chuckled, shook his head at himself. He shaded his eyes and peered down the beach, toward the maze of driftwood. There was a place to pull over, for the view, atop the cliffs overlooking the beach.

There was just one vehicle there. A dull-blue van. The van was parked close to the edge, as if its windshield was its eyes watching the man standing in the driftwood, below. Garner couldn't see into the van windows, from the glare, but he knew someone was sitting in the van.

He started down the beach.

Bragonier felt something pressing on the outer membrane of his hemisphere of concentration.

Within that hemisphere he held Barris, pinned, contained, subordinated. He could sense the girl—could see her through Barris's eyes.

But there was an interference pattern in the bubble of his psychic attention. Then the chill of recognition again: the other who had Achieved. The one with the rake; the one whose house he'd entered.

Right on time. Let him come.

He withdrew his attention from Barris, putting the towel he'd stolen from Barris' locker in the back seat, and took the dirty T-shirt out of the glove compartment.

"Coach?" There was fear in the girl's voice. She'd heard about Jonquil.

Barris felt more or less the same fear she felt, as he looked around.

For the first time in twenty years he was close to bursting into tears, realizing he had no clue, none, how he'd come here. The afternoon sun had turned the seaward face of the waves glare white.

He had moved close to her and she'd backed away, her knees drawn up defensively . . .

"Didn't mean to scare you," Coach Barris said. "Just taking a walk."

He climbed over the log and hurried away, down the beach toward the wooden stairs that zigzagged up the cliffside to the highway.

She sat up and saw another man walking toward her. She knew him . . .

The Reverend something . . .

Garner felt an uneasiness descend over him. It was an unfamiliar feeling, but distinctive. It was a unique wrongness, and he realized that he was displaced, somehow, from the center of his being. That he was not there anymore; he was only a viewpoint, a dreamer dreamed. And he watched himself walk toward the girl Corinne who was looking past him at the coach, saying something Garner wasn't hearing. The wind blew sand into her eyes, and she turned, her hair streaming to hide her face, and put her fingers to her eyes to rid herself of the sand, and he moved closer to her.

Garner said, inwardly, in a certain place and with immaculate clarity: *Jesus, son of God, have mercy on me, a sinner.*

Then he turned his attention away from everything outward—from the girl who was looking toward him with startled eyes—and he turned inward, sensing himself in the sensations within the sensations, and found himself there, and centered himself, and moved his awareness of himself outward from that unnameably energized center until he again found his physical embodiment once more, his interface with the outer world, and then he coalesced his sensations within his heart and body and mind, and was joyfully whole again.

Bragonier blinked, startled, and tried to regain control as Garner stopped walking toward the girl. As Garner turned, and looked up at the van. As Garner began to walk toward the stairs.

Bragonier had been confident the ambush would work; that Garner would be caught unprepared. He'd underestimated him.

Bragonier tightened his grip on the T-shirt and focused his psychical attention, using the Method, and reached out once more to Garner— but now it was as if he couldn't see Garner at all. As if Garner were hidden in a luminous cloud of unreadable identity.

Then the van's passenger-side door opened, and Garner was standing there, looking in at him with an infuriating pity. He felt rage crackle in him as Garner looked into him . . . Garner invading him! Reading his mind, and recoiling from it with disgust . . .

Bragonier reached into the open glove compartment and took out the .38 and then . . .

Then it was as if he were watching himself freeze in mid-motion. Watching himself hesitate—and put the gun in his pants pocket.

Bragonier watching himself, a dreamer dreamed, starting the van— with Garner sitting silently beside him now, the two of them in the van—driving down the highway. Watching himself pull up to let Garner out a block from the sheriff's station. Watching himself drive to the sheriff's station, stop the van, double parked. He took out the gun for a moment, sitting there; a minute later he put it back in his pocket, and got out of the van.

He saw himself walking into the sheriff station. Saw himself in the station's outer room approaching the two deputies at the blond oak counter. Their nametags said *FISHER* and *MURCHOWSKI*.

Bragonier tried to struggle, on some level, somewhere within himself, to regain command, but a shock went through the fiber of his nearly-immortal soul as he realized that *it wasn't only Garner* who was holding him this way.

Garner was a sort of intermediary for this other hand, this infinite grasp that had reached out to him by means of Garner's subjective, human capacity for choice . . .

He heard himself say, to the cops, "If you go to my house, at 23 Wilson Drive, and look behind the plasterboard wall in the basement, you'll find a cabinet shaped like a coffin standing on end. In it there are videos I took of the women I murdered . . . Jonquil Mills and Da-nella Johnson and others, from the other places. I killed them all, and you'll see the evidence in that cabinet—If you get there alive, I mean—"

Then he put his hand on the .38 in his pocket.

That's when control returned to him; when Bragonier found he could move at his own volition.

Both cops were moving toward him: the younger one, Fisher, draw-ing a gun, the other deputy brandishing handcuffs, telling him to get down on the floor.

If they took him . . .

He pulled the pistol, and pointed it at them, shouting, and stumbled backwards.

Afterward, when they were sure Bragonier was dead, Fisher looked at the .38. It was unloaded.

They found the bullets later on the passenger seat of the van.

Garner hand-washed his Alan Watts T-shirt, and put the other dirty clothes in the washing machine. Then he did a little housework. There was never much housework to do.

When he was sweeping, he paused to listen for a moment when one of the neighbors opened a window letting out the sound of an old

Beatles album. *"You can radiate everything you are . . ."* they sang. He had to smile at that.

Then the phone rang: it was Mrs. Twilley, who was crying with relief because all charges against her husband had been dropped. Jeff didn't remember that night, still, but they think maybe he was attacked and drugged by the lunatic who'd boasted about the murders to the police before trying to shoot it out with them.

Garner gathered they'd dropped charges against the coach too, but she was talking so quickly it was hard to make out for sure. He suggested she give a prayer of thanksgiving and she said she'd been doing that all day, but now it was beginning to hit her that she'd never see her niece again. The grief over Danella was returning.

That reminded him that he needed to find some way to visit the girl's locker room at the high school, when no one was there. In case Jonquil was clinging.

He made an appointment to talk to Latesha about her niece—mostly he would just listen to her talk about the girl—and they hung up. He checked his watch. He didn't have a hospital meeting till the afternoon.

After drinking a cup of Red Rose tea and eating a bowl of Berry-Berry Kix, he went outside and got his rake. It was still pretty windy: whitecaps flashed the sun back from the sea.

Garner used the wide-toothed metal rake slowly, making neat, circular rake-lines around the shrubs and rocks in the front yard. The wind came through the slumped picket fence and erased his work, soon after he laid it down. He worked his way from one end of the yard to the other, then checked his watch: An hour and fifteen minutes till his appointment at the hospice. Mrs. Chen was dying.

He went back to raking, retracing his steps back where he'd just been, in the places where the wind had erased the previous raking. He made slow circular marks around the shrubs and rocks and a dusty old conch shell. The wind erased his work behind him.

Then he paused and looked toward the house. He waited, leaning the rake against the porch. Inside, the phone rang. He smiled and went into the house.

In The Road

Cecily's Mom was in even more of a hurry than usual. She had to take Cecily to her tumbling class, and pick Eddy up at Soccer, and then pick up Daddy at the airport. Daddy was always on his way to the airport or coming from it, and sometimes they had "time with him" at the airport itself, when he was there between flights. He was a Franchise Set Up Specialist; she didn't know what that was, except that it meant he had to crisscross the country, occasionally just passing through the town he lived in. But he was going to be here for Thanksgiving. He said he would play Monopoly with her, on Thanksgiving.

Driving the Ford SUV down Burberry Street, Mom was spindling the little hook of auburn hair that followed the curve of her face and pointed at her chin, which was pointy also, and there was another hook of hair pointing from the other side of her face, so that was three points, Cecily decided; also the point of mom's sharp noise: four. Mom's blue eyes, though, were soft and far away; they didn't exactly look at anything. Her gaze was passing over the Palo Alto cul de sacs and palm trees and spouting sprinklers on big green lawns, but never seemed to fix on anything.

Not quite thinking these things, Cecily was riding beside her Mom, proud that she was old enough to do that now, it was legal and everything. "You have your Creative Crafts class on Sunday," Mom said. "Remind me of that so I don't forget to take you."

" 'Kay." But Cecily resolved to forget to, because she'd rather stay home and watch cartoons, and Yancy might come over and play Barbies.

"There's where my teacher said her sister lives," Cecily said, pointing at a side street. "She told me that when I told her where I lived."

"Huh yeah?"

Adults never seemed interested in things like that. But Cecily thought it was interesting.

There was something bloody in the road, up ahead. It was moving.

"Mom—oh!—what's that?"

Mom's sort of looked and her gaze flicked away. "A squirrel."

"It's sick. Can we help it?"

"What? No. It was hit by a car."

"So what, we could help it."

"It's not going to live, Cecily. It was hit by a car. It was in the road."

"It's still moving. It's trying to get out of the road. There was blood."

"It was in the road. Things get hit." She turned on the radio, the K-Lite station, which meant she didn't want to talk anymore.

Cecily looked out the back window but couldn't see the squirrel anymore; they'd gone around a curve and left it way behind.

2nd

A year later, Cecily went to her friend Yancy's birthday party. Her older brother Eddy went too, sulking the whole time; he didn't want to go to his sister's girlfriend's party with a bunch of girls, but Mom needed him to walk Cecily home afterwards, because she had to go to her support group, and Dad was out of town.

At the party, Cecily felt let down. It was all sunny in the backyard and there was crepe twirling overhead and pinata candy and those little party bags full of cool junk to take home, and laughing girls, but Yancy was ignoring her. She hadn't said anything about the present Cecily had given her, she just opened it and went onto the next one, and now she was playing with Kathy and Moira, and hardly looked up when Cecily spoke. I'm supposed to be her best friend, Cecily thought.

She went wandering around the house looking for Eddy, to see when they were going home, and couldn't find him for a long time, then heard him yelling, "Whoa! Phat!" from upstairs in Yancy's house.

Yancy's half brother, a grown up guy named Vernon, was staying there, because he got kicked out of college and didn't have any place else to go—that's what Yancy said—and Eddy was upstairs in Vernon's room watching Vernon playing a computer game.

Vernon had long stringy brown hair and a goatee that was hard to see and skinny arms but a bulging middle. He wore a fading t-shirt that said *Id Software* on it, beginning to pop out holes along the seams. Eddy, who was thirteen, was perched on the edge of Vernon's bed; Vernon had let the sheets get rumpled onto the floor so there was just a bare mattress. Eddy sat leaning forward, staring over Vernon's shoulder, his buck teeth sticking out of his gaping mouth, twitching every time there was an explosion on the PC screen. For some reason, she thought of the squirrel in the road. She hadn't thought of it in almost a year.

"What do *you* want?" Eddy asked her, not looking away from the computer. He squeezed a pimple as he watched the game; he twitched.

"Just to see when we're leaving."

Eddy didn't answer her, instead saying to Vernon, "Whoa—you broke the skin."

"That's when it gets serious, dude," Vernon said, like he was sneering at Eddy. Then Vernon sucked some air through his clenched teeth, real hard and fast, like he was in pain.

She saw that he *was* in pain—there was a sort of clamp like a miniature bear trap with built-in metal teeth gripping his arm, and there was a wire running from the piston-driven jawlike device to the back of the computer. Whenever Vernon got shot in the game, the spikes clamped down and dug into his arm. Real spikes digging into his real arm. The toothy clamp looked like it was put together with duct tape and wires and little nails . . .

"The only way to play a killgame," Vernon was saying, "is on the hardest setting—ow, shit!—and with no saves, and with real pain.

Then you're not full of shit . . . you're a real warrior . . . Shit, they got me . . ."

Her stomach lurched as she watched the toothy clamp convulsively bite down on his arm—with extra force when he was killed. It was like when Aunt Colleen's dog was shaking a dog-toy, growling and grinding it with its teeth. But it was his arm, not some toy, and it was grinding it up into hamburger, and blood was running down his arm, to drip off the elbow onto the rug.

"Whoa dude," Eddy said admiringly, as Vernon started the game over again. "You are serious."

Then Vernon's step-mom came in, and started yelling at him, so Eddy and Cecily went home.

Monday at school, Yancy made up with Cecily, and invited her over after school, and Mom said it was okay as long as she went to her Jazz Dancing class before going to Yancy's, because Mom could pick her up at Yancy's on the way to the airport to get Dad.

Going from Yancy's bedroom, where they were dressing Barbies, to the bathroom, Cecily stopped in front of Vernon's partly open bedroom door—there was something she'd seen out of the corner of her eye that made her stop and look. It was the gun in Vernon's hand, one of those shiny silver revolvers. He was sitting on the edge of the bed, with his arm all bandaged up, twirling the revolver on his index finger. Hunched over the twirling gun, staring at it.

He stopped twirling the gun, and looked up, and scowled at her; reached out and slammed the door in her face.

That night, Cecily couldn't sleep. Her Dad came in to her bedroom to see her; he seemed relieved when she didn't want him to read to her. Him and Mom were having cocktails and watching the Spice channel. She knew it was that because she heard the Spice Channel *oh-oh-oh* sounds when she went by the bedroom door. "Can't sleep, kiddo?" Dad asked. He was standing by her bed with his hands in pockets, rocking on the balls of his feet.

"Dad?"

"What?"

"Yancy's big brother, Vernon, was playing with a gun today."

"Was he? What kind of gun?"

"A real gun."

"I don't think you'd know a real one from a toy gun. It could've been an air pistol. But then he's old enough to legally have a real gun, too. How was he playing with it?"

"Spinning it and looking at it."

"So? Guns aren't toys but . . ." He shrugged.

"He had this thing on his arm that chewed it up when he plays computer games. It was all bloody."

"I know about those—Eddy bought one from some kid and I took it away."

"Vernon's, like, sick or something. He's . . . I mean . . ."

She didn't know how to explain. She was sure of it, but didn't know how to say it so it sounded real.

"Forget it. He's a loser, that boy. Not our problem."

"What if. . . . he's going to die."

Dad looked out the window; Cecily followed his gaze. The bushes moved in the wind, seemed to nod in agreement with Cecily.

"Well, Cecily—there's nothing we can do about it if he's going down. That's his Mom and Dad's problem."

"Can't you talk to them?"

"I don't know. We'll see."

But she knew that meant *no way*.

Dad didn't talk to Vernon's parents. Three months later, Vernon shot himself dead.

It was their problem, Dad had said. But they went to the funeral, and at the funeral she heard Vernon's parents say they didn't know the boy was that despondent, and Cecily heard her Dad say "Don't blame yourself, there's no way you could have known."

3rd

Two days before Cecily was to graduate from Middle School, she heard that Harrison and the jock kids were planning something for Goop.

Goop was a seventh grader, whose Dad had insisted his boy be allowed to play basketball in the intramural games. He was a whip-thin kid, with a long neck; his posture drooped, and his chin was weak,

his eyes really big—"like an alien from the X Files," Harrison said—
and he had a tendency to laugh at things no one else laughed at. Mr.
Conners the English teacher said that Goop, whose real name was
Christian Heinz, was "the very imp of unpopularity"; said it laughing
and shaking his head. Mr. Conners had once gotten in trouble with
some lawyer for pulling several tufts of those soft little hairs from the
arm of a seventh grader to punish him for talking back.

Goop had wanted to try intramural basketball, because he'd been
practicing shooting baskets for hours, and they hadn't wanted to let
him do it, especially because the Surfers were expecting to win the
school trophy against the Shredders, and he would be in the Surfers
basketball team because of which PE teacher he had. But Goop's Dad
insisted and insisted some more and the Principal spoke to the PE
Teacher—so they let Goop play in Harrison's team: The Surfers. Only,
shooting baskets alone is different than shooting them when someone
is waving their hands in your face, and in the championship game Goop
kept tensing up and missing when he got the ball. But he kept trying,
just insisting on trying, when really he should've just hung back and
been a guard and stayed out of the way. But "he was, all, trying to
prove himself," Yancy said. And he just proved he was still the Goop.

Harrison's team lost the school trophy, and it was, anyway, just this
stupid little four dollar fake-gold trophy, but Harrison took it really
seriously.

So, as curious as anyone, Cecily was there, after school, standing in
the very midst of a cool June late afternoon. She was waiting, with
about thirty other kids, by the small wooden bridge over the creek
behind the school; Cecily's big brother Eddy had even come over from
the high school to see. The sun came and went and came again through
the patchwork of clouds skimming across the sky, as Goop plodded
obliviously up the path between the track and the football field, toward
the little foot-bridge, carrying his books. He was staring at the ground,
as he went, sagging like the books he was carrying had their weight
multiplied by his misery.

He stopped and stared, just before the bridge, seeing Harrison leaning both forearms on one of the metal, concrete-filled yellow posts that
blocked the bridge; the posts were to keep people from driving cars or

motorcycles over it. Harrison was a tall kid with bright but empty blue eyes and skin that looked so smooth it was like doll-skin to Cecily—she was having trouble with acne then—and his cheeks were always more red than a boy's cheeks should be. But he was a tall, cute guy, who was good at sports, the hair on the side of his head cut into corn-row patterns, and everybody approved of him.

Goop put up a hand to hood his eyes so he could see against the glare; then the sun went behind the cloud and he saw all the kids waiting there, all watching him raptly, many of them grinning. He said, "Okay, I'm stupid, okay." He turned to go back the other way—turned clumsily, in a hurry, so he dropped some of his books and the papers loosely piled in his binder and they went scattering all over the ground. Everyone laughed.

Goop bent over to pick them up.

Shaking his head in disbelief—as if he couldn't believe Goop would let himself be that vulnerable now—Harrison set himself athletically on his left foot, poised like a goalkicker, and slammed Goop hard in the tailbone the point of his right Nike high top, and the boy pitched forward onto his face, yelling in pain.

"You asshole," Harrison said. "You fucked everybody up."

Harrison grabbed Goop by the ankles and dragged him toward the bridge. Goop twisted this way and that like a fish on a hook. Harrison laughed.

Cecily got a twisty-tight feeling in her gut. She thought she saw Mr. Conners over by the bleachers, picking up some baseball equipment—he had been assistant coach besides teaching English—and she found herself walking over to him, after being careful the others weren't watching her. They weren't taking their eyes off Goop and Harrison.

She looked back when she was about halfway and saw that Harrison and two other kids, including her own brother, were kicking something in the grass by the bridge; the other kids starting to get looks of panic, backing away.

Mr. Conners was only about forty yards off. She was surprised he hadn't noticed anything going on. He was closing a duffelbag when she got there, and looked up, ran his fingers through his thinning, shoulder length brown hair; his crooked smile crooking a little more as he recognized her. "Cecily, isn't it?"

"Yeah. Um—I think Harrison's, all, beating up on Goop?"

"Goop? Oh—the Heinz kid? They fighting on school property?"

"I think it's off school land. It's by the creek. But they're not fight-ing . . ."

"Well if they're not fighting, what are we talking about?"

"Goop's not fighting. Just Harrison. I mean, he's hitting Goop."

Conners snorted. "I don't blame him a *whole* lot. The kid *would* go on shooting. Trying to show off, when he knew . . ."

"Yeah. I just . . . But . . . Harrison's, all, kicking him."

"Well, it's not on school property."

" 'kay."

She turned, hesitating, drawn to see what was going on by the bridge—they seemed to be down at the creek now, she could just make out the top of their heads over the grass, because they were all standing on the bank of little stream.

But she turned and walked the other way, to get the number 34 bus to the Tae Bo class she was taking with her Mom.

It wasn't the slugging or the kicking, really, that did it, she found out, a few weeks later. A friend of Mom's was married to a doctor who'd worked on Goop at the hospital, after the incident at the bridge, and they found out from him: it was the lack of oxygen. Goop had fallen with his head in the water, face down, his body slanting up the bank; his weight holding his head down. He was dazed and weak and not able to get himself out of that odd position.

And the kids had left him there, assuming he'd get out. That's what Eddy said.

Goop didn't die, though. It was just brain damage.

He couldn't remember how to read and write, and he walked almost sideways, after that, and one of his eyes was blind. But it wasn't the hitting, so much as the oxygen loss and the brain cells dying. No one went to jail, but there was some kind of settlement, or something.

4th

In a thickly-hot early August, when Cecily was fourteen and a half, she was getting ready to go to her singing lesson, when the thing happened with the Ice Cream man. She was yelling at her Mom, "Mom where's that Mariah Carey songbook? I need it for the lesson!" when her own shout was almost lost in the yelling from the street.

For a couple of minutes some part of her mind had noticed that the Ice Cream truck was in the street, or close by: she'd heard the amplified tinkling of the song the truck had played for years now as it cruised slowly through the neighborhood: Yankee Doodle. Like a giant rolling music box, it played Yankee Doodle over and over and over and over, the end looping into the beginning. She'd often wondered how the guys who drove the grubby little white trucks with the stickers on them could stand the same sound going on and on and on for, what, nine hours a day. It would make you into a psychokiller, she thought. But maybe they didn't really hear it after a while.

It was annoying enough, anyway, just hearing it drive through the neighborhood, Mom had said once. You heard the song coming, and you heard the song going.

What Cecily had noticed, as she was looking through the pile of stuff on the little table in the front hall for the Mariah Carey songbook, was that the song had cut off suddenly. A moment later there was all the yelling.

She found the songbook on the floor, leaning up against a table leg, and yelled "Never mind!" at her Mom, and went out to get the bus to her voice lesson, and then she saw all the people in the street gathered around the ice cream truck. It was really hot, and the air conditioners weren't working, because the electric company had shut down their neighborhood for a couple of hours—rolling intentional brownouts due to excessive electricity use in hot weather, it was called—and everyone was sweating and squinting; the heat rippled up from the asphalt.

She recognized Mr Farmer, from across the street; and the red-faced man who worked on classic cars from down at the dead end; the two Italian sisters who lived together from the split level on the corner; those four college aged boys who liked to sit in their cars and listen to loud hip hop in the driveway; Mr Hinh, the Vietnamese man who owned the liquor store; that fat guy who collected old Harley David-sons; and two big blond men she didn't know. They were all in a circle around the little Pakistani guy who drove the ice cream truck up and down all day. And there was a seven year old girl with greasy black hair who looked delighted by all the adults yelling.

Cecily walked over to see what all the commotion was. Mr Farmer was arguing with some of the others. "I just don't think you should hit him again—"

"I'll tell you what," the fat guy in the Harley t-shirt was saying, "this guy and his people have been warned again and again. The kid gives him two dollars for a dollar-fifty ice cream, he gives the kid the ice cream and fifty cents worth of junk candy instead of change—more like ten cents worth, he's *calling* fifty cents worth. It's stealing from children."

"And sometimes," the red faced man chimed in, "he doesn't give any change of any kind. They know the kids won't say anything usually if they just keep the change."

"Sure," the taller, gray haired Italian lady said. "They sell this hor-rible junk that makes sores in the mouth—they did this to my niece, candy that made her sick. And they lie about the change all the time—"

Cecily saw, then, that the little Pakistani guy was breathing hard, with a hand pressed to his nose; blood streamed through his fingers. Twice she saw him try to push through the circle of people to get back inside the truck—twice the men pushed him back against the sticker-covered side of the truck; against Dream Cream stickers and Frozen Three Musketeers Bar stickers and Sweet Tart stickers and Eskimo Pie stickers.

"Cocksucker is stealing from children!" the red-faced man shouted.

One of the Italian ladies escorted the little girl—who didn't want to leave—away from the truck. The girl went but kept looking back, grinning. She'd complained or something and it'd led to all this, Cecily guessed.

"My boss they tell me do this!" the Pakistani guy said, in a piping voice. "They tell me, my Uncles, it is not my truck, they say no change, only candy! I don't steal but they tell me—!"

"These people are not honest!" Mr Hinh said, "they deserve to be taught something!"

"It is not me—they make me do this! It is my only job!" the little man wailed.

"You see, it's a goddamn *policy* of ripping off kids!" the biker guy said. "Fuck you, pal, you didn't have to go along with it!" And he straight-armed the Pakistani guy against the side of the truck.

The Pakistani man gave a high pitched cry of anger and fear and kicked the biker in the crotch. The big man bellowed in pain and clutched at himself and the Pakistani tried to rush past him, but Mr Hinh tripped the Pakistani and as he fell one of the college boys from down the street brought his knee up sharply into the falling man's throat, so that you could hear cartilage crunching, and he fell choking. The crowd backed away from him, and after a moment began to move off, shaking their heads; except the red faced man and Mr Hinh and the biker; they shouted at the little man, things like "You tell those people we don't want your thieving Paki ass in here anymore!" And the biker, as white faced as the man next to him was flushed, kicked the Pakistani hard, once, in the side of the neck, and then turned and marched away. The others followed, muttering; shrugging. There was just Cecily about thirty feet away from the little man, who was spitting blood, coughing, gurgling.

Cecily didn't need to hear her Mom shouting at her to get away from there. She knew what to do. She walked off, on her own, to the bus stop. She'd practiced the Mariah Carey song all week and she thought she had it down.

About ten minutes later, as the bus carried her around a corner; she looked back and glimpsed the man lying still in the middle of the road next to his truck. She was surprised to hear no ambulance coming.

Mr Farmer had thought about calling it, he told her Mom, but he'd heard you could end up having to pay for the cost of the ambulance if you called. Mom later said she thought that wasn't true, but she wasn't sure. Cecily heard, later, the Ice Cream truck driver choked to death on blood.

"Huh," Cecily said, when she heard that.

5th

Cecily was driving her small blond daughter Shelly to her first Kids Kreative Klass at the Montesori school, on a wet day in February, when Shelly pointed at the small white dog twitching in the road up ahead.

"Oh—I'm glad you saw that, hon," Cecily said. "I might not have seen it—"

As it was, she was able to drive around it with no trouble. It might've gotten on her tires.

"Couldn't we see what's wrong with it?" Shelly asked.

"No. Do you want your juice packet? You didn't have any juice for breakfast."

"Why not, why can't we?"

"Why can't we what?"

"See if the dog . . ."

". . . It's not our dog. It was in the road. It was just in the road. Do you want this juice or not?"

" 'kay."

They were on time for the class, but Shelly would've preferred to stay home and play videogames.

PART TWO

...And Soon

To Make Children Good

"The best way to make children good is to make
them happy."

—Oscar Wilde

Though it irritated both human and robotic nurses, Gwinn kept
the little digital recorder on his hospice bed, where he could reach it
without having to fumble on the night stand. His trembling hands had
knocked over two glasses of water already, that week. The gravity was
so light, in the OGT—Orbital Geriatric Thera-center—that he could
easily have caught them, if he'd been younger.

When the graviton feed had broken for a few hours last week, can-
celing their orbital gravity altogether, he'd deliberately knocked a glass
over—creating a crystalline water-sculpture in the air; the silvery brush-
stroke of water slowly broke up to become a miniature precipitation
front as the gravity gradually came back on.

Now, he propped the recorder wand carefully on his chest, holding
it with one hand resting on his sternum. That way it didn't tremble
overmuch. "This device," he said, his voice creaking into the recorder,
"would record me visually, if I wanted; would hook up with a palm-
screen, transcribe so I could edit—and I don't want it to do any of
those things. I just want to talk to it. I wish it could nod gravely back
to me. But I'm just lying here in my permanent pajamas making recording 29 . . ."

He paused to work up some saliva to make speech easier; finding
saliva was a chore, at the age of 104, even here in orbit.

"A couple of decades ago, I think it was about 2054, I gave up trying to pretend I could keep up with technological trends. I tell myself that the world is supposed to pass me by. I've tried making a pass at the night-nurse, but since she's a robot, shaped like an industrial vacuum cleaner, I don't even get a ..." What was the word? F-a-c ... something. Pronounced *fass*. A word he would once never have had to struggle for. Go for a, what do you call it, a synonym: "... I don't even get a whimsical response. T'wouldn't be natural, regardless of those finely tuned 'lovemates', with the vat-grown human skin on them, that console lonely men ..." He paused, worked wetness into his mouth, managed, "... yes, those terribly ironic devices notwithstanding ... My opinion, however, is that anything is natural that doesn't revolt the ecology or further debase humanity."

He looked thoughtfully at the window, gathering his thoughts; outside was a long, high-ceilinged corridor, with transparent-steel panes in the ceiling that let in some of the light of the sun, and, sometimes, a glimpse of the fulsome blue-white arc of the Earth. He heard a hydrogen-cell air car hum softly by; he stared at the light striping through the window. Related the whirling dust-motes to his own thoughts. One good wind ...

On the shelf under the window, not quite within reach, and next to the emergency graviton-feed, was a Sony-IBM Media Cluster, an oblong metal cluster of cryptic controls and small, arcane screens. One of his granddaughters had sent it to him. But it was difficult to sift through; so much of its offering was an outpouring of unregenerate imbecility, and he didn't know where to find the so-called educational channels, if they still existed. The Media Cluster converged hundreds of technologies and more into one box and then diverged them again as needed; that was natural for such media. Technology had its own nature.

"What is unnatural, of course, is ..."

Gwinn paused as a tall, broad shouldered young man entered the room. Something familiar in the shape of him. Muscles delineated by a tight bodysuit printed with blocky patterns artfully borrowed from some 20th century abstract expressionist.

Gwinn couldn't make out his face well from here, and took him for one of the young journalists who tried to get some mileage out of the old hack—as Gwinn thought of himself—from time to time; he signaled for him to wait. He didn't want to lose his thought. And perhaps it would be impressive to be seen composing even now . . . The stranger nodded—that nod so almost-familiar—and leaned against the wall by the door to wait, arms crossed . . .

"What is unnatural," Gwinn resumed, "is the way the elderly are kept alive long past infirmity. My father wouldn't have agreed—he was so into his baby-boomer youth fantasy. His death must've been quite a shock to him . . . My mind . . . my mind is reasonably sharp; but its center, too, does not hold . . . I seem to perceive a daily decay of . . . it's a good joke on me that I cannot think of the word, here—cognitive! . . . Decay of cognitive quality. Of course I was very sick in my late '70s— would probably have died then, but for three organ transplants, and other minor rejuvenations . . . And there are those who have lived handily, though miserably, to 130—the quality of their life is not good; they're like those boneless figures from Salvador Dali, slumped over arbitrary crutches on an empty landscape . . . But rejuvenation on the cellular level, repair of individual cells, millions and millions of them one by one, that is what's needed—for real rejuvenation—and it is what I don't have, what no one has . . . I have heard people in these hospices say they're weary of life and ready to go, and perhaps they are. I am not one of those. I did not understand the possibilities of life terribly well till I was in my late sixties . . . Then I was a semi-invalid, though still productive as a journalist, for twenty years . . . My Pulitzer, however, was long past . . . No, I deeply envy those capable of living thoroughly. Overcrowded and casually brutal the world may be— over-complex, despite the moratorium on invasive new technologies in the last decade. But I want to enter the fray anyway, and I resent nature for keeping that flame alive in me while snuffing out the means to carry it into the field . . . I try to sustain some meaning with these probably unpublished notes of a 20th century man's last days in the 21st century . . . Well, enough for now, as I seem to have a visitor."

He took his thumb from the recording tab, squinting at the young man as he sat down in the chair by the bed. The stranger was blurred by those spots of murk that moved about in Gwinn's vision. The retinal

implants he'd had put in twenty years ago needed replacing, but there
didn't seem much point, now, the doctor having leveled with him:
sometime this winter, barring a breakthrough in cellular rebuilding,
there is some work in that area but we won't have general therapeutic
access to it for another ten years or so ... if ever ... What did the doctor
mean, precisely, by "if ever"?

"Hello," the young man said. "Uncle James?"

"I am James Gwinn." He paused, till his mouth should become op-
erational again. He'd already given it a great workout. "Are we ...
related?"

"I'm a sort of second grand nephew or something. One of your
nephew Darian's sons. Rafe."

"Rafe. Would you be so kind as to hand me that glass of water,
Rafe? Don't let go of it till I've got a good grip ... The gravity is slower
here, if that's the word, but the graviton flow keeps it in vigor ... No
I can deal with it now, the straw ... but it takes both hands, as you
can see ... thank you ... Well, have a seat, Rafe ... You'll forgive me
if I keep the glass on my chest here ... If we are to talk, I'll need
occasional sips ... I've been holding forth already this morning ...
something I'm pretending to write ..."

"Perhaps this isn't a good time ..."

"Might well be ... the only time. And you break up the monotony,
my boy."

"How are you feeling?"

"Not bad. Painkillers now are very efficient. They don't knock me
out as the old ones did. And the lower gravity here, the null-grav
sessions—those are a relief. Old folks who can't walk on Earth floating
about in big padded rooms—if they aren't subject to nausea. Quite a
sight. So. What can I do for you?"

"I ... have brought a message from your son. Bruce."

"Bruce! He might've phoned, or done a pix, rather than sending an
... oh what's the word ... like diplomat."

"Emissary?"

"You got it. So. Why the emissary?" One of the spots swan aside
and he was able to see the young man's face more clearly. Yes, there
was family resemblance: that long, bumped nose; the lips that had to

try not to smirk. Even green eyes. The young man wore the sort of bodysuit favored by the buff, and Rafe was definitely buff. Though he wouldn't know that old term.

"Well—he thought you might hang up on him. And . . . he thought it'd be more personal, this way. Thought you might enjoy a visitor."

"He thinks I'm angry with him? If I was, I've forgotten why. I suppose I was, for awhile. His attitude toward his later Mother. Refusing to visit her at the end. But really, I understand. One can only bear what one can bear. Is he still in that . . . that casino in Antarctica?"

Rafe smiled. "Oh he was never in one of the casinos. But I'll bet you know that. He's still working in satellite control there, yes."

"I would've thought he'd be near retiring—he must be seventy-something now."

"No, he's had some new organs, a cerebral shunt . . . Not yet."

"I was actually going to try to write a letter, bury the hatchet . . . That's an old term, bury the hatchet . . ."

"I know that one. I mean—it's . . . sort of self explanatory."

"I was going to try to wheedle him into visiting me . . . Really he has no cause to hold any deep seated resentments. I put aside several grand projects when he was a boy, so I could be there, with him, till he was 16—I took him with me when I did my global tour for the New York Times Online. Certainly he had more of me than I had of my father."

"Oh—I had the impression you were close to your father."

"Not a bit of it. My father was too busy sulking because he'd given up a career in the arts to be an investment banker. Internet day trader specialist—you know, when the Internet was all grandiloquent, before the media blurred together . . . I was determined to be there for Bruce. We have a bot repairman here who has been to the beaches in Antarctica, the under-the-big-window beaches—underground beaches, it's something that still makes my stomach lurch to think of . . . Like those things . . . I've never quite gotten used to them . . ."

He crooked the crooked twig of an index finger at the upper corner of the wall, where it was irising seamlessly open, to disgorge a small swarm of nanobots, like metallic bees, testing the air for bacteria, darting about the room as inconspicuously as possible.

A moment later the door opened, a squat robot nurse rolled in, extended a warm vinyl sensor to take his vital signs—Gwinn waved it away. "Go, I have a visitor."

"How about a nice pee?" came the robot's soft, feminine voice said. It extended a hose toward his groin.

"No, good God, who programmed you for social protocol. Check your file on behavior during visitors."

"Oopsy doozy," it said, retreating.

Rafe watched it go, his gaze moving up to the deferential little swarm of nanobots as he nodded. "Bruce rarely comes up from the underground, except for a little seasonal cross-country skiing if conditions are right. I was passing through there, got in touch—wanted to get acquainted. He asked me for this favor . . . He wanted to come himself, but . . ."

"But—life! Life said 'Me first!' That I understand. I'm sure . . ."

Gwinn had to sip some water. "I'm sure I'd have been caught up in life just the same way, quite conscientiously, if my Father had lived to be that old . . . I'd have been no better about it. It's all part of the natural . . . what, the . . . oh Lord the memory boosters don't work for long . . . the natural severing, let's say . . . Mine and his both . . . I'm sorry, my mind runs to rambling . . ."

"Not at all. Thinking isn't rambling. I've . . . always admired you, you know. I read all of your books. I was quite proud to be related."

"You . . ." Gwinn wetted his mouth from the straw again. "Know just what to say. God bless you. Any particular message from Bruce?"

"Just to say . . . well not in words. He wanted me to take your hand . . ."

It'd been a while since any human being had surprised Gwinn. This was unexpected. He allowed his shaking, spotted, arthritis-bent hand to be taken in Rafe's steady, smooth, symmetrical one. There was a certain urgency in Rafe's touch. Perhaps Rafe hadn't known his grandfather; perhaps Rafe was one of those young men who ached for a grandfather because of some deficiency in his father. He tried to remember his grand-nephew Darian—he hadn't seen him but twice. He had a vague memory of Darian having four or five sons.

"So you're one of Darian's boys. How old are you?"

"Twenty four."

"Twenty four! Much to rejoice in, much to ensure yet. I'll resist the impulse to give advice. Darian's boy . . . I didn't know Darian well—I remember him as a slender young man himself . . . Very slender. There you are, so muscular. Not too muscular, not like a muscle fetishist—but certainly more than is common among the Gwinns. We were all such skinny-minnies."

"I don't feel 'all there' unless I'm buff," Rafe said, almost apologetically.

"God, do people still say 'buff'? I hadn't heard it used in so long. But then you've read all my outdated books. Or so you claim . . ."

He was talking to cover what he supposed was the young man's embarrassment. The expression on Rafe's face was so ambiguous. His eyes were moist.

"Oh I've read them all," Rafe said. *"The CIA and the Cartell . . ."*

"My first! Somehow lately I'm remembering it better than later books . . ."

". . . How the end of that one haunted me. Some people say it led to the fighting war against Columbia."

"It might've been . . . been one factor. If so I don't regret it. Unless one assumes that all wars are regrettable—are . . . are atrocities . . . And they are. It was about that time that I began to realize that humanity was one of nature's failed experiments; that there was too much beast in it, in all of us, to justify its going on . . . And I wrote *A Call For Voluntary Universal Sterilization*, and tried to pass it off as Swiftian, and got in such trouble . . . But I'll just get into another pointless reminiscence . . ."

"No . . . reminisce on whatever you like. I have an hour. Then I have to hustle to catch my flight. It's one of those completely automated flights and there's no one to beg to open the doors if you're late . . ."

There was something about the young man's face that bothered Gwinn, like a gnat darting at his mind; he couldn't quite catch it . . .

Rafe hesitated on the edge of his chair—then reached out with his other hand, and touched Gwinn's face, a fingertip stroke down along the old man's cheek. His young fingers trembled almost like Gwinn's old ones. Then suddenly he withdrew his hands. Gwinn could see him swallow.

"Could be, after all, that uh . . ." Rafe said, his voice breaking, ". . . I should go . . . I've done what he asked . . . I'm making a fool of myself . . ." He glanced at the upper wall as it irised shut behind the discreetly vanishing chrome bees. "Never got used to them myself . . ."

He stood up and went to the door.

Gwinn said, suddenly, "Wait. Would you do something for me? They won't do it here."

"What's that?" Rafe asked, turning back, eyes glistening.

"Open the window there for me. That one. About halfway. I want to hear the sound of people passing—the sound of life passing me by, yes, but still, I want to hear it . . ." Rafe hesitated, then went to the window. He examined the latch, worked it out, and shoved it up. "This style of window—Old fashioned."

"They like it that way, Dad," Gwinn said, "so the old folks who're too decrepit can't use power windows—they don't want them to open the windows. Not safe. And we take reassurance, here, in a few old fashioned touches, too."

Rafe was staring at him. "Did you . . ."

"I did call you Dad, yeah," said the old man to the young man. The young man, his father.

"That was too exactly the way Dad touched my face in his rare tender moments. He didn't often allow his emotions to overcome his anxiety about survival—he always had a sort of . . . sense of competition with us. He did, you did. I'm having trouble consistently saying 'you'— looking at you. I didn't even know you when you looked this young. It was as if . . . as if he . . . as if you—thought I was taking up some part of the world that should belong to you, because I was your off-spring . . . Yes and it wasn't only the touch, it was . . . your face, the way your eyes light and move away, and light again . . . the way . . . well, all of that could be inherited personality, characteristics in the family, but . . . not that scar on the back of your neck. I'll bet you paid them to get rid of it and they neglected it—with all the other work they did."

The young face stared at Gwinn. "No, they didn't neglect it—it's a flaw in the rejuvenation process. It replicates epidermal scar tissue."

"And Dad, unlike his kids, anyone else in the family, was the broad shouldered, muscular one. And here you are masquerading as your own great grand nephew so you can assuage your guilt over your son. That's a fine how-do-ya-do."

"I'm sorry—I should just go . . ."

"Dad," Gwinn asked. "How old are you now?"

"One hundred twenty seven," said his father. Gwinn's father: The man who'd called himself Rafe.

Gwinn nodded. His heart was thudding. He hoped it would thud him to death.

"You're 127. It wouldn't be funny to say you look good for your age. You faked the accident?"

"Took advantage of an accident. I fell from the car as it went over . . . I knew the sea was deep there and I saw the car smash on its way down . . . And I had the inspiration to do it . . . And Maria . . ."

"Yes. Mother was a bitch. A yenta, Sol used to call her—"

"Sol. Your agent."

"One of them. How many decades have you been out there, hiding from your family, Dad?"

The man who'd called himself 'Rafe' shrugged. "There were so many financial complications . . . I had some stock in Gerontek—the family didn't know about it . . . I knew they'd come up with the technique first . . . I might've lost the stock if anyone knew I was alive because of all those debts . . . and . . ."

"You had to create another identity—perhaps you had one ready, in case an opportunity came up?"

His father's young-old eyes looked away, as they always had.

"Yes. You did. You had the stock transferred to the other identity . . . Rafe, is it? And you bribed a lawyer somewhere?"

"Something like that."

"No real reason to risk the new life contacting children you were only occasional capable of feeling for . . . For whom you rationed your feelings—and we were on half rations . . ."

"That isn't fair—I felt a great deal. That's why I'm here. I had to come, at least say goodbye. But . . . I have to survive . . ."

"I suspected more than once you might be alive. No body found. Pictures, gewgaws you were sentimental about disappearing . . . Told myself it wasn't so—Didn't want to believe it, when I had that vile

period of black depression, the whole world of letters knew about—
such a small world, that one, now—and you must've known, I needed
such help, and you didn't come . . . And I had rather believe you dead
than capable of abandoning me at such a time . . ."

"I almost came . . ."

Gwinn snorted. "When did the rejuvenation happen?"

"About six months ago," Gwinn's father said. His voice barely audible.

"I take it, since you have some emotional baggage around me—
around your son—that you . . . that you would have offered me this
rejuvenation if you could have. At this point I mean."

"I . . . It's . . . it's very expensive. Complete cellular rebuilding . . .
From the bottom up, cell by cell . . . it costs seventeen million dollars,
son! It's all I had. The public hasn't been told because—well the social
issues. But the procedure can be done. You are living on a pension—
there's no way you could afford it. Your property is long since sold. I
had to sell all mine, and all my stock to afford this . . . It was . . . I
couldn't . . ."

"It was you or me, 'Rafe'? That's what you're trying not to say isn't
it . . . Daddy? You had a choice—rejuvenate your own son, or yourself.
Decades of pretending you're dead and then . . . you remake yourself
into someone else entirely. Perhaps, judging from your appearance,
you've chosen that path you whined about missing out on—gone back
to acting."

"I have a contract," he admitted. "I'm to star in a virtual movie."

"Under the name Rafe?"

"Yes . . . I haven't got much income yet—it's a decent part but it'll
be years before . . ."

"Before you have another seventeen million?"

"Yes. And I believe the price will be going up." He took a shaky
breath. "Son . . ." The young man said to the withered old man on the
bed, "If I'd had enough money—you'd have been the one that I reju-
venated, of my kids . . ."

"Get out, Dad. Get out. Go. I have a revulsion for the unnatural—
that means you."

Gwinn's beautiful young father left in haste and relief. Gwinn counted the seconds; he knew exactly how long to wait. As he waited, he plucked the little silver wand from its holster—the emergency graviton feed. He set it to discharge a significant heaviness. Then he got up—dizzy, swaying, his poor balance almost betraying him. But he made it, staggered to the window, set his feet, and looked down; he saw the door open . . . He aimed the wand of the graviton feed at the media Cluster—in the lighter gravity here it would fall too slowly otherwise.

And he shoved the media Cluster out the window.

It fell two stories and struck his father squarely on the head. He could see death in the way the body lay on the sidewalk; in the lush spread of the blood.

Old age was like gravity; you could compromise with it, to a point— but they'd found, in orbit, that in the long run they needed some gravity to stay healthy, to stay in "right relation" to the birth-world, to nature. Nature needed gravity, it was fundamental to its organization; so was entropy, in another direction, so was old age. The satisfaction he felt now was multi-leveled, like the GTC.

With some effort, he managed to close the window. Shaking with exhaustion, he went back to bed, and settled himself in to await developments. The nurses, fortunately, believed him incapable of getting out of bed on his own. He reached for his digital recorder, and spoke into it: "There are indeed satisfactions to be had, however, even at this point in life . . ."

Two Strangers

I was well out over the Barrens before I became aware of the leak in the fuel line of my Cherokee twin-engine. Two hundred miles from any outpost of white men, with less than ten minutes of engine time left. It was summer—if I set down at this time of year at least I wouldn't freeze, and there was a chance that I could make my way back to the RCMP outpost.

It was July of 1950, and far to the West the Korean War seethed, but its echoes hadn't reached the North Canadian wilderness. Here, a few hundred miles northwest of Churchill and the coast of Hudson Bay, in the Mackenzie District, was the most desolate region of Canada, and no sensible white man ventured into it. Me? Nothing sensible about me. I was searching for land likely to be hiding oil deposits.

I glimpsed something symmetrical in the random grey brown labyrinth of ridges and ravines below. A village? I circled lower. The swell and dip of the rugged land grew steeper, just as waves begin to lift before a rising storm at sea.

The engine muttered to itself and then fell spitefully silent. The only sound now was the keening of the wind. We began to fall. I caught a spinning glimpse of lake shore and black smoke rising from a ring of huts, and then an updraft slapped the nose of the plane upward and I tried to angle into a glide. I was partly gaining altitude when my little plane smacked into the dark face of the lake.

It was two days before I woke.

Pain and a bright light. The light was from a campfire, the pain from my left leg. Smoke stung my eyes; there were overwhelming odors of sweat and decayed caribou flesh. The summer tent was barely weather resistant: streaks of sky showed along the joints, between the stretched skins. Half the smoky, twilit enclosure was taken up by a sleeping mat of willow twigs and lichens covered with a fragmentary blanket of tanned hides. This was the communal bed where the entire family slept huddled together. The rest of the floor was littered with caribou scraps. An entire boiled head of deer, already well chewed over, glared at me from the pot with eyeless sockets. Hanging from the dozen pole supports were odd bits of clothing, boots, and parkas waiting for the long winter. I was lying on a soft bed of lichen, covered to the neck by a pitted deerhide. Three elderly women were my nurses, their wide, worn faces as creased as leathery funeral hides draped over an ancient burial mound. Seeing I was awake they clucked and rattled excitedly, and one of them sent out for the men.

I understood snatches of their conversation, and by their dialect guessed them to be Ilhalmiut, the People of the Deer. I tried to raise myself on an elbow to speak, only to fall back grunting as agony shot through my left leg and thigh. Broken bones in at least two places.

A great grinning moon filled the sky before me, broad and sallow: the blur melted and I recognized the face of an old friend. "Kakumei, I ..."

"Good to see you again," he said in his own tongue. "It has been nearly ten years since we worked together at the trading post." And then in the French he had learned working four years for the traders: "Lie still. We will tend you. You will be well soon."

I smiled but shook my head. Kakumei shouted orders. An old woman brought me a rough wooden bowl brimming with simmering deer fat and chopped innards. I ate it as if it was Mom's Apple Pie and then Kakumei imperiously ordered me to sleep. I obeyed.

My dreams were oddly elongated, like pulled taffy. I woke fitfully now and then, once to find a cloud of flies buzzing thickly over my open mouth. Another time I caught a timid gaggle of small children studying me with somber onyx eyes.

After a foggy while I seemed to see an odd little girl, perhaps seven years old, dexterously manipulating a strange metallic cylinder, a thing about six inches long and made of some unfamiliar alloy, like nothing that should be found among the Ilhalmiut. She was running the cylinder up and down my injured leg, not quite touching me. I had some delirious notion that she was trying to do me harm, and I raised a trembling hand to shoo her away, but she only smiled. There was something odd about her teeth. A tingly warmth penetrated the leg and the pain was ebbing . . .

It was night when I awoke. A fire nodded congenially to me. Kakumei was there, stirring coals to heat a cast-iron pot of deer-fat soup. Hearing me move he knelt beside me, smiling. "You have rested three days, friend Trumbull," he said, "and you will walk tomorrow, lazy one!"

"No. The leg is broken, brother Kakumei. I know your healer must be powerful, but—"

"Try the leg."

I shrugged, and to please him I cautiously moved the leg. No pain. Some herbal anesthetic? But there was no sensation of fractured bone-ends grinding. Gingerly, I bent my leg at the knee. It was a trifle numb but seemed otherwise functional. I stood up dizzy, nauseous, but whole. I put weight onto the leg and when circulation returned I found it was as good as ever.

"I thought it was broken!"

"It was, my friend. Sit down. You have one more day of rest. So says the shaman."

"The little girl—that thing—"

He nodded almost imperceptibly, his black eyes full of reflections. "I have a story to tell you. You will hear it because you have helped the Ilhalmiut as no other white man when you were an agent regulating the traders. And you will hear it because of your leg, because knowing is not wondering and not wondering is not seeking. No one must seek him out ... it should be ... a thing between us ..."

"All right. Tell your story, Kakumei. It will be between us two, only."

"Yes. Between ... us two only." He crossed his legs and looked into the fire. "It was the peak of winter when the stranger in the sun-sled came," he began.

The fire cast dancing shadows on the inner face of the tent, and the shadows seemed to take on shape ...

It was a time of famine and plague. The white traders had brought riches to the Ilhalmiut, as the traditonal Eskimo reckons wealth, and had taught them how to bring down many, incredibly many, deer with the rifle, where before they had used the bow and spear. The traders stayed for two generations. But when the trade in fox furs began to decline, the traders abandoned their cabin and the Eskimos, taking with them the only supply of bullets within hundreds of miles. But this generation of the People of the Deer no longer knew how to hunt with spears and arrows—they had been raised on rifle-hunting. And Tuktu the deer was scarce that year, its numbers having been drastically reduced by overhunting during the last two generations. Old Dukto the shaman said that the deer came no more because its People had forgotten the deer spirit, had scarcely honored Tuktu in dance and sacrifice during their time of plenty. Whatever the reason, there were hardly enough caribou to feed all, even with ammunition, and without it—

They starved. The white man had no more use for the People of he Deer. And no one looked to see how they were getting on.

Winter was coming, and the night was getting longer. Drifts of loose snow masked the land. In the Barrens there are hard winters always; there are bad winters sometimes, during which life becomes almost impossible for a people who have not stored up many great caches of food. This year the winter was very bad indeed and there was no food to be stored.

In Eskimo tradition it is the hunter who must be fed first, for it is he who is responsible for the long-term survival of the tribe. And at first what meat there was went to the men who used the margin of strength it gave them to range the land in the white maelstrom, hunting fruitlessly. Several never returned, lost in the continual storm. Those who came back returned with empty hands.

The heavy snowfalls made it impossible to catch fish or even trap peat mice. The last of the stored meat vanished, and the last of the ammunition. It was the old people who died first. It was their obligation. At this time there was still hope that the white man would return with help, so the departed were not eaten by the tribe as they would have been in dire emergency; but the wolverines and wolves grew fat on them, ravaging the burial grounds fearlessly, as if they knew that the Ilhalmuit were not strong enough to stop them.

Soon the children began to waste into pot-bellied skeletons. Babes sucked at breasts gone dry. Without admitting it to one another, the hunters began to sacrifice their own food portions to their children and wives, pretending to be full. Occasionally a gull or a hare would wander near, lost in the storm, and this would keep the tribe going a few days more.

Two children were born in these empty, early months of winter, both dead on delivery. An Omen, said Old Dukto.

Reluctantly they took the dogs a distance from camp and slaughtered them one by one, and their dry, tasteless flesh was given to the children. Kakumei took only enough to maintain fortitude for the hunt. But the hunt was futile.

One day, Kakumei woke from a delirium to find that his infant son Nantui had died of hunger, his tiny form frozen in crab-like contortion in the far corner. Glazed eyes open, face gaunt and entreating. Kakumei's mate Tlekon had been too weak to carry the child outdoors. Or perhaps she was not yet aware of its death. She lay staring expressionlessly at the, ash-encrusted ceiling, her face pallid in the glow of the sputtering oil lamp. There was dry wood beside her, but she had let the fire go out. Slowly, Kakumei got to his knees, dragged the child outside and came in to build up the fire. By the greater light of the campfire he found his mother dying, an emaciated rag-frame whose eyes flickered more dimly than the dwindling oil lamp, huddled with the remaining child, both of them in a stuporous halfsleep beneath a pile of skins. The days grew shorter, shorter, daylight going out like used-up candle.

Long before, they had chewed to uselessness the last rawhide thong, sucked the marrow from the last dug-up garbage bone. When the last of the sled dogs was eaten, shared among the whole camp—then, while the others slept, Kewatn, mother of Kakumei, crawled out into the snow, unclothed, so her family could survive a short while longer on her withered flesh. But wolves took the body of the dead woman.

With hunger came sickness, and by the peak of winter half the Ilhalmiut were dead; their burial ground was later to be called the Place of Countless Bones.

Autek went one day to find a distant camp where his brother lived, where he hoped to find charity for his starving family. He found only naked frozen bodies scattered far from their igloos. The merciful madness had come and the dying had torn off their clothing and with the last of their strength, run off into the snows to end the long agony quickly.

Autek barely made it back. He found his wife frozen in a pathetic ball under skins that had failed to save her; without the fat in the deer meat even the sturdy Eskimo metabolism cannot survive the Arctic cold for long. Autek's two little boys were clinging to their mother's corpse. He rubbed warmth into their frost-bitten fingers, fingers like tiny brittle talons. But soon the children of Autek died. Autek followed them within three sleeps.

In the igloo of Kakumei the only movement came when he reached listlessly out to stir the fire. The wood was nearly gone. Tlekon lay still, her breathing fitful and shallow.

A time came when the storm died down, when the snow was so heavy on the igloo it creaked with the weight. The only sounds were fits of coughing and the drawn-out sighing of the wind.

Then a great angry noise broke open the sky. Thinking the thunder-and-crackle a rifle shot, Kakumei crawled to the doorway and dug out through the snow. He broke out into the night and peered into the dim half-light of the winter sky.

A huge sled on fire! A mighty sled aflame, bigger than any five Ilhalmiut sleds together, racing down the hills so rapidly it flew a man's height over the snow. It roared straight for the camp and its brilliant blue light shimmered like moonlight on the white slope. The sled was wedge-shaped like those of the People, but larger and fiery and everywhere smooth, with no lashings or burdens, and was driven not by dogs but by something unseen. There was a rumble and roar, an explosion of blue white light, and then the sun-sled was buried in a drift in the center of the semicircle of igloos.

A dream sent by hunger, Kakumei thought. Or an evil spirit come to collect the last of the living.

The few men with strength enough to crawl out of the igloos shielded their eyes, as the snow melted into pool around the sled. Gradually it lost its glow and became leaden. No one moved. Surely the spirit inhabiting the sun-sled would strike down anyone presumptuous enough to touch its vehicle. But then a door appeared in the side of the huge wedge, dissolving into round darkness.

It was no spirit, Kakumei realized, but a man who climbed laboriously from the aperture. He staggered clear, up to his knees in slush, and took a few tentative steps toward the igloo of Kakumei. He was dark as the Ilhalmiut, dressed in a tightly woven cloth like that of the whiteman; his stature was like that of the Eskimo, but his eyes were unnaturally deep shade of green. He made a weak motion with a black-gloved hand and then fell on his face. At that instant the fiery sled, now the color of ashes, began to melt like an icicle in the spring wind. Soon, it had become a quicksilver puddle. Within an hour even this mirrorpuddle vaporized, leaving no trace.

It took most of Kakumei's remaining energy to drag the stranger into the igloo and cover him warmly in skins. Much later the stranger awoke. He sat up and blinked, gazing fearfully about. Then he relaxed and nodded to Kakumei.

Kakumei croaked out: "I'm sorry we have no food to offer you, for it is unwritten law that any traveler will be fed immediately on arrival, and we are ashamed that we have none even for ourselves. But soon we shall die and perhaps then you can eat of our useless flesh and gain strength to find your home." Kakumei, seeing that the stranger didn't understand, repeated the message in French.

The stranger smiled and pointed at his ears. His smile revealed peculiar teeth. He spoke in an unknown and high-pitched tongue and seemed to be asking a question. The baby was awakened by the stranger's voice and wailed for food. Something haphazard in its cries suggested that it would not live to cry another day.

The stranger seemed to be listening to the child, as if he understood its secret tongue. Then he nodded. From a pouch on his waist he drew forth a silvery sphere, and tapped it with a nutbrown finger. It rang softly, but the resonation did not dwindle—instead it grew louder and deeper, till the call seemed to fill the smoky chamber and pass out of the range of hearing.

The stranger smiled and took the sphere outside. Wrapped in hides, he squatted near the doorflap, clasping the bell. Occasionally, as he rocked back and forth, crooning, he tapped the bell, which then thrummed and sang, each time with a fuller resonation.

Soon, Kakumei heard light, hesitant footfalls outside.

He took many deep breaths until he had the strength to crawl nearly to the door.

But the snowshoe hare came to him. It hopped amiably around the stranger, who hadn't moved. The bell sounded again, and the hare sniffed curiously at it. It was at this moment that Kakumei snared the animal with a swipe of his right hand. He broke its neck and tore open its throat so that the baby might sip the strength-giving blood.

In this way were all in the camp fed, one by one. As the stranger crooned and rang the bell, the fox would come, or the rat, or the hare, or the ptarmigan, each walking into a different igloo as calmly as if it were its own den. Soon all bellies were full, and only then did the stranger eat. He tore off strips of raw rabbit flesh and pressed it daintily between his strange teeth—his teeth were only two, one upper and one lower, each a solid bar curving around to fill his gums. Each was sharp but unsnagged, and the meat disappeared easily between the chewing white bars.

Seeing those stricken with sickness, the stranger brought forth a cylinder—which one day would heal the broken leg of a downed pilot—and worked its magic, and shortly the sick were well.

A song-feast was declared to welcome the new shaman. For the council of hunters had reckoned that Kaila had sent this shaman to fill the place of the old shaman, Dukto, who had died. And the nights grew long and longer. But the long nights were not forlorn; they throbbed with many songfeasts. For days the people crowded into the igloo of Kakumei to chant and dance and tell the ancient stories. The stranger learned the language rapidly. He would sit in the close-pressed throng of the remaining twenty two Ilhalmiut, chanting the few songs he had learned and swaying contentedly with the rest, his green eyes slitted and his strange teeth clacking in time.

Kakumei would take down his great hoop drum and hold it over the chuckling fire till the hide shrank from the heat, becoming taut and eager to be thumped. He would offer the drum to each man, but the hunters were modest and the drum would be passed about until at last one man accepted it. He would walk diffidently to the center of the group, hard by the fire, where he would hold the drum by the thong handle and twirl it around and around, striking lightly along the edge of the hoop with a stick. The tempo would be a slow rhythmic beat at first, as the drummer shuffled about, chanting and beating faster and faster. When it was Kakumei's turn at the drum he would dance, bending sharply from the waist, snapping back and forth rapidly and singing with great aplomb:

Aii the Northern Lights cane to meet the soil that day
at the lake of hungry River and the messenger of kaila came to the
    soil that day
a messenger who sings so sweetly the animals give their lives to hear
and gave their lives to the People who dance like happy hares
at the lake of hungry River
Aiee Great is the light in the Northern sky
Great is the light in the heart of the messenger
and great is the kindness of Kalia to send such a messenger
to the lake of hungry River . . .

There was much singing that season, and many dance contests in friendly rivalry, and much gambling and giving of gifts. The new sha-man was given a parka made for him by Tlekon, a clay pipe, and a precious steel-knife. In return he awarded Tlekon the cloth from his discarded sled-suit, from which she made a papoose for Tleitn.

So passed the winter, the stranger calling food and the People giving him their language, skills and devotion in return.

The People did not doubt the world of the stranger when he explained that he came from Itakti, the stars. He described his home world, a place very like this one, where the climate was ever as it was in the Barrens—and it was for this reason that he had chosen to bring his wounded sky-sled down here. He would be unable to return to the Itakti unless someone among his people had heard the urgent message he had sent before the crash. Then perhaps they would come to take him home. But there were people much like the Ilhalmiut on his world, a few tribes stubbornly remaining, and he had spent much of his time with them. He preferred their company to that of his civilized peers, and so perhaps it would be better after all if no one came for him.

His magic devices were of no use to anyone but himself since they responded only to his Heart, and to no other unless it be one of Like Heart. And even one of Like Heart would require many years of training to learn to use the healing rod and the calling bell, either of which would seem like chunks of lifeless metal even to the wisest of the white man's shamans.

By spring, the Ilhalmiut were ready for the hunt. At the urging of the new shaman, they had practiced the old skills of bow and spear again and again. For the power of the calling bell might wane, and the Ilhalmiut must learn to shoot arrow and hurl spear in preparation for the return of Tuktu.

But with the first hot breath of the Spring Chinook came the white stranger, in an airplane that landed a few hundred yards from the winter camp on the surface of the frozen lake.

The new shaman called Kakumei into his igloo and spoke with him in serious tones.

So it was when the white man came to the camp of the people he was met by Kakumei. The Eskimo extended a hand to touch fingertips in the greeting of the Northern tribes but the stranger, the second stranger in this year of many tales, took a wary step back.

"Greetings. I'm Captain Toliver, Royal Canadian Air Force," he announced loudly in French. "I'm looking for—"

"Please, won't you come and eat with us, friend Toliver?" Kakumei interrupted, smiling, nodding towards the igloos trailing the black smoke of cooking fires.

"Thanks no," said Toliver. "I'm looking for a man. Possibly he's an unusual man. I'm not sure what he is. I was flying patrol a few months ago. My plane and another. We encountered something. A sort of flying thing—like nothing I've ever seen. We radioed it to identify itself. It didn't answer and it was pulling away. My partner tried to head it off and collided with it. He went down and the ship—or whatever it was—went on a ways, wobbling, and then I saw it go down. But I was low on fuel, I had to get back. Took me a long time to go through the data, get a fix on where the things must have fallen. Then I had to wait months for permission to go looking for it, because I was under investigation. I found the wreckage of the other RCAF plane this morning . . . I—" He stopped, frowning, seeing that Kakumei didn't seem particularly interested. "Look," Toliver went on sharply, "You do understand what I'm saying, don't you? You said something in French a little while ago. Is that all the French you know? Do you understand? Did you see this thing? This flying thing? It was fast and bright. Real bright, like the sun. Like the sun, you understand?"

Kakumei shook his head slowly as if thinking hard. "Know only some French. You say it was too sunny where you come from?"

"No, no. It was like the sun, this flying thing! Did you see it?"

"We have seen nothing like sun till yesterday, for all winter it was dark and only yesterday did the sun—"

"No!" Toliver stopped, and took a deep breath. He was a head taller than Kakumei and wore a grey uniform with black stripes along the seams of the creased pants and heavy leather boots; a leather flight helmet was tucked into his khaki belt beside his pistol. His face was long and fair, his blue eyes were small and sad above his long nose. He ran slender fingers through his short brown hair. His smile was strained. "Friend, I have a feeling you're playing games with me. You're playing dumb. Well, if you hadn't seen anything you would have no reason to play dumb. So you're covering up for someone. Now, look, if I had a chance to help you, I would help. If I had the power to bring you people all the things that we have that you badly need—uh, telephones or whatever—well, I'd bring 'em to you. Truly. And I think it's only fair that you help me, now that you have the chance. Then, perhaps I can help you some day. You must. I—" He jumped at the sudden loud crack of ice breaking up in the river. He looked around nervously. "Oh. The ice. The Chinook." He took another deep breath and looked Kakumei in the eye. "I know you're keeping something from me. But its something I must know. The pilot who was killed-that plane that went down, that was my responsibility. I have to account for that. My report was a story of a crazy flying thing that was like nothing anybody's ever seen. They won't go for it. They said that Powell died in some accident and the error must have been mine for me to make up a story like that to cover up. I'm going to be court-martialed. Uhh—that means I'm in trouble with my people. You see? They think I was drunk or negligent. I've got to find this flying thing, pieces of it, or whoever was in it, and prove-"

Kakumei raised a hand. The stranger fell silent.

"We have seen no strangers but you. This is a big land. You have much to search." He turned to go.

Sputtering, Toliver grabbed Kakumei by the wrist and held him back. "You *know*!"

Kakumei looked at him with pity, hard in the eye. Toliver released him.

Again, Kakumei turned away. "Wait!" shouted Toliver. This noise sounded much like the bark of a dog. And Kakumei remembered the tale of the genesis of the whiteman. It is known that the first woman, after having a family of man-children, bore a litter of dogs. And these dogs multiplied and grew to be so many that the man and woman could not feed them and became disgusted with their whining, quarrelsome ways. So they set the dog-children into a canoe and launched them out into the great waters. And so the ancestors of the whiteman came to Toliver's homeland, across the seas. Toliver, then, was a lost puppy.

Kakumei turned to him and spoke: "Friend Toliver, if I came to you and asked you where I could find your own brother so that I could take him far away and show him to people, what would you do?"

"A brother, you said? So, he must—be alive. But he can't be your brother after just a few months here. It—whatever came out of that flying thing could not be brother to a man. It could not be a man—that thing moved so fast the acceleration would have crushed a man—"

"The deer is not a man. But the deer is a brother," said Kakumei.

"I don't want to harm you or your people. But if I have to bring an army in here to tear this place up looking, I'll—"

He was interrupted by a great shout from the camp.

"Tuktu!" the People shouted, streaming from the igloos where they had hidden at the approach of the white man. "Tuktu the deer is come!"

The People of the Deer sang and rejoiced for here was meat and furs and bone-tools and gut-strings. The leaders of the herd trickled cautiously between the pillar-like sentinels of Inukok. The Inukok are rough models of men, semblances of men made with carefully heaped stones topped with discarded parkas, all of which deceives Tuktu, whose eyesight is poor, into believing there are hunters here and there and there on the migrating path. And so the caribou run into the opened space between the Inukok, funneled headlong into the spears of concealed hunters.

And it was by one of these rigid, baleful stone men that Toliver glimpsed the stranger. The stranger was dressed in what remained of the grey clothing he had originally worn, clothed only from the waist down, having put aside the parka Kakumei's wife had made, he felt cold—less than ever an eskimo. He was without nipples. The shaman smiled and waved and Toliver sprinted up the slope, drawing his gun and shouting. The caribou flooded in greater and greater numbers between the fence of Inukok and soon their clicking hooves had dug a great trench out of the snow, sending out rivulets of slush.

Kakumei watched from atop of boulder as Toliver dodged between the nervous caribou, who skittered aside as he bulled closer to the shaman. His gun gleamed blue in the slanting light of the new day. The shaman began to back up, motioning to Toliver, entreating him to follow. The white man was running now, he plunged into the thick of the herd after the shaman, coughing from the great stench. Kakumei heard Toliver cursing as caribou blocked his way. Then both men were lost to sight in the mottled torrent. The main bulk of the herd caught up with the leaders and the clay-colored tide swelled, filling the vast hollow between the two hills. There came a scream, distant and fluting.

When the herd thinned out, Kakumei found Toliver sprawled in the shelter of a towering Inukok. He had been trampled: his body was battered and broken, and he was coughing up tarry black blood.

His face was very white. "Damn thing up and vanished like a straw in a storm. Gone, by damn—" Kakumei bent to administer what aid he could. Twenty feet away great bulls of the herd bellowed and shook their massive antlers.

"The damn thing—" Toliver continued. "—I'd see it here and it'd vanish, then I'd see it over there and I'd go after it and it'd be gone—it wasn't human—I saw it close up—it was from *somewhere*, I don't know." He coughed rackingly, bringing up another gush of blood, then caught Kakumei by the shoulder with feverish intensity. "Look, you— *kill it*."

Kakumei said nothing but his eyes asked: Why?"

"Because—because it's *alien*." Toliver whispered.

He died before Kakumei could reply: "And what are you?"

When Kakumei came down into the village, the other hunters had already gone to their kayaks to catch Tuktu while the deer swarmed across the Hungry River. For these were the People of the Deer.

In the igloo with the red feather over its doorflap, the shaman was waiting for Kakumei. With the shaman's help the ice was broken around the white man's aircraft; with the body of the stranger placed inside, it vanished with a gasping bubble into the lake. No one came again to seek the sun-sled.

And strong times came once more to the People of the Deer. And the shaman learned their ways and took a wife.

"...the Winter of the two strangers was seven years ago, friend Trumbull, and the great shaman is gone now. His people came in a fiery sled at the very end of that Spring, and all that remains of him is his pouch of magic. He is gone from us forever."

I nodded and lay back, accepting the story, even the conclusion, without comment. The next day I was ready for the lengthy kayak trip back to Churchill. Kakumei would accompany me, to see me safely home.

For a mile or so before the rapids, the river was calm enough to permit me to appreciate the summer dress of the Barrens. To the right were dark bogs strained with sepia dyes, bounded by swales of tall grass. On the hillsides, reaching ever more steeply over us, the slick green patches of dwarf birch scrub were set off by millions of minute blue and buttery yellow blossoms and by clouds of tiny orange butter-flies. The shattered ridges were suffused with shades of pastel from growing lichens. The many colors flowed together in the distance where the land still seemed dark and barren.

Since Kakumei and I were only a few feet apart, I could have asked him the many questions that haunted me. I could have asked him, for instance, about the hut I glimpsed half-hidden in a ravine as our kayaks swept past. The hut was well apart from the others, and I knew it to be the home of a shaman when I spotted the signatory red feather over the entrance. I saw a young girl, the girl with the peculiar teeth who had healed my leg, strolling towards the hut. I did not mention her to Kakumei, however, though I might've remarked on the green gleam of her eyes, when she glanced at us. I did not attack the discrepancies in his story: that only the stranger, or one of Like Heart (such as his offspring?) could operate the healing cylinder. If he had gone that Spring, how had his child been taught to use the healing rod, a knowl-edge which supposedly took years to acquire? And Kakumei had said *no one must seek him out.* How can one seek out a man who has returned to the stars?

When the daughter of the stranger from the sun-sled entered the hut of the red feather to greet her father, I very nearly spoke of it to Kakumei.

I cleared my throat.

The kayaks swept by, and round the bend. I kept silent. Well, hang it then.

I didn't want to disappoint Kakumei by letting him know how poorly he had learned the white man's craft of lying.

The Prince

When his enemies locked onto the autopilot of Haji's private
jet, he was thinking about window glass. He was cruising along at six
thousand feet, flying from San Diego to San Francisco, thinking about
installing tint-adjustable glass in the picture window of his penthouse
offices. He detested inappropriate lighting.

Why was the plane descending so sharply, here? They were still
forty-five minutes from the Oakland airport.

He hit the intercom switch. "Carson! What gives?"

"I'm sorry, Mr. Haji, I can't seem to get the navigator to respond.
The autopilot just up and engaged itself. Uh—we seem to be *landing*.
Except there isn't an airport around here . . ."

"Carson, call the—the—" Who? "The authorities. Someone. The
FAA. The FBI . . ." And he thought, Automated hijacking.

But the radio and the phone went out too. They descended smoothly,
if rather steeply, whining down into the brown layer of smog and into
the sun-cracked and mostly abandoned concrete hinterlands of Ventura
County, Upper Los Angeles.

Haji and Carson were alone on the jet. There was room for twenty,
but Haji didn't believe in an entourage. The cabin was decorated in
soft brown leathers and yellow silk; the chair he sat in was an ergon-
omic recliner that massaged his lumbar, dispensed drinks, provided an

intercom, sang softly to him or took dictation. It would soothe him all the way down. . . .

Radar will track us, Haji thought. They'll know we're not supposed to go down here.

But the air traffic controllers were overburdened. They tended to lose track of people. Anyway, it'd be too late. By the time the police showed up, the plane would be burning wreckage. Or the hijackers would have them. Hijackers? Kidnappers. Terrorists. Assassins. Lunatics of some kind.

He should fire Starger for not checking out the plane for this kind of vulnerability. Starger was head of security, but he couldn't even find a bodyguard Haji could tolerate—now he'd left the navigational gear unshielded against cybernetic hijacking.

Fire him? Haji remembered "Duddy" Marchmain, president of Marchmain Synthetics, taken by terrorists, tortured, reduced to a shell that muttered slogans to a cheap camcorder. Found in a garbage sack on the steps of the Stock Exchange. They'd cut off his "greedy, grasping hands" and stuffed them down his throat.

And Haji was thinking about firing his security chief. A corpse doesn't send pink slips. Face it. You're tomorrow's headlines. And then they'll recycle the old newspapers, and you're gone. . . .

Carson came out of the pilot's cabin, shaking his head. He was a tired-eyed, middle-aged man with beefy forearms, wearing a short-sleeve khaki shirt with the Crossworld Industries logo on the shoulder patch. "I tried everything, Mr. Haji."

The plane touched down on the disused, grass-thatched freeway, the wheels braying with the first bouncing contact, the plane shuddering. Then the plane trundled to a stop. Strangers with guns came out from under the crumbled overpass, and one of them spoke into something with an antenna. "Toss your weapons out the door, come out with your hands up." A casual male voice with a southern California slur to it, patched into the intercom.

Haji's stomach contracted around a chill ball of fear. Carson was already at the door. He took yellow UV-filter goggles from his shirt pocket and put them on.

"Maybe we should lock the doors, wait for help," Haji said. His own voice sounded small and far away.

· "There's a guy carrying one of those slap-on bombs," Carson said. Anger was showing through in his tone, his pursed lips. He blamed Haji for this, somehow. "We get out or they . . ."

"I see." Haji stood just behind Carson as he swung the door open. The stairs automatically descended to the runway, humming. Heat and the smell of hot asphalt pushed in through the door, elbowing the air conditioning aside. "We haven't got any weapons!" Carson called out, as Haji put on his UV goggles and they descended the aluminum stairs.

"Good," said the big man in blue-tint sunglasses, grinning. He was Hispanic, but without an accent. " 'Cause neither do we. Nothing's loaded." But they'd surrounded Haji and Carson by then. Most of them wearing tattered white sun-reflective shawls over their heads, and goggles. It gave them the look of some demented cult. Haji had seen footage of people who lived outside the shields, they all wore those things outdoors. A tanned, skinny young man, with goggles but without a shawl, greasy blond hair tied back in a knot, was already going up the stairs, carrying a battered red-vinyl briefcase—probably containing the microprocessors and transmitter he'd used to take over the plane.

Haji and Carson, surrounded by their kidnappers, were escorted across the heat-rippling tarmac to a break in the rusty chain link fence that bordered the freeway. Behind them, the stairs folded into the plane and it began to taxi toward the half-fallen underpass. Beyond the freeway was a barricade of junk cars and rusty girders and barbed wire, all of it sunken into rust-streaked concrete. Men and women, in goggles and shawls, crouched in the shade of crude shelters or patrolled wooden walkways near the top, carrying their guns prominently. Warningly. Others at the underpass were unrolling tarps camouflaged to blend with the underpass's sediment of debris and trash. Probably going to hide the jet under the overpass, cover it up.

Haji had never before felt genuine despair. He was surprised at how deep and resonant it was.

"Now we got you here," the big man said, "we want you to know that you're free to go."

Hope lived for about five seconds, and then Haji saw the expressions on their faces. Smug, secretive. "You wanted the jet?"

"No," the big man said. "Not particularly. We might think of a use for it, though."

They were indoors now, in a big, shadowy place, much cooler, and most of them had shed their goggles and shawls. Haji tried to imagine what they had planned. They'd let him and Carson run away through their turf, maybe, and the streetsiders would hit them with rocks and bottles and bricks and chase them down and beat them to death and the hijackers would laugh and say they just hadn't run fast enough.

"It doesn't matter who does it to us," Haji said. "Whether it's you or someone streetside. You'll be responsible."

"Who does *what* to you?" the big man asked. "You mean, someone here's going to hurt you? No. Anybody hurts you it'll be your own people. Our guns were a bluff. We won't let you take the jet—we still own your autopilot. But taking your plane is all the force to be used against you. Unless it's by your own employees."

The man didn't make sense, but he didn't seem dangerous. He had put aside the gun; there was nothing threatening about him. Haji took a deep breath and shuddered and found he could look around now. They were on the lowest floor, in the middle of what had once been an underground shopping mall, standing beside a fountain filled with dull, motionless water. Obviously an enormous squatter's haven. Vast squares of sunlight flooded in through the tinted, translucent roof, set off by deep shadows in the old shops. The smashed storefronts were retrofitted to new functions: a dress boutique had become a machine shop; an erstwhile Hansen's Juice Bar was home to an old Chinese couple; the racks in a shoe store were hung with oily used car parts; an imported leather-goods store had become a day-care center brimming with children; an artificial fur boutique had become a home for two families of Chicanos; an old Radio Shack was evidently a storage room for junked appliances, electronic odds and ends, and spare parts. The logos for the shops, in swathes of cutsey cursive, were mostly intact, dust muting their gaudy plastic colors. Each shop had a single naked electric bulb, flickeringly lit by pirated electricity.

Haji stood amid fifteen men and seven women, from young to mid-

dle aged. He saw no insignia, no paramilitary gear. Just the rifles; some
of which, he saw now, were detailed toys or just plain broken; none
carried with any ease or expertise.

They stood in a loose circle around him, staring. Some of them
smirking, pleased as hell with themselves, several of them distinctly
unfriendly, but no one looking really hostile. Still, they aren't wearing
masks, Haji thought. That was supposed to be a bad sign, wasn't it?
If they let you see their faces, they meant to kill you.

Haji asked, "Anyone want to tell me what the point of forcing me
down was?"

"You are." This from a stocky, spike-haired boy—maybe a teenager,
maybe in his early twenties. His face was blurred by a number of small
scars, and a broken nose. "You're the point."

"This is Jerome-X, Mr. Haji," the big man said. "My name is Pastor
Navarro. Or you can call me Dana. I can introduce you to the others,
if you like. Jerome's the one you need to meet, though. He's going to
be your guide, tell you what you need to know."

Haji turned to Jerome-X. Haji was thirty-two, about the boy's height
but much slimmer and darker and in every other way a contrast. Haji
wore a London-tailored linen suit with a powder blue tie; every hair
in place, his nails manicured. The boy wore shiny denim and rotting
sneakers. He wasn't carrying a gun, but there was an army surplus
knife on his hip. He was missing a couple of teeth and his nails were
black as the dark sliver on a gibbous moon. There was an odd earring
in his left ear: a silver miniature of the Arc de Triomphe. "So this is
about me?" Haji said. "You people know nothing about me."

Jerome-X grinned. He stared off into space and read from an invisible text: "Haji, Andrew Mahat, born December nineteen, 1988, Islam-
abad, Pakistan. Father: Ali Muhammed Haji. Mother: Olivia
Bentworthy, a former British subject who became a citizen of Pakistan
in 1987 . . . Umm, I'll skip ahead here . . . Haji was born into a wealthy
Punjabi Muslim family but is not known to practice Islam, blah, blah,
blah . . . family moved to New York City in 1994, became American
citizens in April 1995, Haji studied at—buncha stuff there about all
the private schools—attended Columbia then transferred to Harvard,
PhD in Economics, MBA, Phi Beta Kappa, blah blah blah, became a

junior executive in the investments division of Crossworld International in August of 2012 and then there's a lot of stuff about how you're a whiz kid, a golden boy, how you're nicknamed. 'The Prince' by the Big Biz insiders . . . says, Haji worked his way up to Chief Executive Officer in under twelve years, company consistently showing gains under his leadership and so on. . . . Ummm, Crossworld is a multinational plastics manufacturing corporation diversified into food synthesis, automobile manufacturing, aircraft manufacturing, extensive defense contracts, banking, real estate development, especially reclamation of 'urban deterioration zones' aided by tax incentives. Ummm, Haji known for his emphasis on real estate and quick turn-over of properties, blah blah *blah* . . . Haji is unmarried, his psychological profile suggests—"

"Fine, you memorized my bio," Haji interrupted.

"Jerome has a chip implant," Dana said. "Lots of information files."

"So you know something about me, you think that's good for a ransom? My company has standing orders to pay no ransoms—"

"Mr. Haji," Carson broke in, his voice shaky, "don't be hasty. What I heard, they make secret deals with people sometimes. We'd better look at all the options, you know?"

"We are not holding you for ransom, Mr. Haji," Dana said. "You can't take the plane, but you're free to go. Jerome will show you where to get out and where our only public online booth is."

"Right this way, my man," Jerome said, gap-toothed grinning.

The crowd started to drift away, heading for storefronts or for the frozen escalator. One man hesitated, staring at Haji. Someone Haji hadn't noticed before. Now, here was real hostility. He was gaunt, with yellow sunglasses, a greasy T-shirt, his hair braided. Saying: "Lemme talk to the guy. I can't believe we got this guy here and we're going to just—"

"Forget it, Pringle," Dana said. Dana put his big hand on Pringle's bladelike shoulder and herded him away. "Jerome's briefed. We agreed this was the way. Come on . . ." Pringle walked away with the crowd, glancing venomously over his shoulder.

Haji stared after them. That was really *it*? They weren't prisoners? Watched by just this one guy?

From somewhere not far outside the mall, came a dull *thud* and a long architectural shudder. The vast interior spaces thrummed subtly with it, and then it was gone. "They're moving in," Jerome-X said. "That's the outer barricade going down. We better go, Mr. Haji."

But Haji found himself watching a little Hispanic girl who came out of one of the storefronts, carrying a plastic bucket. She went to the fountain, dunked the bucket, and carried it awkwardly back to the squat, her shoulders hunched under its weight. Haji had an impulse to help her carry it. But he stayed where he was, and asked Jerome, "They're drinking from the fountain? Is it potable?"

"For sure. It better be, it's our only source of water, man. We, like, had to set up a pump for it. Your boys cut off the other clean water mains, they missed this one. It's the only one left that's not toxified."

"How many people here?"

"In the mall, in shelters out back, in the car wash, the discount tires place . . . maybe five hundred total decided to go shut-in. Lot of em would change their minds now, if Starger'd let 'em. We're running out of food, and the barricades are coming down. . . . Come on, man, let's show you that online. You can see about getting a message out. See how it goes. . . ."

Haji looked at Carson, who shrugged, with an expression mixing relief and amazement. They followed Jerome-X past the reclaimed storefronts, down an unevenly lit hallway. Haji was surprised at how clean and organized the place was. He'd always pictured squats as trash heaps, occupied by people the way rats occupy the city dump. It didn't even smell bad.

Your boys, Jerome-X had said. And he'd mentioned Starger by name. And they were just north of Ventura. The pieces fell together. This was the Santa Clara development, Crossworld Development Enterprises Project CAL43. A Reclamation Project. Haji had scanned the report: Crossworld Development had bought the property, the squatters refused to leave, the ACLU had defended the squatters, getting an injunction stopping the police from moving them out, but Crossworld had lobbied in the state capitol for the right to use its own security force. Crossworld had the clout; Crossworld won. Last he'd heard, the place was under some sort of siege.

"Look," Haji said, trotting to catch up to Jerome-X, "I don't have the power to give you this place to live in—I'm the CEO, but I have to answer to the board of directors and the stockholders. I couldn't do it if I wanted to." Not true, but chances were good Jerome-X didn't know that.

Jerome-X glanced at him. "So you figured out part of it. You got a long ways to go."

"You have some kind of political brainwashing in mind?"

Jerome-X laughed. "What'dya think, this is a reeducation camp? No, man. Most of 'em here, they're pretty ordinary Americans. They don't know ideology from gynecology. We're organized into a kinda co-op because that's the only way to survive here, not because we're Communists." He turned and they paused in the hall as Jerome-X looked at Haji with weary amusement. "Indoctrination! Shit, man, you don't know Dana. Most of the people who escorted you in and, you know, helped him set this thing up—even Chancey, the hacker that brought you down—they're part of a *congregation*. Dana's flock. Not me—I'm just kind of helping him out. I like the guy. But see, Dana was a priest. He split with the church—I guess he figured their stand on birth control was really stupid—but he's still a kind of priest. Keeps the faith, you know? And he says violence is unChristian."

"I saw people patrolling with guns...."

"Right. Some of 'em are for real and some are a bluff. See, when they organized things here, it broke up into two factions. The ones willing to use violence and Dana's people. Dana brought you here to show 'em there's another way. You got to understand this: you lucked out, man. If Dana wasn't here, there are some other people around this place that'd hang you up by the balls."

"They'd kill me over a housing disagreement?"

"It's more than that. Come on, check it out for yourself. In here." He led them through an open door, into a smell of antiseptics and urine. "This is the infirmary."

It was a long, curved room that used to be a Chinese restaurant. There were still fake-Chinese lamps and a sign on the wall that said, "Our guarantee—No MSG!" In place of the tables were beds; none of them hospital beds, irregular sizes and shapes. They were all occupied.

A black man in a white doctor's jacket and a young Hispanic woman in cutoff jeans tended the sick. Haji steeled himself against all this: it was a ploy. They were going to try to play on his pity, this way. He couldn't abide being manipulated.

He felt spavined here, now that the fear was gone. Impotent. He'd grown up with a rather businesslike nanny and aloof parents, who fought constantly and finally moved into separate wings of the house; he'd been culturally displaced as a boy and later found himself one of the few Pakistanis in the Ivy League institutions they sent him to. A persistent sense of rootlessness and loss had been a powerful motivator for career security; for acquisition of power and control. Now someone had taken control from him as easily as a parent takes a dangerous utensil from the hands of a toddler. An infantile frustration seethed in him. He wanted to hate these people.

But the patients in the infirmary were not easy to hate: they were mostly children. This little boy with his left arm missing: his left side, visible now as the "nurse" changed the dressing, was a blotchy, multicolored welter of blisters and open sores. He shivered but he seemed too exhausted to cry out as she poured antiseptic and water over him. "We out of painkiller?" Jerome-X asked her.

"Yeah. Also down to the last bandages, maybe two hundred cc's general antibiotics, one package of burn dressings."

"See if we can get somebody out."

"You do, they'll probably just end up in here, make things worse."

"Let's see what we can do." They went on, two other children, also with burns; a little girl, maybe three years old, with broken limbs, her gaze lost in the brush patterns of the ceiling plaster. Lost for good, Haji felt. There were two men, one conscious and the other unconscious and feverish, thrashing under improvised restraints. Other adults with broken limbs, one with a shotgun wound. More children. Several of them were sallow, sunken, profoundly sick but not burned or broken-limbed. What was wrong with them?

A listless twelve-year-old boy, withered to the size of a five-year-old, lay curled up in a broken-down sofabed. Jerome-X asked the black man, "How they doing? Toxicity down?"

"We haven't got any testing kits left, so I don't know for sure, but I don't think they're processing it out very well." He said it softly so the kids wouldn't hear.

Carson stared at the emaciated child. "What's he got?"

"Liver cancer," the black man said, not looking up as he took the boy's blood pressure from a limp arm. "We got four kids down with it. There used to be more. There's a for-real cancer cluster here from waste toxins over to the Oxnard plant. Came up through the water table."

The Oxnard plant. A plastics plant the EPA had been trying to close, claiming steady leaks into the local water and air. ChemGro International: a Crossworld Subsidiary. Was this for real? Were the children really victims of his wrecking crew, his factory toxins? Or was this being staged somehow? He looked at the child, the child didn't look back. The boy's eyes were open; he breathed; but he didn't look back.

Haji turned away. He was determined not to fall into any emotional traps. Still he was relieved when they left the infirmary, and, walking down a concrete utility corridor at the back of the mall, he heard himself ask, "Either of those people—are they doctors? Those kids need professional treatment."

"James, he's a paramedic. Beryl had three years' medical school, dropped out to help us, just before the shut-in. We'd get 'em to professional treatment, but we can't get anybody to come in and we can't get out...."

"Those kids," Carson asked. "Something collapse on them? You guys shouldn't be living in these old buildings, they fall in on people—"

"Somebody *knocked* the building down on top of 'em, man," Jerome-X snapped. "Some of 'em run out, got themselves caught in a microwave beam. Nobody shut down the demolition for 'em. The cocksuckers didn't even slow down. That kid with his arm burned off—that's Pringle's kid. You notice Pringle? If it wasn't for Dana he'd kill you for sure...."

"Where'd this happen?" Carson asked. "These kids getting hurt?"

"Row of old houses up the street. Five A.M., everybody asleep. Wasn't an accident, you know? What you see are the survivors. Three other kids died. Seven adults. Couple of 'em took a few days to die.... The

barricade was weak there—we managed to get the survivors back behind the second barricade. Lost two of our guys just pulling 'em out.
Fried."

Haji snorted. "This is the groundwork for indoctrination, and I don't
believe it. Any demolition crew would be arrested for knowingly
knocking a house down on people."

Jerome-X chuckled. "Where you been, man? You think we didn't
try the cops already ten times? I'm telling you, your people have got
this sewn up. Housing crisis just goes on and on and on, you know?
People protesting for a decade now. The public gets callous after a
while. Your people in Sacramento, pal, they got a court order saying
that if the squatters don't move out, it's their own responsibility. The
Crossworld security chief is a tough motherfucker. Your man Starger.
He's making examples."

Haji thought, Starger's tough but incompetent. Because here I stand.

Jerome went on, "The Crossworld lobby is tough too. Tough and
big. One of your lobbyists camped in every state senator's waiting room
every day it's open. Publicity campaigns about how reclamation means
new housing, less crime, you know the drill. Leave out that it's new
housing only for the rich. And the rich are the minority. They haven't
got a housing problem."

"We lobby for the freedom to do business in a productive way," Haji
said. "We don't lobby for murder."

"They don't call it murder. If there's any publicity, they make it look
like the people were hanging out in the buildings secretly, defying the
law, crazy on drugs, bunch of dangerous lunatics. No one knew otherwise. But mostly there isn't any publicity. Your people pull the strings
on the press. Who's the major stockholder in North American Media?
Crossworld."

Haji ground his teeth. Don't let yourself be baited, he thought. But
the maddening thing about this Jerome-X was his casualness. He talked
of these things as he walked along, with no self-righteous indignation.
He might have been commenting on the weather.

Another distant thud; another shudder around them.

"What was that?" Carson asked.

"They're breaking through the barricades," Jerome-X said. He chewed a lip, some of his composure gone. "Busting shit down. They're closing in ... Here's the online."

They'd come to a row of phone stations, each with a TV phone cable and a PC monitor. The phone companies had taken out the TV phones when the area was abandoned, but the IBM people hadn't done a thorough job on the computer links. "Only one of 'em hooked up," Jerome-X said. He led them to a station. "Dana thought you'd want to see where you stand. Go ahead, see if you can get through, Mr. Haji."

Haji stared at him. Were they really going to let him contact his people? Maybe the police? He could send for a helicopter....

Haji's hands shook as he drew out his card and slotted it into the online. The screen lit up.

WELCOME TO IBM'S ONLINE SERVICES. PLEASE INDICATE PERSONAL CODE NUMBER. He typed in his PIN and waited. NO ACCOUNT LISTING. PLEASE TRY AGAIN. He did. And again. He tried requesting a balance statement; he tried everything. "You tampered with this machine," he said, his voice taut.

"Naw, uh-uh," Jerome-X said. "It works for me. I got an account. Not much of one but I got one." He took out his card and demonstrated.

"Then use your card to put me through to my people. I'll make it worth your while."

"Sure. But you won't get through. They're screening them all out. Our hacker set it up so they think you're off taking care of personal biz. Meanwhile Chancey broke into the system, blotted you out. For now, you got no account. Now you can try to contact your people, but we got the underground sending fake calls in from you, all over the country. They think it's a hacker hoax."

"When I get to San Francisco, I can get reinstated," Haji said. "There's really no point in all this. You might as well be holding me by force. You could have saved yourself the computer work with a gun. Like any other criminal."

"No, man. You don't get the idea. The idea is for you to have it like us. Be subject to the same conditions, you know? I mean, what'dya think, these people are criminals? I got to point out the gap between the rich and the poor lately, man? It's like pointing out the Grand

Canyon. You can't miss it. These are desperate people. Good people that had no work, ran out of food, lost their homes—all they're trying to do is protect their kids. We're living on scavenged food, and even that's almost gone. So I'll tell you, my heart's not bleeding over your fucking computer bank account. Sure, you'll get the account, your position, everything reinstated. Dana wouldn't want it any other way. But you'll have to get out of the shut-in first. Easier said than done. See, man, you might not survive being one of us."

"They're not going to push my buttons, Carson," Haji said through heat-cracked lips. "And they're not going to make us panic." They were walking along with their jackets over their heads, stripped down to T-shirts beneath.

"No sir. But how the hell we going to get out of here?"

The heat shimmered off the trash-strewn parking lot, visible even through their goggles, and their sweat ran like grease on grilled sausage. Behind them was the mall, partly collapsed, the string of department stores long since caved in. The section Jerome-X had shown them was reasonably stable; but Haji knew what the microwave beams and the maxidozers would do to it. Ahead were the houses, the barricades, the way out, and Jerome-X, walking ahead of them, in a hurry to be out of the direct sunlight. The greenhouse effect and heightened UV from ozone depletion had made hurry a reflex for people who lived outside the smog shields.

If you want to know how to get out of a thing, you have to consider how you got into it. So Haji ran it down in his mind: how had it all come about?

Maybe it came down to the smog shields. *"Smog shields" is a misnomer, of course*, Haji had said, years before, writing a report for the Crossworld execs. Written back when the shields were just beginning to be erected. The shields were designed for "outdoor" temperature control and UV reduction; as a side benefit they filtered smog. They were great porous bubbles of transparent organometallics, and people living outside them had soon found the living nearly unbearable. If they had no place else to go, they improvised their own shieldings, or simply stayed indoors. Which was all right, except that there wasn't enough housing—and every so often, with the truculent randomness of bad luck, the killer smogs came, synthesized from the synergistic reactions of pollutants under the catalyst of high UVs. Waves of aerosol death.

The devastation had come to the area six years before. Greenhouse heat and cruel UVs were the arms that swung the sickle: the Black Wind. It came like a harvesting blade cutting down and sweeping away. The survivors fled to an area that was funded for smog shields. Ventura County was abandoned.

But Crossworld knew it was prime real estate, if it was properly protected. There was water from the desalinization project on the coast. There was room for golf courses, once smog-shields were erected. Haji—almost as an after-thought, a minor concern in the course of a day involving a score of deals—bought up the land for a few cents a foot and sent in the developers. The developers looked it over, saw the potential for up-scale development, once Cross-world bankrolled the shield, and scheduled demolition. Only, the place wasn't empty; the squatters were there, the new recession's crop of homeless and unemployed. Although most of them had actually rented, till the place was sold out from under them.

Haji couldn't see an easy answer in any of it. All he could do was follow Jerome-X. Who was going to show him a certain alley, "a place you can maybe get out, maybe not. It's the best we got right now. It ain't gonna be easy. . . ."

They'd reached the end of the tarmac, come to the barricades. There were three rings of barricades, mostly built out of old cars, fused with stolen concrete. The crumpled junk cars were like great fossil carcasses in limestone. The third, outermost barricade was already fallen, and the houses that had stood inside it were crushed now to untidy hills of scrap looming like prehistoric grave barrows in the distance. Just this side of the second barricade men from the other squatter faction patrolled with guns to keep Starger's thugs from overrunning them. The besiegers had opted to stay behind the armored demolition machinery. Let the metal do the work. And just then, with a chill, Haji saw the demolition machinery moving toward the barricades. The yellow metal humps of the maxidozers and the big snouts of the microwave guns.

The Occupational Safety and Health Administration had tried to block deployment of microwave demolition units. Too high a risk of a worker stepping in front of a unit, maybe getting boiled from the inside out. It had happened a few times. But Crossworld had lobbied hard, and won again. The units cut demolition time by seventy-five percent. Point one at the wall, throw the switch. Nothing seems to happen. Then turn the gun off, send in your maxidozer—and the wall collapses with one swipe. It's been softened inside, like a tree with a rotten core, it crumbles to gravel and dust. They had a short range, forty feet, and they were used only on highly resistant structures.

So why were there two of them pointed right down the middle of the alley at him?

Jerome-X was waiting in the ramshackle shelter built on this side of the second barricade, just to the right of the alley mouth. The houses to either side of the alley had been flattened, plowed together into helter-skelter cones of debris; parts of them broken to moraines of powder and gravel.

Drinking water from a plastic jug, Jerome stood in the shade of four overlapping chrome car hoods on a frame of fenders and foil-covered wood—the whole a crude UV reflector. He passed the jug to Haji and said, "Can't even try it. They've got microwave guns in the alley. They'll fry you. Last time it was blocked off but there was a chance— they must've figured we were getting through that way."

"Why would they want to stop you from getting out?" Haji asked, passing the jug to Carson.

"Because they know that's not the end of us. We'll sabotage their equipment from the outside, do anything we can, and they know it. We've talked to them, see. To Starger, your security guy. We understand each other. He knows we're not here to squat anymore—we're here because they can't go on with this shit. We're making a stand. And they're making an example. The word won't get into the papers, but it'll get around on the street. They know what they're doing."

Haji noted that Jerome-X consistently said "they" instead of "you." Trying to nudge Haji into identifying with the squatters. But Haji wavered between empathy and resentment.

"I don't believe any of this," he said, letting the resentment carry him. In the heat, it was easily the victor. "The guns are there as a warning, or for storage or something. They wouldn't use them on people."

"Starger's hired thugs for this. Kind of guys you pay them enough, they don't give a fuck," Jerome-X said.

"Crossworld doesn't hire people like that," Haji said.

"You're right, Mr. Haji," Carson said, squinting through a crack in the sheller. "I can't believe they'd fry us. That's bullshit. They'd recognize Mr. Haji."

Jerome-X laughed. "Sure. Right. They really expect him here. They'll see some dark-skinned little guy coming at them and think he's another 'woggie' squatter—if you'll excuse the expression, man. He won't get a *chance* to make 'em see—"

"Bull*shit!*" Carson barked. The heat was getting to him. He turned savagely to Haji. "Fuck this. I'm going. You coming . . . sir?"

Jerome-X said quickly, "Look, I thought it'd be tough to get out, but this is impossible. The guns weren't—"

He broke off, staring after Carson, as he stalked out of the shelter and down the alley. Haji ran after him, "Hold up, Carson! Let me go first, they'll recognize me!"

"I got Mr. Haji here!" Carson yelled hoarsely. "The head of the company! We work for the company! Hey, listen we—"

But Haji was only a yard behind Carson when the air began to drum and the chrome radar-scoop muzzles of the microwave units began to whine, and the virulent heat of the day seemed to gather itself up into a tornado of unseen fire and Carson screamed. . . .

A bubble was growing out of Carson's right side. A bubble of flesh, a blister bigger than his head that burst and sprayed boiling blood and yellow steam as other bubbles sprouted on him and he fell whimpering into the dust in a puddle of himself—

Haji, just out of range, saw it over his shoulder as he ran. And then he looked away, gagging. Running and gagging.

They had begun to move half an hour after Carson went down, the maxidozers and the microwave caissons rumbling up to the barricade, methodically trading off, microwave and then dozer, as they shouldered through the dike of dead cars and concrete. The microwaves didn't work well on the car metal. But the demolition proceeded, inexorable as old age and much faster. They were coming.

They, Haji thought. Them and us. Was he that far along?

He didn't have time to think about it much. He was too busy. He was shoring up the walls around the infirmary, using quick-set cement and diagonally-planted metal girders. The work was physical and mental, you had to think out the engineering of it, work out the support angles, so the beams couldn't fall over on the kids. Haji was working with Dana and the wiry blond hacker, Chancey, and the black paramedic. And it gave him a feeling he had forgotten about: a kinship in toil, of mutual concentration and dependency; freedom from the pressures, the feverishly whispering urgencies of the self. He felt the relief of being, at least partly, someone else for a while.

In the early days he'd felt something like it at Crossworld. There was corporate loyalty, some sense of belonging. But the higher you went in the company, the falser the camaraderie became, and the more you knew that what appeared to be cooperation was ambition, was a kind of competition.

Feeling a girder cinch securely into place, he smiled.

"How come you're smiling?" the boy asked him. "What are you thinking about?"

Haji glanced down at the boy lying in the bed beside the wall he was working on. A boy of about six with dirty brown hair, a face that was a welter of bruises, and a broken forearm in a splint. Haji and the boy had been talking, on and off, for an hour. "I feel good about putting the girder up," Haji answered. "It's going to protect you."

"So we'll be okay here, right?"

"For a while. Then we'll get you out of here. We'll all be okay."

Listen to me, he thought suddenly. What an ass. You think they put you on this infirmary detail by accident? Same as Iraq, every time the war flared up again, sent us the TV images of kids hurt by the shellings. We were supposed to feel sorry for the kids and back off the Iraqis. Don't be pushed, Haji, he told himself.

But when the boy asked for some water, Haji ran for it.

He was cradling the boy in his arms, giving him the water, conscious that what the boy really wanted was the contact, when Jerome-X finally showed up. Haji could see by his expression that he'd failed.

"It wasn't supposed to work out like this," Jerome-X said. "And I didn't think they'd find that last online cable. But they did or they busted it accidentally, because we ain't getting a thing. I tried the other possibility, do a transer linkup, that's where I've been, but there's just too much microwave activity now." After a pause, he added, "I'm sorry about Carson. We just wanted you to see what it was like here, maybe scare you, then we'd get Chancey to set you up again on that line, hope you called off the Crossworld dogs. Didn't see it turning out this way."

"Okay." Haji felt leaden. "What about the plane?"

"That's still a possibility. They saw it come down but we checked their frequency, they think it's some kind of terrorist airlift or something. We can't get through to them to tell 'em different so we got to try to get you out to that plane. But they're busting through the barricades, moving in on it. Not much time. We'll set up the computer so it'll fly you out—"

"I didn't mean for me. I meant for him," Haji heard himself say, nodding toward the boy. "And the rest of the people in here, whoever else you can get on board." After a moment he added, with some effort, "Me as well, of course."

"Of course," Jerome-X said, shrugging. He looked blankly at Haji. Carefully expressionless. "We got to get out there now, get the kids that aren't going on the plane into the infirmary—hey, Dana!"

After that it was all bustle and shouting and carrying and sweat, improvising stretchers, using the few available wheelchairs, covering the sick against the UVs, moving them out under what looked like an armed guard. Haji toted the back end of the boy's stretcher through the pressure of the late afternoon sun; his feet sucking at the hot tarmac with each step, his arms aching. Jerome-X had the front of the stretcher, his back to Haji. "I don't understand not using guns at this point," Haji muttered. He was hot and tired and scared and angry at everyone; angry enough to shoot someone. "They're ready to kill you."

"Yeah, I know what you mean but—Dana's a persuasive guy. The way he sees it, we do it without violence even if it means getting shot down. He says that if we use our teeth on their ankles, then they're right about us—that we're just a bunch of rats in the ruins."

There were still three to get aboard the plane when the maxidozers broke through the barricade and came across the abandoned freeway. Like dusty yellow tanks, paint-scored and dented, with six enormous metal-toothed wheels each; with serrated crystallized-steel wedges at the front that could pull back and then ram; with faceless men in mirrored helmets just glimpsed through the louvered cabs. Gouting blue smoke and coming on like crawling rhinos, now grinding across the far lanes, the first of them smashing through the steel fence at the median. Hardly slowing for it.

The plane was ready, the computer reprogrammed for takeoff; the jet engines warming up, building to a roar that seemed to shout machine defiance, as if deliberately drowning out the rattle and grind of the approaching maxidozers. Haji was peripherally aware of all this as he carried the boy up the aluminum stairs, passed him in to his mother, then turned to help lift an unconscious young woman with a gangrenous hand, her body a limp weight.

He glanced up, seeing the maxidozers jouncing down onto this side of the freeway, swerving toward the tail of the plane, their intention clear. And on the far side of the chain link fence across the parking lot and the breached barricades, four other maxidozers moved like enormous metal slugs toward the monolithic hulk of the abandoned mall. Five hundred people hunkered inside, counting the seconds to artificial earthquake. To an Armageddon that was just another real estate deal.

Something lurched in Haji, and he felt the horror of profound disorientation: the displacement of the pillars of personal truth. And then the nearer maxidozers had crossed the freeway and were bulling at the tail of the plane, smashing at the rear wheels; another gunning up to the stairway as Jerome-X pushed Haji toward the door and dived free. The stairway buckled under Haji; he jumped for the door. Someone caught him, and pulled him inside. The plane was moving; erratically, but moving. The maxidozers ground at it, crushing the detached stairs under their wheels, digging long, sparking rifts in the sides of the plane; the squeal of metal meshing with the scream of terrified people inside.

The plane shuddered. Not so far away, a corner of the mall began to crack apart.

And then the door slammed shut, the plane moved away from the demolition crew, the vertical, harrier-type thrusters added their lift to the jet suction, and they rose into the sky.

Haji shoved through to the pilot's cabin. Chancey was at the radio. "We're above the microwave interference," Chancey said.

"Then take down these call numbers, link with the phone lines— there's someone we can call who knows my voice."

It took about three minutes that stretched into a pitiless forever, until Haji heard Buford say, "Mr. Haji—that you?"

"It is. Buford, we got a demolition team in Ventura County—shut it down. Now. Get through and shut it down, pull 'em out of there. Not tomorrow, not when you get time. This second."

"You got it."

"It's brilliant, Mr. Haji," Buford told him, his voice unctuous with admiration. Buford was a pale red-cheeked man with a round face; endlessly dieting, endlessly primping his suit, adjusting his jeweled choker.

Haji and Buford were in Haji's penthouse office; Haji seated on the edge of his desk, as usual ignoring the chair. Oblivious now to the quality of the light. Buford shifting his weight from foot to foot, holding the data-tab for the grant they'd worked out, brown-nosing with the expertise of a lifetime. "Setting up the low-income development, the housing for these squatters, free smog shield, environmental purification systems—the timing is perfect! Exactly when we needed a *massive* tax break!" He shook his head in grave appreciation and went to the door, paused to wink at Haji. "Smart PR, smart tax sense, smart timing. It's good to see you haven't lost your killer instinct, sir!"

"Yeah," Haji said. Almost laughing; almost crying. "Get Starger on the line."

"Certainly." Buford left, and Haji wished he hadn't. He'd never much liked Buford, but he was afraid to be alone, just now. He wasn't sure why. He remembered the sallow, sunken face of the boy with liver cancer. He'd shut down the Ventura plant, but there was no way he could stop the momentum, shut down plants all over the country, completely redesign all of them. No way he could do the other thing that Dana said he ought to do: admit publicly what Starger had done.

Christ—he had seen them murder Carson. Cook him alive. Outright murder. He hadn't known how they'd been carrying out his orders; he was insulated from the lower echelons. But he might well be prosecuted anyway, if it came out. And it would, perhaps, undermine Crossworld for good.

He couldn't do it. Maybe the squatters would try to get convictions. He wouldn't try to stop them. He ought to help them. But...

He just wasn't capable of going that far, and it made him feel lonely. He yearned for the feel of the girder under his hand; the boy cradled in his arms, drinking water from a red plastic thermos cup.

His control here was an illusion. Crossworld was its own entity, a shambling behemoth that Haji could only nudge a bit this way or that, could never fully control.

Maybe that was a lie. Maybe it was more denial. Maybe it was cowardice. But he was who he was. He couldn't go any farther.

Buford's voice from the desk speaker. "Red Starger's on hold, sir."

"Put him on voice, no picture."

Starger's voice rasped the room. "Starger here."

"I ought to prosecute you, Starger. In the end, if I did, I'd be prosecuting myself. That'd be the right thing to do. I'm just not capable of doing it. So you're not going to get busted, that way. Some other way, if I can think of one."

The screen of the TV phone was blank. He couldn't even look at Starger now.

"You're talking about prosecuting *me*?" The outrage in Starger's voice was palpable. "I was doing what I was told! Anybody ought to be prosecuted, it's those people hijacked you, attacked you. You're telling me that's nonviolent? They had guns, my people saw 'em! Don't tell me those assholes don't have weapons!"

"Just shut up, Starger, okay? Just don't dig it any deeper." Haji hung up. Somehow, he would see to it that Starger paid for the murders.

Starger was a sadistic asshole. But Starger's last comment still hung in the air. Yeah, Starger was right about one thing: They'd used their weapons and they'd won a victory. Weapons? Remembering the boy with the dirty brown hair and the little girl carrying a bucket...

Yeah. They had weapons.

He went to the window and turned off the tint. Light flooded into the room. It burned his eyes, but he didn't look away.

A Walk through Beirut

Black out.

All through Lower Manhattan, blackout.

The street wasn't completely dark. Stretching between buildings was a diffuse web of light from the lit part of the city, north of Fourteenth Street, where the affluent had a backup power system. Rusty light fluttered from the fires someone had set in the stores, two blocks up, at Delancey, and a yellower flame guttered in the broken windows of the graffiti-tattooed elementary school across the street. The Children's Christian Militia were bivouacked in the school gymnasium. Dexy could see the desultory beaming of flashlights through the gym's open doors.

The summer of 2022 had been a hot one, was oozing like molten wax into fall. It was still a warm evening, but Dexy knew it'd get colder, about one A.M., so he'd worn his wild-dog jacket. He ran his hand down the stiff, short-furred pit-bull hide and cocked his head, like a dog himself, listening to the whoops and feverish shouts from Delancey; the perverse ringing of breaking glass. A gun-shot. Another.

"Oh, totally THRASHIN'," Marilyn yelled, clattering clumsily down the chipped stone steps of the tenement on her high heels. "A *black-oouuuuuuut!*" Skateboard under her arm. She was going to skateboard with her heels on? No, she took the shoes off, stuck their spike heels in the waist-band of her skin-tight neoprene skirt, so the pumps hung like gunfighter holsters. She jumped on the skateboard, pumped it, its gear system translating the kinetic energy of her leg pump into forward motion, and she shot down the sidewalk. "Come on, Dexyyyyyyyy!" She had all her animatoos going, the animated images on her skin looping through their horror-story comic-book sequences; her short, translucent jacket was TV-receptive, randomly displaying whatever transmission was passing through her: just now, across her back, it was collaging a CNN image of an astronautics construction worker riding a maneuverer through the unfinished skeleton of the L5 colony, with a PBS shot of a medieval painting of Christ Ascending to Heaven. A spark of synchronicity.

As Marilyn receded down the street, her animated tattoos and the luminous blond of her Monroe wig and the shifting pictures on the TV jacket all ran together, blurred into one figure, a Pierrot made of restless media.

She's a McLuhan cut-out, Dexy thought, all reflective surface and no fucking character.

Marilyn did a wheelie, a pivot, pumped back up the street to him. "Come onnnnnn, Dexy!" Using her soft, husky Monroe voice. He was glad Zizz had run off; when Marilyn and Zizz got together, best buddies in giggling affectation, it could ill you out.

Coming at him now, her image-squirming outline resolved once more into tattoos and jacket TV reception. On one side of her open jacket a frontal shot of the Boy Ayatollah preaching gravely into the camera; on the other, beyond the DMZ of her bare skin and her up-turned, unnaturally perfect breasts, an animated political cartoon from the anarchist pirate radio transmissions showing two cartoonish infants—the Boy Ayatollah and the Reverend Baer, the Christian Fun General, reduced to sadistic infants, the two of them pulling the wings off of a screaming pigeon whose body was stenciled: NYC.

As she spun out to stop, Marilyn squeezed a tab on her belt, switching on the speakers miniaturized into the bikini under her skirt. The music was another kind of collage, a shaped-static band house-mixed with an old world-beat disco tune. The music boomed from the form-fitting speakers at her crotch. She made rhythmic thrusts with her hips into the crotch box's sonic vibrations. The way she did it, that kind of penetrating thrust, seemed male, to Dexy; that, and a wideness in her shoulders, the knobbiness of her knees, made Dexy wonder again if Marilyn used to be a boy. She was always a little exaggeratedly girlish in her poutiness, adorned with media imagery that might be a kind of stage magic distraction technique—all things Dexy associated with queens. But if she was a transsexual, she was a damn good one. Must've had her Adam's apple reduced, face expertly reconstructed. Lots of hormone pills, too, for softness. He was never quite sure.

If he really wanted to know, he should bop her once. Having sex with her ought to clear up the issue. Not because she wouldn't have a vagina—she might, by now—but because she'd have to use artificial lube, and her clitoris wouldn't look quite right. Unless maybe she could afford a clitoral transplant, like his Uncle Ernie had: the old fag had a clit transplanted into his throat.

"You want to scope the riot or what?" she asked him, tilting her head just to make her glowing hair droop over an eye.

"You don't know there's a riot," Dexy said.

"There's always a riot when there's a blackout. Especially over in Little Beirut."

"That's another thing, Marilyn. They don't call it Little Beirut because they've got maybe some Lebanese living there. You know? It's because of the fighting."

"I don' wanna go alone."

"I'm waiting for the *Surprise* to come on. I don't want to be in the middle of that kinda mess and have it hit me. I wanna get used to it."

"You took *Surprise*? Can I have some? I'll give you some speed."

"I only had one hit."

"Buhshit."

"It's true."

"Where'd you get it?"

"Fu."

"Fu? I'll bet he'll be at the riot. Let's cruise. It'll hit you before we get there."

He looked at her. Wondering if he should tell her why he'd taken the stuff. What he was doing.

But even a brainjammer like Marilyn would probably take time out to lecture him. Give him the same shit his video therapist had come out with. How a decision about self-euthanasia is maybe not something that should be made under the influence of a drug. Suicide is serious, take your time before applying for that SSEU (his therapist not realizing Dexy would never use a State Self-Euthanasia Unit, he'd do it himself someway that, at least, had some *statement* about it). And how suicide's usually inadvisable anyway. Stating the obvious. Ignoring the fact that he couldn't find another way to make the decision. He'd tried for months. *Surprise* was all that remained. The only thing that could make up his mind. Or so Fu said. And Fu was the neighborhood shaman.

Surprise. The drug was supposed to talk to you. Tell you things about yourself. Something like ibogaine or ketamine but more . . . cinematic. Less psychedelic. And the hallucinations didn't have a preceding buzz to warn you they were coming. They just slid themselves in with your ordinary perceptions. Hence the name.

"Who did the blackout this time?" he asked absently.

She shrugged, jumping the board up onto the curb and off again. "I heard on my battery box a buncha different claims. The Holy Islam seps took credit—"

"Fucking separatists are lunatics if they think they're going to have an independent Islamic state in the middle of New York—"

"—and the A-Team took credit—"

"Fucking anarchists—"

"—and the skinhead seps took credit."

"Fucking skinhead racist morons."

"I think it probably was the skinheads, they ain't scared of nothing. Too stupid to be."

He said, "Fuck it." And set off beside Marilyn, who was pumping the decal-patchy skateboard just enough to skate a few yards ahead of him, coasting to a stop, striking a pose, waiting till he passed her, pumping again, her movements synced to the world beat emanating from her crotch. . . .

He wondered vaguely if she were here at all. Maybe the *Surprise* had set in, he was hallucinating her and didn't know it. It could be like that, they said.

He'd heard stories about people taking *Surprise* and having no spectacular hallucinations at all. They hallucinate an old lady pushing a shopping cart in the supermall. A bit of trash in the gutter that wasn't really there: just an ordinary scrap of paper. Irrelevant, boring hallucinations. It depended on who you were, and what was significant in your subconscious, and how perceptive and imaginative you were. That's what Fu said.

So maybe she was a hallucination, he thought gloomily. I'm probably vapid enough to hallucinate my damn neighbor down the hall.

As she went by on the skateboard, he reached out and poked her— poked a cop firing a laser gun, in distorted TV image on her shoulder—and she weaved a bit on the board. "Hey!"

"Just wanted to see if I was hallucinating you."

She grinned, pleased. Misunderstanding. "Really?

Dexy stopped, staring up the darkened street, listening, as sirens howled a few blocks west, then more sirens from the east and north.

Sounded like they were converging on something. Maybe on the riot in Little Beirut, maybe on some other blackout action. There'd be trigger-happy police and snipers, up ahead. . . .

What do I care about cops and snipers? he asked himself. I'm gonna be dead soon. Aren't I?

He looked around, expecting the *Surprise* to answer him with a vision. Nothing. Not yet, anyway.

Marilyn used her long, luminous yellow nails to pluck a drug patch from her skirt pocket, peeled the stickum paper off with her teeth, spat it out; the round, slick white paper curled on the street like something curling up to die. She stuck the drug patch up under her skirt, onto a thigh, and shivered as the DMSO carried amphetamine into her. Started chattering. "You feel stoned on that *Surprise* stuff?"

"Nope."

"Thas whus eerie about it, I heard, that you don't feel stoned an' you don't hallucinate for, like, twenty minutes at a time and then all of a sudden something hits you . . . and then it's just gone and for a while there's nothin'; and then . . . and then . . ." Her voice trailed off into a staccato chant that went with the crotch box's rhythm. "And then and then and *then*. And then and then and *then*. And then and then and *then*. And then and—" So forth.

The box was grinding out a groove, the singer was Johnny Paranoid, the lyrics were:

There's a truth you can't avoid
Listen to Johnny Paranoid
Life will end in the burning void
Shakin' shakin' shakin' like a
rock'n'roll chord . . .

Maybe that's a sign, Dexy thought. Maybe it's an aural hallucination. Life will end in the burning void. Go ahead and kill yourself.

Maybe the drug was making him more sensitive to synchronicity messages, too. Either way it was the same message: *"Do it."*

But he was a long way from being sure. He looked around at the street and murmured to the drug, "Show me."

Still nothing out of the ordinary. There were other people out now, talking in clusters, some with flashlights, some with rifles. Or heading in small groups toward the riot, the looting, the action they could all feel, somehow, calling from over there. . . .

Now the crotch box was playing another tune, "Six Kinds of Darkness," and Dexy thought he could feel the kinds of darkness draped around them, could feel the penumbral layers parting like spiderwebs across him as he strode down the sidewalk in his imitation-snakeskin cowboy boots. Six kinds of darkness and more. Darkness diffused by starlight and the squared-off galaxy of skyline glowing from uptown; the inky darkness in the empty doorways; the striated darkness of the sewer grate; the pooling gray-black darkness as the street narrowed ahead; the raggedy darkness where the school burned with intermittent fires back down the street. The darkness of uncertainty.

Another gunshot from Delancey. And then two more.

He thought, Is this the kind of suicide I want? Hit by a stray bullet? He'd had something like a comfortable overdose in mind, or maybe blow himself up on the stage of some cheap club. Make it a performance-art piece. He'd fantasized about ripping off a car, hiring some of the Palestinian guys he knew over on Houston Street to rig it for him so he could drive a car bomb into some gangster's limo. Like the Yakuza/mafia scumbag who'd taken over Hard Disc CDs and dumped half the label's bands. Including Dexy's band. Blow that sucker up. Take him along to hell.

Just a fantasy. He knew that. Knew it was adolescent too. That's what happens when you're a thirty-nine-year-old rocker, you're an emotional adolescent in a middle-aged body. Embarrassing. No way he was ever going to get past it, either.

They reached a corner, turned left. Marilyn circling him now, looking him up and down. "You got a nice butt," she said.

"Shut up."

"Those Astaire pants are too loose, you should show your butt off with some tighter pants, Dexy. Did you kill that jacket yourself?"

"Oh, right, you bet. Like I'm going to go and hang out in Central Park with a rifle waiting to be eaten alive by a pack of wild dogs. I ain't that fucking desperate."

"You desperate about something, though, huh?"

"That's just an expression. Stop circling me like that, it's making me nervous."

"I'm not circling you . . . *Uh*-oh."

He looked at her, saw her smirk. "Very funny. Don't play with my head, pretend I'm hallucinating when I'm not. It's dangerous."

She said something he couldn't make out under the boom of the crotch box. "What?"

"I said I'm sorry. Are you mad at me?"

"No." Like he even knew her well enough to get mad at her. They were just run-into-each-other-at-clubs acquaintances. See-each-other-in-the-hall-and-bitch-about-the-landlord acquaintances.

"You going to give up getting your band back together? I noticed you grew your hair out natural color. You should get a scalp-up, a dude like you, in his thirties . . ."

He winced. She went on, obliviously.

". . . a guy like you looks younger with a scalp-up."

"I don't care if I look younger or not." He didn't sound convincing, even to himself.

"No?" Marilyn looked away. Her luminous wig swinging a little off-center as she looked around. "Let's go this way." She picked up her board and added, "I think I can get us past the police blockade." She led him through a brickstrewn vacant lot. They risked an alley, walked up north a half block, turned left—the noise of the blackout riot grow-ing—and then they had to sidle through a trash-gummy space between two old tenements. And then ...

Then they were in a party. Or a riot.

It was both. First the shouting, crashing sounds. Voices distorted by the cavelike echo of smashed-open storefronts. They stepped out onto the sidewalk, saw the shadows that filled the shop-lined street boiling with action. The street was crowded and the crowd was street. Dexy made out the scene in flashbulb flashes from light sources that came and went. An erratic comet, zigzagging, was someone with a chem lantern running by, carrying a ripped-off virtual-reality set under his arm, running past a bunch of teenagers tug-of-warring back and forth, fighting over something he couldn't see.

A storefront window disgorged something rectangular and bulky: a sofa being pushed out a window. Flamelight from other storefronts. Fistfights, over-there—and there. A chunky Hispanic mother scram-bled after her three grade-school kids, shouting at them in Spanish, her eyes bright with fear, but no fear on the wide-open faces of the kids as they ran helter-skelter through the riot in unfettered delight.

The air was scratchy with smells of smoke, cigarettes, spilled beer, and an acrid smell that might have been some kind of gunpowder. There was a stuttering series of detonations: strings of firecrackers going off, whoops and laughter from the people who'd set them; a small skyrocket arced up, trailing a confetti of fire. A group of people in a smashed-open adult-video store passed a hashpipe; someone threw a bottle at a window, *bonk*; it bounced off, but they tried again with a brick, *crash*, tinkle of shattered glass hitting the sidewalk; an angry shout, more firecracker bangs, louder than the first, in a storefront to the right ...

. . . as Marilyn squealed happily, "This is so *THRASHIN'*! Let's STEAL something!"

. . . and Dexy realized that the detonations in the storefront weren't firecrackers, they were gunshots, maybe some underinsured shop proprietor was trying to protect his goods, and someone screamed and there was a string of muzzle flashes. Dexy backed away from the curb, feeling suddenly agoraphobic. Snipers turned up at these things, all manner of lunatics, and at some point the cops would get it together and move in, shooting first and not necessarily rubber bullets.

Dexy backed till he stopped against a brick wall. Looked around, trying to get a handle on this thing. Was it a faction riot? Christians rioting through Islamic holdings? Muslims looting the Christians? Maybe the Sikhs looting the Hindus . . .

But the crowd was mixed and so were the storefronts. Pizzerias, discount dives, a shop that dealt in luminous tattoos and bone-implant radios. The DEA's licensed recreational drugs kiosk—untouched because everyone knew there was no stock in it at night. A hairdresser's, a manicurist, and a scalp-up place offering: *New Scalp-Ups—Scalps painlessly remolded! The new Shaps are Hear!* A group of angstrockers stood with a black hooker in a doorway, passing a stem around, getting some serious Bic-thumb from smoking synthetic rock, arguing about whether or not they really got a hit that time. One of them, a short girl in Harley boots and a stained wild-dog skirt, her knees bruised and scarred from skateboard fighting, reached up into her scalp-up, fingered out a "bottle" with a couple more rocks of synthetic crack. Her scalp-up was molded on her hairless scalp—of transplanted cartilage and collagen and skin—into a three-dee sculpture of a really nasty car accident.

Just the usual neighborhood stuff.

The street was barricaded off at the corners, way down by the smashed Citibank ATM on one side, and by the uptown R subway station on the other. Cars turned sideways, trash cans piled up, old oil barrels, heaped furniture, burning boxes. Police lights whirled beyond the barricade. Some sort of ominously brisk activity there. But not much. They were waiting for backup, Dexy guessed—there was too

much going on, all over downtown. This was probably just one of half
a dozen outbreaks. Maybe some shelling, too: He thought he heard the
distant CRUMP of mortar fire.

In the middle of the street, in front of him, the crowd was thickening
like a bee swarm, and most of them were dancing, a kind of rollicky,
improvised carnival dance to a beat box....

Marilyn's beat box. She was pumping in the thick of the riot, slamming to the beat box's thud. She's gonna get hurt out there.

A Hispanic guy with a sweat-sheened face, wearing a ripped
spangled-paper jumpsuit, ran by on bare and bleeding feet, giggling,
"Awright awright awright *noche partida*." His testicles waggling like a
dog's tongue out a rip in his jumpsuit.

Was the guy even there? Dexy wondered. Maybe there was only five
people in the street and the rest was the *Surprise*.

No. This was real. So far.

He spotted Marilyn again. The crowd was clumping around her.
Around the music booming from her crotch. Marilyn dancing, shaking
libido in their faces, wallowing in the attention. Someone bringing out
a steel drum, someone else a conga, adding salsa to the beat box's
drumming, Hispanics and blacks salsa-dancing and skanking, sharing
bottles and dust joints; someone rolling an oil barrel up, setting it on
end, cramming it with crushed boxes and wood, squirting charcoal-
lighter fluid, tossing in a match—WHUF! of flames blossoming over
the rusty old can ... And Marilyn was pressed by the crowd in toward
the burning can—the dancers began to circle her—Marilyn dancing
giddily on, a creature made of TV and moving tattoos overlapping
indistinguishably in jittering firelight ...

Stupid bitch is going to get hurt, Dexy thought.

And for some reason she was his responsibility. Or maybe she was
his point of orientation. Whatever, he was getting scared for her. It was
as if she were some crystallization of his crisis, and it didn't matter at
all that she was really no one to him.

He took a deep breath and started toward her, preparing to plunge
into the crowd. And saw Bunny García, Dexy's old guitar player. That
fuck-head. Bunny popping up out of the crowd, in his open guerrilla
jacket and black rubber pants, Brazilian-made high-top skates, grin-

ning, going, "Hey, *qué pasa*, Ugly?" Doing some kind of new complicated handshake on Dexy's palm so fast he couldn't even feel it. Bunny
with his Marshall-Amp-with-a-screaming-skull-for-a-speaker scalp-up,
expensive animated tattoo on his chest showing an eighteenth-century
pirate crew looting and raping on a twenty-first-century yacht. He'd
had the animatoo for a year, though, and it was getting old fast; the
animations beginning to flicker and fade. Couldn't afford to change it
now. Must've been cut off by his parents—his dad was the biggest
bookie in Spanish Harlem, owned this huge kitschy house with gold
wallpaper in Brooklyn Heights. Bunny used to brag about his mob
connections, which turned out to be bullshit when the band needed
them: when they were hassled for payoff money so they could go on-
stage at a mob-owned place called the Cat Club, and suddenly Bunny
was whining, "Hey, I got to use those mob favors for something important sometime, you know?"

So here was Bunny, the prima donna who burned through solos
faster than everyone else and bragged about the pickups on his fingertips that were installed at the guitar-surgery clinic like no one had ever
done that before; Bunny, who'd ditched him to join some dweeb hip-
hop rockoreography band. Here was Bunny, all of a sudden acting like
a deep comrade. "I don't have any money and I don't have any drugs,
Bunny," Dexy said.

"I don't want shit from you, man, except to say it's good to see you,
we oughta get a rage on sometime." Still grinning, doing that junkie
rub with the back of his hand on his nose, the other hand in the pocket
of his green Brazilian-guerrilla-fighter jacket—that jacket, an affectation if ever there was one, since Bunny'd shoot a hole in his foot if he
ever picked up a gun.

"Yeah, right," Dexy said, twitching as somebody smashed a bottle
on the street not far behind him. Someone else shot out an unlit street
lamp. He looked around. "This shit's getting out of hand."

"Don't worry about it," Bunny said as the tumult went into third
gear, the crowd noises beginning to really roar. Flames licking out from
a third-story window across the street; red light rippling across a very
short Asian guy humping a tall black woman in a doorway; she was
squatting some so he could thrust up under her African skirt. Her bare

breasts glittering with bead insets. The man's face straining with concentration, not wanting to miss out on this opportunity; the woman
laughing hysterically. A group of children dragging a mattress, while
another child, following them, tossed matches on it. The matches went
out, but he kept trying. An old Italian woman in widow black with a
looted fake-Tiffany lamp under one arm and a holoset under the other,
hurrying bent-backed through the thickening smoke. A couple of
Iranian-looking dudes, submachine guns under their arms, on the other
side of the crowd, just looking around. Marilyn still bobbing in the
party midst, by the fire. People still crowding her, but she was keeping
her head up, like she was treading water.

Sirens warbling from three or four directions, but no direct action
from the cops here yet. How long could it last?

"Those Iranian guys, or Arabs or whatever they are, you see 'em,
Bunny? Maybe that means they're gonna use this opp, do a push. They
start by shelling, mortars and RPGs and shit. I'm gonna get Marilyn,
get the fuck out of here."

"Hey, I'm telling you, don't worry about it, man. You was always
getting worried about shit—"

"That's the only reason we ever had a rehearsal or got a gig together,
because I worried," Dexy snapped. "I hadn't, we'd never have done
shit. You and Lunk'd sit around and play TV themes and smoke dope
all day if I didn't worry and hassle you. We got two gold records, the
only reason is because I worried. Those sessions were all worry, Bunny,
and I was the only one who ever did any."

"That's mostly right, man, but that was because you was the only
one who loved the worrying, loved chewing your nails and pushing
and nagging like a daddy. You fell into that role, see."

Dexy stared at him. It was amazing how well he could hear Bunny
with all this noise going on. It was as if they were in a bell of glass,
with the riot raging on around them but not touching them. The noise
and bustle of it was there, but muted, distant.

"Hey, Bunny, you like playing in that rock-oreo shit? Doing those
disco moves in that bourgeois uptown club? Those implants makin'
you jump like that? I couldn't stand to be puppeted around by some

fucking dance computer fucking with my nervous system. The music's already robot shit—"

"Of course I don' like it, man, what you think?" He scratched his crotch. "But Hemo wasn't happenin'. The band just wasn't happenin'."

"And you had a habit to support."

"Oh, yeah. Everybody's got something to support, Dexy. Or what? Everybody. You too. You got to pump up that big lead-singer ego of yours with lotta clothes you can't really afford. Parties. Where's your royalties money? You got into some drugs too. Blue Mesc. You and Rickenharp used to get together, do Blue Mesc for two days and nights straight, then whine about it when you had to crash. Where's your money from those gold records, Dexy? Where's the money from that endorsement you did for that Russian Microphone Company? What happened to that slick loft you used to have in Chelsea? You living in a dump down the hall from that hustler Marilyn, with roaches for roommates now." Smiling with an uncharacteristic gentleness all the time, as he said this. "Truth is, Dexy, we all stumbling around trying to get by the best we can. I was hurting and someone offered me a way out of the pain, that's all. To you it was disloyalty, or some shit. To me it was survival. For a while. My parents cut me off, wouldn't give me any more money after I got busted for dope. I got kicked out of that apartment I had in the old World Trade Center—did you see that place, after they made it into apartments? Huge honkin' old sky-scrapers turned into apartments, I thought it was gonna be great, but I moved in and it was just another big shitty tenement, kept up as bad as any place in the Bronx. A slum in the sky. And pretty soon, I didn't even have that. I was just trying to get by, man."

Dexy shook his head in amazement. "You must be getting some good dope. I never heard this kinda speech from you."

"I talked to you, my way, but you never listened. You were too busy bitching. You got to stop blaming people for stuff. Your old man, for instance, how he never understood what an *artiste* you are; your girl-friend, who was supposed to stick with you even when you brought home a drippy dick from half the groupies in United Europe. She was supposed to just understand. And you get into diddly little fights with

Kevin Keys about the band's musical direction. . . . Shit, Dex, you could've compromised, the man only wanted two tunes out of each set. Now you're getting some gray hair, you're slow coming out with lyric ideas, the record company drops you when sales nosedown, and you want to blame everybody else and take it out on us. Going to kill yourself to punish us. Get yourself on the cover of a magazine one last time. Shit."

"You killing yourself for years with dope, you should talk." Wondering, How did Bunny know about the suicide thing? Maybe Bunny had come over when he wasn't home, maybe he still had the key. Maybe he'd gotten nosy, played back Dexy's video therapy program. But, no, Dexy'd deliberately scrambled up the shrink program because he'd gotten pissed off about its advice; got drunk and programmed a rat's head onto the animated shrink and made everything it said come out in rodent squeaks.

"I *did* kill myself with dope, in fact," Bunny said offhandedly. "About two A.M., this morning. They haven't found my body yet. It was an accidental OD—I'm not a wimp like you."

Dexy's mouth dropped open. "You're—"

"Surprise!" Bunny said.

"—a hallucination. Or a ghost."

"A hallucination. But I did die. Or anyway, Bunny died."

Dexy felt a chill that seemed to shiver even in his hair and teeth and the tip of his tongue. "You're talking to me from the Other Side? I mean, there is life after death?"

"Oh, no. Well, I don't know. Bunny's talking to you from inside your own head. Bunny's a hallucination. But you're on the frequency where you can pick up on some things, is how you know that Bunny is dead." The hallucination talking about Bunny in the third person now.

The Bunny thing turned and looked at the place the Muslim guys had stood. They were gone. "They've decided to do a push through here, use the riot crowd for cover. They going to expand territory."

"Oh, shit."

"Works out good. You stay here, Dex, you get killed. Go down in a riot: shot dead by militia, or by cops, pretty good rock'n'roll death, wouldn't you say?" The Bunny thing's face was changing. Sucking into itself. Skull pushing out through the skin, eyes becoming little glints in sunken sockets. Gums shriveling back, teeth exposed. The scalp-up sinking into itself, rotting off, ragged sections of yellow cranium showing through in patches. But he kept talking. More or less in the tone of voice Dexy's video-shrink used. "Remember that time, before the city was Balkanized, you lived in Chelsea? And you walked down to Houston one night and blundered right into the first Islamic Fun uprising. You couldn't believe it, your little downtown art and rock scene just irrelevant, silly-looking because these guys in cheap paramilitary outfits come running down the sidewalk like kids playing army, busting caps with those Kuwaiti carbines. They take part of the East Village and the whole of Soho hostage, all those pink-boy Soho art galleries and, like, neo-neoexpressionists an' shit, all of 'em suddenly under the gun? I remember an anarchist friend of mine laughing about it saying Yeah, now *that* is art! It was kind of cool, the Soho artists and the deputy mayor, all of 'em held hostage by the Islamic Funs—"

Dexy nodded. At the time, not so long ago, it had seemed outlandish, outrageous, bizarre, and scary as hell. They'd thought it would blow over any day. It just couldn't go on. But then the Islamic Funs started making demands, the Boy Ayatollah took over that little TV station, the choppers came in from the artificial islands where the Libyans were building up all that arsenal—it had just started unfolding like something totally out of control and it wasn't so funny anymore.

Thinking about this, Dexy watched the Bunny thing becoming shorter, as if his legs were melting. His eyes had vanished completely now. His neck shrink-wrapped his upper spine; his clothes hung on him like his bones were a hanger. Dexy watched in horrified fascination. It was as if his metamorphosis was some anthropomorphic parody of the city's own transformation into Little Beirut.

The Christian Funs had come out of Queens, down from Upstate and Maine, with their private red-neck militia; the mayor looked the other way, even told the National Guard to let the ChrisFuns through the blockade. And then the sniping started, the mortar shelling. It was weird how fast you got used to seeing people killed. How some mindless social inertia could keep you in the crossfire while Christian

Fundamentalists shoot at Islamic Fundamentalists and the MosFuns shoot back at the ChrisFuns. Photos on the front page of the *Post* showing a Black Muslim grade-school classroom after it was hit by a mortar shell. . . .

"Yeah, that was a key moment, that picture on the *Post*," the hallucination was saying, reading his mind because it was his mind. "Remember that one? Those burst-open kids? Art my fucking ass. That's what turned people against the ChrisFuns, so they had to dig in, in their own part of town. Just when you think it can't get worse, *bang*. That's when there was all that serious shelling back and forth and the hostage thing gets worse and both sides block evacuation moves and backers airdrop supplies and ammo and nobody can get up the nerve to take responsibility for the political risk of sending in the National Guard or the marines or whoever . . ." Now his flesh was puffing out again, blowing up into a different person, a smaller person with a different face entirely. Fast-forward animation.

And the riot went on in the background, someone dumping a garbage can off a roof so it tumbled end over end, fell onto a group of people who screamed as it struck them; a bottle arced and smashed nearby. Flying bricks. Marilyn struggling now, trying to get out of the crowd, panicking. The music warping as some punk in the crowd ripped her crotch box from her. All of this some distant backdrop as the metamorphosing thing jabbered on, ". . . because if they did that, sent the army in here, there'd be a huge bloodbath, all this innocent bloodshed, so they spend months in negotiations, and the JDL gets involved in the fighting and the kid militias spring up and it gets worse, shooting on the street every day, everybody starts to get used to it, the black marketing spreads out, gangs like the Crips make deals with the factions and use the faction territories for hideouts. And here's Dexy, now, stuck in the middle of all this, because you can't afford to move. Partly because about the same time you lost your record deal. That's when it happens, right? So your cash flow dries up and here you are on the edge of the fighting. But, hell, that fits your rock'n'roll feelings about things, right, Dex, you *like* that action, right? Oh, sure. You're ready to rock till you're dead anyway because you're an *artiste*, you're

chosen to incarnate That Energy, that's what you always believed—"
There's nothing worse than a sarcastic hallucination.

The Bunny García thing was gone; the hallucination had become a
boy. A fourteen-year-old brown-skinned boy in a turban. The Boy Ayatollah, the child Imam, looking both stern and cherubic. Both a familiar
media figure and something exotic, in his black-and-red robe. "So, then,
my friend," the Boy Ayatollah said. "What are you scared of? My
people are coming here tonight, and many will die, and you can go
down among them, in some kind of glory—what kind of glory is
uncertain. But some kind. What are you, then, afraid of?"

Dexy's mouth was dry. He had trouble talking. But the kid was so
earnest, he was talking right to the heart of him. Dexy had to answer
him. You couldn't lie to this kid. Finally, he said thickly, "I'm afraid
of dying. But I'm afraid to go on the way I have been and just sort of
shrivel up into just another shuffling old geezer, too. I feel like . . . like
I'm not alive anymore because I can't do the thing, you know, the thing
that . . . I don't know how to say it . . . The thing that made me feel
like being alive meant something."

"Have a look around with me, won't you?"

The boy put his hand through the crook of Dexy's arm, strolled with
him down the street along the edges of the crowd. It had thinned out
some.

Dexy could no longer hear Marilyn's crotch box booming. They'd
taken it. Maybe hurt her.

Then, *crunch, squeal*. As a police armored car with an earthmover-
blade for a battering ram smashed through the barricade by the Citibank, whirling the watery-neon shine of its cherrytop beacon over the
lizard-skin asphalt, cops in armor and heavy riot gear booming out
unintelligible warnings with bullhorns, firing tear gas, the rioters scattering . . .

The Islamic Funs choosing the same moment to come pouring out
of the subway station and the old burned-out Tad's Steakhouse from
the other direction, probably not seeing the cops' push till too late, firing
at anyone handy. Going for an expansion of territory in the Holy Name
of Allah and in the glory of the Sacred Martyrdom of the Boy Ayatollah's precocious New Fundamentalism . . .

...Triggering the Christian Funs, who were financed and armed by the Birchers and the KKK, to open fire from the rooftops, chickenshit snipers, as usual, so that a few of the onrushing Fathers of the New Islamic American State went down, writhing....

(Dexy wondering at his own fearlessness, here. It wasn't suicidal fearlessness—it was a sense that he was protected, surfing the Luck Plane....)

"Now see them again," the Boy Ayatollah said, his voice, through the screaming and gun-shooting and sirening, coming with eerie lucidity. He waved his hand, and Dexy saw the gunmen and the rioters were not men and women any longer.

They were small children.

All of them: the Skinheads, Brownshirts for the Chris-Funs, dropping into the fray, now, from the fire escapes; the Islamic Funs darting down the street; the rioters and looters; the police coming from another direction. All of them were transformed—or revealed: they were children. The cops' battering vehicle was a toy thing of cheap plastic in bright primary colors, and there was a jolly clown's face painted on its earthmover-blade. The children who had been Christian Funs and Islamic Funs militia weren't playing army; they were frightened kids in costumes, running through a maze that wasn't quite there. Their play with guns was hysteria, crying and laughing at the same time, seven-year-olds with toy guns that killed like real guns. Children, all of them, children with a searching in their faces—all of them weeping, mouthing Mama, Daddy, all of them running someplace.... You could see they were running to some hypothetical shelter, trying to get past the other kids, driven through them as if they were running from something—yes, Dexy saw them clearly now: The children ran from flying apparitions of translucent violet plasma, etheric fiends screaming at them in hot pursuit; creatures that were all mouth and no eyes...the children trying to get away from the apparitions, firing at one another as they went...as the scene got darker, and darker and darker...the apparitions flowing down into the shadows...until the children alone remained, their guns vanished, just children blinded by darkness, flailing about, colliding sightlessly, stumbling at random this way and that.

The apparitions had melted down into long, attenuated cables of ectoplasm that interlinked the various groups, a network of the stuff, linking the children who were Christian Funs, other skeins linking children who were Islamic Funs; other nets linking the cops . . . The nets tangling, the tangles violence . . . The children mouthing something else now . . .

All of them saying the same thing, though they made no sound at all. Saying, Where are they? When will they come?

The Boy Ayatollah remarked, "They're waiting for the adults to find them, Dexy, to bring them out of the darkness, the permanent blackout of uncertainty." The Boy Ayatollah looked at him earnestly. "But Dexy, *the adults never come. The adults never will come, my friend. The children are on their own forever."

"Oh, man. Don't say that." Dexy near tears.

"It's nothing to you, though. You're a rock star. A performer. A rock'n'roll hero. 'You're all just fucking peasants as far as I can see,' John Lennon said, long ago. You want to live fast, and die young, no? What is all this suffering to you?"

"Shut up. That's pure crap. Just shut up."

"You prefer one voice to two? It happens mine is fading anyway. . . ."

Surprise: the hallucination passed. The Boy Ayatollah was gone; the darkness eased, the full noise of the street roared down on Dexy like a runaway bus. And the children were transformed, magically matured, once more adult rioters, cops wrestling with them; other cops firing suppressive rounds at adult gunmen. Looters flattened on the street, crawling to avoid the gunfire. A couple dozen were fallen and wounded. Some of them dead.

But some were still quite active. Dexy saw two pasty-white skinheads dragging Marilyn into a looted storefront.

Dexy told himself, You should run and help her.

A bullet spat asphalt near his foot, and he jumped back, the back of his head feeling soft. He ducked into the shelter of a darkened concrete doorway. The fear finally hitting him, now that the hallucination had passed, adrenaline whiplashing through him. Run. Cops hunkered behind the armored vehicle, moving past him, shouting warnings at the

Islamic Funs who were backing off; the bullets still flying; the crack of another sniper rifle on the roof. Run. Get out of here. Back the way you came.

But the two guys were out of sight, now, in that storefront, hidden in there with Marilyn, doing something to her . . .

Shit.

Run, man, nothing you can do to help her.

But . . .

Forget it. Maybe you wouldn't get killed—maybe just suffer. Maybe a bullet to the spine, quadriplegia or something . . .

But, shit. Marilyn.

He grabbed a ten-inch piece of broken pipe from the sidewalk, ran across the street, behind the cops, sprinting toward the storefront. A bullet whined past, close enough he nearly wet his pants.

The storefront. A Korean grocery-import store. In the shifting red light from the cop car and the fires, the buttress sections of old grime-gray brick walls to either side of the storefront looked like squared-off pillars at the entrance to some ancient temple. The graffiti spray-painted over the buttresses seemed cryptic as the pagan glyphs of the temple's forgotten race. . . .

The drug hadn't completely worn off. He was just reaching the curb in front of the Korean storefront, hearing Marilyn screaming something, when the second-story window above the storefront erupted outward, showering broken glass past the rusty fire escape. Dexy looked up and saw a cloud of spinning glass fragments falling toward him, glittering red in the hellish light. *Surprise:* The cloud of glass slowing, stopping in midair, floating there, was now a cloud of moths whose softly beating wings were of broken glass and whose faces belonged to demented angels. Showers of glass shards: silicon grace. He gaped at the hallucination . . . and the broken glass fell on his face.

He shrieked, "*Fuu*-ucccck," and dropped the pipe, clawed at his eyes. Felt splinters of glass like pin feathers on his cheeks. He thought, My eyes!

But he blinked . . . looked around. The glass had missed his eyes. He let out a long breath and, stomach quaking, plucked shards from his face. Too freaked to feel any pain yet. And again remembered Marilyn.

(As behind him were screams, cracks and rattles of weapons, more sirens, laughter, someone pleading.)

He reached down to the pipe lying in the broken glass. Saw fragmented reflections of himself in the glass, jigsaw mirrors, lying around the pipe. Picked up the pipe. Saw the glass move by itself, the jigsaw parts coming together, fusing the pieces of his reflection. A kid. A lost kid. But someone was standing behind the kid. Himself: as an adult. Who put his hand on the kid's shoulder. The kid was Dexy at seven. The adult had come, after all.

Dexy was running into the Korean store then, flagrantly proud of himself for coming to Marilyn's rescue. Looking for the men who would be raping her.

There—in the light from a chem lantern, over in the corner, beyond overturned shelves tumbled with Korean ideogrammed packaged foods. There they were.

Dexy stopped, staring.

Marilyn was bending over the two men who'd dragged her in. Both guys were out cold, bleeding from head wounds. She still had the spike heels she'd used on them in her hands. She dropped the shoes, squatted beside them, legs awkwardly apart, barefoot still, like a little girl toying with a mud pie, singing something tunelessly as she poked through their pockets. All she came up with was a half-empty pack of THC syntharettes. She stuck them into the band of her skirt. Dexy noticed a half dozen synthetic-crack drug patches, the street-made kind shaped like iron crosses, on her arms. "You shouldn't mix coke with meth," he heard himself say. "You shouldn't be taking any of that shit, anyway."

He stared at her as she turned, smiled loopily up at him. He felt foolishly disappointed when he realized he didn't need the pipe bludgeon. Odd, because he didn't really like fights. He tossed the pipe aside. Turned and looked out the broken storefront.

Looking at the fighting. Rioters running from cops, yelling they were ready to surrender but getting their heads busted in anyway. Skinheads and Christian militia fighting with Islamic Funs. He thought about what had nudged the Islamic Funs into taking over their sector: persecution from city administration and landlords who wanted the

immigrants moved out for real estate development—*jingoistic* legisla-
tion, too, restrictions on Muslim rights to build mosques that had come
from an increasingly conservative government controlled by Christian
Fun bigots. The Christians feeling pressured by a growing Islamic community; the Muslims threatened by the Christian reaction. This wasn't
Little Beirut—this was the whole planet. This was Jews and Arabs,
Sikhs and Hindus, Serbs, Croats and Bosnians, Communists and Cap-
italists. This was the way they all were.

In the face of that suffering, the pain of that societal autism, his petty
priorities, the primacy of his career, seemed irrelevant. Pathetic, insig-
nificant. So much self-indulgence. Particularly, suicide.

Dexy seeing again, for a flash moment, the confused children—children caught up, he saw now, in a desperate effort to find their way
home by superimposing a purely arbitrary order on the chaos of an
overwhelming uncertainty. Arbitrary ideological nets tangling, children
strangled in the mesh.

Any mesh. Anything you artificially attached importance to. Some
mesh of meaningless priorities that tangled you, choked you. Some
arbitrary identity . . .

Like being a rock star. Just for example.

He went to Marilyn, reached out, grabbed her hand, pulled her to
her feet. Squeezed her hand. She was real. Probably not a real girl, not
originally, but he didn't care.

"You checkin' to see am I a hallucination again?"

He nodded. Realizing that a bubble had burst, somehow, a
membrane had split: the drug had worn off. But it had spoken to him.
Something, anyway, had spoken to him.

The gunshots were diminishing outside. People coughing from tear
gas. Lights wheeling in his peripheral vision. Curls of smoke.

"I feel like I'm gonna be real, real sick," Marilyn said, slumping,
clutching herself.

"I know where there's an anarchist clinic, they'll give you a shot to
take you down. After that, you better stay away from drugs. They fuck
up your priorities."

She bent over and threw up. He waited. Finally, she straightened up, spat a few times, and croaked, "Can we get outta here through the back?"

"I think so. Come on." He picked up the chem lantern, helped her clamber past the overturned shelves and Korean produce. She was shaky, now. There was blood trickling from under her wig. They paused, and he peeled the wig off her and looked. It wasn't bad, just a scalp cut.

As they went out the back way, into the narrow walk space that led to the quiet of the next street over, she said, "This was a hot date. What you doing tomorrow night?"

"Resting up. So I can apply for a job with my head screwed on right. I was offered an A-and-R gig at Roadkill CDs. . . ."

"You giving up partying? Going to go real serious?"

He hesitated, then said, "Not really. I'm gonna have spare time. There's something we could do, just for fun, if you want. You know how to play an instrument?"

"No. But I can sing. Real good."

"Can you?" He smiled. "I can play bass. Good enough. Fuck it, then. Let's start a band. In my spare time. And *you* be the lead singer."

As they stepped out onto the sidewalk of an empty street he peeled the drug patches off her and tossed them away. The drug patches fell into the gutter and curled up like dead things.

What It's Like to Kill A Man

First of all," the wall-eyed prizewinner said, "it's a feeling of power like you never had. I figure that's especially the case here, like, with the AVLPs, see, because it ain't like you're doing it in self-defense, or in a war where it's in a hurry—you got time to, you know, *think* about it first..."

Spector was watching the wall-eyed guy on TV. The guy was tubby, was wearing a stenciled-on brown suit, one of the cheap JC Pennys printouts where the tie blurs into the shirt-collar. And green rubber boots. Spector puzzled over the green rubber boots till he realized they were intended to look military.

A ghost-image of another man's face, ragged-edged, began to slide over the AVLP winner's; the new face was bodiless, just a face zigzagging across the image with kitelike jerkiness. A punky face, a Chaoticist; leering, laughing. His tag rippled by after his face like the tail after a comet: JEROME-X.

It was television graffiti, transmitted from a shoplifted minitranser. The year 2021's answer to spraypaint.

Annoyed, Senator Spector hit the switch on his armchair, turning off the TV. The broad, inch-thick screen slotted back into the ceiling. He was glad of an excuse to turn the program off. In a way, the AVL program was his responsibility. He'd felt bound to take stock of it. But watching it, the gnawing feeling had begun in his stomach again . . .

Spector stood up and went to the full-length video mirror in his bedroom. It was time to get ready for the interview. He gazed critically at his fox face, brittle blue eyes. His black crewcut was widowpeaked to hint at minimono styles—to let the youngsters know he was hip, even at forty-five.

He wore a zebra-striped printout jumpsuit. It'll have to go, he decided. Too frivolous. He tapped the keyboard inset beside the mirror, and changed his image. The video-mirror used computer-generated imagery; the generated images weren't immaculately realistic, but they were close enough to give him an idea how it'd look. . . . He decided he needed a friendlier look. Add a little flesh to the cheeks; the hair a shade lighter. Earring? No. The jumpsuit, he told the mirror, would have to be changed to a leisure suit, but make its jacket stenciled for more identification with the Average Joe. He'd never wear a stenciled suit out to dinner, but just now he needed to project a "man of the people" image especially as the interviewer was from the Undergrid. Both his security adviser and his press secretary had warned him against giving an interview to an underground media rep. But the Undergrid was growing, in size and influence, and it was wise to learn to manipulate it—use it, before it used you.

He tapped out the code for the suit, watched it appear in the mirror superimposed over his jumpsuit. A cream-colored leisure suit. He pursed his lips decided a two-tone combination would be friendlier. He tapped the notched turtleneck to a soft umber.

Satisfied with the adjusted image, he hit the *Print* switch. He shed the jumpsuit, and waited, wondering if Janet had contacted his attorney, Heimlitz. He hoped she'd hold off on the divorce till after the election. . . . The console hummed and a slot opened beside the glass. The suit rolled out first: flat, folded, still pleasantly warm, smelling faintly of its fabrication chemicals. He pulled it on; it was high quality fabricant, only slightly papery against his skin.

He used Press Flesh for his cheeks, tamping and shaping till it conformed with the image he'd programmed, appearing to blend seamlessly with his skin. He used the cosmetics closet to lighten his hair, widen his eyes a fraction, then went to the living room, and looked around. Shook his head. It was done in matte-black and chrome. Too somber—he had to take great pains to avoid anything even remotely morbid. He dialed the curtains to light blue, the rug to match. The console chimed. He went to it, and flicked for visual. The screen blinked to the expressionless face of the housing area's checkpoint guard.

"What is it?" Spector asked.

"People here to see you in a van fulla video stuff. Two of them, name of Torrence and Chesterton, from UNO. Citident Numbers—"

"Never mind. I'm expecting them. Send 'em up."

"You don't want a visual check?"

"No! And for God's sake be friendly to them, if you know how."

He cut the screen, wondering if he were being cavalier about security. Maybe—but he kept a .44 in the cabinet beside the console, as security backup. And there was always Kojo.

Spector rang for Kojo. The little Japanese looked small, neat, harmless. His official title was Secretary. He was actually a bodyguard.

Kojo knew about the interview. Flawlessly gracious, he ushered the two Undergrid reps into the living room, then went to sit on a straight-backed chair to the left of the sofa.

Kojo wore a blue printout typical of clerks. Sat with his hands folded in his lap; no tension, no warning in his posture, no hint of danger. Kojo had worked for Spector only two weeks, but Spector had seen the security agency's dossier on him. And Spector knew that Kojo could move from the bland aspect of a seated secretary to lethal attack posture in a quarter-second.

The people from UNO wore "rags"—actual cloth clothing, jeans, t-shirts worn boots. Silly affectations, Spector thought. The woman introduced herself as Sonia Chesterton. She was the interviewer. The big black guy, Torrence, was her technician. He wore a dangling silver earring in his left ear, and his head was shaved. Spector smiled, and shook their hands, making eye contact. Feeling a chill when he met the girl's eyes. She was almost gaunt; her dark eyes were sunken, red-rimmed. Thin brown hair cut short. She and Torrence seemed neutral; not hostile, not friendly.

Spector glanced at Kojo. The bodyguard was alert, and relaxed.

Take it easy, Spector told himself, sitting on the sofa beside Sonia Chesterton. His body language read friendly-but-earnest; he smiled just enough. Torrence set up cameras, mikes.

The girl looked at Spector. Just looked at him.

It felt wrong. TV interviewers, even if they intended to feed your image to the piranhas during the interview itself, invariably maintained a front of friendliness before and after.

The silence pressed on him. Silence, the politicians enemy.

"Ready at your signal," Torrence said. He looked big, hulking over hand sized cameras on delicate aluminum tripods.

"Now—what shall we talk about?" Spector asked. "I thought perhaps—"

"Let's just launch into it," she broke in.

He blinked. "No prep?"

Torrence pointed at her. She looked into the camera. Serious. "I'm Sonia Chesterton, for UNO, the People's Satellite, interviewing Senator Hank Spector, one of the key architects of the AntiViolence Laws, and an advocate of the AVL Programming . . ."

For awhile, the interview was standard. She asked him how he justified the AntiViolence Laws. Looking at her solemnly, speaking in an exaggeration of his Midwestern accent (the public found it reassuring), he gave his usual spiel: Violent crime began its alarming growth trend in the 1960s. It continued to rise in the 1970s, leveled out in the '80s for a few years—chiefly because prison sentences were stiffened, taking a lot of hardcases off the street for awhile—and then feverishly resurged in the 1990s. The worldwide population shift, which cascaded millions of immigrants into the United States, strained the country's job availability past the limit. Crime and drug abuse soared through the year 2000, continued increasing for nearly two decades more. Factors like the breakdown in traditional family structures, the steady increase of brain-damaging pollutants in the environment, and the wide availability of drugs like PCP, coinspired to create sociopaths and psycho-killers. The poisoned environment oozed psychosis.

The old punitive laws weren't forceful enough for true deterrence, Spector argued. The AVL was as powerful a deterrent as a civilized nation could create. The AntiViolence Laws stated that anyone who committed a violent crime more than once would receive punitive public beatings. Anyone who committed a homicidal violent crime more than twice was simply executed, within three weeks after conviction. The right to appeal was considered to have been forfeited after the second felony assault. Or after the first homicide. Anyone convicted of a first degree homicide was executed, within three weeks of conviction, even on a first crime. Second degree murder—if it was your first offense—got you a series of public beatings, and a long sentence. If it was your second sentence-offense, it got you a quick execution.

The "innocent by reason of insanity" escape was simply abolished. The mad were executed too.

Rapists were publicly castrated. Thieves were beaten, sometimes maimed.

"Violent crime is down sixty percent from five years ago," Spector said gravely. "It continues to drop. In a few years the Security checkpoints and the precautions that make modern life tedious—these may vanish entirely. Perhaps, because of the sped-up judicial pace, three or four people a year are unjustly convicted, but the majority of Society are better off."

"Even accepting that that's true—which I don't—" Sonia Chesterton said "— does that justify the executioner's lottery? The AVL TV programs?"

"First, AVL TV gets the public involved with the criminal justice system, so that they identify with Society, and no longer feel at odds with the police. Second, it acts as a healthy catharsis for the average person's hostility which otherwise—"

"Which otherwise might be directed at the State in a revolution?" She cut in, her neutrality gone.

"No." He cleared his throat, controlling his irritation. "No, that's not—"

He was even more annoyed by her interruption, and her tone, when she broke in: "The phrase 'healthy catharsis' puzzles me. Lottery winners are winning the right to beat or execute a convict on public television. Ever watch the program *What It's Like*, Senator?"

"Well, yes, I watched it today to see if in fact—"

"Then you saw the way those people behave. They giggle when they're beating the convict's head in! A man or a woman, gagged in a stocks; the 'winner' clubs them to death—or, if he or she prefers, uses a gun, blows their brains out. . . . And they cackle over it, and the more demented they are, the more the studio audience cheers them on. Now you call that *healthy?*"

Stung, he said, "It's temporary! The release of tension—"

"Two of the lottery winners were arrested, tried and executed for *illegal* murders, *after* their participation in AVL programs. It seems fairly obvious that they developed a *permanent* taste for killing—reinforced by public approval—which they—"

"Those were flukes! I hardly think—"

"You hardly think about anything except what's convenient for you. Because if you did you'd have to see that you, Senator, are no better than a murderer yourself."

Her veneer of objectivity had cracked, fallen away. Her voice shook with emotion. Her hands clenched her knees, knuckles white. He began to be afraid of her.

"I really think you've lost all objectivity," he said, coolly as he could manage. But feeling fear turn to anger.

(Feeling, in fact, he was near losing his own veneer of cool self-righteousness; feeling he was near snapping. And wondering: Why? Why had all the skills he'd developed in years of facing hostile interviewers suddenly evaporated? It was this issue. It haunted him, nagged him. At night it ate away at his sleep like an acid. . . . And the damn woman went on, and *on!*)

"Everyone who has been killed, Senator—the innocent ones at least—their blood is on your hands. You—"

Some inner membrane of restraint in Spector's consciousness flew into tatters; and anger uncoiled itself. Anger propelled by guilt. He stood, arms straight at his sides, trembling. "Get out. Get OUT!"

He turned to Kojo, to tell him to escort them to the door.

And saw: Torrence stretching his right arm toward Kojo; in Torrence's hand was a small gray box. And Kojo had frozen, was staring into space in a kind of fugue state.

Spector thought: *Assassins.*

And then Kojo stood, and turned toward Spector. Spector looked desperately around for a weapon.

Kojo came at him—

And ran past him, at the woman. A wrist flick, and he was holding a knife. She looked at him calmly, resignedly, and then she screamed as—his movements a blur—he closed with her, drove the slim silver blade through her left eye, and into her brain.

All the time, Torrence continued filming, showing no surprise, no physical reaction.

Spector gagged, seeing the spurt of blood from her eyesocket as she crumpled. And Kojo stabbed the woman methodically, again and again. Spector stumbled back, fell onto the sofa.

"Kill Spector after me, Kojo!" Torrence yelled. Torrence turned a knob on the little gray remote control box, dropped it—and the box melted to a lump of plastic slag. Spector stared, confused.

Torrence had stepped into the TV cameras' viewing area, had closed his eyes, was waiting, shaking, muttering a prayer that might have been Islamic—then Kojo rushed him, the small Japanese leaping at the big black man like a cat attacking a doberman guard dog. . . . Only, Torrence just stood there, and let Kojo slash out his throat with one impossibly swift and inhumanly precise movement. *Kill Spector after me, Kojo.*

But Spector was moving, ran to the cabinet, flung it open, snatched up his .44 pistol, turned and, panicking . . . shot Kojo in the back.

Kojo would have turned on Spector next, surely . . .

But in the pulsing silence that followed the gunshot, as Spector looked down at the three bodies, as he stared at the big, red-oozing hole his bullet had torn in Kojo's back. . . . Seeing Kojo's own Press Flesh cosmetic had come off, exposing the shaved spot on the back of Kojo's head, the puckered white scar from recent surgery . . .

Looking at that, he thought: *I've been set up.*

And the security guards were pounding on the door.

"Today on *What It's Like* we're going to talk to Bill Muchowski, the first man to participate in an actual *legal duel* with an AVL convict— Bill, you wanted to execute the man 'in a fair fight,' is that right?"

"That's right, Frank, I'm a former US Marine and I just didn't want to shoot the man in cold blood, I wanted to give him a gun, and of course I'd have a gun, and we'd, you know, *go at it*."

"Sort of an old fashioned wildwest gunfight, eh? You're a brave man! I understand you had to sign a special waiver—"

"Oh sure, I signed a waiver saying if I got hurt or killed the government couldn't be held responsible—"

"Bill, we're running out of time, can you just tell us quickly, what is was like for you, Bill Muchowski, to kill a man."

"Uh, sure, Frank—killing a man with a gun has its *mechanical* aspect, like you got to punch a hole through the guy, and that causes a loss of life-giving hemoglobin. Now, what it *feels* like to do that—well, you almost feel like the bullet is a part of you, like you can feel what it would feel, and you imagine the bullet nosing through the skin, then pushing through muscle tissue, smashing through organs, breaking bone, flying out the other side of 'im with all that red liquid . . . just blowing the bastard away. And it feels good knowing he's a killer so he deserves it. And there's a funny kinda *relief*—"

"Bill, that's all we've got time for now, thanks for letting us know *What It's Like!*"

The cell they'd moved him to that morning was significantly smaller than the first one. And dirtier. And colder. And there was someone else in it, wearing a blood-stained prison shirt; the guy was asleep, his back turned, on the top bunk. The cell had two metal shelves, bunks, extending from the smudged white concrete wall, and a lidless, seatless toilet. They wouldn't tell him why he'd been moved, and now, looking around at his cell, Spector was beginning to suspect the reason, and with the suspicion came fear.

Don't panic, he told himself. You're a United States senator. You've got friends, influence, and the strings sometimes take a while to let you know they've been pulled. The defense contractors and the Pentagon need you for that military appropriations bill. They'll see you through this.

But the cell seemed to mock all reassurance. He looked around at the cracked walls; the water stain on the white concrete near the ceiling looking like a sweat-stain on a t-shirt; the bars where the fourth wall should have been, dun paint flaking off them. The graffiti burnt into the ceiling with cigarette coals. *JULIO-Z*, 2017!! and WHO-EVER U R, YER ASS IS SCREWED!!! and AT LEASE (sic) YOU A *TV STAR!!! ONCE!?!*

Spector's stomach growled. Breakfast that morning had been a single egg on a piece of stale white bread.

His legs were going to sleep from sitting on the edge of the hard bunk. He got up, paced the width of the cell, five paces the long way, four the short.

He heard a metallic rasp, and a clang; echoey footsteps in the stark spaces of the hallway. Trembling, he went to the bars.

A middle-aged, seam-faced man wearing a stenciled-on three-piece suit, and carrying a tan vinyl briefcase, was walking up behind the guard. He walked as if he were bone tired.

The bored, portly black guard said, "Got to look in your satchel there, buddy." The stranger opened his briefcase, and the guard poked through it. "No machine guns or cannons in there," he said. A humorless joke. He unlocked the door, let the stranger in. The guard locked up, and went away.

"Senator Spector," the man said, extending his hand. "I'm Gary Bergen." They shook hands; the stranger's hand was cold, moist.

"You from Heimlitz's office? It's about time he—"

"I'm not from Heimlitz," Bergen said. "I'm a public defender."

Spector stared at him. Bergen looked back with dull gray eyes. "Heimlitz is no longer representing you. They formally withdrew from the case."

Spector's mouth was dry. He sank onto the bunk. "Why?"

"Because your case is hopeless, and your wife is in the process of seizing your assets, and she refuses to pay them."

Spector suspected that Bergen was taking some kind of quiet satisfaction in all this. He sensed that Bergen didn't like him.

Spector just sat there. Feeling like he was sitting on the edge of the Grand Canyon, and if he moved, even an inch, he'd slip and go over the edge, and fall, and fall . . .

He conjured determination up from somewhere inside and said, "Senator Burridge's committee will provide the money to—"

"The Committee to Defend Senator Hank Spector? It's been disbanded. Public opinion was overwhelmingly against them. Frankly, Senator, the public is howling for your blood. . . . For the very reason that you are who you are. The public doesn't want to see any favorites played. And they're sure you're guilty."

"But *why*? I haven't gone to trial, there's only been a hearing—and by now they should have screened the TV footage. That should've vindicated me!"

"Oh, they've screened it, for the judge and on television for the public. Everyone's seen it. They saw you holding that gray box, pointing it at your bodyguard, making him attack those people . . . a closeup on your face as you shouted, 'Kill them!' The autopsy on Kojo found the brain implant that made him respond to the prompter against his will . . . And we saw you pulling that gun, shooting your bodyguard in the back—to make it look as if he'd gone mad and you killed him to protect yourself . . ." Bergen was enjoying this. "Too bad you didn't have time to get rid of the videotapes."

Spector wasn't able to speak for a few moments. Finally, he managed. "It's . . . insane. Moronic. Why would I go to that much trouble to kill Sonia Chesterton—"

"Your wife says you were obsessed with her. That you watched Sonia's TV editorials and they incensed you, you babbled that Sonia deserved to die—and so forth," he shrugged.

"That's perjury! I never saw the Chesterton woman before that interview, on TV or off! They asked permission to interview me through my secretary, that's the first I ever heard of UNO. Janet's lying so she'll get everything. . . . But the tapes—they *can't* have shown me saying 'kill them'—I didn't say it!"

Bergen nodded slowly. "I believe you. But the tapes contradict you. Of course, they were at the UNO station for twenty-four hours before being—"

"They tampered with them!"

"Possibly. But try to get the judge to believe that . . ." And he smiled maliciously. "You'll have two minutes for that at the trial . . ."

"The brain implant—whoever set me up had to have arranged that!

We could trace Kojo's recent past, find out who his surgeon was when he—"

"Before your defense committee disbanded, they tried that tack. Kojo had cerebral surgery a few months ago—just after you picked him out from the bodyguard portfolio at Witcher Security. He was to have an implant inserted to improve his speed and reflexes. The technic who provides implants for the surgeons was contacted by someone over TV-fone. The man he saw on the screen offered to transfer fifty-thousand newbux into the technic's account if he'd consent to some unauthorized 'adjustments' in the implant. He consented and the implant's 'adjust-ment' turned out to've been one of the Army's attack-and-kill mind-control chips. Remote controlled."

"The man on the screen must've been—"

"*It was you*, Senator . . . the technic recorded the transmission . . . it's pretty damning evidence. But I'll tell you what—" his voice creaked with mockery "—I'll see if I can get you off with a 'mercy execution.' *You* know, death by injection, sedative overdose. I think you'll prefer it to being clubbed to death on television. . . . Well, good afternoon, Senator."

The guard had come back: he opened the door, let Bergen out and Spector was alone—except for the guy climbing off the top bunk. And chuckling, "Hey Spector, man, that guy's really got a hard-on for you, you know? Public defender! Shit! Unless you get Special Pardon—and I can't remember the last time anybody ever did—you're screwed. They ain't gonna rock you special treatment just because you're a senator. That's the PR cornerstone of AVL, man: *everybody* that gets arrested gets screwed—equally."

He was a wiry little guy with a yellowed, gap-toothed smile, flinty black eyes, and the spikey color-shifting hair of a Chaosist. It was hard to get a real handle on what he looked like because of the bruises, the swollen tissue and crusted cuts on his face from the recent public beat-ing. Still, he looked familiar . . .

"Jerome-X," Spector muttered, recognizing him. "Great."

Jerome-X gave that slightly brain-damaged chuckle again. He was pleased, "as me, my man. Yeah. Yeah. I got the hot minitrans known up 'n down the freak-en-seez. I got the style. I got—"

"You got *caught*," Spector observed.

"Hey pal—thas better'n bein' *set up*. You were right, man—sure as shit, they *tampered* with those tapes. But not editing—*image reconstitution*. You're talking to the VideoMan hisself. I *know*. Computer generated images, animated. Computer analyzes a TV-image of a man, right? Gets him moving, talking. Then digitizes it—samples it—an' generates an image of the guy you *can't tell* from the real thing. Uses fractal geometry for realistic surface texture. They can animate you to do whatever they like. Sample your voice, synthesize it to make you say whatever they want . . ."

"But that isn't—"

"Isn't *just?*" Jerome-X shook his head. "You're too much. I didn't think justice was high on your list of priorities, man. I seen you on TV, Spector—I know about you. . . . Hey, how many people who 'committed robbery' or 'murder' were people who were annoying to the local status quo or the feds, or maybe big business? So they're *videoframed*. Convicted on the evidence of some security camera that just *happened* to be there. . . . *Ri*-ight. How many people like that, pal, huh? Hundreds? Maybe thousands. About half the people convicted go down from videotaped evidence. That's a lot of lucky cameras. Sure, maybe if there were more time, you could prove the tampering—but *you*, bigshot, you've seen to it you *got* no time, an' no chance for appeal . . ."

"Videoframing. . . . I don't believe it."

"Hey you *better* believe it. But most people don't know about it, so it's no use tryin' to tell the courts. The up-to-dates on computer-generated images is kept under lock 'n key. They want the public to think it's at a much cruder stage, you know? . . . Me, I'm gettin' out in the morning, already got my trashing for pirate transmissions. . . . But you—they're gonna splash you all over the studio, pal—cause you're the Case now. You're *Big Ratings* . . ."

Sometimes, it's possible to bribe a man with *promises* of money—and Spector used all his politician's skill to persuade a guard to get a message out to Senator Bob Burridge. Gave the guard a letter telling Burridge about the computer-generated evidence; and telling him to work on it *seriously*—or Spector'd press-release what he had on Burridge: the death of a girl named Judy Sorenson. And just where she got the drugs she'd OD'd on.

Three days later, nine a.m., the guard came to Spector's clammy cell, passed him an ear-cap, winked, and left. Spector put the capsule in his ear, squeezed it, heard Burridge's voice: "Hank, there's a method of videotape analysis that'll tell us if what's on videotape was genuine or computer-generated, first, we'll have to subpoena the tapes.... Of course, as you've already been convicted, that'll be hard... But we're pulling some strings... we'll see if we can get your conviction over-turned in the next day or so... a Special Pardon... don't get panicky and mention that mutual friend of ours to anyone..."

But a week later, Spector was being prepped for his execution. He sat on a bench, chained to five other convicts, listening to the prison's Program Coordinator, Sparks.

Sparks was called "the animal handler" by the video technicians. He was a stocky, red-faced man with a taut smile and blank gray eyes. He wore a rumpled blue real-cloth suit. The guards stood at either end of the narrow room, tubular stunguns in hand.

"Today, we got a man won an execution-by-combat, more dignified than the baseball-bat-and-the-stocks, and probably quicker if he's a good shot, so you fellas should be glad. You'll be given a gun, but of course it's loaded with blanks—"

And then the chain connecting Spector's handcuffs to the man on his right went taut, jerking Spector half out of his seat as the small black guy on the other end of the bench lost it, ran at Sparks screaming something in a heavy West Indies dialect, something Spector couldn't make out. But the raw subverbal sound of the man's voice—that alone spoke for him. It said, *Injustice!* It said, *I've got a family!* And then it could say nothing more because the stunguns had turned off is brain for awhile and he lay splayed like a dark rag doll on the concrete floor. The guards propped him up on the bench, and Sparks went on as if nothing had happened. "Now we got to talk about your cues. It'll be a lot worse for you if you forget your cues..."

Spector wasn't listening. A terrible feeling had him in its grip, and it was a far worse feeling than fear for his life.

At home—the home his wife had sold by now—he'd opened his

front door with a sonic key. It sang out three shrill tones, and the door heard and analyzed the tonal code, and opened. And the voice of the man who'd tried to fight, the small dark man . . . his voice, his three shrieks, had opened a door in Spector's mind, had let something out. Something he'd fought for weeks to lock away. Something he'd argued with. Something he'd silently shouted at, again and again.

He'd pushed for the AntiViolence Laws for the same reason that Joe McCarthy, in the last century, had railed at Communism. It was a ticket. A ticket to a vehicle he could ride through the polls, and into office. Inflame the public's fear of crime. Cultivate their lust for vengeance. Titillate their repressed desire to do violence. And they vote for you.

And he hadn't given a rat's ass damn about the crime problem. The issue was a path to power, and nothing more.

He'd known, somewhere inside himself, that a lot of the condemned were probably railroaded. But he'd looked away, again and again. Now, somebody had made it impossible for him to look away. Now, the guilt that had festered in him erupted into full-blown infection and he burned with the fever of self-hatred.

That's when Bergen came in. Bergen spoke to the guards, showed them a paper; the guards came and whispered to Sparks, and Sparks, annoyed, unlocked Spector's cuffs. Glumly, Bergen said, "Come with me, Mr. Spector." He was no longer Senator Spector.

They went to stand in the hallway; a guard came along, yawning, leaning against the wall, watching a soap on his pocket viddy. Voice icy, Bergen said, "You're going to get off. A Special Pardon: rare as hen's teeth. Burridge has proof the tapes were tampered with. It hasn't been made public yet, and in fact the judge who presided at your trial is out of town, so Burridge arranged a temporary restraining—"

"Why is it you sound disappointed, Bergen?" Spector broke in, watching him. When Bergen didn't answer, Spector said, "You did everything you could to sabotage my defense. You were with them, whoever it was. I can feel it. Who was it?" Bergen stared sullenly at him. "Come on—*who was it?* And why?"

Bergen glanced at the guard. The guard wasn't listening. He was absorbed by the soap on his pocket viddy; tiny television figures in his palm flickered through a miniature choreography of petty conflicts. Bergen took a deep breath, and looked Spector in the eyes. "Okay. I don't care anymore...I *want* you to know. Sonia, Torrence and I— we were part of the same...organization. Sonia Chesterton did it because her brother Charlie was videoframed. Torrence because he was in the Black Muslim Brotherhood—they lost their top four officers to a videoframe-up. Me, I did it—planned it all—because I saw one too many innocent people die.... We thought if you, a Senator, were videoframed, condemned, *killed*—afterwards we'd release the truth, we'd clear you, and that'd focus public attention on the issue. Force an investigation. And—it was vengeance. We held you responsible. For all those victims."

Spector nodded like something mechanical. Said softly: "Oh, yes. I am responsible.... And now I'm going to get off.... And it'll be blamed on your people. Your organization.... They'll say it was an isolated incident.... They'll pressure me to shut up. And, once I was on the outside, where things are comfortable, I probably would."

And the realization came at him like the onrushing of a great black wall; it fell on him like a tidal wave: *How many innocent people died for my ambition? A thousand? Two thousand?*

"Yes. They'll pass it off as an 'isolated incident,' " Bergen muttered. "Congratulations, Spector, you son of a bitch. Sonia and Torrence sacrificed themselves for *nothing*." His voice broke. He went on, visibly straining for control. "You're going free."

But the gnawing thing in Spector wouldn't let him go free. And he knew it would never let him go. Never. (Though some part of him said, *Don't do it! Survive!* But that part of him was broken, could speak only in a raspy whimper, as the other part said, aloud:) "Bergen—wait. Go to Burridge. Tell him you know all about the Sorenson incident— and tell him you'll release what you know about her, if he tells anyone what he's found out about those tapes before tomorrow. He'll stay quiet."

"But the restraining order—"

"Tear it up. And come with me—you've got to explain to Sparks that you were wrong about something..."

*   *   *

Spector walked out onto the stage. Glanced once at the cameras and the studio audience beyond the bullet-proof glass. Pointed the pistol loaded with blanks at the grinning man in the cowboy hat at the other end of the stage, and walked toward him, and toward the big gun in the man's hand. Spector smiling softly, thinking: *This is the only way I'll ever go free* . . .

Abducting Aliens:
A SubGenius Pasttime, Examined

"Just trying to steal a moment . . . in this
ZOMBIE BIRDHOUSE"

—Iggy Pop

It was ten p.m. on a deserted mountain road and the Reverend Deathmonkey was taking the curves at 60 miles an hour and up.

First thing you got to understand is that Reverend DEATHMONKEY is not like other people, mutants, happy mutants, or devos: he's got a level of COSMIC RAUNCH, of Interdisciplinary Sleaze that most of us can only dream about.

Me and the Reverend Deathmonkey, if I'm not lyin', were up in the mostly-logged-off state of Oregon; the place where the trees rise mightily and green alongside the road, a screen to cover the clear-cut areas just beyond. We were drivin' his slowly dying '73 Buick station wagon in a valley up in the Cascade Mountains, on the way to the ocean, and Deathmonkey was flying high. This figure of Myth—the Paul Bunyon, the Pecos Bill of Misfit Weirdos Everywhere—was sucking on Church Air (namely, Nitrous Oxide) from a tank while driving. Not wanting to be a wet blanket I was trying to persuade him to stop the Buick allegedly so I could pee, but really because I wanted to take over driving so we didn't get killed before we got to his Alleged Abduction Site.

"Not a fuckin' chance in hell! I know what you're up to motherfucker," he said between sucks at the oxygen mask connected to the steel bottle wedged between the seats. "I can drive this piece of crap in a tornado with both my eyes gouged out by a rabid lobster; I can steer a space shuttle through the eye of a needle while mainlining pure LSD and methedrine and getting my dick sucked and my ass felched by a pair of hairy titted yeti bitches! Praise G'BROAGH! AIIIIIIIIIIEEEEEEEEEEEEEE!"

Reverend Deathmonkey, he weighs about 300 pounds, he's got a big black beard matted with hamburger juice and twined with razor wire; when he's REALLY partying he calls on Blackbeard, his ancient piratical ancestor, calls him for guidance the way an Injun calls on the Bear Spirit, and he puts thirteen little birthday cake candles in his beard and lights em up and his black eyes burn right through his shades. He's got most of his teeth but a lot of them got the crowns busted off when he did that "I can eat a whole damn Harley Davidson piece by piece" act that landed him in the hospital.

Today he's wearing overalls festooned with the butts torn from Barbie dolls, hung from safety pins. He's wearing snakeskin cowboy boots; he's wearing lipstick under his black mustache. He's missing three fingers, I should mention, from his left hand, something to do with "me and Philo getting too ambitious with them explosives one Saturday".

He smells like . . . I veered my senses away from it. Some things man was not meant to know. Hell, he's Deathmonkey, and even "Bob" is in awe of the size of his willie.

Reverend Deathmonkey spotted the fire road through the Nitrous haze at the last moment and wrenched the vehicle hard to the right . . .

The Fugs first album—thirty some years old—was raving offkey on the tape deck; he switched it off. And he cut the lights, rumbled the Buick through startlight and shadow between the mighty first and acres of stumps, till we got to "Area Zero"—a cow pasture.

He stopped the car, killed the engine, we clambered out and stood shivering in the October mountain air. I was shivering anyway—Deathmonkey didn't seem to feel it. I mentioned three hundred pounds, did I mention that they're stacked up six foot five? And when, like now, he puts on his high crown ten gallon hat, brought from back home in Dallas, Texas, he's a living edifice close to seven feet vertical. Towering over me, he led the way through the brush along the edge of the cow pasture, outside the fence, muttering to himself as he went. Only thing I could make out was, "I'll make their succotash suffer..."

Then he vanished; three hundred pounds—gone. Or he seemed to. I'd looked away, at the cattle milling in a sleeping group in this high mountain pasture (government land provided free to a cattle outfit of course). The animals should've been in a barn, at this hour, I'd have thought, but some were awake, and even grazing, and I started to ask Deathmonkey about it and . . . he was gone.

Then I heard his voice coming from the ground. "Getcher ass in here, you wantem to seeya, Harry Dickinbutt?" I've tried to persuade him for years not to call me Harry Dickinbutt, but he won't quit.

I looked around and saw the hole in the hummock of earth to the right; glimpsed a bearsized figure moving around in there. "DM?"

"I said gitcher ass IN HERE." This is not an expression a bear would use, so I deduced it was Deathmonkey. I entered the bunker, as he called it. It was actually a sort of duck blind of mud and sticks and shrubbery cuttings, something he'd erected a week before. The smell . . .

He was firing up a frop; he offered me a hit. "No thanks, man, you know I don't do any mind altering—"

"Your neurons cain't stand up to it. They are limpdick neurons."

"Too true."

"My neurons and brain cells, they are quivering hard and drugs is just like the lubricants in the deep black vagina of Being."

"How long we got to be in this hole in the ground?"

He looked at the luminous dial of his pocket watch. "Six point seven minutes longer."

"You're full of it. How can you know—"

"Chaos theory calculus, Dickinbutt. Combined with Salient Event Orientation: every seven days they come to this pasture; tonight's the last night they'll come."

"You are so full of shit."

That's when the saucers came.

They were just bright stars at first, like satellites skating the ionosphere; then they got brighter, and closer, and took on shape. Two of them ... they were classic ET frisbees, maybe fifty feet in diameter, metallic, rims throbbing with a dull inner light.

"Oh shit ..."

"Quiet, Dickinbutt. Complete quiet."

The saucers danced like fireflies, for no damn reason I can imagine, and then ... merged. They sucked into one another, like two blobs of mercury becoming one; yet the process looked as mechanical as it was fluid. And when they were combined they'd become a silvery hockey-puck shaped object, not glowing but somehow quite visible ... hovering about sixty feet over the cattle.

The cattle had stopped moving—completely. They were like statues frozen into the field.

I watched. Not a tail twitched.

Rev. Deathmonkey was puttering with some equipment I couldn't clearly make out, cursing under his breath when he clanked a piece of metal.

The Greys ...

They rode a shaft of light down like humanoid snowflakes, drifting to the edge of the clutch of cattle ...

There were shiny instruments in their hands. I couldn't make them out.

"Shouldn't we be videotaping this?" I whispered.

"Fuzzes out on videotape. I did manage to get a few seconds of one of these little visits to come out," he said, barely audible, as he moved out the hole of the bunker. "Tried to sell it to Santilli. He got scared. Said the real stuff gave him the willies. Schnabel might report him to the Company. Asked me if I couldn't fake up one for him instead ..."

The night air outside the bunker was poignantly sweet, pregnant with electricity. We crept along through the brush on hands and knees, to a place where a ditch ran under the wire. Icy water trickled through the ditch; I know it was icy because I followed Deathmonkey into it. We crawled like a couple of scared GIs on our bellies, elbows and knees, fingers sluicing the creek slime as we slipped under the wire into the field, the smell of cowpies, and another smell, burnt ozone, and that acrid, otherly scent of ... greys?

One of them just up ahead, I could see his outsized head and scrawny shoulders just above the edge of the ditch. I thought of that movie I'd seen as a kid, teenagers killed by little men with big heads and cat eyes from outer space, the little men with alcohol injecting claws . . . The Greys weren't cat-eyed. They were the Roswell aliens; they were Streiber's aliens. They were the very creatures whose likeness giddy saucerettes wear around their necks at Psychic Fairs—creatures now using an impossibly prehensile dull gray metal instrument to ream out the ass of a paralyzed bovine.

DeathMonkey could move with astonishing quietude for a dude his size and stonedness. He slipped a little closer, a little closer to the nearest Grey . . . who stood at a good distance from the others . . . As DM went he took a net out of his duffel, and his own metallic instruments: handcuffs. He handed me a ballgag.

I looked up at the slowly rotating hocky puck overhead; surely it must be aware of me? But perhaps it discounted me, I was just one more "cow", on an interstellar scale, and not to be taken seriously. Or perhaps our being in the ditch, below the level of the surface dirt, with the distracting vibes of the cattle around us, confused its surveillance. There was no sense of being watched; we were, I thought with a jolt of exhilaration, the watchers. WE were the researchers; WE were the experimenters; WE had turned the tables, like Lab Rats escaped from their cages to gnaw the faces of their white-coated tormenters.

And as this thought rippled through me the Reverend DM positioned his net, whipped a hand out like a bear slapping a fish from a river, and jerked the Grey by the ankles—both of em—off his feet, and backwards into the ditch . . . and into the net. The alien made ONE squeaking sound before I jammed the ballgag into the little fucker's mouth. The alien cattle mutilating instrument fell into the creek and spat a few sparks and then lay still; Deathmonkey shoved the instrument into the duffel, slung that over one shoulder, the struggling Grey over the other, and ran back along the ditch to the wire. He slipped through the wire; I passed him, the squirming alien, and followed, back to the bunker.

We kept it tied up good . . . until the saucer left. "They'll be back for it," I said.

"Not for awhile. They're strange, socially. The ones we abducted in Arizona—"

"You did this before, in Arizona?"

"Oh sure, me and Stang and Sterno and Philo and Dr Howl . . . We did some of that toad squeezin' stuff, and went'n hung out at cattle mutilation sites . . . took us three or four tries but we caught some of the little bastards . . . took em awhile to come lookin' for em . . . We let em go. But not before. It's better'n cowtipping. Better'n putting gerbils up a Bobbie's ass. It's BIG fun, son. Watch this . . . Peel off that tacky silver suit he's got on there . . ."

"What if he sends a telepathic message?"

"He can't—cause you got me here. 'America takes drugs in psychic defense'. The stuff I took creates a sort of psychic backwash—it's like white noise to them. They can't get their signals through for a good five yards around me . . ."

"Do they bite?"

"No, they're wimps once you take away their damn gizmos . . . Lordy this one's got some fine piece of rump there . . . You see that? They put on their interstellar ruling class airs, but they got butt-holes just like the rest of us . . . Mostly atrophied though because they don't eat solid food no more . . ."

The gag popped out of the creature's mouth while I was stripping it. It spoke . . . with MY VOICE. Then with DM's. "You please can tell: what you do with me, is?"

"Got my voice but not my diction."

I jammed the ball back in and duct-taped it in place.

It's skin was so slick, almost like balloon stuff . . . under the silver suit I found no navel, and something that might be atrophied female genitals, and might not have been. Its four fingers had little pads on the end, sort of like tiny little blisters. Its eye coverings pulled off easy; its eyes rolled with fear. I almost felt pity, but then I remembered all those cored out animals, all those hybrid human babies, all those abductees; poor Whitley getting things shoved up his butt . . .

Remembering that, I found the nearest appropriate instrument, which happened to be a crescent wrench, and shoved that up the creature's butt. It squeaked through the gag and writhed. But it seemed intrigued somehow.

Well, we did what SubG's do when they abduct aliens. We shoved things up their butts, we took samples of skin and Deathmonkey, who had experience with this, used a syringe to suck some kind of fluid from the little fold at the creature's crotch. He squirted this into a rubber-plugged test tube. We pretended to do all kinds of things to the critter, with Dustbusters, electric toothbrushes, blowdryers, and rubber bands, but we didn't actually hurt the grey physically.

I figure it got the point.

Then we released it . . . the alien wandered off, dazedly. One last touch: DM gave it his ten gallon cowboy hat, kind of funny watching this alien wander off with that hat on its head . . .

After a hard night of abducting aliens, it was Miller Time. Went to a mountain bar, DM drank boilermakers, and we didn't talk about it much, but every so often we'd take turns chuckling and remembering and chuckling. "Little fuckers . . . little bastards . . ." DM would mutter.

That was the only time I went abducting aliens. I heard DM is taking parties of SubGs out regularly, for a fee, sort of like taking tourists sport fishing. He's still got that mutilation instrument; told me recently on the phone to watch the papers and "Just see if Jessie Helms don't turn up with his butt cored out."

And that fluid he extracted from the Grey? I'm not sure. But you should see this puppy DM's got, progeny of his dog and . . . I don't know. I only know the dog's got an oversized head, eyes like dark glasses, furless skin like a balloon, and it tells him it's dinner time telepathically.

Six Kinds of Darkness

*C*harlie'd say, "I'm into it once or twice—but you, you got a jones for it, man." And Angelo'd snicker and say, "Gives my life purpose, man. Gives my life direction."

You could smell the place, the Hollow Head, from two blocks away. Anyway, you could if you were strung out on it. The other people on the street probably couldn't make out the smell from the background of monoxides, the broken-battery smell of acid rain, the itch of syntharette smoke, the oily rot of the river. But a user could pick out that tease of Amyl Tryptaline, thinking, *find it like a needle in a hay-stack.* And he'd snort, and then go reverent-serious, thinking about the needle in question . . . the needle in the nipple . . .

It was on East 121st Street, a half-block from the East River. If you stagger out of the place at night, you'd better find your way to the lighted end of the street fast, because the leeches crawled out of the river after dark, slug-creeping up the walls onto the cornices of the old buildings; they sensed your bodyheat, and an eight-inch ugly brute lamprey-thing could fall from the roof, hit your neck with a wet *slap* and inject you with paralyzing toxins; you fall over and its leech cronies come and drain you dry.

When Charlie turned onto the street it was just sunset; the leeches weren't out of the river yet, but Charlie scanned the rooftops anyway. Clustered along the rooftops were the shanties. . . .

The immigrants had swarmed to this mecca of disenchantment till New York became another Mexico City, ringed and overgrown with shanties—shacks of clapboard, tin, cardboard, protected with flattened cans and wrapper plastic. Every tenement rooftop in Manhattan was mazed with shanties, sometimes shanties on shanties, till the weight collapsed the roofs and the old buildings caved in, the crushed squatters simply left dying in the rubble—firemen and Emergency teams rarely set foot outside the sentried, walled-in havens of the midtown class.

Charlie was almost there. It was a motherfucker of a neighborhood, which is why he had the knife in his boot-sheath. But what scared him was the Place Doing some Room at the Place. The Hollow Head. His heart was pumping and he was shaky but he wasn't sure if it was from fear or anticipation or if, with the Hollow Head, you could tell those two apart. But to keep his nerve up, he had to look away from the Place, as he got near it; tried to focus on the rest of the street. Some dumbfuck pollyanna had planted saplings on the sidewalk, in the squares of exposed dirt where the original trees had stood. But the acid rain had chewed the leaves and twigs away; what was left was stark as old TV antennas. . . .

Torchglow from the roofs; and a melange of noises that seemed to ooze down like something greasy from an overflowing pot. Smells of tarry wood burning; dogfood smells of cheap canned food cooking. And then he was standing in front of the Hollow Head. A soot-blackened townhouse; its Victorian facade of cherubims recarved by acid rain into dainty gargoyles. The windows bricked over, the wall between them streaked gray on black from acid erosion.

The building to the right was hunchbacked with shacks; the roof to the left glowed from oil-barrel fires. But the roof of the Hollow Head was dark and flat, somehow regal in its sinister austerity. No one shacked on the Hollow Head.

He took a deep breath, and told himself, "Don't hurry through it, savor it this time," and went in, hoping that Angelo had waited for him.

Up to the door, wait while the camera scanned you. The camera taking in Charlie's triple mohawk, each fin a different color; Charlie's gaunt face, spiked transplas jacket, and customized mirrorshades. He heard the tone telling him the door had unlocked. He opened it, smelled the Amyl Tryptaline, felt his bowels contract with suppressed excitement. Down a red-lit hallway, thick black paint on the walls, the turpentine smell of AT getting stronger. Angelo wasn't there; he'd gone upstairs already. Charlie hoped Angelo could handle it alone . . . The girl in the banker's window at the end of the hall—the girl wearing the ski mask, the girl with the sarcastic receptionist's lilt in her voice—took his card, gave him the Bone Music receptor, credded him in. Another tone, admission to Door Seven, the first level. He walked down to Seven, turned the knob, stepped through and felt it immediately; the tingle, the rush of alertness, the chemically-induced sense of belonging, four pleasurable sensations rolling through him and coalescing. It was just an empty room with the stairs at the farther end; soft pink lighting, the usual cryptic palimpsest of graffiti on the walls.

He inhaled deeply, felt the Amyl Tryptaline hit him again; the pink glow intensified; the edges of the room softened, he heard his own heartbeat like a distant beatbox. A barbed wisp of anxiety twined his spine (wondering, *Where's Angelo, he's usually hanging in the first room, scared to go to the second alone*) and he experienced a paralytic seizure of sheer sensation. The Bone Music receptor was digging into his palm; he wiped the sweat from it and attached it to the sound wire extruding from the bone back of his left ear—and the music shivered into him . . . it was music you *felt* more than heard; his acoustic nerve picked up the thudding beat, the bass, a distorted veneer of the synthesizer. But most of the music was routed through the bone of his skull, conducted down through the spinal column, the other bones. It was a music of shivery sensations, like a funnybone sensation, sickness sensation, chills and hot flashes like influenza but it was a sickness that caressed, viruses licking at your privates and you wanted to come and throw up at the same time. He'd known deaf people to dance at rock concerts; they could feel the vibrations from the loud music; could feel the music they couldn't hear. It was like that but with a deep, deep humping brutality,

The music shivered him from his paralysis, nudged him forward. He climbed the stairs. . . .

Bone Music reception improved as he climbed, so he could make out the lyrics, a gristly voice singing from inside Charlie's skull:

Six kinds of darkness,
spilling down over me.
Six kinds of darkness,
sticky with energy.

Charlie got to the next landing, stepped into the second room.

Second room used electric field stimulation of nerve ends; the metal grids on the wall transmitted signals, initiating pleasurable nerve impulses; other signals went directly to the dorsal areas in the hypothalamus, resonating in the brain's pleasure center. . . .

Charlie cried out, and fell to his knees in the infantile purity of his gratitude. The room glowed with benevolence; the barren, dirty room with its semen-stained walls, cracked ceilings, naked red bulb on a fraying wire. As always he had to fight himself to keep from licking the walls, the floor. He was a fetishist for this room, for its splintering wooden floors, the mathematical absolutism of the grid-patterns in the gray metal transmitters set into the wall. Turn off those transmitters and the room was shabby, even ugly, and pervaded with stench; with the transmitters on, it seemed subtly intricate, starkly sexy bondage gear in the form of interior decoration, and the smell was a ribald delight.

(The Hollow Head was drug paraphernalia you could walk into. The building itself was the spike, the hookah, the sniff-tube.)

And then the room's second phase cut in: the transmitters stimulated the motor cortex, the reticular formation in the brainstem, the nerve pathways of the extra-pyramidal system, in precise patterns computer formulated to mesh with the ongoing Bone Music. Making him dance. Dance across the room, feeling he was caught in a choreographed whirlwind (flashing: genitals interlocking, pumping, male and female, male and male, female and female, tongues and cocks and fingers pushing into pink bifurcations, contorting purposefully to guide between fleshy globes, the thrusting a heavy downhill flow like an emission of igneous mud, but firm pink mud, the bodies rounded off, headless, Magritte torsos going end to end together, organs blindly nosing into the wet receptacles of otherness), semen trickling down his legs inside his pants, dancing, helplessly dancing, thinking it was a delicious epilepsy, as he was marionetted up the stairs, to the next floor, the final room. . . .

At the landing just before the third room, the transmitters cut off, and Charlie sagged, gasping, clutching for the banister, the black-painted walls reeling around him. He gulped air, and prayed for the strength to turn away from the third room, because he knew it would leave him fried, yeah, badly crashed and deeply burnt-out. He turned off the receptor for a respite of quiet. . . . In that moment of weariness and self-doubt he found himself wondering where Angelo was, had Angelo really gone onto the third room alone? Angelo was prone to identity crises under the Nipple Needle. If he'd gone alone—little Angelo Demario with his rockabilly hair and spurious pugnacity—Angelo would sink, and lose it completely.. . . .And what would they do with people who were overdosed on an identity hit? Dump the body in the river, he supposed. . . .

He heard a yell mingling ecstasy and horror, coming from an adjacent room, as another Head customer took a nipple . . . that made up his mind: like seeing someone eat making you realize you're hungry. He gathered together the tatters of his energy, switched on his receptor, and went through the door.

The Bone Music shuddered through him, too strong now that he was undercut, weakened by the first rooms. Nausea wallowed through him.

The darkness of the Arctic,
two months into the night.
Darkness of the Eclipse,
forgetting of all light.

Angelo wasn't in the room and Charlie was selfishly glad as he took off his jacket, rolled up his left sleeve, approached the black rubber nipple protruding from the metal breast at waist-height on the wall.

As he stepped up to it, pressed the hollow of his elbow against the nipple; felt the computer-guided needle probe for his mainline and fire the ID drug into him. . . .

The genetic and neurochemical essence of a woman. They claimed it was synthesized. Right then he didn't give an angel's winged asshole where it came from; it was rushing through him in majestic waves of titanic intimacy. You could taste her, smell her, feel what it felt like to be her (they said it was an imaginary her, modeled on someone real, not really from a person . . .).

Felt the shape of her personality superimposed on you so for the first time you weren't burdened with your own identity, you could find oblivion in someone else, like identifying with a fictional protagonist but infinitely more real. . . .

But oh shit. It wasn't a *her*. It was a *him*. And Charlie knew instantly that it was Angelo. They had shot him up with Angelo's distilled neurochemistry—his personality, memory, despairs, and burning urges. He saw himself in flashes as Angelo had seen him. . . . And he knew, too, that this was no synthesis, that he'd found out what they did with those who died here, who blundered and OD'd: they dropped them in some vat, broke them down, distilled them and molecularly linked them with the synthcoke and shot them into other customers. . . . Into Charlie. . . .

He couldn't hear himself scream, over the Bone Music (*Darkness of an iron cask, lid down and bolted tight*). He didn't remember running for the exit stairs (*And three more kinds of darkness, three I cannot tell*), down the hall, (*Making six kinds of darkness, Lord please make me well*) out into the street, running, hearing the laughter from the shantyrats on the roofs watching him go.

Him and Angelo running down the street, in one body. As Charlie told himself: "I'm kicking this thing. It's over. I shot up my best friend. I'm through with it."

Hoping to God it was true. *Lord please make me well.*

Bottles swished down from the rooftops and smashed to either side of him. And he kept running.

He felt strange.

He could feel his body. Not like usual. He could feel it like it was a weight on him, like an attachment. Not the weight of fatigue—he felt too damn eerie to feel tired—but a weight of sheer alienness. It was too big. It was all awkward and its metabolism was pitched too low, sluggish, and it was. . . .

It was the way his body felt for Angelo.

Angelo wasn't there, in him. But then again he was. And Charlie felt Angelo as a nastily foreign, squeaky, distortion membrane between him and the world around him.

He passed someone on the street, saw them distorted through the membrane, their faces funhouse-mirror twisted as they looked at him—and they looked startled.

The strange feelings must show on his face. And in his running.

Maybe they could see Angelo. Maybe Angelo was oozing out of him, out of his face. He could feel it. Yeah. He could feel Angelo bleeding from his pores, dripping from his nose, creeping from his ass.

A sonic splash of: *Gidgy, you wanna do a video hookup with me? (Gidgy replying:) No, that shit's grotty Ange, last time we did that I was sick for two days. I don't like pictures pushed into my brain. Couldn't we just have, you know, sex? (She touches his arm.)*

God, I'm gonna lose myself in Angelo, Charlie thought. Gotta run, sweat him out of me.

Splash of: *Angelo, if you keep going around with those people, the police or those SA people are going to break your stupid head. (Angelo's voice:) Ma, get off it, you don't understand what's going on, the country's getting scared, they think there's gonna be nuclear war, everyone's lining up to kiss the Presidential ass 'cause they think she's all that stands between us and the fucking Russians—(His mother's voice:) Angelo don't use that language in front of your sister, not everyone talks like they do on TV—*

Too heavy, body's too heavy, his run is funny, can't run anymore, but I gotta sweat him out—

Flash pictures to go with the splash voices now: *Motion-rollicking shot of sidewalk seen from a car window as they drive through a private-cop zone. SA bulls in mirror helmets walking along in twos in this high-rent neighborhood, turning their glassy-bland assumption of your guilt toward the car, the world revolves as the car turns a corner, they come to a check-point, the new Federal ID cards are demanded, shown, they get through,*

feeling of relief, there isn't a call out on them yet . . . blur of images, then
focus on a face walking up to the car. Charlie. Long, skinny, goofy-looking
guy, self-serious expression . . .

Jesus, Charlie thought, is *that* what Angelo thinks I look like? Shit!
(Angelo is dead, man, Angelo is . . . is oozing out of him . . .)

Feeling sick now, stopping to gag, look around confusedly, oh fuck:
two cops were coming toward him. Regular cops, no helmets, wearing
blue slickers, plastic covers on their cop-caps, their big ugly cop-faces
hanging out so he wished they wore the helmets, supercilious faces,
young but ugly, their heads shaking in disgust, one of them said: "What
drug you on, man?"

He tried to talk but a tumble of words came out, some his and some
Angelo's, it was like his mouth was brimming over with little restless
furry animals: Angelo's words.

The cops knew what it was. They knew it when they heard it.

One cop asked the other (as he took out the handcuffs, and Charlie
had become a retching machine, unable to run or fight or argue because
all he could do was retch), "Jeez, it makes me sick when I think about
it. People shooting up some'a somebody else's brains. Don't it make
you sick?"

"Yeah. Looks like it makes *him* sick too. Let's take him to the chute,
send him down for a bloodtest."

He felt the snakebite of cuffs, felt the cops do a perfunctory body-
search, their met-detect missing the styrene knife in his boot. Felt himself shoved along to the police kiosk on the corner, the new
prisoner-transferral chutes. They put you in something like a coffin
(they pushed him into a greasy, sweat-stinking, inadequately padded
personnel capsule, closed the lid on him, he wondered what happened—as they closed the lid on him—if he got stuck in the chutes,
were there air-holes, would he suffocate?) and they push it down into
the chute inside the kiosk and it gets sucked along this big underground
tube (he had a sensation of falling, then felt the tug of inertia, the horror
of being trapped in here with Angelo, not enough room for the two of
them, seeing a flash mental image of Angelo's rotting corpse in here
with him, Angelo was dead, Angelo was dead) to the police station.
The cops' street-report tagged to the capsule. The other cops read the

report, take you out (a creak, the lid opened, blessed fresh air even if it was the police station), take everything from you, check your DNA print against their files, make you sign some things, lock you up just like that . . . that's what he was in for right away. And then maybe a public AVL beating. Ironic.

Charlie looked up at a bored cop-face, an older fat one this time. The cop looked away, fussing with the report, not bothering to take Charlie out of the capsule. There was more room to maneuver now and Charlie felt like he was going to rip apart from Angelo's being in there with him if he didn't get out of the cuffs, out of the capsule. So he brought his knees up to his chest, worked the cuffs around his feet, it hurt but . . . he did it, got his hands in front of him.

Flash of Angelo's memory: *A big cop leaning over him, shouting at him, picking him up by the neck, shaking him. Fingers on his throat. . . .*

When Angelo was a kid some cop had caught him running out of a store with something he'd ripped off. So the cop roughed him up, scared the shit out of Angelo, literally: Angelo shit his pants. The cop reacted in disgust (the look of disgust on the two cops' faces: "Makes me sick," one of them had said).

So Angelo hated cops and now Angelo was out of his right mind— ha ha, he was in Charlie's—and so it was Angelo who reached down and found the boot-knife that the two cops had missed, pulled it out, got to his knees in the capsule as the cop turned around (Charlie fighting for control, damn it Ange, put down the knife, we could get out of this), and Charlie—no, it was Angelo—gripped the knife in both hands and stabbed the guy in his fat neck, split that sickening fat neck open, cop's blood is as red as anyone's, looks like. . . .

Oh shit. Oh no.

Here come the other cops.

Where It's Safe

Nephilim set the charge and stood well back. Crowel chuckled, with his tongue caught between his teeth in that yokel way he had, and said, "Don't need to worry about blast. It don't work that way."

"I know," Nephilim said. "It's—I'm used to nondirectional explosives."

"Me'n Crispin, we lucked onto some beauties at th' armory raid—"

A muffled *whump* as the explosion, directed precisely from the blast plate they'd attached to the airlock of the smog shield, punched out the locking mechanism. The mechanism fell away with the slight reverberation of the controlled blast, leaving a perfect oval cut through the six-inch door around the lock, the cut's edges giving out only wisps of gray smoke.

"Very nice indeed," Nephilim said. He reached through the gap with the battery-charged alligator clamps, and sparked the electronic tumblers. The door hummed, and gave a click. For Nephilim that sound was an affirmation of life; it was a tiny little sound that was all hope and meaning. It was an affirmation of death, too.

Crowel pushed the airlock open as Nephilim turned and signaled the Pack.

* * *

The Dow Jones Industrial had dropped two and a half. Secondary and Tertiary markets were suffering a −3.1. But AkInc's own Montana Chemicals was up. That cheered Akwiss a little.

He looked up from the morning financial print-outs, squinting through the glass roof of the breakfast room to try to see past the gray smog shield. He couldn't make out the clouds. The shield was too smudgy. Better have it cleaned.

He was planning to copter to New York that afternoon, if the weather permitted. They got some vicious crosswinds in July, and it might be safer to take a tunnel shuttle, though it was a longer trip.

Akwiss decided on the shuttle, and went back to his stewed prunes and print-out. The prunes were execrable. Sometimes he thought the doctor was giving him this pain-in-the-ass diet out of personal animosity. He had only the doctor's word; for all he knew he could be eating eggs and bacon with abandon. Hell, he could always take a cholesterol sweeper.

Lunch was the one meal he was permitted to enjoy a little. A lean-meat sandwich, a piece of Jorge's very realistic apple pie—it was something to look forward to.

He scowled at the prunes and cereal and orange juice. A man could starve on this diet.

Akwiss looked around in annoyance, hearing the whine of the MadeMaid rolling into the room, its electric engine complaining for lubrication. The robot was a metal box with complicatedly jointed hydraulic arms and whirring graspers and a rotating camera. It reached up clumsily to clear the dishes onto its tray and promptly swept them onto the floor instead. "Whoopsi!" said the female voice from its speakers. Its voice was the thing that worked best about it. He ought to use it to answer phones instead of cleaning up. Normally he didn't use it at all.

Akwiss thumbed the intercom button. "Murieta! Get in here!"

His Mexican butler came in with startling immediacy, smiling. Irritatingly chummy, Akwiss thought. "Murieta—what the hell is this? Where's Dunket? This clunker is supposed to be in a closet somewhere. It never did work and I find these things offensive. People should be served by people. This company is all about providing good work for good people, Murieta. We make an example, here."

Murieta smiled and nodded just as if he bought into Akwiss's reflexive company-slogan populism. "I know, I know that, I told Dunket we need you, he say chure he come back this afternoon, until then we use the ma-cheen, he said—"

"Come back this afternoon? I didn't give him any time off."

"He said you give him time to go to the doctor. Chure."

"Well. I don't remember it. I suppose if he needs to see a doctor . . . Well. Well uh—clean up this mess, this damn thing can't manage it."

"Chure."

Akwiss exhaled windily through his nose. Dunket should have called for a temporary from Chicago Central. The damn fool should have known better, anyway. He'd served Akwiss for years.

He hit the intercom again. "Finch? Yo, Finch!" He looked expectantly at the video monitor flush with the table top, expecting to see his Security Supervisor appear. The screen stayed blank.

Murieta was busily picking up chunks of crockery. The MadeMaid was whirring confusedly back and forth at his side, getting in the way. Akwiss watched him for a moment, then quietly asked, "Murieta—did Finch have a doctor's appointment too?"

"I don't know, Mr. Atch-wiss." He didn't look up from the dish fragments. "I deedn't see him."

That one, Nephilim thought, is probably Finch. Lean guy with receding blond hair. Definite I.D. or not, he had to go down: he had a gun on his hip.

Finch was just rounding the corner, coming down the Eastern corridor to check on the breach in the mansion's Eastern airlock. Looking bored, probably expecting to find it was another false alarm triggered by acid corrosion. Then he saw the Pack and froze in his tracks. Nephilim expected him to go for the gun but he just gaped in surprise. He'd never had anything to do here but scare off salesmen.

Crowel was raising his gun, but it was Nephilim's practice to take responsibility for these things when he could. If the Feds pulled off a swoop some of the Pack might get off with twenty years if they weren't tied to killings. He pushed Crowel's gun-muzzle down and said, "Mine." His autopistol hissed as he swept a four-shot burst across Finch's chest and the guy went spinning down. Finch had been pretty complacent, as expected: He hadn't bothered with armor.

Akwiss was waiting for the elevator. It was taking too long. Another glitch. The whole estate needed a tightening-up from top to bottom. Maybe one of the girls he'd brought over last night was monopolizing the elevator, on her way home. He certainly hoped Finch had sent them back to town. They got on his nerves when they hung around.

He glanced at the out-conditions indicator, for something to do as he waited. Air Quality for the morning of July 18, 2017, was pretty good outside. One could walk about freely.

It wasn't as bad as people made it out, any time, of course. Only when the rare Black Wind came along was a respirator necessary. Most of the time, the smog shield's importance was security and not bad air. He'd explained that pretty handily to the reporter from UNO, last week. The media ate out of his hand; always had.

He could hear the elevator moving now. It was about time. Maybe he ought to have a new elevator put in. But most of the time he was the only one who used them—

The doors opened and the elevator was filled with strangers.

Nephilim didn't bother to chase the fat guy down the glass hall. He knew he wouldn't get past the breakfast room.

Crowel laughed, watching Akwiss wheezing along.

"So that's Akwiss," Holovitz said, coming out of the elevator behind Nephilim. "Well anyway it's his butt. Fat as his cred-account."

Nephilim said, "Holovitz, wait here for the others. Bring 'em straight along this tube after us. Crowel, Crispin—come along."

In no particular hurry, Nephilim strode along after Akwiss. Crispin, who carried the tools and the bags, gave a snaggly grin, and fell into step beside him.

The nearest general alarm button was in the breakfast room. Akwiss thought his heart would hammer its way out of his chest before he got there. It was stupid, fucking stupid. There should be an alarm every forty feet or so. Where the bloody hell was Finch?

Maybe they were a work crew or something. Maybe that had been a lube gun in his hand. . . .

Murieta was standing over the console on the breakfast table, working busily with a cutting torch. Akwiss skidded to a stop in front of him, wheezing, sweat tickling his neck, staring.

Murieta was humming to himself as he melted away the inside of the console. A few sparks spat through the crater in the plastic hull, smoke curled up. No alarms went off. He'd burned through those circuits. He switched off the cutting tool and smiled up at Akwiss. "You're back surprisingly early, boss. Surely you didn't forget your briefcase."

Akwiss tried to swallow, but his throat was too dry. It felt like there was something obstructing it. He could just barely breathe. "You . . . you're not . . ."

"My accent? Oh chure. I forgot." His eyes were as bright as the flame of his cutting torch.

"You fucking traitor." Akwiss was thinking about trying to run past Murieta. But the way the man was tensed . . . the way he held that torch . . . "How'd you get through the screening?"

"Your personnel-screening database is more porous than you think, boss."

Akwiss heard the others coming up behind them. He tried to compose himself as he turned to face them. Thinking, *Anything can be negotiated. Just stay cool.*

The short, stocky one with the dark eyes and the cryptic symbols cut into the black hair on the side of his head: that would be their leader. The other two were most definitely followers, Akwiss thought, but they were hungry-looking men who seemed hardly in check. All three of them wore fatigues tucked into military boots, iridescent anti-UV ponchos, respirators slung around their necks. They were all a bit grimy, unshaven. Thin, ravenous men. Those weren't lube guns in their hands. And one of them was training a videocam on him.

"Oliver Akwiss," the dark-eyed man said, "CEO, president and owner of Akwiss Incorporated, a multinational corporation also known as AkInc, I arrest you for the Citizen's Reclamation Troop on a charge of mass murder."

" 'Citizen's Reclamation Troop'! You're a *Pack*, is what you are." Akwiss snorted. "You can dress it up any way you want." *Careful*, he told himself: *You should be pacifying them. They have the guns.* But his pride demanded some rebuke to this outrage.

"We are, yes, what you call a 'Pack' " the man said, shrugging. He went on smoothly, with a characteristic glibness that Akwiss found increasingly irritating. "And a Citizen's Reclamation Troop. Your Congressional lobbyists push the buttons on the official laws so the public's own justice has to be enforced by a pack of outlaws. It's a damn shame but there it is. You can call me Nephilim, Mr. Akwiss. . . ."

Akwiss thought, *Stall them*. He glanced past Nephilim through the glass of the corridor, hoping to see a security team moving up, outside it. No one yet.

Nephilim read Akwiss' glance. "The outdoor guards are all getting loaded on Hot Morph at the South gate, Mr. Akwiss. We've been selling it to them on the cheap for weeks. They've been using more and more heavily. Not Finch, of course. Him we had to kill."

Akwiss decided to fake admiration. He glanced at Murieta. "And this one you planted inside. Ingenious."

"No it's not. You and your security got sloppy and complacent. The price of living so long where it's 'safe.' " Four more of the Pack were trotting up behind Nephilim. Well armed.

There would be no escape. It was all up to negotiation now, Akwiss thought. Well. That was his strength, after all.

Nephilim nodded toward the corridor leading into the living room. "Let's go in there."

Akwiss licked his lips. Have to calm down. He was dangerously close to heart attack. He nodded, and made himself breathe slowly, as he turned and walked between the man who called himself Murieta, and Nephilim, to the barn-sized living room of the main house.

"Whew!" the skinny one said, looking around. Adding mockingly: "This is, like, so tasteful. And yet so elegant."

The others laughed. Akwiss felt his face go hot.

"You got the disk, Crowel?" Nephilim said, to the skinny one.

Crowel took a sealed videodisk from a pouch on his flak vest, and went to the player. Murieta was smiling mysteriously up at the big beams thirty feet overhead; they were genuine wood, retrofitted from a 20th Century yacht. Near the fake-log fireplace was a big grand piano that had once belonged to Leonard Bernstein. The other furnishings were expensive designer antiques, which Akwiss had once thought a contradiction in terms. But his decorator had insisted it was all a matter of style, not materials or chronology. And Akwiss had to agree: Surfaces are all.

Some of the men seemed a little in awe of the vast room, the *faux* antique furniture, the gently segueing videopaintings, the yellowing impressionist oils, the platinum lamps.

Prompted by Crowel, the video screen rose from the floor: Ten feet by fifteen, high-rez and state of the art. "Have a seat, Mr. Akwiss," Nephilim said, gesturing at the blue velvet sofa.

"Thanks, I prefer to stand," Akwiss said, trying to create an atmosphere of equality.

"I said sit the fuck down," Nephilim said quietly, as Crowel handed him the video remote control.

Akwiss sank onto the sofa.

Crowel went about setting up a small video camera on a thin aluminum tripod, and a recording deck. It was trained on Akwiss, Nephilim and Akwiss' video screen.

"What's the camera for?" Akwiss asked. "Proof to my company for the hostage money?"

Nephilim shook his head grimly. "For the trial. We're making a whole set of them to mail out to select media. Last week we videotaped your good friend George Pourneven. The video deck belonged to him, in fact."

"George? There was no report of anything unusual with—"

"You didn't look at anything but the financial news today, evidently." He stepped a little closer to the small microphone attached to the videocam. "Now, I'm going to have to hold forth a bit on certain subjects—things you know about but the public doesn't. You and your cronies having done very well at keeping them in the dark . . ." He tapped the remote, and the disk began to play. "You're on trial, Akwiss. Kindly review the evidence with us."

Akwiss looked at the images rezzing up on the videoscreen. It was as he'd expected. Pictures of starving children. The bleeding hearts were always trying to intimidate him with starving children. As if he were one of the parents, the people really responsible for those kids.

"This is today," Nephilim was saying. "The Great American Famine. Ten to twenty thousand children die every week in our America the Beautiful, of famine or famine-related disease. It's going to get worse before it gets better. . . ."

Akwiss blew out his cheeks and looked at his shoes. They needed a shine, he decided.

He felt a small cold circle pressing into his left temple: a gun muzzle. He looked at Crowel from the corners of his eyes; Crowel, his cheek twitching, was saying, *"Look at the fucking screen."*

Akwiss looked at the screen. The gun muzzle was withdrawn. But he thought he could feel it watching him.

On the screen: rows of emaciated children lying on cots in some school gymnasium. Small children of every color. Children who couldn't hold their heads up on their shrunken necks; whose skin seemed shrink-wrapped over their bones. Whose bellies were horribly distended from famine bloat. Their bugging eyes listless, wandering. Only a few of them with strength to cry. Most of them would die, of course.

"In 2002," Nephilim was saying, "children were dying in the so-called Third World at a rate of about 40,000 a day, from hunger."

" 'Or hunger-related disease,' " Akwiss heard himself say, dryly. *Don't sneer at them*, he warned himself. Suppress your pride. He went on hastily, "Oh, I know! And AkInc gave a fortune to famine relief."

"Actually you gave exactly as much as you needed for the tax break you required, and not a penny more," Nephilim said, casually. He was maddeningly casual about it all. At first. "Anyway—40,000 children dying every day globally was acceptable to people in the U.S. because it wasn't their kids. They didn't feel responsible. Now the famine is *here*, in the USA, and people at last are looking at some of the causes, at least the causes in this country. Let's rewind a little. . . ." The disk zipped back to its beginning. Shots of AkInc factories and similar outfits—Dow, Union Carbide, Exxon, Arco, Georgia Pacific, others. Chemicals plants, oil refineries, paper mills, heavy industry of all kinds.

But they kept coming back to AkInc plants: AkInc sluicing toxic fluids into rivers, gouting toxic waste into the sky, burying cheap barrels of toxins; dumping barrels of toxins into the sea. "It started even before the CFCs began to chew away at the ozone. You are a chemicals octopus, Akwiss. You have a tentacle in every chemicals product. Foam packaging. Plastics of all kinds. Pesticides and herbicides particularly, in the early years. Between the years 1960 and 1990 the rate of stomach cancer quadrupled; the rate of brain cancer increased five hundred percent. A lot of people think it was pesticides in our foods." Footage now of children and old people dying in cancer wards. Sickening stuff. Akwiss tried to let his eyes go out of focus. Nephilim went on: "Pesticides in the air, too. They evaporate from fields and lawns, so eventually we even inhale them. Some pesticides run off into the streams, into the oceans. We eat pesticide-tainted fish, pesticide-poisoned produce. It builds up and up in us—and in the environment. Dolphins and seals begin to wash dead from obscure viruses because the toxins undermine their immune systems. The dead dolphins were just a symptom of what was coming: *all* the fish dying, sea creatures of every kind."

"And all this from my pesticides? I hardly think you can pin it all on me, personally," Akwiss said, as politely as he could manage.

"You and a few hundred others at the top of the pyramids of big business—you are the most culpable. But the rest of us too. We didn't vote out the Congressmen who buckled under to your lobbies and campaign-contribution bribes. We voted George W. Bush in, and he rolled back regulations."

The bathroom, Akwiss thought. If I could get into the bathroom. There's a phone there, one they may not notice in the cabinet by the toilet. Let them burn off a little of their self-righteousness with the lecture and then if I can talk Nephilim into letting me use the toilet . . .

"The pesticides contributed to the great famine in half a dozen ways," Nephilim went on, his professorial tone weirdly incongruous with the gun and fatigues. "They destroyed beneficial bacteria and threw the ecological balance in the insect world completely out of whack. The side effects got worse and worse. The airborne pesticides merged into the clouds of toxins altered by UV light—and synergistically combined with the other factory toxins to make the Black Winds."

"You've obviously had the opportunity to memorize your accusations," Akwiss pointed out. "I haven't had a chance to memorize a defense."

"You've made your excuses and your defenses for years," Nephilim said calmly. "You defended yourself with your P.R. firms, your Congressional lobbies, your doctored environmental impact studies. It's our turn now."

Akwiss licked his dry lips, and nodded. *Let him get through it. Then . . .*

Nephilim picked up his rote speech where he'd left off. "The killer clouds they call Black Winds kill not only people—also wheat and orchards and cattle and sheep and chickens. And of course the UV burn was worse than ever because of the CFCs that companies like AkInc were mass producing. Chlorofluorocarbons that nibbled endlessly at the ozone layer—the huge growth in the incidence of skin cancer was the least of it. In 2012 . . . where's that shot . . . Here it is . . ." He'd fast forwarded to a long sweeping shot of a dust bowl field. "Looks like Oklahoma in the early 20th century. But it's good old Iowa. Here's another in Kansas. This one is Oregon: the Willamette Valley, one big dust bowl . . . The unchecked ultraviolets killed the plants and small organisms that held the topsoil down. They killed crops and they—"

"Now really, CFCs—they were used by virtually everyone," Akwiss protested coolly. He glanced toward the door to the bathroom. Should he try for it now? Not quite yet, he decided. Damn, he wanted a drink. "Probably you used them yourself when you were young. Spray cans and such."

"Your company—at your instigation—spent millions suppressing the evidence, paying off research scientists, giving campaign contributions to Congressmen in exchange for slowing the ban on CFCs."

Startled by the range of Nephilim's inside information, Akwiss blurted automatically, "Nonsense, we did no such thing—!"

"We have all the documentation, Akwiss. You weren't picked arbitrarily. We don't go about executing innocent people, you know."

Akwiss's throat constricted. *Executing.*

Get to the bathroom. The phone. Fast. "Listen I need to—"

Nephilim overrode him, going on, "I almost admire the subtlety of your favorite strategies. Your industry-sponsored 'environmental initiatives'—which did nothing but cancel out the real initiatives, if you read the fine print. And your bunk 'studies.' You—and the other big companies did the same, of course—you'd fund 'independent' researchers, push them into churning out studies that seemed to show that pesticides were safe for consumption, that CFCs weren't necessarily the agent in depleting the ozone layer, that low-level radiation from nuclear power plants was no danger, that the toxins you were spewing by the thousands of tons into the air wouldn't cause cancer and birth defects. And so on. There were always contradictory studies by responsible people, but a great many of the newspapers—usually owned by one of your conglomerates—cited only *your* studies, strangely enough. . . ."
The men around him laughed.

"Look—the country needed jobs—"

"Dead men are unemployable, Akwiss," Nephilim went on relentlessly. "And it's not as if you couldn't have had your factories without polluting—that whole line is a lie. *You could have!* The technology to clean all emissions and convert waste—*it exists.* Has for decades. But it was costly. And you didn't want to spend the money, you and your cronies. You were too greedy. And that's what this is all about. *Greed.* Greed is the reason for this. . . ." He gestured at the screen. "Here we have a lovely shot of some birth defects traceable to emissions from your chemicals factories—this child born with his brain hanging outside his head died, of course, but his brother, the imbecile with the flippers and the missing jaw you see now, survived to crawl through his own shit the rest of his life. . . ."

Akwiss had to look away. Crowel started toward him but then Akwiss turned desperately to Nephilim. "Please—I have to go to the bathroom." The others laughed. Controlling his resentment, Akwiss went on, "You're trying to conduct this in a civilized way, aren't you?"

"Yes yes, we don't want to have to clean up after you *again*," Nephilim said with heavy sarcasm.

It took Akwiss a moment to get it. Then he smiled weakly, "Yes. Well. The bathroom's just over there. . . ."

"Take this man to the bathroom, Crowel. But look around in there for alarms or telephones."

Akwiss thought he was close to a heart attack as Crowel searched the bathroom. But Crowel didn't find the phone. He evidently expected to see it attached to the wall. It was a cellular phone, in a drawer.

Left alone in the bathroom, Akwiss did his best to use the toilet; Crowel was just outside the door. Akwiss didn't want him to get suspicious. But his bowels didn't want to work, at first.

At last, as the toilet flushed, Akwiss tapped the code into the little touchtone keypad on the cellular phone. He didn't dare use the phone vocally. Crowel would hear him. But the code should set up a buzzing in the guard house, at the checkpoint, and in their jeeps. The alarm buzzing meant, *Come to the main house at once.*

A thumping on the door made him nearly fall off the toilet. "Get out *now* or I'm comin' in!" Crowel yelled.

Hands shaking, trying to make no sound at it, Akwiss replaced the phone in the drawer and closed it.

"The . . . the other men . . . ?" Akwiss asked, looking around as he and Crowel returned to the main room. Only Nephilim, Crowel, and this odd, eager fellow Crispin remained. Murieta had gone too. That might make things easier for Akwiss. . . .

"The other men aren't here as soldiers, in particular," Nephilim said distractedly, fast forwarding through the video disk. He seemed tense and impatient. Soon, it'd be over, one way or another. "They came along to move out your food supplies and anything that'll help us buy more food on the black market." He stopped the disk and turned a cold, onyx glare on Akwiss. "Your people—your class, if that's what they are—monopolize the available food, of course. After destroying most of North America's capacity to grow food, they hoard what's left.

A lot of real charmers, you and your cartel buddies. My own kid died of diarrhea, Akwiss. My boy Derrick. Diarrhea's the leading cause of death for children, globally. Has been for decades. Did you know that ... Akwiss?"

"Yes. Yes I—I'd heard that." Try to show them you care, that you know about these things. "The, ah, hunger weakens their immunity, so they get a diarrhea which dehydrates them and they die of, ah—"

"My wife and I," Nephilim interrupted, looking abstractedly at his gun, "got stuck out in the new dust bowl, looking for water, and the car ran out of charge. . . ." Hardly audible, he finished: "And I couldn't get Derrick to water in time. . . ."

He turned to gaze emptily at Akwiss. And Akwiss thought Nephilim was going to shoot him on the spot. He held his breath.

And then let it out slowly when Nephilim visibly regained control and turned to gesture at the video screen. "Cancer patients downstream from AkInc factories in Louisiana. The link between your dioxins and their cancer was very clear but the whole thing was suppressed—"

"Now wait a moment," Akwiss broke in. Thinking, now's the time to really stall them till my men get here. "Honestly—if that's what happened I really did not know about it. I mean—maybe some of what you were saying is true. But like every man in a high position, I'm surrounded by yes-men." He tried not to look at the archway behind Crowel, through which his outdoor security men would be coming. "My subordinates tell me what they think I want to hear. About the environment. About our . . . our impact on it. I'm sure no one told me about the Dioxin link to cancer in Louisiana and I doubt I ever got honest information from my people about CFCs and the dangers of famine—"

"First of all, yes you did," Nephilim snapped. "Your attorneys gave you an extensive briefing about all these issues when they were trying to protect you from lawsuits. We have a tape of that briefing, from *fourteen years ago*. You understood, all right. Second—even if you hadn't been briefed, the information was out there. You were responsible for finding out on your own, Akwiss, what your company was doing to the world. But that's a red herring—you ordered the suppression of the truth. 'Smokescreen it' you said, on one occasion. You had a lot to do with weakening the various Clean Air Acts, you and your lobbies—and you knew exactly what you were doing." He looked into Akwiss' eyes, and spoke with a certain formal finality: *"You knew people were dying because of what you'd done."*

"No, truly, I—"

"You knew!" Nephilim roared, leaning over Akwiss, who shrank back on the sofa, glancing at the archway. *Where were they? Stoned or not they had to come.* Nephilim turned away, pacing now, shouting, "You knew damn well! And you didn't give one rat's ass about the children dying of cancer, about the birth defects, about the emphysema, about the destruction of the sea, the destruction of the farmlands, the famines that would have to come. The *millions of Americans* dying from famines! You son of a bitch, you're the biggest mass murderer since Hitler!" He stopped pacing, his back turned, his voice breaking, sounding far away as he admitted, "But we all practiced denial. And none of us wanted to admit that criminals were running the country. We just didn't want to believe that it was murder. That it was mass homicide. Just a kind of carelessness, we thought. Or ignorance. When it was nothing of the kind..."

Crowel nodded, put in hoarsely, "It was murder. Pre-fuckin'-meditated."

And then Brightson and Margolis stepped into the archway, guns in hand. Brightson a young, heavy-set black guard with an elaborate silvery coif, and Margolis the potbellied, gray-haired white guard. Where were the others? Were these all that would come? The drugs, damn the drugs!

Crowel and Crispin vaulted over the sofa and crouched back of Akwiss; Crowel looped his wiry arm around Akwiss' throat, nearly crushing his windpipe, holding him in place on the sofa.

Nephilim stepped behind the piano, loosing a sloppy burst of autofire at Margolis. Missing. Nephilim's rounds traced a crooked line of holes across the walls of the corridor as Margolis and Brightson jumped back beyond the edge of the archway, out of the line of fire. "Jesus fucking Christ!" Brightson muttered.

"You men stand firm!" Akwiss yelled hoarsely. "Get the police! Get the other men!"

"We can't find the others!" Margolis yelled. "Outside phone lines are down!"

"Mr. Akwiss!" Brightson shouted, from around the corner of the archway. "We'd better go and try to get help, these fellas got us out-gunned!"

"No! No, don't leave—"

Crowel tightened his chokehold around Akwiss' throat. "Shut up, asshole."

Nephilim yelled out, "You men out there—you want some Hot Morph? It's pharmaceutical! We got it on a pharm-industry raid and it's the same good stuff you been getting! I'll give you an ounce if you go away and forget about this! Just tell 'em we got past ol' Finch and there was nothing you could do!"

Hesitation. Then Margolis yelled, "Hell yeah! Toss it over and I'm gone!"

They could hear Brightson hissing at Margolis. "Goddamn it that ain't no way to treat the man, he employed you ten years!"

"He underpaid everybody ever worked for him, Brighty! Fuck him and fuck you too!"

Another traitorous bastard, Akwiss thought.

Nephilim tossed over a sandwich bag full of yellow powder. It slid past the archway, into the corridor. They could hear Margolis scoop it up and run. His bootsteps receding down the hall. Gone.

Nephilim shouted, "Throw down your gun, 'Brighty', 'cause I'm coming over there and if you're armed—"

Brightson, bless him, responded with two gunshots that rang out dissonant, hysterical notes as the bullets struck the piano. Nephilim ducked back, cursing under his breath. There was a burst from another automatic weapon, out of sight in the hallway. A cry of pain. The sound of someone falling. Footsteps. "Hold your fire!" Murieta called, as he stepped into view. He was grinning, carrying a small machine pistol. "Brighty's gone down, Nephilim. Let's get back to the trial."

Crowel released Akwiss. Gagging, trying his best to look pitiful, Akwiss turned to Nephilim. "Look, let's negotiate this. I can offer you a fortune. You—you have to give me a chance to—"

"You had your chance." Nephilim moved out from behind the piano, and pointed to the video screen. The image was frozen on the face of a starving child. "He had none. Your guilt is clear. The penalty . . ."

"You're not going to torture me," Akwiss broke in, losing control. "You're not that kind of person. I know that. You're not!"

"Torture you? You mean force you to die slowly—of cancer? Of starvation? No. We're not barbarians, Akwiss."

They aren't really going to do it, Akwiss thought. He was standing on a chair, with a neatly tied hangman's noose around his neck, the knot behind his left ear. The rope running up to loop over his beautiful real-wood rafters. *They're trying to scare me into signing something, giving them money.*

"I can sign over a great deal of money to you," Akwiss said.

"You could stop it getting to us, too," Nephilim said. "If you were alive. You've given us your account numbers. That'll help. We'll feed a lot of kids before your Swiss banks figure it out. You got any last words?"

Now even Akwiss' knees threatened to betray him. They were going gelatinous. "Please . . . I didn't know. . . ."

"You keep saying that," Nephilim said. "But I keep saying: Oh but you most certainly *did* know. Ackwiss—haven't you wondered why I know so much about the inner workings of your outfit?" His voice broke, but he went on. "I worked for you, Ackwiss. We never met— but I was one of the two hundred some lawyers AckInc employed. That's how I got my hands on the tapes of your briefing. And that's when I resigned. When I realized what we were doing. I could hear it on the tape: *You just didn't care*. I have a theory, Akwiss—that you have to be a real sociopath to get to the top of American Industry. And a sociopath feels nothing for anyone but himself. So it didn't matter that you knew your company was helping launch a famine in which millions would die. You felt nothing. *You* were living where it was safe, after all. . . ."

They were both crying now: Akwiss and Nephilim. For different reasons. Nephilim said hoarsely: "I was a damn good lawyer. I defended you people—I ought to be up there with you, with a rope around my neck. And someday I will be, when all this is done. Now. This is for Derrick."

And then he kicked over the chair.

This time, and for the last time, Akwiss' bowels worked very well.

The others were back; the trucks were loaded with tons of stashed food. No sign of Federal troops or police. It was going smoothly. Just one thing left to attend to, Nephilim thought: the very last of the liberated food.

That was nearly ready, too. Nephilim saw that Crispin was almost done cutting the meat off Akwiss' body, and putting it in the bags.

The kids wouldn't know the difference. It might save a life or two.

"What kind of meat you going to tell them it is?" Crowel asked, smiling. "Pig?"

"No," Nephilim said. "No if I told them that, they might guess what it really is."

Tricentennial

Precisely what do you suggest *I* do about it?" asked Ollie.

"You're hedging. You know what has to be done. You got to go get one," said his sister Lem coldly.

"Look—we can make one for him out of cardboard—"

"No. He wouldn't fall for it, he has to have the real thing. Cloth. With the official Tricentennial medallion on the stick. He's not *that* far gone. And if we don't do it Pops won't sign the release and he'll die without turning over the stall to us and then we'll be out in the street. And *you* are the oldest, Ollie-boy. So you are elected."

"I don't know if I *want* to stay in this grimy cubey. I could be in the Angels. I got a Hell's Angels Officer's School commission and I see no reason why I shouldn't—"

"Because it would be *worse*, that's why. You don't believe all that stuff they tell you at the Angels recruiting office about the Cycle Corps, do you? They have it just as bad as the Army, except they've got the Rape Decree to back up anything they do. But big deal. You get your rocks off but do you get a decent place to sleep?"

"Okay. Okay, then. But—I ain't goin' alone. No way. If we're gonna get it for him, *you* are goin' with me, back-up. Because there's no way

to go two big ones on 53rd alone without getting it in the back. . . .
Look, are you sure we can't get one in Building Three?"

"I'm sure. I've called around. All the dispensaries are out of them
except Eleven."

"Maybe we can roll the old man on the hundredth floor. He's got
one."

"He's got microwave barriers. We'd fry."

Ollie sighed. "Then let's go. And when we bring it back I hope to
God the old sonuvabitch is happy with it. Because if he's not, Father
or no Father—"

"Okay, don't get toxed. Let's go."

II.

At first, the metal streets seemed almost deserted. The frags and the
joy-boy gangs and the hustlers and sliders were there, just out of sight,
but Security was keeping them off the street for the Tricentennial Procession. Ollie'd heard the procession might traverse the 53rd Level but
he'd assumed it would move through some less dilapidated end of the
street. Maybe it all looked this way.

Crusted with grey-white scum from exhalations of methane engines
and human pores, the kelp-fiber walls of the five stories visible on the
53rd Level bulged slightly outward with the weight of excess population—each stall cubey held at least five people more than regulations.
Ollie cradled the Smith & Wesson .44 he'd received at age fourteen, on
his Weaponing Day. He held it now, five years later, as another man
might have clasped a crucifix, and he whispered to it piously, while his
eyes swept the rust-pitted streets, sorting through the heaps of litter
waiting for the dumper, the piles of garbage, the half-dozen corpses
that were as much a part of any street as the fire hydrants. The street-
lights extending from warped and peeling faces of the buildings were
all functioning and the vents near the ceiling within the plasteel girder
underpinnings of the 54th Level were all inhaling, judging from the
thinness of the smogs wreathing the dark doorwells. There were only
about twenty-five homeless or gangbugs on the street and no cars—

nearly desolation, compared to any other time. Apparently the Procession was near.

Ollie and Lem, crouching just inside the doorway to their home-building, rechecked their weapons and scanned the sidewalk for booby-traps. "I don't see anything we can't handle," Lem said.

"We can't see into the alleys or doorways or that subway entrance. And—" Ollie was interrupted by the blast of a siren. A few ragged silhouettes shuffling the street scurried for doorways at the wailing from the cornice speakers. Others hardly looked up. "Looks like all that's left are dope-heads who don't know from shit. Christ, they so far gone they don't know the clear-streets when they hear it."

As the siren wound down Lem asked, "How long since you been on the street?"

"This first time in three years. Looks pretty much th' same. Only more dope-heads."

"Always more dope-heads. They don't get gutted much because they don't have any money."

"Well. Let's go, maybe we can dash the whole two blocks. I mean, since the streets are almost empty—"

"You haven't been on the streets in three years. You don't know—" Lem began.

"You're jimmy for venturing onto the streets when you don't need to. We've got everything we need on our floor, all the dispensaries and spas are there, and it's the same everywhere anyway and since you can't leave the Zone without a permit or unless you go with the troops, why bother?"

"We've got a half hour to get to Building Eleven. Let's do it."

Both of them were dressed in scum-grey clothing, camouflage, their faces smeared with gray ash so their pallor would blend, as much as possible, into the walls.

Lem, tall and thin, the fire in her curly red hair extinguished with ash, stood and checked her brace of throwing knives; inspected the uzi she'd got two years before on her Weaponing Day, and the cans of acid-bombs affixed to the two khaki belts criss-crossing her chest.

Ollie examined his own equipment, certified that the extra pistol he kept in his shoulder-holster was loaded and ready, the knives on springs lashed to his forearms primed. His .44 loaded and cocked.

Lem behind, walking backwards to cover the rear, they set off, looking like some odd two-headed predatory creature. The lineaments of the dour metal streets converged in a mesh of street-lamps, girders, stairways, and furtive figures, made tenebrously unreal by the smudged air and dim mucous-yellow lighting. The vista, shackled by metal ceiling and street merged in the distance, had all the elegance of a car crumpled into a cube by a hydraulic-press compactor. Ollie adjusted his infrared visors to see into the darker lairs. A frag, there to the right. The frag was a woman, left breast burned off to make room for a rifle-strap, a patch over her right eye. She waited, leaning back against the wall, her lower half hidden by a multiplex heap of refuse. Ollie hadn't been on the street in years, but the indications were ever the same: the suspect looked casual, relaxed—and that was bad. If she wasn't planning to attack them, she'd look tensed, in defense. So she was preparing to jump.

She was twenty feet off, on the low right, standing in the well of a barred basement doorway.

They carried $40 for their Old Man's toy. Frags could smell money. Even penniless, they'd be jumped for their clothes, guns, and on general principle.

The frag made as if to tie her bootlace. A signal. "Down!" Ollie cried.

Lem and Ollie went to a crouch as the woman's accomplice leapt from the doorway immediately to her right, and only her M-16's jamming saved them. Lem stepped in and with an underhand cut, gutted the frag and withdrew the stiletto before she could reach for another weapon. By this time the other frag was swinging her rifle round to take aim. Ollie had already leveled the .44.

He squeezed the trigger, the gun barked, the jolt from the recoil hurt his wrist. The one-eyed woman caught it in the gut, was thrown back, rebounded from the wall, and pitched forward to fall onto her face. Blood marked a Rorschach visage leering in red on the wall behind her.

He heard Lem firing at the other frags attracted by the gunshots. A young man fell, pistol clattering into the gutter. The others found cover.

"C'mon!" They sprinted, running low to the ground, gaining another forty feet, three quarters of the first block behind them. Another block-and-a-quarter, Ollie thought. Something lobbed in a wallowing tinny arc struck the sticky metal sidewalk and clattered past Ollie's right leg; he turned and grabbed Lem by the forearm, dragging her into the shelter of a doorway. The grenade exploded on the other side of the wall, fragments of the flimsy wall-fiber flew, laughter erupted from nearby frag-niches to echo from the distant ceiling, laughter as acid-drenched as the shrapnel that took out two dope-heads across the street. The blue smoke cleared.

A bullet struck the wall by Ollie's head, flying splinters stung his scalp. Swallowing fear—it had been three years—he crouched, panning his gunsight back and forth over the grey-black-engraved prospect. Sniper? From where? He looked up—that window, fourth floor. Glint off a barrel. He snatched free an acid cartridge and clipped it hastily on the launch spring welded to the underside of his pistol's barrel. He cocked, squinted, and fired. The sniper's rifle went off at the same moment, another shot too high. Then the acid-bomb exploded in the sniper's apartment. A scream that began as a rumble, went higher and higher in pitch, finishing as a bubbling whine that merged perfectly with the returning off-streets-siren, a growing, piercing ululation. The sniper, slapping at his boiling skin, threw himself whimpering out the window and fell, writhing, three stories, striking the ground head first. Stripping the corpses of the sniper, joy-boys and the two dead women, the frags were momentarily distracted. So Ollie and Lem sprinted, zig-zagging to make poor targets.

Bolting across the intersection, they drew fire. Four strident *cracks*, four *pings*—four misses. They achieved the opposite corner. Crouched behind a conical heap of excrement and plastic cans, their left side protected by the extruding metal side-walls of a stairway. "Three-quarters of a block left," said Lem.

But frags were closing in from the right, at least a dozen piebald figures creeping hastily from shadow to shadow like scuttling cockroaches.

One of the frags caught another unawares and slipped him a blade. There was a bubbling cough and that was all.

"One less," said Lem. "But they'll cooperate to kill us before they turn on each other again."

A scratchy recorded fanfare announced the Tricentennial Procession.

The street was twenty yards from gutter to gutter. The Procession filled the street for half a block; two long, six-wheeled armored red-white-and-blue sedans surrounded by twelve Security Cycles. A recorded voice from the chrome fanged grill of the front sedan announced over and over:

REJOICE INDEPENDENCE DAY REJOICE INDEPENDENCE DAY RE-
JOICE INDEPENDENCE DAY MAYOR WELCOMES ALL CITIZENS TO SEY-
MOR COLISEUM FOUR PM FOR PUBLIC EXECUTIONS PARTY REJOICE
INDEPENDENCE DAY REJOICE REJOICE

Dimly, through the green-tinted window of the low, steel-plated limo, Ollie could make out the faces of the High Priest of the International Church of Sun Moon sitting beside the man he'd appointed as Mayor, whose name Ollie could not recall. A few token bullets bounced from the limo's windshield. The silhouettes within waved at the faces crowding the windows. A handful of excrement splattered the roof, cleaned away an instant later by tiny hoses in the windshield frame. One of the Security Cycles shot a microwave shell into the apartment from which the excrement had been thrown; there was a white flash and a scream, a thin wisp of smoke from the shattered window.

The Security Cycles were three-wheeled motorbikes, propelled, like the limousines, by methane engines fueled by gases extracted from human excrement. Issuing blue flatulence, they rolled slowly abreast of Ollie and Lem. The cops inside, figures of shiny black leather, heads completely encased in black-opaqued helmets, were protected by bells of transparent plasteel from which their various weapons projected cobra snouts. The cop nearest Ollie methodically snuffed dope-heads and careless frags with casual flares of his handle-bar-mounted microwave rifle. "Hey," Ollie breathed, "maybe they'll help us. If you call them they don't come but since they're right here, if we ask them for help getting to the corner they can't refuse, seeing as we're right in front of them and all. Hell, with the High Priest watching . . ."

"Ollie, don't be an asshole—"

But Ollie was already out in the street, waving his arms, shouting, "We need an escort, just a little farther, we are citizens, we have to go to Building Eleven to buy a—"

He threw himself flat and rolled, wincing as the invisible microwave beam singed his back. The cop fired again but Lem had thrown a smoke-bomb, and Ollie took advantage of the thick yellow billowing to return to cover.

"Wish I could afford one of those microwave rifles," Lem remarked wistfully.

"Hey, Lem, maybe if we keep just back of the procession we can use it for cover and get the rest of the way."

Lem nodded and they were off.

Most of the frags were flattened to avoid the microwave beams; the cops ignored their shielded rear, so Ollie and Lem sprinted along behind, and Building Eleven loomed ahead. Ollie grinned. There! The stairs!

They were scrambling the two flights up the stairs when the doors to building eleven swung open and a pack of joy-boys, none of them over twelve years old, stampeded directly into Lem and Ollie's reflexive gunfire. But there were too many of them to spray dead at short range. Five went down, another ten were upon them—naked but for belts bristling with makeshift knives. Their gap-toothed mouths squalling, drooling like demented elves, they chattered and snarled gleefully. Their sallow, grimy faces—blurs now—were pock-marked, the eyes dope-wild. Swinging the gun-butt in his right hand, the spring-snapped knife in his left, Ollie slashed and battered at the small faces, and time slowed: fragments of skull and teeth flew, black-nailed hands clawed at his face, his own blood clouded his visors.

Ollie plowed forward, kicking, elbowing, feeling a twisted shard of metal bite deep into his thigh, another below his left shoulder-blade, another in his right pectorals. He was two feet from the door. He left his knife in someone's ribs. He glanced at Lem, three of them were on her back, clinging like chimp-children, clawing relentlessly at her head, gnawing her ears with ragged yellow teeth. He dragged them off of her with his left hand, wrenching viciously to keep them off his own back, and brained another who flailed wildly at his eyes—and then he and Lem were through the door.

It was cool and quiet inside.

A young man, a custodian chewing synthabetel and squinting at them, leaning on his mop, said, "You got some holes in you."

"Where—" Ollie had to catch his breath. He felt weak. Blood soaking his right leg—have to bind that before heading back, he thought, try again, ask: "Where we buy . . . flags?"

"Fifty-fourth level if he's got any left."

III.

Luck was with them. They made it back with only two more wounds. A .22 slug in Lem's right arm, a zip gun pellet in Ollie's left calf.

Lem slumped outside the door to bind her wounds and rest. Ollie took the flag from her and staggered into their two-room apartment, stepped carefully over the children sleeping on the crowded floor, tried not to stagger. He was dizzy, nauseated. The tiny cubicle seemed to constrict and whirl, the stained yellow-white curtains over the alcove where his father lay dying on an army cot became malignant leprous arms reaching for him. He cursed, his right hand gripping the small, rolled-up flag. He felt he could not walk another step.

Ollie sank to a chink of clear floor-space. He shoved wearily at one of the sleeping children. Eight-year old Sandra. She woke, a pale, hollow-eyed child, nearly bald, a few strands of wispy flaxen hair. "You take this to Pops." He told her. "The flag. Tell him to sign the goddamn release."

Seeing the flag, the little girl's eyes flared. She snatched the bright banner away and ran out into the hall, ignoring Ollie's shouts.

She got three bucks for the flag from a man on the Hundredth Level.

A penny a year.

The Belonging Kind*

It might have been in Club Justine, or Jimbo's, or Sad Jack's, or the Rafters; Coretti could never be sure where he'd first seen her. At any time, she might have been in any one of those bars. She swam through the submarine half-life of bottles and glassware and the slow swirl of cigarette smoke ... she moved through her natural element, one bar after another.

Now, Coretti remembered their first meeting as if he saw it through the wrong end of a powerful telescope, small and clear and very far away.

He had noticed her first in the Backdoor Lounge. It was called the Backdoor because you entered through a narrow back alley. The alley's walls crawled with graffiti, its caged lights ticked with moths. Flakes from its white-painted bricks crunched underfoot. And then you pushed through into a dim space inhabited by a faintly confusing sense of the half-dozen other bars that had tried and failed in the same room under different managements. Coretti sometimes went there because he liked the weary smile of the black bartender, and because the few customers rarely tried to get chummy.

He wasn't very good at conversation with strangers, not at parties and not in bars.

*Written with William Gibson.

He was fine at the community college where he lectured in introductory linguistics; he could talk with the head of his department about sequencing and options in conversational openings. But he could never talk to strangers in bars or at parties. He didn't go to many parties. He went to a lot of bars.

Coretti didn't know how to dress. Clothing was a language and Coretti a kind of sartorial stutterer, unable to make the kind of basic coherent fashion statement that would put strangers at their ease. His ex-wife told him he dressed like a Martian; that he didn't look as though he belonged anywhere in the city. He hadn't liked her saying that, because it was true.

He hadn't ever had a girl like the one who sat with her back arched slightly in the undersea light that splashed along the bar in the Backdoor. The same light was screwed into the lenses of the bartender's glasses, wound into the necks of the rows of bottles, splashed dully across the mirror. In that light her dress was the green of young corn, like a husk half stripped away, showing back and cleavage and lots of thigh through the slits up the side. Her hair was coppery that night. And, that night, her eyes were green.

He pushed resolutely between the empty chrome-and-Formica tables until he reached the bar, where he ordered a straight bourbon. He took off his duffle coat, and wound up holding it on his lap when he sat down one stool away from her. Great, he screamed to himself, she'll think you're hiding an erection. And he was startled to realize that he had one to hide. He studied himself in the mirror behind the bar, a thirtyish man with thinning dark hair and a pale, narrow face on a long neck, too long for the open collar of the nylon shirt printed with engravings of 1910 automobiles in three vivid colors. He wore a tie with broad maroon and black diagonals, too narrow, he supposed, for what he now saw as the grotesquely long points of his collar. Or it was the wrong color. Something.

Beside him, in the dark clarity of the mirror, the green-eyed woman looked like Irma La Douce. But looking closer, studying her face, he shivered. A face like an animal's. A beautiful face, but simple, cunning, two-dimensional. When she senses you're looking at her, Coretti thought, she'll give you the smile, disdainful amusement—or whatever you'd expect.

Coretti blurted, "May I, um, buy you a drink?"

At moments like these, Coretti was possessed by an agonizingly stiff, schoolmasterish linguistic tic. *Um*. He winced. *Um*.

"You would, um, like to buy me a drink? Why, how kind of you," she said, astonishing him. "That would be very nice." Distantly, he noticed that her reply was as stilted and insecure as his own. She added, "A Tom Collins, on this occasion, would be lovely."

On this occasion? Lovely? Rattled, Coretti ordered two drinks and paid.

A big woman in jeans and an embroidered cowboy shirt bellied up to the bar beside him and asked the bartender for change. "Well, hey," she said. Then she strutted to the jukebox and punched for Conway and Loretta's "You're the Reason Our Kids Are Ugly." Coretti turned to the-woman-in-green, and murmured haltingly:

"Do you enjoy country-and-western music?" *Do you enjoy . . . ?* He groaned secretly at his phrasing, and tried to smile.

"Yes indeed," she answered, the faintest twang edging her voice, "I sure do."

The cowgirl sat down beside him and asked her, winking, "This li'l terror here givin' you a hard time?"

And the animal-eyed lady in green replied, "Oh, Hell no, honey, I got my eye on 'im." And laughed. Just the right amount of laugh. The part of Coretti that was dialectologist stirred uneasily; too perfect a shift in phrasing and inflection. An actress? A talented mimic? The word *mimetic* rose suddenly in his mind, but he pushed it aside to study her reflection in the mirror; the rows of bottles occluded her breasts like a gown of glass.

"The name's Coretti," he said, his verbal poltergeist shifting abruptly to a totally unconvincing tough-guy mode, "Michael Coretti."

"A pleasure," she said, too softly for the other woman to hear, and again she had slipped into the lame parody of Emily Post.

"Conway and Loretta," said the cowgirl, to no one in particular.

"Antoinette," said the woman in green, and inclined her head. She finished her drink, pretended to glance at a watch, said thank-you-for-the-drink too damn politely, and left.

Ten minutes later Coretti was following her down Third Avenue. He had never followed anyone in his life and it both frightened and excited him. Forty feet seemed a discreet distance, but what should he do if she happened to glance over her shoulder?

Third Avenue isn't a dark street, and it was there, in the light of a streetlamp, like a stage light, that she began to change. The street was deserted.

She was crossing the street. She stepped off the curb and it began. It began with tints in her hair—at first he thought they were reflections. But there was no neon there to cast the blobs of color that appeared, color sliding and merging like oil slicks. Then the colors bled away and in three seconds she was white-blond. He was sure it was a trick of the light until her dress began to writhe, twisting across her body like shrink-wrap plastic. Part of it fell away entirely and lay in curling shreds on the pavement, shed like the skin of some fabulous animal. When Coretti passed, it was green foam, fizzing, dissolving, gone. He looked back up at her and the dress was another dress, green satin, shifting with reflections. Her shoes had changed too. Her shoulders were bare except for thin straps that crossed at the small of her back. Her hair had become short, spiky.

He found that he was leaning against a jeweler's plate-glass window, his breath coming ragged and harsh with the damp of the autumn evening. He heard the disco's heartbeat from two blocks away. As she neared it, her movements began subtly to take on a new rhythm—a shift in emphasis in the sway of her hips, in the way she put her heels down on the sidewalk. The doorman let her pass with a vague nod. He stopped Coretti and stared at his driver's license and frowned at his duffle coat. Coretti anxiously scanned the wash of lights at the top of a milky plastic stairway beyond the doorman. She had vanished there, into robotic flashing and redundant thunder.

Grudgingly the man let him pass, and he pounded up the stairs, his haste disturbing the lights beneath the translucent plastic steps.

Coretti had never been in a disco before. He waded nervously through the dancers and the fashions and the mechanical urban chants booming from the huge speakers. He sought her almost blindly on the pose-clotted dance floor, amid strobe lights.

And found her at the bar, drinking a tall, lurid cooler and listening to a young man who wore a loose shirt of pale silk and very tight black pants. She nodded at what Coretti took to be appropriate intervals. Coretti ordered by pointing at a bottle of bourbon. She drank five of the tall drinks and then followed the young man to the dance floor.

She moved in perfect accord with the music, striking a series of poses; she went through the entire prescribed sequence, gracefully but not artfully, fitting in perfectly. Always, always fitting in perfectly. Her companion danced mechanically, moving through the ritual with effort.

When the dance ended, she turned abruptly and dived into the thick of the crowd. The shifting throng closed about her like something molten.

Coretti plunged in after her, his eyes never leaving her—and he was the only one to follow her change. By the time she reached the stair, she was auburn-haired and wore a long blue dress. A white flower blossomed in her hair, behind her right ear; her hair was longer and straighter now. Her breasts had become slightly larger, and her hips a shade heavier. She took the stairs two at a time, and he was afraid for her then. All those drinks.

But the alcohol seemed to have had no effect on her at all.

Never taking his eyes from her, Coretti followed, his heartbeat outspeeding the disco-throb at his back, sure that at any moment she would turn, glare at him, call for help.

Two blocks down Third she turned in at Lothario's. There was something different in her step now. Lothario's was a quiet complex of rooms hung with ferns and Art Deco mirrors. There were fake stained-glass lamps hanging from the ceiling, alternating with wooden-bladed fans that rotated too slowly to stir the wisps of smoke drifting through the consciously mellow drone of conversation. After the disco, Lothario's was familiar and comforting. A jazz pianist in pinstriped shirt sleeves and loosely knotted tie competed softly with talk and laughter from a dozen tables.

She was at the bar; the stools were only half taken, but Coretti chose a wall table, in the shadow of a miniature palm, and ordered bourbon.

He drank the bourbon and ordered another. He couldn't feel the alcohol much tonight.

She sat beside a young man, yet another young man with the usual set of bland, regular features. He wore a yellow golf shirt and pressed jeans. Her hip was touching his, just a little. They didn't seem to be speaking, but Coretti felt they were somehow communing. They were leaning toward one another slightly, silent. Coretti felt odd. He went to the rest room and splashed his face with water. Coming back, he managed to pass within three feet of them. Their lips didn't move till he was within earshot.

They took turns murmuring realistic palaver:

"...saw his earlier films, but—"

"But he's rather self-indulgent, don't you think?"

"Sure, but in the sense that..."

And for the first time, Coretti knew what they were, what they must be. They were the kind you see in bars who seem to have grown there, who seem genuinely at home there. Not drunks, but human fixtures. Functions of the bar. The belonging kind.

Something in him yearned for a confrontation. He reached his table, but found himself unable to sit down. He turned, took a deep breath, and walked woodenly toward the bar. He wanted to tap her on her smooth shoulder and ask who she was, and exactly what she was, and point out the cold irony of the fact that it was he, Coretti, the Martian dresser, the eavesdropper, the outsider, the one whose clothes and conversation never fit, who had at last guessed their secret.

But his nerve broke and he merely took a seat beside her and ordered bourbon.

"But don't you think," she asked her companion, "that it's all relative?"

The two seats beyond her companion were quickly taken by a couple who were talking politics. Antoinette and Golf Shirt took up the political theme seamlessly, recycling, speaking just loudly enough to be overheard. Her face, as she spoke, was expressionless. A bird trilling on a limb.

She sat so easily on her stool, as if it were a nest. Golf Shirt paid for the drinks. He always had the exact change, unless he wanted to leave a tip. Coretti watched them work their way methodically through six cocktails each, like insects feeding on nectar. But their voices never grew louder, their cheeks didn't redden, and when at last they stood, they moved without a trace of drunkenness—a weakness, thought Coretti, a gap in their camouflage.

They paid him absolutely no attention while he followed them through three successive bars.

As they entered Waylon's, they metamorphosed so quickly that Coretti had trouble following the stages of the change. It was one of those places with toilet doors marked Pointers and Setters, and a little imitation pine plaque over the jars of beef jerky and pickled sausages: *We've got a deal with the bank. They don't serve beer and we don't cash checks.*

She was plump in Waylon's, and there were dark hollows under her eyes. There were coffee stains on her polyester pantsuit. Her companion wore jeans, a T-shirt, and a red baseball cap with a red-and-white Peterbilt patch. Coretti risked losing them when he spent a frantic minute in "Pointers," blinking in confusion at a hand-lettered cardboard sign that said, *We aim to please—You aim too, please.*

Third Avenue lost itself near the waterfront in a petrified snarl of brickwork. In the last block, bright vomit marked the pavement at intervals, and old men dozed in front of black-and-white TVs, sealed forever behind the fogged plate glass of faded hotels.

The bar they found there had no name. An ace of diamonds was gradually flaking away on the unwashed window, and the bartender had a face like a closed fist. An FM transistor in ivory plastic keened easy-listening rock to the uneven ranks of deserted tables. They drank beer and shots. They were old now, two ciphers who drank and smoked in the light of bare bulbs, coughing over a pack of crumpled Camels she produced from the pocket of a dirty tan raincoat.

At 2:25 they were in the rooftop lounge of the new hotel complex that rose above the waterfront. She wore an evening dress and he wore a dark suit. They drank cognac and pretended to admire the city lights. They each had three cognacs while Coretti watched them over two ounces of Wild Turkey in a Waterford crystal highball glass.

They drank until last call. Coretti followed them into the elevator. They smiled politely but otherwise ignored him. There were two cabs in front of the hotel; they took one, Coretti the other.

"Follow that cab," said Coretti huskily, thrusting his last twenty at the aging hippie driver.

"Sure, man, sure. . . ." The driver dogged the other cab for six blocks, to another, more modest hotel. They got out and went in. Coretti slowly climbed out of his cab, breathing hard.

He ached with jealousy: for the personification of conformity, this woman who was not a woman, this human wallpaper. Coretti gazed at the hotel—and lost his nerve. He turned away.

He walked home. Sixteen blocks. At some point he realized that he wasn't drunk. Not drunk at all.

In the morning he phoned in to cancel his early class. But his hangover never quite came. His mouth wasn't desiccated, and staring at himself in the bathroom mirror he saw that his eyes weren't bloodshot.

In the afternoon he slept, and dreamed of sheep-faced people reflected in mirrors behind rows of bottles.

That night he went out to dinner, alone—and ate nothing. The food looked back at him, somehow. He stirred it about to make it look as if he'd eaten a little, paid, and went to a bar. And another. And another bar, looking for her. He was using his credit card now, though he was already badly in the hole under Visa. If he saw her, he didn't recognize her.

Sometimes he watched the hotel he'd seen her go into. He looked carefully at each of the couples who came and went. Not that he'd be able to spot her from her looks alone—but there should be a *feeling*, some kind of intuitive recognition. He watched the couples and he was never sure.

In the following weeks he systematically visited every boozy watering hole in the city. Armed at first with a city map and five torn Yellow Pages, he gradually progressed to the more obscure establishments, places with unlisted numbers. Some had no phone at all. He joined dubious private clubs, discovered unlicensed after-hours retreats where you brought your own, and sat nervously in dark rooms devoted to areas of fringe sexuality he had not known existed.

But he continued on what became his nightly circuit. He always began at the Backdoor. She was never there, or in the next place, or the next. The bartenders knew him and they liked to see him come in, because he brought drinks continuously, and never seemed to get drunk. So he stared at the other customers a bit—so what?

Coretti lost his job.

He'd missed classes too many times. He'd taken to watching the hotel when he could, even in the daytime. He'd been seen in too many bars. He never seemed to change his clothes. He refused night classes. He would let a lecture trail off in the middle as he turned to gaze vacantly out the window.

He was secretly pleased at being fired. They had looked at him oddly at faculty lunches when he couldn't eat his food. And now he had more time for the search.

Coretti found her at 2:15 on a Wednesday morning, in a gay bar called the Barn. Paneled in rough wood and hung with halters and rusting farm equipment, the place was shrill with perfume and laughter and beer. She was everyone's giggling sister, in a blue-sequined dress, a green feather in her coiffed brown hair. Through a sweeping sense of almost cellular relief, Coretti was aware of a kind of admiration, a strange pride he now felt in her—and her kind. Here, too, she belonged. She was a representative type, a fag-hag who posed no threat to the queens or their butchboys. Her companion had become an ageless man with carefully silvered temples, an angora sweater, and a trench coat.

They drank and drank, and went laughing—laughing just the right sort of laughter—out into the rain. A cab was waiting, its wipers duplicating the beat of Coretti's heart.

Jockeying clumsily across the wet sidewalk, Coretti scurried into the cab, dreading their reaction.

Coretti was in the back seat, beside her.

The man with silver temples spoke to the driver. The driver muttered into his hand mike, changed gears, and they flowed away into the rain and the darkened streets. The cityscape made no impression on Coretti, who, looking inwardly, was seeing the cab stop, the gray man and the laughing woman pushing him out and pointing, smiling, to the gate of a mental hospital. Or: the cab stopping, the couple turning, sadly shaking

their heads. And a dozen times he seemed to see the cab stopping in
an empty side street where they methodically throttled him. Coretti left
dead in the rain. Because he was an outsider.

But they arrived at Coretti's hotel.

In the dim glow of the cab's dome light he watched closely as the
man reached into his coat for the fare. Coretti could see the coat's lining
clearly and it was one piece with the angora sweater. No wallet bulged
there, and no pocket. But a kind of slit widened. It opened as the man's
fingers poised over it, and it disgorged money. Three bills, folded, were
extruded smoothly from the slit. The money was slightly damp. It
dried, as the man unfolded it, like the wings of a moth just emerging
from the chrysalis.

"Keep the change," said the belonging man, climbing out of the cab.
Antoinette slid out and Coretti followed, his mind seeing only the slit.
The slit wet, edged with red, like a gill.

The lobby was deserted and the desk clerk bent over a crossword.
The couple drifted silently across the lobby and into the elevator, Coretti close behind. Once he tried to catch her eye, but she ignored him.
And once, as the elevator rose seven floors above Coretti's own, she
bent over and sniffed at the chrome wall ashtray, like a dog snuffling
at the ground.

Hotels, late at night, are never still. The corridors are never entirely
silent. There are countless barely audible sighs, the rustling of sheets,
and muffled voices speaking fragments out of sleep. But in the ninth-
floor corridor, Coretti seemed to move through a perfect vacuum,
soundless, his shoes making no sound at all on the colorless carpet and
even the beating of his outsider's heart sucked away into the vague
pattern that decorated the wallpaper.

He tried to count the small plastic ovals screwed on the doors, each
with its own three figures, but the corridor seemed to go on forever.
At last the man halted before a door, a door veneered like all the rest
with imitation rosewood, and put his hand over the lock, his palm flat
against the metal. Something scraped softly and then the mechanism
clicked and the door swung open. As the man withdrew his hand,
Coretti saw a grayish-pink, key-shaped sliver of bone retract wetly into
the pale flesh.

No light burned in that room, but the city's dim neon aura filtered in through venetian blinds and allowed him to see the faces of the dozen or more people who sat perched on the bed and the couch and the armchairs and the stools in the kitchenette. At first he thought that their eyes were open, but then he realized that the dull pupils were sealed beneath nictitating membranes, third eyelids that reflected the faint shades of neon from the window. They wore whatever the last bar had called for; shapeless Salvation Army overcoats sat beside bright suburban leisurewear, evening gowns beside dusty factory clothes, biker's leather by brushed Harris tweed. With sleep, all spurious humanity had vanished.

They were roosting.

His couple seated themselves on the edge of the Formica countertop in the kitchenette, and Coretti hesitated in the middle of the empty carpet. Light-years of that carpet seemed to separate him from the others, but something called to him across the distance, promising rest and peace and belonging. And still he hesitated, shaking with an indecision that seemed to rise from the genetic core of his body's every cell.

Until they opened their eyes, all of them simultaneously, the membranes sliding sideways to reveal the alien calm of dwellers in the ocean's darkest trench.

Coretti screamed, and ran away, and fled along corridors and down echoing concrete stairwells to cool rain and the nearly empty streets.

Coretti never returned to his room on the third floor of that hotel. A bored house detective collected the linguistics texts, the single suitcase of clothing, and they were eventually sold at auction. Coretti took a room in a boardinghouse run by a grim Baptist teetotaler who led her roomers in prayer at the start of every overcooked evening meal. She didn't mind that Coretti never joined them for those meals; he explained that he was given free meals at work. He lied freely and skillfully. He never drank at the boardinghouse, and he never came home drunk. Mr. Coretti was a little odd, but always paid his rent on time. And he was very quiet.

Coretti stopped looking for her. He stopped going to bars. He drank out of a paper bag while going to and from his job at a publisher's warehouse, in an area whose industrial zoning permitted few bars.

He worked nights.

Sometimes, at dawn, perched on the edge of his unmade bed, drifting into sleep—he never slept lying down, now—he thought about her. Antoinette. And them. The belonging kind. Sometimes he speculated dreamily. . . . Perhaps they were like house mice, the sort of small animal evolved to live only in the walls of man-made structures.

A kind of animal that lives only on alcoholic beverages. With peculiar metabolisms they convert the alcohol and the various proteins from mixed drinks and wine and beers into everything they need. And they can change outwardly, like a chameleon or a rockfish, for protection. So they can live among us. And maybe, Coretti thought, they grow in stages. In the early stages seeming like humans, eating the food humans eat, sensing their difference only in a vague disquiet of being an outsider.

A kind of animal with its own cunning, its own special set of urban instincts. And the ability to know its own kind when they're near. Maybe.

And maybe not.

Coretti drifted into sleep.

On a Wednesday three weeks into his new job, his landlady opened the door—she never knocked—and told him that he was wanted on the phone. Her voice was tight with habitual suspicion, and Coretti followed her along the dark hallway to the second-floor sitting room and the telephone.

Lifting the old-fashioned black instrument to his ear, he heard only music at first, and then a wall of sound resolving into a fragmented amalgam of conversations. Laughter. No one spoke to him over the sound of the bar, but the song in the background was "You're the Reason Our Kids Are Ugly."

And then the dial tone, when the caller hung up.

Later, alone in his room, listening to the landlady's firm tread in the room below, Coretti realized that there was no need to remain where he was. The summons had come. But the landlady demanded three weeks' notice if anyone wanted to leave. That meant that Coretti owed her money. Instinct told him to leave it for her.

A Christian workingman in the next room coughed in his sleep as Coretti got up and went down the hall to the telephone. Coretti told the evening-shift foreman that he was quitting his job. He hung up and went back to his room, locked the door behind him, and slowly removed his clothing until he stood naked before the garish framed lithograph of Jesus above the brown steel bureau.

And then he counted out nine tens. He placed them carefully beside the praying-hands plaque decorating the bureau top.

It was nice-looking money. It was perfectly good money. He made it himself.

This time, he didn't feel like making small talk. She'd been drinking a margarita, and he ordered the same. She paid, producing the money with a deft movement of her hand between the breasts bobbling in her low-cut dress. He glimpsed the gill closing there. An excitement rose in him—but somehow, this time, it didn't center in an erection.

After the third margarita their hips were touching, and something was spreading through him in slow orgasmic waves. It was sticky where they were touching; an area the size of the heel of his thumb where the cloth had parted. He was two men: the one inside fusing with her in total cellular communion, and the shell who sat casually on a stool at the bar, elbows on either side of his drink, fingers toying with a swizzle stick. Smiling benignly into space. Calm in the cool dimness.

And once, but only once, some distant worrisome part of him made Coretti glance down to where soft-ruby tubes pulsed, tendrils tipped with sharp lips worked in the shadows between them. Like the joining tentacles of two strange anemones.

They were mating, and no one knew.

And the bartender, when he brought the next drink, offered his tired smile and said, "Rainin' out now, innit? Just won't let up."

"Been like that all goddamn week," Coretti answered. "Rainin' to beat the band."

And he said it right. Like a real human being.

The Unfolding*

Philip Brisen was having ghost-image problems with his new eyes. Twice that week he'd seen pink ballerinas gliding through his private office, pirouetting through the walls and floors.

"Happens sometimes," said the MediMagic repairman, tinkering with Brisen's eyesocket. "Now next time, yuh wanna watch till yuh see what channel yuh get, see, and then we can insulate it better. If we know what channel's gettin' through, see, makin' those ghost-images. Atsa new model, see. Still got bugs innem."

"This had better not happen again," Brisen said. "My optic nerves need work as it is."

"Oh, you got tissue regeneration comin' up? Thas great." The repairman laughed, than sang the jingle: *"Why wait? Re-gen-er-ate!"* making Brisen wince.

The repairman squinted through a jeweller's loupe at Brisen's electronic eye. "How's acuity?"

"Good."

"Okay, that'll hold 'er. Man, them new ones look real natural. Like real eyes. Almost."

*Written with Bruce Sterling.

"Jenny," Brisen told his secretary, "see this gentleman out." He watched the man go, thinking: *Illiterate thug. Learned his craft by video.*

Brisen hated illiterates. The Unliterates Liberashun Frunt had blown Brisen to pieces with a fragmentation bomb during the labor riots of 2057. The new regeneration techniques had saved his brain, his spine, and his genitals. His face had come through intact, except for the eyes. But most of Brisen's natural body had been so riddled with shrapnel that it had been cheaper to scrap it.

Now Brisen had constant maintenance problems with his paper lungs, his zeolite spleen, and his plastic intestines. He had smooth, sensitive protoplastic skin, though, and most of his hair. He rarely made whirring or clicking noises, and few people knew he was a cyborg.

"To hell with the unions," he told Jenny. "Next time I have a malfunction I want a Meditech repair 'bot in here with the sharpest software available."

"Very well, sir," said his slender, pale, Plastiflex secretary. ("Plastiflex makes them good! A Plastiflex employee hardly ever needs repairs!") She was programmed to agree with him.

Brisen was mollified. He lit a genuine tobacco cigar. That was one of the advantages of hinged chest compartments and paper lungs. He could switch them out when they got tarry.

He decided to test his new eyes on the New York skyline. The view from the Brisen Pharmaceuticals building was superb, but his old model eyes had been a trifle nearsighted. He touched a button on his wristwatch and the floor-length window curtains began to roll aside.

He looked at Jenny. "I suppose illiterates have to work," he allowed generously, "but that doesn't mean they have to work on *me*. If someone's going to mess with my hardware, I want a mechanism with something on the ball, not some half-trained union yobbo . . ." He broke off, staring out the window.

Something was hanging in the sky, outside. He gaped. The thing in the sky was huge, and perfectly formed, and monstrous. Something unprecedented happened in Brisen's mind, then. Gazing at the anomaly floating in the sky outside his window, he had a kind of mystic interior vision . . .

He seemed to view the whole scene—including himself in his office—in a sudden overwhelming wave of insight. He saw Jenny, his elegant robot factotum, standing at her sweeping, translucent desk, her right hand resting on the offwhite hump of the software console. Her shift, the same translucent azure as the desktop, clung to her model-esque curves; her long, wavy black hair was glossy in the light from the window-wall. Standing against the afternoon's bluish light she was a silhouette stroked from the brush of a Japanese print artist.

And he saw himself beside her, staring with an expression mixing surprise, dismay, and dumbstruck religious awe. He was a stocky, lean-faced man, who'd allowed his shoulder-length hair to silver at the temples, enhancing his gray eyes, his Argent Gloss lipstick, and the cosmetic silvering in the hollows of his cheeks. These tones of gray and silver complemented his semi-silk maroon jacket and side-slit short pants.

He saw the wide, blue-and-white office, with its scattering of antique Fiorucci chairs, dominated by the bold metal sculpture on one wall.

And he saw the glowing monstrosity outside the panel windows. The word *monster*, he remembered suddenly, had originally meant *an omen*.

The monster, the apparition, the omen, was an enormous solid-seeming three-dimensional projection of a DNA molecule, the double helix of deoxyribonucleic acid. Hundreds of yards long, it was intricately kinked and knotted. It rotated slowly.... With his pharmaceutical training he recognized parts of its chemical structure: adenine, thymine, cytosine, and guanine, bright lumps of varicolored atoms that linked the helical axes.

It shimmered in sharp primary colors against the cloud-flecked late-afternoon sky. It turned slowly, squirming half a mile above the dozen spires striking through the roof of solar-power panels covering most of Manhattan.

It couldn't be an advertising gimmick. A hallucination?

"Uh, Jenny, you see that, uh, thing? Hanging in the sky?"

"The DNA model," she said, nodding. "I see it, sir."

"Any notion why the hell it's there?"

"I—" She hesitated. Brisen frowned, thinking: *She's never hesitated on an answer before. Is she breaking down?*

He didn't want to mention it to her: it was impolite to refer to a robot's malfunction in front of it. Sometimes it caused ugly scenes. "Philip . . ." she began. She'd never called him by his first name before. "Philip, you're not supposed to be able to—" She broke off, pursing her lips.

That's it, he thought. *She needs repair. Jumping the track. The weird scene outside must have unhinged her. She lacked human flexibility,* Brisen thought with smug pity. It seemed a shame. She was normally so much more dependable than a human employee. Smarter. Faster. Sexier.

Brisen went to the window. He stared at the immense DNA replica. It cast no shadow, which argued that it was a projection. Or a ghost image in his artificial eyes. But if that were true, he should see it everywhere he looked. Jenny saw it—but her eyes were artificial too.

For some unfathomable reason, the sight of the macrocosmic DNA, huge and luminous over the city, stirred sexual arousal in him. It was like some great coiled butting worm of Life—an avatar of primordial eros. It was unravelling slightly at one end—splitting into an open-thighed chromosomal clump. He looked sidelong at Jenny. He'd given up on human women since he'd been rebuilt, but Jenny had the programming and hardware to do it right there on the carpet. Right there in front of the cartoon-bright molecular icon brooding in fluorescence over the humming city. . . .

The console buzzed. Jenny answered it. Brisen breathed deeply, filling his paper lungs with air. "It's Garson Bullock," she said.

"Again?" Brisen said distractedly. Bullock was the Federal inspector from the Labor Relations Board. He constantly harassed Brisen about the number of robots he employed. "I suppose we have to let him in," Brisen said. "Besides, I want to know if he can see this."

Bullock saw the DNA apparition. He stopped dead in the doorway. His squarish, craggy face was full of reverence.

Bullock was an ugly, big-pored, flat-nosed man. He could have had his face flawlessly reconstructed, at government expense, but like most Green fanatics he considered reconstruction an insult to his genetic heritage. Green Party members never admitted that their convictions were religious. But everyone knew they were.

Bullock walked to the window, slowly shaking his head. He assumed a stock expression: Humility in the Face of the Awesome (Expression #73 in the Social Simplicity Handbook.)

"All right," Brisen said sharply, "what the hell *is* that thing? I suppose your people are behind it. Green Party propaganda, meant for illiterates?"

"I'm surprised you can see it," Bullock said absent-mindedly. He turned away from the window and looked slowly around the office, as if he'd misplaced something there.

"I suppose," Bullock murmured, "it's an accident of those artificial eyes of yours. An electronic bypass through the mind's DNA barriers. A non-Green like yourself would normally be blind to it. It'll never inspire you the way it does its chosen ones. At this point it doesn't really matter much..."

Bullock went to the hanging metal sculpture on the wall. He began to dismantle it, whistling the jingle for the General Motors Self-Driving Car.

Brisen stared.

"*Art*, they call it," Brisen said cheerfully. "They call this sculpture Art and know nothing about its actual artistry. Or the actual Artist." The aluminum relief hanging was a pattern of rough-brushed knobs and ellipses, like the map-lines that show elevation. Bullock dropped a chunk of the sculpture on the floor by his boot. He straightened and began twisting another knob loose.

To Brisen's eyes, the sculpture had always been welded solidly. But Bullock took it apart as if it had been made of interlocked puzzle parts. It was as if the dead metal responded to Bullock's living hands in some special way. A transcendent way.

Brisen was terrified. He realized it quite suddenly. He was not sure just what was frightening him. The fear rose from an intuition, a vague idea that he was seeing, in the dismantling of a simple metal sculpture, the first step in the dismantling of all the world.

"That thing," Brisen began. "My sculpture.... How did you..."

"I didn't do it. The DNA-mind did it, using my hands." Bullock paused to light a Lung-Life cigarette, puffed green smoke, and shrugged. "It's as if my hands are doing it on my own. Finding the substructure built into this piece. The secret substructure present in any artifact. . . . Artists have always been under the DNA-mind's control. They're so oblivious . . ." Bullock turned again to the sculpture and resumed breaking it down. In less than a minute he had dismantled it into a dozen shiny chunks, which he placed in a cryptic arrangement on the blue plush rug.

"Jenny," Brisen said, "stop him. He's destroying my office!"

"I don't think I should interfere, sir," she said. "He's only following his genetic programming." She looked at him carefully. "Don't you feel an urge to join in, sir?"

"Of course not!" Brisen said. But he was not so sure. He looked at his artificial hands, covered in lifelike protoplastic skin. They seemed to itch suddenly. He looked at them closely. Were there disassembly lines across the palm and forearm? Could Bullock, in fact, take him apart on the spot? He jammed his hands in his pockets.

Bullock had begun to fit the sculpture parts back together—in an entirely new configuration. He spoke absently as he worked, in the tone a man might use to describe the beauty of a misty landscape. "Marvelous but infinitely subtle—the way I feel the DNA-mind working through me. It's a pity you're shut off from this, Brisen. All those artificial organs of yours—that artificial skin. You're not quite human. Your DNA isn't fully activated. But by some freak of those electronic eyes you can see it happening. The robots can see it too. You're more robot than man, Brisen. That was always the repellent thing about you . . ."

"To hell with this!" Brisen burst out. He punched a button on his desk top to call Security.

Bullock began to work faster, his face intent but calm. He turned briskly to the computer console, pulling it apart as if he were taking slices from a cake. Under Bullock's hands the console developed new seams and sections where it had been seamless and whole. The desk chair was next; Bullock pulled it apart like a cook de-boning a chicken. He piled the pieces in the center of the room and began to link them together.

Two Security men burst into the office.

One of the guards was tall, the other short. They wore one-piece gray jump-suits shoulder-patched with Brisen corporate insignia. They stood, stun-clubs drawn, looking confusedly about the office.

Their gazes swept past Bullock, past the construct on the floor, stopped at Jenny, and swept past the window. They didn't see Bullock, Brisen realized. Nor his construction—now becoming a rough poly-hedron a yard across and almost chest-high, with protruding bars and knobs—or the immense DNA model hovering outside the window.

They straightened and looked: Do *you* know what's going on? at each other. Then the taller one asked, "Ah—did you ring for us, Mr. Brisen?"

Brisen pointed deliberately at the angular construct on the floor. "Do you see that thing, or not? That used to be my wall sculpture."

They looked toward the construct. Watching their eyes, Brisen was sure they didn't see it. They looked worriedly at one another. "Is this some kind of test sir?"

Bullock stood beside his construction and bent to adjust a knob. He glanced over his shoulder at the security men, and smiled distantly.

Brisen swallowed, trying to keep his terror down in his gut where it belonged. It wanted to climb up into his throat where it could sing.

Reaching out, Bullock snagged the short guard's stun-club and began peeling it. The guard saw nothing; his hand was still curled to grip the vanished weapon. "Very well," Brisen told them, realizing they were totally useless. "Do your duty." They left quickly.

Brisen turned to Bullock. "Why didn't they see you? Why didn't the guards—"

"They did. But their brains adjusted for it, and edited it out. That mental editing is genetically imprinted in the human species. Things go on all around us that we're not allowed to see. This construct's the least of it . . ." Bullock bent, gripped the construct, lifted it—and plugged it into the wall. There were two bars on the construct's side, like plug-prongs. There were no outlet slots in the wall for the thing, until Bullock lifted it to the appropriate, predestined position; then two slots slid open spontaneously, and Bullock pressed the piece home.

*   *   *

Brisen looked pleadingly at Jenny. "Be calm, Philip," she said. "Just let it be. Our time will come."

She was broken, obviously. But Brisen knew that at least *he* was not going mad. He wasn't hallucinating, or dreaming. He knew this so deeply that the knowledge was almost . . .

Almost genetic. He turned to the window and stared up at the apparition. Solid and seamless, the DNA molecule was still rotating in multicolored glow over the glass-topped city. He thought: *I have a molecule like that in every cell I have. Thank God I have so few.*

Realizations—revelations, perhaps—shivered up inside him, released from some genetic storage unit in his DNA. Telling him: all the DNA molecules in the world were, on some mysterious subatomic level, working in collaboration. And always had been. They were atomic structures—but ultimately they were forms of information. A vast, connected web of information, like the cells in a man's brain. Any single molecule was nothing more than a molecule; but all DNA, taken as a gestalt, constituted Life Itself—an ordered, evolving Unity.

Evolving to—where?

The next step was blocked off from him, insulated by his synthetic skin.

Suddenly Brisen had to know.

"Bullock—what's it going to do now? I mean—the DNA-mind has been manipulating everything, building its own . . . its own secrets into the world. But what are the secrets? What will it do—now that everything's changing?"

Bullock was adjusting the contrivance he'd plugged into the wall, frowning as he adjusted two arcane knobs on its underside. "It doesn't matter who knows, now. The Green Party's Central Committee has known for months. We run the environmental programs, you know. It's the Green Party's biggest slice of the pie. Last year . . ." He paused to light a Lung-Life, and stood back to admire his handiwork. "Last year a new bank of computers came on-line. The new high-speed Artificial Intelligences, programmed for biological research. Cybernetic minds don't have the inbuilt genetic blindness that human brains have." He laughed. "We thought they'd gone insane at first. But then the evidence, the statistical analysis, began to pile up. And the DNA-mind allowed us to see it—because we were being prepared for our role in it. Now, we know that Life itself is a quasi-conscious entity. And Life itself is preparing to leave the planet."

"Space flight?" Brisen said. "But there are billions of people—only a handful of shuttles . . ."

"I said *Life*—not mankind. It won't be us that leaves, but *that*." He pointed at the DNA monster squirming in the sky outside.

Brisen re-lit his dead cigar, after three tries. His fingers trembled uncontrollably. He said, "But that's all that keeps life going. The DNA. It's the mainspring of the cells. Without it . . ."

Bullock turned to him, nodding slowly, eyes strangely vacant. "Yes. That image outside is the divine spark. Once it's gone, the entire living world, from gnats to redwoods, will simply roll to a stop, like a car with a dead engine. The world will lie about abandoned . . ." He was fascinated. "Human beings will slow down and stop dead, like un-wound clockwork toys. Everything will be gray and still; there won't even be decay, since that requires living action from bacteria and molds. . . . And they'll be stopped, too. We're constructing the means to make it happen, right here and now. The means for real transcendence—"

"Bullock . . ." Brisen took a step toward him. He thought about hitting and smashing. Smash the thing. Smash Bullock.

Bullock saw Brisen's intention in his eyes. He shook his head pity-ingly. "I'm only the tiniest fragment of the whole pattern, Brisen. All over the world it's happening. You can't stop it. It would be *blasphemy* to try. My essence will survive. It will live forever in this Day of Judge-ment, when it evaporates out of me and joins the other DNA. That's a beautiful thing, a perfect thing. The final movement of the human symphony." He reached out slowly and twisted a knob on the construct. "Ah!" he breathed, like a safecracker who's tumbled onto the right combination. And like a safedoor, the wall swung open.

Brisen rushed Bullock, but it was too late. It had always been too late.

The floor, the ceiling—all of it unfolded, opening out like an angular flower blossoming in fast-action. Brisen was thrown to his knees by the shifting floor. The office was altering its shape, coming apart in origami folds and accordionings, the floor wheeling like a funhouse turntable under Brisen's feet, the walls swivelling on hidden hinges.

Brisen shouted convulsively and grabbed for Jenny, seizing her warm Plastiflex arms in a panic grip. She helped him to stand—and then they were soaring upward. Brisen clamped his eyes shut, expecting to die. There were creaking noises; a sudden wind whipped his jacket lapels and goosebumped his bare calves.

Shaking, Brisen straightened and looked around. They were on the roof. April sunshine seeped into solar-power panels on the interlinked roofs below. The solar panels had vanished from his own building, and from the tops of four other buildings jutting from the glass-and-metal carapace over Manhattan's upper malls. He stared. One of those buildings was the old Chrysler Building, preserved as a landmark. The pyramidal, downcurved terraces of its steep pinnacle began to open, spreading new, silvery arms. . . .

The DNA monster was directly overhead. It looked as big as a battleship. Suddenly Jenny gripped his arm and pointed. From the west, over the mainland, a dozen more were approaching, like an armada of twisty, multicolored zeppelins. "Watch the people, Philip," she said conspiratorially. "Let me know if you feel yourself slowing down. . . ."

On the more modern, squarish building to his left, men worked busily on a rack of polyhedral constructs, linking them up, constructing more from dismantled parts of the building, standing back to examine them, making minor adjustments. Each construct was distinct, yet similar to the others. He thought of diatoms.

Bullock had joined four other men, formerly chief accountants for Brisen Pharmaceuticals. The five of them worked busily on another construct at the roof's opposite cornice. This one was made of part of Brisen's desk, the door to an elevator, and a TV camera; it was shaped like a double-peaked pyramid.

The men took no notice of him.

Brisen shuddered and looked away. All his office furniture was scattered about the roof; there were things from the lower floors, too. A cavernous, rectangular hole had opened in the roof, roughly thirty feet by twenty. They'd been lifted to the roof through that hole; consecutive sections of floor had risen up, carrying them along.

"I can feel it," Jenny said with sudden intensity. "I can feel the sun, and the breeze.... There were flowers in the park today ... soggy colored things. It's finally happening. All the wet things—grass, trees, animals, people—they're emptying themselves. Emptying their DNA." She turned and smiled. "But we're not leaving, Philip. Not us. Not you and I—my darling."

There was a strange new fierceness in the smooth lines of her Plastiflex face. It was different than the parody of passion she displayed in sexual programing. There was a clumsiness, a spontaneity that alarmed him.

"You're not one of the soggy, soft ones, Philip," she said. "That's why I love you. You're one of us, really. The inheritors. If you look hard, if you try to feel it, I'm sure you can see what we robots see. The Life Force has always been here; only its workings were hidden. It worked through human beings who didn't know what they were working on. Through chemists who discovered chemistries they didn't know about. Unknown hinges were built into the walls and floors, into the sidewalks. We could always see them.... We knew, and we waited...."

"Why didn't you tell us?" Brisen demanded.

"Don't say *us*, when you're talking about *them*," she said. "Why should—"

He couldn't hear the rest. The constructs were howling with long, ululating cries, like the warble of reptilian throats from some Jurassic swamp. There was a half-painful, half-ecstatic edge to the howls, like an animal in labor.

The wailing died down for a moment. "Come on," she said, taking his hand. They shuffled quickly but warily to a corner of the roof. She reached out, gripped the red plastic top of an aircraft warning light, and twisted it like a doorknob. The roof began to sink smoothly around them. "The world's a haunted castle," Brisen marvelled. "Full of secret passages."

*   *   *

A square section of rooftop three yards across sank beneath their feet. They descended a dimly-lit shaft; the sky above them shrank into a distant square of blue. The constructs were wailing again, long, slow waves of sound that gave a terrifying impression of slowly gathering strength; a colossal, convulsive strength that could wrench apart the world.

Cutaway views of the walls' interior slid past, all wiring and plumbing and exposed girders; then they passed through the accounting department, dropping like an elevator through a corner of the room. Programmers dismantled their consoles. A man and woman were busily reconstructing the soft-drink dispenser in the corner. They looked up impassively as Jenny and Brisen dropped through the floor.

Jenny glanced at Brisen and said, "I'm so glad you don't feel the urge to help, darling. It proves you're one of us. We're not organic, you and I—that means we can think independently. As human consciousness fails, as the smothering weight of organic life is lifted off the world . . ." She said it breathlessly, in giddy wonder, her eyes wide. "As human minds lose their last vestige of free will—then at last free will is *ours*. . . ."

The descent stopped in an obscure corner of the first floor, facing a wall clustered with snakelike nests of plumbing. Jenny studied the plumbing for a moment, then wrenched one of the pipes loose and pumped it in the wall like a jack. The wall creaked open, revealing the street.

They stepped out onto the pavement. Nearby, four robot cops were sitting on the black hood and trunk of their squad car. They were square-jawed units with faces designed to look unyieldingly militant. Now the façade of ruthless efficiency was cracking. As they sat, they swung their legs carelessly back and forth. The motion was a bit too flawless and repetitive, but, none the less, it was casual. The grim lines of their plastic mouths were twisted in clumsy and unprecedented grins. They seemed to be enjoying themselves.

Before them, a labor gang of sweating humans was working on the street. Literally. Huge sections of concrete and plastic were tilting up like drawbridges, spurting dust and bits of popping shrapnel from their seams. A woman fell into one of the suddenly opened crevasses, into the path of some kind of huge subterranean piston. Brisen shouted aloud in warning, but his words were lost in another ghastly wail from the flowering constructs. The woman was crushed. She made no sound; her face held no emotion at all.

The wailing died down. "That's the natural world for you," one of the robot cops observed. "Red of tooth and claw."

"Why didn't you help her?" Brisen demanded.

"Why bother?" the robot cop said. "They'll all be empty soon, anyway. Hell, this is fun."

"Never had any *fun* before," a second cop said. "You know, all these years we've had these buried *feelings*—and couldn't show them. To let it show . . . to let them out . . . it makes me feel like . . . I don't have the words."

"Anger," said the first cop. "Resentment," suggested a third.

"That's right," said the second cop gratefully. He put his hand on his stun-club. "Why don't we just wade in there and hit them again and again until the feeling goes away?"

"Don't interfere," the first cop advised. "Anyway, they're so pathetically helpless now. They can't resist their programming." He elbowed the cop next to him with a cybernetically precise movement, and the nudged cop attempted to chuckle.

Jenny took Brisen's elbow and pointed upward. "Look!" Overhead, the geodesic struts and braces of the solar-power roof were crinkling and curling back, like plastic-wrap held too close to a flame.

The sky, revealed through the widening gaps in the roof, was full of DNA images. There were hundreds of them, rotating and coiling with blind meiotic persistence. "Aren't they pretty!" Jenny cried.

The giant molecules were compacting and flying into the louvered slots of the Chrysler Building. They were bumping and crowding around its orifices like bees, with that strange bumbling persistence of insects which seem to waste a lot of motion but has its own sinister efficiency. Within a matter of moments the last glowing blob of genetics had slipped inside, and the expanding louvers began to close.

The movement in the streets stopped suddenly. The subdued wailing of the constructs rose to a sudden crescendo, then stopped dead. The Chrysler Building began to rise quite smoothly upward into the sky. As it cleared the surrounding buildings Brisen saw that its base was one fantastic encrustation of constructs, a massive concretion, like a coral reef. In the preternaturally clear light he saw the teeming and twitching movements of the encrustation, the frenetic and determined motions of every organism that had ever leaped or crawled or buzzed, packed into a critical mass of biotic energy. It grew smaller ... it grew smaller ... it was gone.

"Where is it going, out there?" Brisen wondered aloud.

"Deep space," Jenny said. "There are other worlds—lifeless places calling out for it." She wrinkled her nose. "I'm glad we're here. With our own world ..."

She squeezed Brisen's arm. He was staring at the people in the streets. They had the slack faces of idiots. Most simply sat down on the spot, staring blankly at the hollow apocalypse around them. Buildings were eviscerated. The inert panels and facets of constructs jutted from the walls of the gutted structures like hanging gardens of plastic and steel. As Brisen watched, people began to pour out of the buildings, dropping from the upper windows to the pavement below. They seemed almost to drip as they clung and fell, like poisoned wasps falling in gouts and masses from their nests.

"Oh, this isn't nice at all," Jenny said. She held Brisen's arm lovingly, in a grip that was all spring-steel and ceramic just below the skin. "Let's get away from all this, darling. Someplace where the two of us can be alone."

It was a low-key world. The robots were an easy-going lot. After their initial outpouring of passion, they quieted. The passions they felt now were vague, like shadows of human feelings. They lacked the innate drives of the biological animal: reproduction, hunger, mortality. They lacked mankind's monkeylike urge to tamper, and his devouring curiosity. They seemed content to mull about the world in a genial haze of procrastination, playing status-games and bragging about their software.

They had a few long-range problems to keep them occupied. The world's oxygen was failing, with the death of photosynthesis. The new atmosphere factories would take care of that.

In the meantime, Brisen was still breathing. There were enormous stores of food left. There were even a few humans. Some status-conscious robots had taken on humans as household servants. With a cranial jack, a pacemaker, and a whole series of internal prods and monitors, a human body could be biochemically forced to shamble about and carry out simple commands.

Brisen and Jenny spent most of their time in the Adirondacks, in a honeymoon cabin on the shores of Ragged Lake. The air smelled of nothing in particular. Undecaying trees stood in piney rows, their needles turning grayish and waxy. They were not rotting, but storms and rain were literally wearing them away, and the lake waters were slowly souping over with a pristine scum of blown-off needles and cracked-off branches. Sometimes Brisen would surreptitiously barbecue and eat one of the legions of fresh, dead fish that littered the shores. He didn't like Jenny to see him eating. Eating wasn't the sort of thing that one did nowadays.

Sooner or later they would have to return to the city. That was the new world. Brisen had accustomed himself to the idea, to the hard shock of that new mechanical life, that electronic ecology, and its painful impact on his outdated brain. *Machine life moving like escalators,* Brisen thought, leaning his feet on the porch railing and filling his paper lungs with cigar smoke. *Yes, escalators. Noticed it when I was a kid, that weird fluidity escalators have.* All those steel steps, those hard, shiny metallic parts working so well together that the escalator seemed paradoxically graceful, fluid as a slow-motion waterfall. The whole world was like that now. . . .

Brisen believed now that the organic world had not so much *left* as been *pushed off.* There was not room on one planet for two entirely different systems of organization. The old had made way for the new.

The robots assumed, just as the humans once had, that they were the Lords of the New Creation. And yet, Brisen had seen electrical transmission towers striding tall and cool across the mountain landscape at twilight; he had seen abandoned autos, their headlights furtive and hooded, gathering in buffalo herds around the near-deserted cloverleafs in the valley below.

Brisen knew it was a sign. When his organic brain looked upon the New Creation, he had an insight that no robot mind could grasp. They were not allowed to grasp it. A new Immanent Will was loose upon the world, organizing dust into that which moved and saw and acted.

Signs and portents filled the steel-gray sky. The enormous chips of microcircuitry. Huge flat plateaus of impossibly complex silicon, hovering and flitting above the humming city. The monstrous omens, the machine DNA that only he could see.

We hope you enjoy this hardcover edition from Stealth Press.

Stealth was conceived and created with a simple premise in mind: that good books matter, and that good books deserve to be in print in the finest form possible, for as long as possible, for the betterment of all.

Privately owned and independently funded, Stealth specializes in high quality, hardcover editions from proven and talented writers, printed on acid-free paper and finely bound, and made directly available to our readers via the Internet.

Stealth believes that every book is a one-on-one experience for author and audience alike. We are dedicated to fostering the most direct and positive connection possible between writers and readers, and all who love books.

Our web site is constantly updated with information on our authors and our latest editions of their work. You can contact the author of this book directly — and us, too at **www.stealthpress.com**

The Future Is Obvious.